Praise for

The Art of Peeling an Orange

“Few books these days gob smack me, but *The Art of Peeling an Orange* certainly did. It’s vividly written, suspenseful, darkly humorous . . . and it’s one of the most twisted and twisting love stories I’ve ever had the pleasure to read. And right when you think you have it pegged it digs deeper, with more and more layers. Avilan is an exceptional writer. Her story moves fast, covering . . . a lot of emotions. And yet her attention to detail is extraordinary even at the fairly breathless pace . . . those details only add to the clip of her storytelling. I saw every painting. I smelled the oils and the drawing utensils. And I could hear the scratching of the sketching. That is how acutely she describes the art world. It comes to life on the page in ways that are astonishing.” *—Jeff York, The Examiner*

“If you want the lure of obsession fueled by the madness of lust right before it collides with the creativity of a wild woman and the finesse of a Courtly scribe, Victoria Avilan’s your girl and *The Art of Peeling An Orange* is your Book of the Year! In this anything-but-staid re-imagining of the mythic trope of those lusty would-be Greek lovers, Orpheus and Eurydice, *The Art of Peeling An Orange* . . . is true to the spirit of the Greek drama—except it’s West Hollywood.”

—Historical romance author T. T. Thomas

“Once in a blue moon I find a book like this. This is a work of art to adore, to devour, to enjoy and re-read after a while just to see if I’ve missed anything or see it with fresh new eyes . . . very well-written in a sophisticated, profound manner in a lovely style, and will speak to most as it’s also down to earth and realistic at the same time. Also most artists will be able to relate to one or more of the characters . . . The erotic scenes are tastefully done, yet sexy and romantic.”

—Fantasy author Natasja Hellenthal

“This book was incredible! I was hooked from the start and did not put it down till I was finished, I simply could not! After a night dreaming of these women, this story, I then read it again. This book ran the gamut of emotions and senses. The story’s sustenance was hypnotic, addicting, breathtaking, mysterious, sensual and so full of nuances, apprehension and twists that you never saw coming. Even with the sweet release the drama

never ceased. By book's end I was well and truly spent. This is one of those books that when you finish and surface to face the real world you can not believe it has not changed. Surely the world can not be the same after such an experience. Thank you so very much Ms. Avilan, for this wonderful encounter. ”
—Ameliah Faith

"West Hollywood is an unlikely setting for a Modern Gothic story, but in Victoria Avilan's tale a group of modern WeHo bohemians becomes entangled with one of Hollywood's most glamourous stars and her dangerous secrets. I've called this Modern Gothic as I can't think of a better way to describe Avilan's mix of realism, surrealism and the supernatural. Madness is a key feature of the Gothic genre and I found myself alternately trying to decide if anyone at all was sane and expecting to find the first Mrs. Rochester in an attic somewhere . . . Anna's story is suspenseful and intriguing as it starts to untangle. The layers of secrets surrounding her life and Greg's death are exciting and complicated. *—InkedRainbowReads*

The Art of Peeling an Orange

a novel

Victoria Avilan

Shaggy Dog Stories

Cover image and design by Victoria Avilan
Author's photo on back cover by Suzanne Gross
Edited by Beth Hill
Published by Shaggy Dog Stories

The Art of Peeling an Orange : a novel / Victoria Avilan. – 1st edition.

ISBN-13:978-1514257654 (paperback)
ISBN-10:1514257653
ASIN: B00S70EG00 (eBook)
Library of Congress Catalog Card Number: TXu 1-951-245

Contact email : victoria@vicavilan.com
Author's website : www.vicavilan.com
Visit Victoria Avilan's author page on facebook

Also by Victoria Avilan
A Small Country about to Vanish

Acknowledgements

For your mentoring through the UCLA Writers' Program and for words of wisdom that etched new grooves in my brain, I thank you, my dear friend and teacher, Claire Carmichael, Writing Guru Extraordinaire.

Editor Beth Hill, thank you for your brilliant insights and valuable advice. Nili Sachs, thanks for occasionally attempting to restore my sanity. My BFFs Patricia Gisler, Jeff and Suzie Gross, thank you for your constant help throughout the process. Special thanks to Teresa Bernau, Kathleen Harrigan-Hamamoto, and Kevin Amick.

Mocha, Indie and Max—for warming my feet when I write and for wagging when I don't.

My beloved wife Tracey Dodd, thank you for letting me be, for being my first reader and editor and the reason for everything.

I thank my loving father Uzzi Levy, who gave me wings and showed me how to fly; and my mother, Miryam Levy, the beautiful artist who handed me a paintbrush before I learned to walk, and taught me everything I know about art and beauty.

I love you all. You made the writing of this behemoth possible and worth the effort.

For Tracey

"We have art in order not to die of the truth."

Friedrich Nietzsche

The Art of Peeling an Orange

Prologue

High beamed headlights blinded him through his rearview mirror. Why were they chasing him? They all kept too close behind in news vans, surrounded him on motorcycles, swarmed over his head in helicopters, a cloud of angry insects.

Why couldn't they leave him alone? He was a broken man, a dying man.

The freeway was red and white and darkness.

His head exploded with both their images, two incredible women who didn't know each other, but knew him too well. He chanted their names with the *clank, clank, clank* of the speed bumps, his mind feverish in the flurry of red tail lights.

He fumbled for his cellphone, one hand on the steering wheel.

He scrolled down and texted.

A network of freeway bridges emerged from the blackness like a giant octopus and loomed above him in the clear night's air.

He wanted to add another word. Then a motorcycle neared his window and someone snapped a flash photo. And another flash. His headlights fell on the wall that shot at him at high speed.

Just like that, it was over.

Part One

1

Anna Garibaldi was nothing to me until the funeral. We had nothing in common but the man in the casket, the man she had the right to mourn as her *dearly departed.* I had no such right.

She stood still in the darkness of the church, her pale hair pulled away from her just as pale face and her white hand gently caressing the raised casket. She seemed to me like a heroine in a Greek tragedy. I took out a black marker and quickly sketched her impression, this vision of grief, on the palm of my hand.

Suddenly sunlight broke in through the clouds and streamed down from slits in the Gothic ceiling, showering the widow with the golden rays of a saint in a Renaissance painting. And she was neither a saint, nor the tragic heroine, but rather a dark and majestic mythological Goddess. Her other name, the Divine One, came to my mind. Now I craved a white canvas and a palette of the deepest midnight blues and the inkiest jet blacks, those ominous shades that paint the earth and the sky when the moon is full.

Hers was to be the only eulogy. Who could have competed with the powerful words of a best-selling novelist? Who else cared about the deceased?

I cared.

"Only months ago my dear Guido was an unknown," the widow said in the famed contralto she used on talk shows when introducing one of her books or films.

International was the only way I could describe her voice, with its unique mix of the romance languages, mostly Italian. Even in grief public speaking was in her comfort zone. Her audience was hooked. A killer first line was her forte.

A killer, I thought.

A small smile relaxed her lips when she said, "I recognized Guido's enormous talent the moment I met him."

Guido. I couldn't listen to that farce of a eulogy, to that rich contralto saying, *my husband* and *my protégé*. My knuckles turned bone white as I stopped myself from lashing out at her with my bare hands, messing up that perfect hair, ripping the huge sunglasses off her famous face to show a full church the absence of her tears.

The rock in my heart turned to molten lava and squeezed its way up into my feverish throat and out of my eyes with the first tears, and out of my mouth with the spit I wanted to put in her perfect oval face. I wanted to . . .

I tuned out her eulogy and drifted away back to the happy days before my almost-wedding. I thought of my white gown, of how it had hugged my straight figure just right, giving me the shapely dream curves I'd always wanted. How my dark curls with their natural highlights fell to my shoulders, framing my face to form a Pre-Raphaelite illusion.

Now all was ruined, my wedding gown, my hair, my life. And she was to blame for it.

As she spoke, I thought of the goofy way I'd smiled at my own reflection, almost pretty and giddy, because I was about to marry my best friend, my childhood sidekick. When I'd skipped downstairs in my bare feet, two stairs at a time, eager to show them my gown, rather than squeals of delight, I was met with silence. They had bad news.

The man I loved had left me for another, a famous woman. An infamous woman. This woman, with her golden hair and her hourglass figure and the divine shower of rays engulfing her. This woman—now his widow, now calmly speaking his eulogy.

How? I wanted to shout and crush her calmness into pieces. How did he get himself into this mahogany casket, the rich corpse of a trophy widow?

I was choking back the tears, trying to block out her words. Even as I didn't listen, little by little I paid attention, only because there was nothing else to do. Her voice trickled its way into me like sweet, warm liquor, lulling me into a state of relaxation, taking me along with the crowd on waves of reactions, now a chuckle, now a gasp at another vivid description of Greg. His joy and generosity came through her words—the way he would sing off-key on purpose, the way he'd bring the house down with his out-of-the-blue one-liners, the way his eyes blazed with love for me. No, for her.

In a church filled beyond capacity with a crowd that flowed into the street, the woman who ruined my life spoke directly to me, or that was how it felt. She had robbed me of the man I loved, but her powerful words gave him back to me. A floodgate opened and I cried for the first time since he died.

Zoe and Kyra held onto my arms. Robert smoothed my hair. All three surrounded me with their love, as they had since Greg had abandoned me for this woman.

The church was silent except for her voice, some sniffling and the occasional blowing of a nose. I gazed down, my tears dripping.

"Goodbye, my dear Guido." The widow ended her eulogy.

I couldn't take it any longer.

"His name was Greg. Greg, Greg, *Greg!*" I cried out, my voice cracking from lack of use.

The spell was broken. Rows of heads turned. Men and women stared with horrified eyes.

"Carly, sit down," Zoe whispered, wrapping her skinny arms around my waist.

Kyra and Robert tried to force me back into the pew. I remained standing, overcome by red-hot rage, trembling with emotions I'd suppressed long enough.

The widow raised a hand, signaling to the mumbling crowd to settle down.

"Funerals are made for grief," she said. Then to me, "Speak up. Who are you?"

Anger choked me. "Why is he lying cold . . . dead . . . and you . . . you are still alive?"

"I ask myself the same question," she said, her voice steady. Her stare from behind the dark glasses drilled a hole into me.

"Shut it, Carly," Kyra whispered.

I could not shut up. "How in only six months . . . did he go from being *your husband* and *your protégé* . . . to being dead?"

"Tell me your name," she ordered.

"Tell her nothing," Kyra said.

The widow made a barely noticeable gesture with her hand, and her bodyguard, a huge woman, started down the aisle toward us.

"Quick," Kyra urged. "Let's go."

I was glued to my spot, staring paralyzed at the approaching human mountain, when my three companions simply lifted me off my feet to the sound of rumbling disapproval in the crowd.

As I was carried out—unlike Greg, alive and kicking—a crazy idea crossed my mind, one of many that had assailed me recently. The widow was Hades. She had access to Greg even in death. And if I wanted to have him back I should charm my way to her underworld and beg for my beloved as Orpheus begged for his Eurydice.

2

They buried him at the Hollywood Forever Cemetery. I buried him in my heart. Kyra, Zoe and Robert told me every detail about the stoic widow, the humanist minister, the Garibaldi family plot. The dead party, aka the "celebration of life," took place at the Beverly Hilton and was apparently phenomenal. Robert described orgasmic lemon drops and éclairs that exploded in one's mouth.

Since they'd carried me out I missed the rest of it and drove straight home with my belly full of hate, the widow's face fresh on my mind, and a rough impression sketched in the palm of my hand with a black marker. I had to purge the grief and the anger from my system the only way I could, by painting.

I had a vision of that angelic face, that perfect figure, clad in blue and engulfed by sinister darkness. For me she was Hades, ruling the underworld, a place of loss and pain and death. My fingers ached to start.

The painting's background was viscid black, just as I imagined the water of the Styx. Her hair, with its rich tones of gold and platinum, was down to her waist. Her pale face was shaded with cerulean blue—strong, striking features, square jaw, straight nose. I left out the dark glasses, but as I hadn't actually seen her eyes, they remained undefined and shadowed.

Instead of a brush I used only a palette knife, to give the background depth and the features an edge. It took me a few days to get the image right. When I was done, I turned the finished portrait toward the mirror and examined its reflection —a test I used to detect imperfections and see the work with new eyes.

Such raw hunger radiated from the canvas, I shuddered. She was so alive. Yet something was missing.

Who was she really?

Anna Garibaldi.

The tabloids called her the Divine One, *La Divina*. Whatever she touched turned to gold, and she did everything—act, direct, sing, dance, write. She'd get bored and shift her focus at the top of her game. She'd started as a runway model and an interpretive dancer. Those who saw her dance never understood why she'd stopped. She had a velvet voice, but she performed only for close friends at private parties. Her novels became instant bestsellers. She wrote and directed for television and stage. All her art films were black and white, despite their colorful names. Her last, *Divine Darkness*, was nominated for an Academy Award. Indie, Palme d'Or and Emmys were all under her belt, yet she kept reinventing herself.

Her age was irrelevant, though she looked to be forty. She could have been four hundred, considering all the lives she had lived.

I'd never watched any of her films or read her books, but in the entertainment capital of the world one couldn't escape constantly reading her name, seeing her photos and hearing how she had surpassed with her talents even the dead legend, her mother, Irena Garibaldi. You only had to stand in the grocery line to find a glamour shot of her on the cover of at least one fashion magazine in her signature Garibaldi Eyewear. She loomed over the freeway in shampoo ads, her hair arranged in an intricate, sculpted design and held up by simple chopsticks or elaborate accessories.

The painting I was scrutinizing in the mirror, this product of my catharsis, was not glamorous, but rather sinister. This particular image was mine to hate. I'd given the effort all I had.

As a final touch, I dipped my thinnest sable brush in crimson and shaded the left side of her head with a thready curve suggesting a menacing religious halo. Nothing was missing now.

I raised my gaze to my own reflection.

Metal clips held my hair piled on top of my head with neither glamour nor design. My ruined wedding gown had always been loose; now it hung in vertical folds from my collarbones down my Modigliani-thin body. Psychedelic brush strokes covered every inch of formerly virginal white. Sorry, Robert. You cried when you saw what I did to your creation, but the dress suits me better as blotting material. My haunted eyes and the palette knife clutched in my right hand made me look insane. What a curious self-portrait I'd make.

I painted portraits for a living—people of all ages, kids, pets, whole families. I could see beyond the obvious—shapes, colors, lines of laughter or sadness—and into my model's inner life. I flattered my sitters with kinder, happier faces than those given them by nature. After all, that was the reason they chose to pay me. I took pride in my work.

This portrait was different. No one sat for me. No one commissioned me. No one would see it. I painted it from memory and it was mine to destroy. The time had come to settle unfinished business, creator to creation, avenging angel to powerful demon.

"Anna Garibaldi," I whispered to my personal Hades, for the first time daring to utter the hated name. "You could have had anyone, but you seduced the only man I loved."

I resented her widow status, her right to mourn my man so publicly, so famously, to choose how and where to bury him and what to engrave on his headstone. We were *Carly and Greg* for as long as I could remember, and she'd made him forget me. I blamed her for trapping him in her evil net. I blamed her for his death.

Greg died in a car crash on the way to see me. I'd loved him since childhood, yet I had no rights in his death. His black widow kept all his belongings, even items that were gifts from me, including the silver ring I'd given him, engraved with both our names. She'd kept the cellphone on which he'd texted a hurried, loving message, asking for my forgiveness.

I'd memorized those three sentences. A short one. A long one. A short one.

Coming to pick you up. Have something to show you that will make you forgive everything. You are the only one.

Greg's last text message left a fatal question in my mind, a great mystery. He'd been coming to see me, to show me something. But what? We all analyzed the text ad nauseam. I'd been fixed on that third sentence. *You are the only one.*

While I'd said nothing to my nearest and dearest, secretly I believed he'd one day come back to me. And I would have taken him back, no questions asked. I would have consoled him and protected him from Kyra's wrath, from Zoe's ridicule. They would have had to suck it up and take him back as a friend.

Another thing they'd never know is how many times I tried calling him in those six months between the time he'd left me and the time he died. He never answered the phone. Did his wife take the phone away? I imagined him as her slave and her prisoner, never as her lover. Never that. Not if I wanted to survive this break-up. I told myself he'd been miserable, unhappy. That he had to risk his life retrieving the phone to text me, stealing the car keys to come back to me. Then he died, and I just knew that his wife had killed him.

I kneeled down and rested my forehead against the wet canvas.

"Anna Garibaldi," I repeated, tears in my voice. That name had the sound of sacrilege. "I lost him twice because of you."

"Carly."

Zoe rushed to me. I hadn't heard the door.

"Don't cry, sweetie."

"Ever heard of knocking?" I asked, toughening my voice. "You dudes fuss around me like old ladies." I wiped my tears. My hand came away covered in blue paint and snot.

"I knocked," Zoe said, eyeing the painting. "Wow, this is cool."

"This is going," I said, making a move to blot out the painted face. Zoe, strong and quick from years of working in the emergency room, grabbed my shoulders and pulled me away from it.

"*Blue Madonna*," she said, crossing herself. "But you're Jewish!"

I was silent, allowing Zoe time to study the portrait. She didn't take long to realize what she was looking at. From the corner of my eye I saw both her hands go to her cheeks.

"This is no Madonna. This bitch destroyed you."

"Right."
She kept staring at it. "She's your best."
"Don't get too attached," I said.
"Already?" Zoe asked, amazed. "Who bought it?"
"Hades."

3

I had no intention of driving on the Sunset Strip, stopping at Bookworms or landing smack in the middle of *G* in the fiction section. Yet those things happened and they were Anna Garibaldi's fault because she ruled the shelf. All eight of her novels were in my face in the order of their publication. What choice did I have?

Terra Bruciata, or *Scorched Earth*, was her first, a journey of self-discovery originally written in Italian. I picked it up, promising myself only a peek at her glamour photo, to see if my painting was close in resemblance. I read half of Terra Bruciata standing up and the other half, sitting on the carpeted floor. Its page-turning speed left me breathless.

I managed to fit all eight paperbacks into an awkward embrace and carry them to the counter.

"A book club assignment." I felt the need to justify my obsessive purchase to an indifferent cashier, a Marilyn Manson wannabe with multiple piercings.

Manson tossed all the books into a colorful bag and scratched his inflamed earlobe. As inflamed as I was. I counted eight earrings, one for each Anna Garibaldi novel.

At the Starbucks across from Bookworms, I tore ravenously through the second novel, *White Horizon*, letting an untouched Americano cool down in front of me. I'd never before read so fast.

That evening I waited for Zoe to leave for another night shift, then I continued my feverish page turning at the kitchen table.

Anna Garibaldi's style was stream of consciousness with the freshness of a first draft. I was taken by her passion, her sense of both sorrow and *joie de vivre*, her eagle eye for details, her generosity. Had she been an opera singer, she would have lost her voice to excess long ago. She opened doors wide based on one sound, one touch or one whiff of fragrance.

In the course of a week I read all the novels in the order of their publication. I read each book twice. The first time, to find out what happened. The second, to enjoy what she'd coaxed from the language. Each book built on its predecessor. Each prepared for the next. All eight as a whole were an epic experience. All eight had alternate endings, a tragic one and a happy one.

A deep vein of sorrow patterned her fiction. The woman who had everything had lost something irreplaceable. As I tore through the books, chain reading, I searched for my dead beloved in the darkness of her world. What had she lost that had made the way she expressed herself so generous? Entire phrases burned holes in my belly and stayed with me.

I was hooked. I almost forgot that English was not her primary language. She was probably far more brilliant in French and Italian. I almost forgot that she was my enemy. Then came the first nightmare to remind me.

I dreamed I was an eagle, flying over a dead terrain. The sun above me was a big black hole in a stark white sky. I couldn't tell up from down. Something big and more basic than air was missing. The world, I realized, was colorless. All the pigments were gone and without my reds, greens and yellows, I was suffocating, dying.

I woke up air hungry, my face wet with tears. I turned on the light and immersed myself in color—the bedspread, my paintings, the books in my bookshelves. I needed, craved, those colors. Garibaldi's fiction frightened me. *Scorched Earth, White Horizon, Pale Sky* were written long before she had met Greg; still they mirrored her world. Was my beloved lost within those labyrinths of cavernous darkness, wandering and calling my name?

4

"My dear Carly,

Ten years is a significant age difference. I'd been protective of you even before we lost Mom and Dad. Now Greg is also dead, I'm writing the truth I never got to tell you. You may not want to speak to me again after you read it, but I'm writing it for you, as well as for myself. Consider this a love letter from your adoring big sister."

"*Ugh!*" Kyra said in frustration. "This sounds so stupid, she'll laugh."

She threw the crumpled letter into a growing pile of false starts around the overflowing wastepaper basket. She paced the room, restless, stubbing her big toe on the Oxford Dictionary, cursing, fussing. She needed to write it all down even if Carly never read it and the exercise only served to get the story out of her own system. But first, food.

There was nothing in her fridge except a leathery old pizza from the night Lulu broke up with her, a jar of green olives covered in gray fuzz from when Zoe mixed drinks for all of them. A container of unidentified Chinese food stunk up the place. She threw it all into the trash. Nothing in the freezer, not even ice cream. What a mess she was for a well paid professional. What would her clients think if they saw how she lived?

Kyra clicked open a can of beer and took a small sip. She stood for a moment, pressing the cold, wet can against her burning cheek, frustrated and worried, because how did you tell the horrible truth to someone you loved, especially to your sister, whose life you had ruined?

Her desk was its usual mess, with coffee mugs stuck to its surface and piled high with books she was supposed to read. Nothing too exciting: Jung and Adler and some experimental contemporaries. She was half way through Freud's *Die*

Traumdeutung in the original German, but that was just fun reading, as she was fascinated by dreams and their interpretation.

She gulped her beer and graced the world with a thunderous belch. Then she picked up the legal pad, rested one bare foot on the lowest drawer and began another miserable attempt at a confession.

"Dearest Carly, your crying at the funeral was a healthy sign, but when Garibaldi started praising her dead husband and you lost your temper, it took all three of us to seat you back down.

She allowed you to complain, I'll give her that. You left early, so you didn't get to see how the Divine One sashayed behind the casket, with the huge bodyguard, that brick shithouse on steroids, ambling next to her. I assumed that was the first time she'd walked behind Greg.

I promised truth, so here's the first scorcher: seeing her up close, I understood what happened to Greg. I could have high-fived his dead ass. Falling for her had to have been a no-brainer. Her beauty is startling. Her voice is music. Her walk is a dance. Her sunglasses—she was never seen wearing one pair twice—are a hoot. And her hair . . . Famous people have a thing about their hair.

Here's the thing. Handsome men like Greg are as common as dirt for La Divina. I know why he fell for her, Carly, but what on earth did she find in him?

What did you find in him, other than childhood friendship?

When you and Greg decided to get married, I believed it a big mistake. As you know, about marriage, I'm right there with Oscar Wilde: *Bigamy is having one wife too many; monogamy is the same.*

I was against it for another reason: you two were childhood sweethearts and neither of you had dated others. I said nothing at the time, and I should shut up now so as not to speak ill of the dead. Yet for all I know, you'll never read this anyway, so I'm writing for myself and I need to put it all out there.

I loved him as a friend, but as a husband, I believed you could do better than Greg. He as much as admitted that to me one night at the G-Spot. I was already annoyed, because my friend and sometime foe B. J. had just found out about my second Ph.D. She kept saying, 'What's up, Doc?' to me in that voice, acting totally stupid and passive aggressive. She thought Greg was my date and that I was switching teams.

Anyway, after two beers for Greg, one tequila shot for me, and five *What's up, Doc*s from B. J., Greg confessed that he had an inferiority complex when it came to you.

'Drop the qualifier,' I said quietly into my drink.

He was so busy feeling sorry for himself, my insult went over his head.

There was no complex; he was simply inferior to you. He could recognize good art, he knew a hell of a lot about it, but his talent was shit when you dated him, it was shit when he painted his muse, Anna Garibaldi, and when serious collectors bought his paintings way before they'd dried, his talent was still shit. Where the critics saw gentle expression, I saw weakness of lines due to weakness of character. I know how you hate it when I speak against him—bear with me while I'm getting to the point.

I figured he was suffering pre-marital jitters, because he turned into a drunken mess and the truth came out of him like verbal diarrhea. I hear the tearful confessions of strangers for a living, and it takes a lot to upset me, but Greg upset me then. His confession mirrored my own ugly thoughts.

I would have openly agreed with him, had I not stopped after that one Jose Cuervo. I had to fall back on professional nodding, humming and biting my tongue. I remained sober. I memorized his words so I'd be able to open your eyes one day. Did you know he planned to manage your career? Translation: he was going to let you work while he counted your money. Problem was, even at managing finances he was inferior to you.

I kept quiet—my first mistake. I should have openly objected. What I never forgave, even as I stood at his open grave, was the way he broke up with you, or rather didn't even bother to do. If hell exists, I hope the motherfucker is burning in it.

The rest tomorrow,
love you,

Kyra."

She shoved the legal pad into the drawer and quickly slid it shut, as if it could come alive and jump at her.

The rest tomorrow.

That, if she could bring herself to write down the rest.

5

Zoe still wore her green scrubs when she came into my room with coffee and the morning paper.

"Will you ever learn to knock?" I snapped at her, another colorless nightmare lingering inside my sleepy head.

"I did."

She didn't, but the coffee absolved her. Zoe would never knock, and I would always snap and immediately forgive her, just because she was Zoe.

The two of us had become fast friends during my short career as a nursing student. We'd studied together for finals. Then I dropped out of the nursing program in favor of life drawing, portraiture, and art history. My nursing career was over before it had begun, luckily for my future patients since I was too disorganized to be a nurse and my real love was art. Zoe and I remained best friends. When she needed a roommate to help pay her mortgage, I moved in with her and took the room upstairs. It had been five years now, and we both loved the arrangement.

Zoe saw the books strewn on the floor. The glamorous author smiled beatifically behind a pair of diamond-clad sunglasses from the back cover of *White Horizon*.

"All her books?" Zoe glared at me with disbelief. "Why are you making yourself crazy, painting her portrait, reading this shit? She ruined your life."

"That's why."

She picked up *White Horizon*. "Is she any good?"

"That's the problem," I said. "Brilliant."

Zoe dropped the morning paper on top of my blanket and sat cross-legged on the bed. "Here's another one for you—listen to this." She read out loud from the paper's book section. "Famous novelist brings beloved dead husband back to life with erotic poetry. *A Silver Ring* by Anna Garibaldi is saved from pornography only by its elegant expression."

The cover was a photo of a hand, its pinky adorned with a shiny silver ring that matched my own.

"The nerve!" I protested, spilling hot coffee on my white sheet. "I paid four bucks for two of those when I was twelve!"

Both rings had crude engravings of Greg's name and mine, done on the spot at a street fair while we munched on spicy hot dogs. We both later wore them on our pinkies. I used to take mine off only when working extra-messy oil pieces with my fingers. Greg never took his off, at least not when we were a couple.

Zoe said, "Your two-buck ring has just become a priceless *objet d'art*."

"I'll get it back," I growled, "if I have to rip it off her finger."

"Good luck with that," Zoe said.

An hour later I found myself at Bookworms. It didn't take me long to find Garibaldi's poetry collection; I tripped on its garish, over-the-top display, ending up face down on the floor with a life-sized cardboard cut-out of the alluring author on top of me—extravagant sunglasses, complex hair structure, feather boa and all the rest.

"You're not the first who tripped today," said Marilyn Manson in his bored voice. He reassembled the cardboard cut-out exactly in the same spot. I wanted to point out the obvious to him, but didn't. Let more customers disgrace themselves.

A Silver Ring by Anna Garibaldi was already a bestseller.

I leafed through the thin paperback. The text was in two languages, the Italian translation of each poem on the adjacent page. The grainy cover shot became grainier as I stared at it. It was hard to tell whose hand it was, hers or his. Mine? I compared the book's ring to the tarnished silver ring on my hand, inspecting the blue oil pigment under my fingernails.

More than anything, I wanted to be disgusted by bad writing. She could write fiction, indeed, but poetry was a whole 'nother thing.

I should have known better.

With the first stanza I recognized greatness. I read each poem carefully, all of them. Like Beethoven's *Ninth Symphony*, this ninth and last book was by far Garibaldi's greatest, the erotic climax of all that had come before. That last poem, the title poem, was Garibaldi's "Ode to Joy."

The poem was as brief as an afterthought. Four lines captured the rainbow of human emotions. In those few words I realized how much she'd loved him, and that Greg had never taken the ring off his finger. That latter realization filled me with happiness. I closed my eyes and imagined telling her about the ring, its importance. Rubbing it in and laughing when she cried.

"Miss, are you okay?"

A short balding man in an Hawaiian shirt offered me tissues. I was the one crying.

That night I read the whole book again.

In my dream she stood by my bed, pale and angelic, wearing that tight black suit from the funeral. Her eyes saw deep into my core. *You loved him*, I said, *but he was mine till the end.* I told her about my Greg and what he had meant to me. I told her how she had robbed me of my happiness. She listened quietly and then she ran a warm hand over one side of my face, down my neck, lower. I discovered I was naked.

My own gasp of dread woke me up. The book was open on my face, and even the smell of its new pages was raw sensuality. What was happening to me?

I skipped down to the kitchen. With trembling hands I mixed myself a Baseball Bat 911, a mean martini with extra twists. Zoe claimed it killed her emotions.

Mine remained alive and sizzling.

"Fuck you, Garibaldi." I drank the slush straight from the pitcher sip after icy sip, emptying it into my burning throat. "Damn," I cried out, hating her even more when brain freeze doubled me over with excruciating pain.

Zoe found me at the kitchen table, reading it for the third time and picking at a bowl of cereal. I quickly closed the book. Big mistake. Garibaldi's glamour shot stared at us from the back cover. I sat on it.

"Whose face are you sitting on?" Zoe asked with a yawn, slumping into a chair.

I ignored her. "Did you have a nice night shift?"

"You can get used to having your soul sucked out, but you wouldn't call it nice."

She leaned back against the wall, drained and pale with exhaustion. I saw the dark bloodstains on the front of her scrubs and knew what she'd never put into words, that another stranger might have died in her arms last night.

"You need the breakfast special?" I asked.

"Nine. One. One."

The Baseball Bat 911 was created long ago on a certain night Zoe and I wanted, needed, to forget. We'd been studying together for our pathophysiology final—the upper respiratory system—when Zoe decided to try her new stethoscope on me. She'd listened to my heart and lungs, then I listened to hers, and next we were necking, then kissing, then playing doctor in her four-poster bed. Our affair lasted about five minutes and was a unanimous failure.

"At least we won't die wondering," Zoe had said. "Let's mix a new cocktail."

A lifelong friendship was born, along with our co-creation, the illustrious Baseball Bat, which we considered a noncredit school project. Our failed lesbian endeavor had left Zoe certain of her heterosexuality and me wondering what else was out there. Kyra claimed that one time didn't make you gay, only curious.

Zoe waited for me to get up. Quickly she snatched the poetry book from the chair, proving she wasn't as tired as she looked.

"Whatcha reading this smut for?" She flipped through the pages.

I snapped the thin volume away from her, my face burning. I didn't want her in my business.

"Why are you paying this woman for her books when you can barely make the month?"

"Next week I get paid for that family job." I dropped a Kalamata into her drink. "I'll pay you the rent."

"Good," Zoe said. "For once you charge people."

"I worked pro bono *once*," I said.

Five-year-old Timmy had sat for a portrait he wanted to give his mom for her birthday. He offered me ten bucks, his entire savings. I'd said a hug would do.

"You don't see me work for free," Zoe said.

"What do you call that Heimlich maneuver you did at Rocko's?"

"Life and death don't count."

"Now you sound like a real nurse," I said.

"Reassuring." She gave another dainty sip, then knocked the drink back and burped out loud. She stared at the book with disgust, and the dark circles of fatigue around her eyes made her seem ill. "It isn't only Greg. Something dark has gotten into you."

She was right. I drank the leftover martini straight from the shaker. Alcohol made me remember I had something to tell her.

"And something dark wants to get into *you*."

Zoe sat up, alert. "Robert's back from Florida?"

Her boyfriend worked for Montblanc as a window display designer, traveling around the country.

"If it isn't him, someone else used his keys and snored in your bedroom all night."

She got up. "I'll find out what's wrong if I have to overdose you with Sodium Pentothal."

"Go to your boyfriend," I said, laughing. "And pity my celibate ears, you two. Keep it quiet for a change."

I read the poetry book at Starbucks again, then for the fifth time in my study, in the midst of half-finished canvases, strewn paintbrushes and the tang of turpentine. I read the whole thing in the Italian, a language familiar to me because I was an opera junkie. I learned the last poem by heart, to bathe myself in the essence of the Divine One. To find Greg in her world.

Despite my deep hate for Anna Garibaldi, I couldn't keep away from that book. The poems—erotic, sensual, dark—lured me, pulled at all my senses. I could taste the words on the tip of my tongue, smell their musky fragrance, feel their soft caress on my skin. If I blocked the traffic noise on Santa Monica Boulevard, I could almost hear a sultry whisper, her famous voice, reading the words.

Greg and her.

I imagined the two of them on the dance floor, her leading in a sexy tango. *Slow, slow, quick, quick, slow*. I could see them at the breakfast table, crunching toast, pouring coffee for each other, his dark, passionate eyes, those eyes that loved me, now burning with love for her. I saw the powerful seduction of their bond. I imagined them in bed, her leading again . . .

This was too much.

The sun was setting. It had been six hours since Zoe joined Robert in her bedroom. I worked on one of my green landscapes, feeling lonelier than ever and on my way down the road of desperation. I was a shit for lying to Zoe about the rent. She would again have to pay the mortgage by herself. It wasn't the first time one of us picked up for the other, but I felt bad just the same.

White envelopes of unpaid bills were piled on my desk. The sight of them didn't help my melancholy. I decided to be brave, go downstairs and admit to my best friends the sad truth that I was broke.

I made a fresh pot of coffee, poured three mugs and stirred them with cinnamon sticks. I knocked on Zoe's bedroom door, a tray in my hands.

Robert's groggy voice answered, "Come in."

I squeezed myself into the warmth between them on top of the blanket. Mental pictures flashed in my memory of that one night with Zoe, here in this very room a million years ago.

"Did we get a dog?" a sleepy Zoe asked. "Oh, it's you. What's up?" She reached out for her mug and sipped loudly.

I lay on my back, stared at the ceiling and just said it. "I'm broke. I can't pay you the rent, Zoe. The money from that family portrait wasn't much to begin with and is long gone on art supplies and on the books of that bitch who ruined my life."

"Screw the rent, Carly," Zoe said. "Tell mama what's really wrong."

"Here it comes," I said, looking away from Zoe's gaze. "I wanted to . . ."

I was going to tell them how I wanted to confront Anna Garibaldi because I was certain she'd killed Greg, but I couldn't.

Robert was good at finances, so instead I said, "Can you, will you, check my bank account with me, see if there's a way to apply for a personal loan?"

"Sure." Robert put down his coffee and reached for his laptop. "Sign on. Once we see what we're up against, we'll work it out together."

I loved the way he used *we*. I hesitated, embarrassed to let even my best friends see my pathetic balance. I signed onto my bank account and waited for my password to be verified.

"What the hell?" I rubbed my eyes in disbelief, thinking my vision was distorted from reading too much poetry. I screamed.

Zoe and Robert stuck their faces close on both sides of me. Then black coffee splashed everywhere on the white bedspread as their shrieks joined mine.

"Call Kyra," I said. "We need someone who can think straight."

6

"Don't ever use those words on me," Diane mumbled, her shaky fingers playing with the brown polka dots on the faded gray couch.

"Again, Diane," Kyra said. "Calmly, clearly. Be assertive."

Diane wiped her tears with the edge of her beige sleeve and repeated the words, still mumbling, but looking Kyra in the eye.

"Better. Now prouder."

"*Don't ever use those words on me.*"

Kyra gasped out loud. "Good, that gave me a chill. You looked formidable, strong."

"Strong? Me?" She pointed at herself.

"Definitely," Kyra said. "Keep this attitude and have fun watching what happens to all the bullies in your life—your husband, your kids, your co-workers. All of them."

Diane blew her nose into a tissue.

Kyra glanced around her office, at the hodgepodge of furniture gathered from garage sales. The old desk, the boring couch with the brown polka dots. The place needed an overhaul, a Zen redesign with bright colors. There was nothing soothing about those brown polka dots, nothing tasteful, nothing here suitable for a therapist's office, except the framed pastel on the wall.

That pastel drawing was different. It was beautiful. Carly painted it when she was six. She rendered Mom's casket next to Dad's headstone in stark black and whites, and in the midst of all that grief two girls in spring colors, a big girl and a little one, holding hands, looking at each other with love and light. Carly's small, warm hand in Kyra's, her gaze of trust up at her big sister. What six-year-old had such a mind for colors? Kyra thought.

At sixteen she had become Carly's guardian, and it was more than a mere legal term. She'd always loved her little sister as though she'd given birth to her. Once both their parents were dead, Kyra had become Carly's mother and father, best friend, confidant. They were everything to each other. In this drawing Carly's gifts and skills are already apparent, in the way she captures Kyra's short, spiky hair, her wire John Lennon glasses, her monumental size. But how she understood colors, the drama of colors, at such a young age was beyond Kyra.

"The drama of colors," Kyra said.

"What?" Diane's voice jolted her back into the moment.

Kyra was distracted. It was wholly unproductive, and it certainly wasn't fair to her patient.

She had an idea. "You need retail therapy."

Diane seemed shocked, as one would, realizing her therapist had lost her mind.

"A new attitude starts with clothes," Kyra explained. "Go buy yourself a power suit."

"What, now?" she asked, fumbling with her beige purse.

"A bright red T-shirt," Kyra said. "Tight jeans with back pockets. And boots. Big, bad boots."

Diane didn't move.

"A doctor's order," Kyra said, smiling. "This session is on me."

"Yes, Doctor." Diane smiled back, the first smile Kyra had seen in ages.

As she locked up, her gaze went to the lettering on the door.

Kyra Rosen, Ph.D., Psychotherapist.

This plaque, those letters after her name, her whole life suddenly seemed hollow. She felt small and insignificant. An impostor.

What right did she have to pry into people's lives, to listen to their honest confessions, to guide and direct them, when her own sister couldn't trust her anymore? She listened to people every day. Was good at it and got paid for it. Yet her nearest and dearest could not open up to her, and she couldn't blame her.

Carly had been abandoned at the altar and she, Kyra, was the one responsible. Greg was the only other person who knew exactly how it had happened, and now he was dead, so, inadvertently, Kyra was responsible also for his death. Carly didn't ask about it, but one day she may, and Kyra will have to tell her how she had ruined her life.

The plaque on her door should read, *Dr. Kyra Rosen, total fuck-up*.

Wracked with guilt, Kyra took her own advice. On the way home she stopped at the Boot Barn, and immediately fell in love with a pair of cowboy boots. They had spurs and buckles in all the right places and they cost more than Kyra had any business spending on a single item, but she planned to live in them until they fell apart. It was hard to find shoes for a six-footer like herself, what with her huge paws and her fussy stylistic demands. She wore them out to the street, enjoying every metal clunk they made. The world smiled at her again.

Her second stop was the G-Spot, the center of West Hollywood, to see who was there and to show off her purchase. Then she planned to go home and prepare for Tuesday's lecture on sex and violence.

Bruna leaned against the door and snapped at everybody. Her sunburned face twitched.

"Hi, Bruna Bear," Kyra said, stretching up to kiss the cheek of the only human female taller than her.

"Hey, Doc," said Bruna, her deep baritone softening. Bruna had had a crush on Kyra since that time Kyra allowed her, for laughs, to frisk her.

"How's your cute little sister?" she asked.

"Hanging in there."

"You think someone loves you, then *wham-o*," Bruna said. "Tell her we feel for her."

West Hollywood had no secrets. Kyra didn't exactly want to small-talk the ups and downs of Carly's life, then she remembered something.

"I saw your dead ringer at the funeral," she said. "The left side of her face twitches when she's mad, like the right side of yours."

"Hildi is my mirror twin." Bruna spat into the corner through a large gap between her front teeth. The spittle nearly hit Kyra's new boots, but she jumped in time.

"Wow, your twin works for Anna Garibaldi," she said, immediately full of regret for possibly stirring up old demons.

"Yes, and I'm stuck here." Bruna made an extravagant gesture toward the dark wooden façade on which someone had knocked down the *S* and left *G- pot.*

"Don't you two switch places sometimes, for kicks?" Kyra asked. "Carly and I have the exact same voice, and we sometimes fuck with people on the phone."

"Me and my bitch sister don't talk," Bruna said, bitter. "Hildi is too wrapped up in that important job to fit me in."

Kyra would have bought her a drink since she'd upset her, but her phone chimed the clinking-glasses ringtone, announcing a new message.

Come for tea, Zoe texted.

Tea time had nothing to do with Buckingham Palace. Mostly it meant pitchers of that shit they called Baseball Bat 911. Kyra didn't know what Zoe mixed into it, but the hangovers were amazing.

What's wrong? she texted back, blowing a kiss to Bruna as she started for the Jeep.

It's about Greg, Zoe texted. *Carly and Greg.*

On my way.

Kyra picked up her pace, wishing she'd bought a larger size boot. Her clunky new boots were all of a sudden too tight on her running feet, the metal spurs too loud with each footfall.

Carly and Greg. Mentioning the two in the same sentence had been taboo for the last few months.

What happened to Greg could have happened to anyone—La Divina was irresistible—but he didn't even have the decency to break up with Carly. Together since early childhood, and not even a phone call. Not one. Carly was discarded and forgotten.

Most people have a nervous breakdown when catastrophe barrels into their lives. Carly had been stoic when he deserted her and stoic when he died. She'd rejected sympathy as one would reject poison. Instead, she acquired a new artistic direction, a new style reflecting her personal tragedy. For instance, she took one pastoral landscape and threw blood-red blots on it. When she was done taking her anger out on that painting, it resembled that Jungian nightmare of death and dismemberment.

Greg became dead to Carly, but not to Kyra. Carly's work helped her keep an illusion of sanity; Kyra's didn't.

She had tried calling him a few times to give him a piece of her mind, but her calls were declined. He knew that she knew what happened, unless his brain rot had set in early on. Kyra imagined that he had given up all his friends for the same reason he allowed the Divine One to change his name. He'd become a joke. Even the name his wife had given him—*Guido*—was used in a derogatory manner.

Soon thereafter the art world discovered Greg Wheeler, aka *Guido*, aka *Mr. Garibaldi*, because, to add insult to injury, he'd suddenly flamed with creativity. Not that he had sprouted a real talent. Rather, he'd found art as some found the Lord, through epiphany. His medium was oil on canvas, his muse was his powerful new wife, who presented his artless paintings in the most lucrative galleries of Beverly Hills and New York. They sold like a hot new gadget before Christmas. He was a joke indeed, a trendy joke. Anyone who was someone wanted to own a *Guido*.

When Greg became the new object of mass fascination, Kyra, the art snob, actually studied his works. Here's another irony: the woman most known for her beauty had become his model, yet his nudes of her were as sophisticated as the mudflap girls.

The story of their love flooded all sorts of media. On TV interviews they never sat in separate chairs, always in a loveseat holding on to each other, and Greg being so affected and full of himself, he made Kyra gag. Painting was his new *metier* and Anna Garibaldi was his muse, or *musa*, as he'd pronounce it, steeped in pretense and condescension. His talent was a flat line. He was funny with his friends, but his sense of humor committed suicide way before he got himself killed, when he started using fat expressions like *having a metier* and *capturing the Zeitgeist*.

"*Musa* my ass, you shit," Kyra would yell at the TV when Carly wasn't around. "What about my sister?"

As for Carly, Greg was off limits for criticism or jokes. It was painful, because snide remarks would write themselves. Kyra learned to bite her tongue until it hurt, as did Zoe and Robert. She should have invested in Kank-A, the way her whole mouth constantly ached from not being allowed to cut loose.

Of course, not all was peachy in Greg's marriage. His famous wife, as the rumor went, had a frightening temper. There was that television interview in which she'd insulted him. They all watched it, all except Carly. And there was a humiliating scene at one of his art shows the week he was killed. An attempt was made to hush it up, but the tabloids were worse than ever.

Carly would have felt so much better had she joined them and laughed at him and at the unfolding grand operatic drama of their marriage. The Greg Kyra knew and loved would have made fun of himself. A paradox and an irony.

"You don't speak against the dead," Carly said once.

"Only his sense of humor died," Robert answered.

The quiet way Carly glared at poor Robert, he could have turned to stone. It was as if nothing he had ever done for her mattered.

And then two weeks ago Greg really died, and the vault was sealed forever on what a piece of shit he was.

Kyra was often mistaken for the tougher sister because of her size, her butch appearance and her big, bad mouth. Yet Carly was really the one to be wary of. She was tough to a point of pigheadedness. Kyra knew her limits with her sister.

Kyra's tires screeched to a halt. Carly ran out to greet her, short of breath. Her long hair was bunched up like a bird's nest on top of her head, and the ruined wedding gown she had turned into a blotter dress was even baggier than the week before, when Kyra had last seen her. Carly was wasting away. The green streaks of oil paint on her cheek were the only color in her otherwise pale face. She smelled of turpentine.

"You should change your perfume, princess." The green paint on her cheek was still wet when Kyra tried wiping it off. "And the brand of your make-up."

"Come." Carly pulled her like a bag of laundry up the stairs to her study.

Greg's black widow wielded power and authority from that extraordinary piece they named *Blue Madonna*. Below it, Zoe and Robert were staring at a laptop. They greeted Kyra with excitement and pointed at the screen. It was a bank account page.

"Fuck me," Kyra said, counting more and more zeros.

7

"Fuck me," Kyra kept saying, so many times I started to worry about her.

"Nice new boots," Zoe said.

My sister tore her gaze away from my engorged bank account and glanced down at her feet. "Thanks. Who cares?"

"No one. You had to be rebooted," Zoe said.

Robert's baggy pajama bottoms sagged off her slim hips and made everything she said sound funny. We were laughing. Nervously.

"Did you sell something fabulous?" Kyra asked.

"No, but we have a theory," I said. "Look at the date of the transaction."

Kyra did. "Exactly two weeks ago. How did you not see it for that long?"

"Never mind that," I said. "Remember what happened, Kyra? Think!"

Kyra wrinkled her forehead. "The day he died!"

"Exactly!" A strange triumph seized me. "This is still our joint account! He transferred the money the day he died. Remember his text message? He was trapped and unhappy in a miserable marriage and he was coming back to me."

"I guess he wasn't as useless about finances as I thought," Kyra muttered to herself, infuriating me. "But why transfer the money? Why not first come and see you and make sure you were on the same page?"

"This is the cherry on the cake of my theory. Greg knew he was going to die. She was killing him, poisoning him, and he knew. I'm going to the police to tell them everything I know. She is going to prison."

"*Whoa, whoa,* does anyone else hear my sister talking crazy?" Kyra stood, arms akimbo, her spiked black hair falling into her eyes. "I hate her too, but you can't go around accusing people willy-nilly."

I said, "The money is evidence, so is the poetry book she conveniently published, what, a mere week after his death?"

"Conveniently? She is an author," Kyra said.

"But her timing, the planning needed. Unless she self-published, which she doesn't. Obviously she wrote the poems during the early months of the marriage, while planning his murder."

Kyra said, "He died in a car accident, texting you! Good thing he didn't take anyone else out with him."

I raised my gaze up to *Blue Madonna*. "I'll see in her attitude if she's guilty of murder."

"How exactly will you see that, Miss Law and Order?" Kyra asked.

"I'm a portrait artist. I can see into my sitter's soul. I'll confront her and tell by her reaction. Then I'll demand Greg's ring back."

Zoe laughed out loud. "Will you threaten her with a number ten drawing pencil or with a charcoal white?"

"I'm serious."

A plan was forming in my obsessive mind. I was going to somehow confront her. But how and why? My belly ached at the prospect of a meeting. Would I say, *You loved him, but all the while he wore my ring*? Would I request that she tell me about his last months? Would I fall at her feet and thank her for her loving eulogy?

I hated her for the influence her words had on me, for the way her books intrigued me and her poems inflamed me. The last and shortest poem made me downright desperate. But for what?

Before my life went to shit, I had no interest in her books. Now I was hungry for every word. There was no reason to ever see her again, yet I was dying for a close look.

Kyra said, "You plan to go to one of the most powerful women in Hollywood, who is more protected than the Mona Lisa, and demand a ring that belonged to her late husband?"

"It has sentimental value." I stuck my ringed pinky up. The sight of my almost black ring and the blue paint staining my fingernails was pathetic and so was I.

"She's Italian." Zoe fastened her huge pajama bottoms. "She'll have the *Cosa Nostra* chop off your finger for your matching ring and stick it up your ass before they drown you in the toilet."

"Slow down, Zoe," Kyra said, wincing along with me at the mental picture.

Zoe didn't give up. "Before you get anywhere near the bitch, and *confront* her, a gang of Amazons will eat you alive and spit out the bones. What's wrong with you?"

They were so predictable. One saved lives for a living and the other calmed lunatics, but both were losing their cool. I let their reactions wash over me and give my private madness the colors of the rainbow.

"I hate to spoil your drama."

Robert, always an intent listener, typically reserved speaking for emergencies. He was our fashion consultant, our hair stylist, our zen coach, our financial advisor. When he spoke, we listened.

"This all may be a bank error, and if it isn't, you'll have to pay taxes on it at the end of the year."

"I don't need his stinking money," I said, testing my own feelings and theirs. "I'm going to throw it in her rich and famous face."

"What?" Kyra and Zoe cried out in unison.

Robert ignored them. "If, indeed, it is from Greg, the money is rightfully yours."

"How so?" I asked.

"It was his last wish that you have it."

"His last wish, as far as I'm concerned, was to marry me."

Kyra and Zoe started again, but Robert raised his hand to shush them.

"Carly, you're all over the place with this," he said, calm. "You'll demand Greg's ring; you'll accuse her of murder; you'll throw Greg's money in her face. I'm not telling you not to meet her, but be clear on the why. Laser-sharp mental focus is power."

Focus.

"Here's the thing," I said to the three people closest to me. "I may be a little out there, but I feel like, well, you know, Orpheus."

"We know Orpheus," Zoe said. "He's that Greek dude who resuscitated his dead chick."

"He didn't actually succeed," Kyra said. "He messed up because he loved her too much and he turned too early, and—"

"Right," I said. "Well . . . " I hesitated. How could I admit just how crazy this was? "I won't rest till I've crossed the Styx, faced Hades and reclaimed my beloved. I know this sounds like metaphoric mumbo jumbo, but I need your support."

Greek mythology did it. Zoe and Kyra relaxed their faces. Robert sighed with relief.

"Shoot an email to her agent and ask for an appointment," Robert said. "You have nothing to lose."

"She can't give you Greg back," Kyra said, "but play nice and she may give you the ring."

Zoe warned, "No mention of the money."

"I'll see about that," I said.

"Never!" Zoe cried out, letting go of her pants.

A tickle of hysterical laughter started in my chest.

"What's wrong with you?" Kyra eyed me with concern.

"Zoe . . ." I pointed, unable to speak. Her pants were on the floor, revealing a red thong that was supposed to be sexy, but drooped off her little butt.

Our dramatic mood was broken. Now I had to get them out of my room. "I can't think straight without a drink. Zoe, cover up your bony ass and make us a pitcher of slushy Bats."

Slushy would buy me more time.

"It's nice to see your sour *punim* smiling for a change," Kyra said.

"Call me when it's ready." I nudged them out.

They were all chatting excitedly on their way downstairs. Zoe was already in Hawaii, sipping mai tais and gazing at hot surfers as she helped me spend the money. Kyra said that I was finally getting paid for what the bastard had put me through. Soon I heard the blender crushing ice in the kitchen. The ice had to be crushed first then all the ingredients added slowly in a certain order.

I sat still, battling with myself not to follow them downstairs. I had something to celebrate, didn't I? Greg had loved me even when he was married to a famous, great beauty. He'd left me all his money when he knew he was dying. He'd died on his way back to me, hadn't he? His widow should keep his ring—she had no idea what it symbolized anyway—and I should dump all her books in the local library and be done with it. Move on.

Yet my life wasn't that simple. My self-esteem was tied to the man who had abandoned me at the altar.

I took out one of my letterheads and wrote, "*Dear Ms. Garibaldi.*" The loathed name, the formal *Dear*, made my hand shake so violently, I had to rip the paper up and start again. I kept it short.

"Dear Ms. Garibaldi,

I would like to make an appointment with you.

Regards,

Carly Rosen."

For some reason beyond me, I quickly snapped a few photographs of *Blue Madonna* with my cellphone. I downloaded them to my laptop and chose the least sinister version of those shots, the one not exactly true to color, with its background more blue than black. I made an eight by ten print. With my heart pounding out of my chest, I placed the print and the letter in a manila envelope, and addressed it to Anna Garibaldi in care of her agent, whose name and address I found online. I marked it private and confidential.

"It's ready," Zoe called from downstairs, sounding silly, having obviously enjoyed a few tastes of her potent mix. "We want to toast you and all your new stinking money."

What am I doing? I took the envelope with its contents to the shredder, pressed the shred button, but then released it.

Still barefoot, wearing my paint-stained blotting dress, I ran downstairs. Jolly laughter came from the kitchen. I hesitated another split second, then hurried out the door and across the street. I dropped the envelope into the blue mailbox, the point of no return. Immediately, I tried to fish it out, but it was too low, too deep in the dark underworld of irretrievable letters.

8

I craved her response, I dreaded it, I fantasized and dreamed big nightmares inspired by her fiction. I knew that her response would never come. The divine Anna Garibaldi surely employed a cabal of secretaries, or deadly brutes with geared-up spears, who had treated my letter as trash.

In my new works I used not only a paintbrush, but my fingers and my palms and the backs of my hands and the palette knife—big strokes, thick layers. When the paint dried, I could see the painting with my eyes closed by running my fingertips on its surface.

In each idyllic landscape I planted something from my nightmares. A calm ocean resort, with playful dolphins and bathers and their colorful umbrellas, was threatened by a giant black wave. A serene mountain scene with red-roofed houses was gradually washing into a gloomy, colorless terrain in black, white and grays. A foreboding storm cloud took the shape of a cloaked figure.

"Greg's black widow?" Kyra's short hair was spiked up in a new, thornier style.

"Hair glue?" I asked.

"No hair product at all," she said, dropping all eight of Garibaldi's books on my bed. "This black and white detailed descriptions makes my hair stand on end." She threw my pillow on top of the author's angelic face.

"Can I pick your brain?" I asked. I'd tell Kyra my recurring dream and she would solve it, decimate it, and put my mind to rest.

"You actually want my *help*?" Kyra asked, unable to hide her excitement. "I'm flattered."

Kyra's genuine interest and intense listening skills made her a rising star as a psychotherapist. She could have just as easily become a priest or a police detective. She simply made one want to confess. So far I held back, knowing that she blamed herself for what had happened to me. I wasn't ready to hear the truth just as she wasn't yet ready to tell me. Maybe our time has come to talk seriously.

"Promise to treat me like any of your clients," I said.

"Two hundred an hour," she said. "Hop into my Wrangler. We'll talk on the way downtown."

It was the miserable rush hour. The 110 freeway stretched bumper to bumper for miles as I told Kyra about the nightmares and the attacks of vertigo I lately suffered in high places. "I can't even look down at my feet!"

"Jung says that everything in your dream represents you," Kyra explained. "The eagle, the colorless world, the black water, the black sun, the white sky are all you, whatever they mean to you. White and black are the play between knowledge and mystery."

"What's Freud's take on it?"

"Freud is all sex. Your dreams give expression to erotic wishes. Your black body of water, the black killer wave, the black cloak—even your own nakedness—are all associated with love, protection and enveloping female sexuality."

"Which means what, Dr. Rosen?" I said.

"Nothing a good fuck can't fix," Kyra said. "You've been a nun for a long time."

"Is this how you talk to your clients?"

"Seriously, get out more, meet new people. Hey, what about this Friday? Be my date on New Year's Eve."

"Okay," I said. "Fix me up with one of your girlfriends."

"I have a list of women waiting for you to switch teams."

"Tempting."

The G-Spot would be crowded, sweaty and loud, but anything was better than spending my first New Year's Eve without Greg and alone. The midnight kiss used to be such a big deal for us, wherever we chose to be.

"I'll teach you the beer bottle trick," Kyra said, excited.

"What's that?"

"Something you do when you run out of pick-up lines."

"You'll never run out of words!" I laughed out loud. My sister was a hopeless one-night-stander. "Tell me more about what sucks the colors out of my dreams. Give me more Freud and Jung. What's your theory?"

"You live art," she said. "You drink, eat and breathe color. When you imagine your private hell, it is colorless. What a fucking parking lot. Our time is up, Ms. Rosen."

I wanted more professional Kyra. I was ready to hear the truth about what happened the night Greg had dropped me, but the traffic was getting on her nerves.

"It must be a gigantic accident," I said, searching AM channels for a traffic report. "Maybe we can bypass the thing."

I landed on Juliana Crown's Book Talk.

" . . . new poetry collection by best-selling novelist Anna Ga —"

"Asshole!" Kyra screamed out the window. "Quit honking and get off my tail. No one's moving!"

"Eat something," I said. "You're unbearable."

I took a partially eaten hamburger out of a shopping bag and unwrapped it for her. The commercials were on for two long minutes. Then Juliana Crown said, "We're back with author Anna Garibaldi and her poetry collection, *A Silver Ring*."

The next voice, a silky contralto with hints of both Italian and French, twisted my heart and squeezed out its blood. It was the voice from the funeral. The voice from the eulogy. The voice from my nightmares.

I pointed at the radio. "Listen, Kyra."

"I'm listening, princess. What?"

"It's her."

Hamburgers are not meant to be eaten while driving. A piece of meat went the wrong way down Kyra's throat. She started coughing. The whole thing in its wrapper flew out of her hand and rained bits of bread, mushrooms and meat on us. Kyra would likely forget about it until two days later, when the Jeep started reeking of decayed meat.

"Those poems were all written in one week. The week my dear Guido and I fell in love."

That week.

The week Greg had left me hanging out to dry, she was writing poetry.

"To think you managed to write . . ." Juliana chuckled.

"Yes, love and poetry," Garibaldi said with a sigh.

Juliana said, "Is the silver ring an actual ring or only a euphemism for sexual intercourse?" Juliana asked.

"Actual," Kyra and I said in unison.

"My dear Guido never took it off his little finger. A silent agreement between us kept me from asking about it. I knew the ring was an important part of his past and that he would tell me in time. The day he died, in the emergency room, I was handed both his wedding ring and the silver ring."

Juliana asked, "Did Guido keep many secrets from you?"

"I can't complain," she said. "I had a few of my own."

"Do you mind sharing?"

Anna Garibaldi's throaty, sensual laughter ran chills down my back.

"You'll have to read between the lines." Her voice cracked. Was it laughter, tears, or an act? I couldn't tell.

My sister fidgeted, restless. I had no idea what she was up to until Juliana said, "We have Kyra on the line."

I glared at her in amazement. How had she managed to call without my noticing?

"I know that ring," Kyra said. "My sister has a matching one, and both are engraved."

"Kyra, quiet!" I begged.

"Is your late husband's silver ring engraved?" Juliana's voice came from the radio.

"Not that I know of."

"Ms. Garibaldi," Kyra said with venom. "You are a boyfriend-stealing, husband-killing black widow."

Kyra seemed totally demented, wearing a piece of limp lettuce in her hair.

"Stop it," I cried out. "Juliana, hang up on her!"

"Hypocrite patron of the arts," Kyra continued, ignoring me. "You'll pay dearly one day!"

A double click told us Kyra was disconnected.

"I'm sorry you had to hear that," said Juliana on the air.

"I am flattered by outbursts." Garibaldi had a smile in her voice. "Effective poetry evokes deep emotions. You should see some of the mail I get from fans, sometimes haters."

She probably considered my letter fan mail! What a fool I'd been for expecting a response.

9

I knew this New Year's Eve at the G-Spot would be a mistake. Beefy Bruna had her hands full, blocking any more people from squeezing into the bar. Her eyes lit up when she saw Kyra.

"Happy New Year, Bruna Bear."

"May we find true love this year, Doc," Bruna said.

"Amen." Kyra grabbed her huge face and kissed her lightly on the mouth. "In case we aren't together at midnight," she said. "Now let us in."

Bruna's right cheek twitched when she moved aside.

Most of West Hollywood was packed into the place. It was steamy hot and too noisy for me. All those amorous lesbian couples made my loss and grief unbearable. I scanned the crowd, searching for Greg, as I did around every street corner, in every store and restaurant.

Last year at this time he was mine, alive, I thought. My eyes filled with tears. Now he was dead. In her Land of the Dead.

Did she miss *her dear Guido*, as I did? I doubted it. She probably had someone new to kiss at midnight.

"So weird, seeing all my exes in one small place." Kyra's shout barely overcame the volume of the ear-blasting music. "Here's Sibyl, who tells the future when she's stoned, which is all the time. And here's Dolly and hi, Mimi!"

Mimi's thumb was on the rewind button, playing the autoerotic scene from Garibaldi's *Divine Darkness* on the huge flat screen. By the fifth time the beautiful Leila, played by the exquisite Juliet Blair, pleasured herself while eating a plump orange, even Kyra had had enough.

"Mimi, sweetie." Kyra took her hand and kissed it. "I remember this skinny thumb. Give it a rest. Let's have one party with fewer than seven hundred rewinds."

Mimi smiled up at her and shaped her lips into a kiss. I watched the exchange, amused, wondering if anyone here in the heart of WeHo had not gone through Kyra's boudoir, that boudoir with its surround sound and red throws and red curtains for the right mood, and that incredible antique headboard she'd found in India, hand carved with scenes from the Kama Sutra. Sex was Kyra's religion, her church was the G-Spot, and her sanctum sanctorum was her bedroom.

B. J. ogled me shamelessly and winked, looking tough in her leather biker gear, a silver chain around her neck.

"What's up, Doc?" she asked Kyra in that stupid voice. "Why are you kissing my new girlfriend?"

"For old time's sake," Kyra said.

I turned around and stopped dead. My heartbeat quickened. My enemy, my destroyer, was here, only a few feet away! She was so elegant and out of place wearing a blue dress, her blond chignon pinned up with one black chopstick and those bejeweled sunglasses sparkling in the lights. If I went down on my knees and managed a glance at her feet in this dense crowd, I'd surely find stilettos the same shade of royal blue as her dress.

I squeezed Kyra's hand. I couldn't speak or breathe or stay here.

My enemy turned to face me. She had a huge Adam's apple, a five o'clock shadow and a hairy chest. I was immediately relieved and then a smidgen angry for being duped. Not Anna Garibaldi, but one of her eager impersonators.

What was I thinking? The Divine One would never spend New Year's Eve in this neighborhood dive. She probably celebrated somewhere fabulous, in style, with a select few adoring friends, sipping Dom Perignon in an undisclosed penthouse suite fifty floors above Times Square, wearing the latest creation from Garibaldi Eyewear on her pale face.

I imagined her in a vast open balcony, and myself approaching from behind her. It would take only a tiny push. She wouldn't expect it. She'd topple over, sunglasses propelled away from her face. Next, she'd be dangling out the fiftieth-floor balcony, her fingers grasping, holding on for dear life. Only the wind and her dying ears would hear me say, *This is for stealing my life*. I'd have the upper hand. I'd grin into her pleading eyes and slowly push her dainty hands off the edge, finger by manicured finger. Each finger would leave bloody tracks, each fingernail would make a scraping noise as I flicked it off and away. I would laugh out loud, like the villain in an opera, as my gaze followed both my enemy and the Times Square ball plunge in slow motion down the length of the sleek building and into the colorful lights and celebration.

The music was interrupted. In that sudden silence all the colors were sucked out of my daydream. I was myself suspended above a barren, colorless world, dizzy and disoriented from my visions of sweet revenge.

"Princess." Kyra pulled me close. I rested my forehead on her strong shoulder and cried.

The buzz of anticipation, then the countdown. A crescendo of shouting voices reverberated, pushing the first of January into place. Blinding lights flickered into my eyes. My head exploded. The year of twice losing Greg had come to an end, yet my memory of him was still a gaping, bleeding wound.

"Greg," I cried out, adding my enemy's name silently, "*Anna*."

They were both on my mind. Both inaccessible. Both tempting me wordlessly into dark places.

10

Two months passed since Greg's death. His memory was fresh on my mind and I missed him every day and night. I felt cheated. Cheated by *her*, his glamorous widow. I kept myself busier than ever. The money remained in my account, untouched, minus what I'd owed Zoe. I was working the last touches of a family portrait. The family members all had prominent ears, including the twin baby girls. I didn't change the size of their ears, but a play of light and shadow made that feature less striking. I was imagining how pleased they'd be by the finished product when my phone rang.

It was the generic harp tune, not assigned to anyone in particular. I had less than half an hour to get ready for dinner at Rocko's, so I let it ring. I added a stroke of blush pink to soften the babies' faces.

The harp tune sounded again, persistent.

"Give it up," I said out loud. "I don't need anything."

On the third ring a sense of urgency seized me. I dried my hands on my blotting dress and reached for the phone, tipping over a glass container of turpentine. It crashed to the floor.

"Carly Rosen, please," said a velvety contralto.

The sound of that voice, as smooth as it was, punched me in the stomach. I opened my jaws to keep my teeth from grinding into powder. I tried speaking, but nothing came out. I was curled on the floor in the fetal position, the phone clutched to my ear.

"Is Ms. Rosen there?" she asked again.

"Speaking." The word came out of my mouth. I think it did.

"Anna Garibaldi," she simply said, as plainly as one would any other name. "Your note only now arrived. My agent takes the concept of snail mail quite literally."

She waited for my response. When none came she said, "You asked for an appointment."

Did she respond to every lunatic who asked for an appointment?

"I did," I whispered, my throat and lungs scorched by the fumes of turpentine.

"My driver will pick you up tomorrow at five," she said unequivocally.

Driver? I could see where this was going. The Divine One was used to making the rules. She didn't even ask whether or not I'd be free. What if I had plans for tomorrow at five? Was I supposed to cancel my life for Her Majesty? I'd tell her to go to hell. I would be busy the whole week.

"Five p.m.?" came out of my stupid mouth.

"Yes, and bring the original," she said, no *please* even intimated. She disconnected.

The original of *Blue Madonna*, I assumed. Did she want to buy it? Burn it? Break the canvas over my head?

I sat motionless for who knows how long, a feeling of impending doom circling my head like a big, black bird. I stared at the phone, wondering if life had ceased all over the planet or only inside my heart.

The cellphone blinked two text messages, one from Kyra and one from Zoe, then the screen darkened.

Why did she call me, why did I answer, and why exactly did I write to her in the first place?

Night fell. I don't know how long I sat on the floor, staring at my phone, saying, "If you were a smart phone, you'd tell me what to do."

Someone turned on the light.

"We waited for you at Rocko's," Zoe said. "Did we have another earthquake? What's all this glass?"

Kyra's new boots were in my field of vision, their shiny surface reflecting a distorted version of my face. She lifted my chin, giving my face a questioning look. "What's up, princess?"

"What does one wear for an appointment with Hades?" I asked.

11

I remained seated on the floor, talking about an original and the underworld and what to wear. From their puzzled faces I guessed I was speaking gibberish.

"Here, wear this," Kyra said.

She took off her sweatshirt and gave it to me. I pulled it over my blotting dress and its smell of fresh soap calmed me down a little. Kyra—while soaking up the turpentine and picking up the broken glass—sent Robert to mix Baseball Bats and Zoe to light the logs in the fireplace.

Then the drinks were ready and the four of us huddled by the fire. Warmth and alcohol usually snapped me back into place. I felt my sanity returning with the first sip of the potent cocktail.

"I've just had a phone call from A-A-Anna G-Garibaldi." I stuttered the name.

Robert choked on his drink.

"She called you out of the blue?" Kyra asked.

"I wrote her," I said, biting my lip.

Zoe fell face down on the Navajo rug, saying, "She is all lawyered up, you dimwit."

"Why would she need a lawyer?" I asked.

Zoe sat up, took a gulp of Baseball Bat and let loose one of her extra-loud burps. "Greg's money, of course. She wants it back."

"How do you know it was really her?" Kyra asked. "B. J. crank calls people all the time."

I swallowed hard. "The voice was sophisticated, and your friend B. J. is an idiot. That's how I know."

All three of them hummed in agreement.

"What did she sound like?" Kyra asked.

"Arctic, bossy, demanding." I pulled down the hem of my blotting dress to cover up my bare feet. "She's sending a driver to pick me up. She said she wants the original, I guess of *Blue Madonna*."

"There you go," Robert said, still coughing. "Give it to the driver and be done with it."

Zoe and Kyra agreed again.

"Do any of you work for free?" I asked. "I'll give her a good price."

"Greg paid you enough," Robert said.

"She doesn't know it," I said.

Kyra asked, "Where would her driver drive you?"

"She didn't give me a chance to ask," I said, restless, refilling their empty glasses with a second round. "A law office in Beverly Hills, the underworld, or a secluded mountain road where I'd be beaten to a pulp by Zoe's Cosa Nostra and left for dead."

"Go find out what her damned problem is," Zoe said, "and then tell us."

Kyra made one of those professional throat clearing sounds. "You want my little sister to get into a strange car with a strange man and be taken who knows where to confront a powerful woman known for her atrocious temper? Carly, you're not going."

"Your *little sister* is twenty-nine," I said. "Problem is, I don't know whether I should wear my hiking boots or my fuck-me heels."

"Wear this thing." Zoe gestured toward the blotting dress. "You may need camo."

At that Robert looked away. He'd never said a word about it, but my wedding dress—which he'd worked so hard to design and make—had turned into a cleaning rag for my paint brushes. That was a sore spot for him.

"I'm coming with you," Kyra said. "La Divina will have big Hildi. You'll have me."

I said, "As long as you keep your mouth shut and let me handle this."

"Wear hiking boots," Zoe said. "Both of you."

Robert took over hair and fashion. First he let my hair down and pulled on its ends, frowning. Next were my hands.

"I hope you didn't spill all the paint thinner; your hands are a mess." He took the silver ring off my finger and handed it to Kyra. "Give this thing a polish."

A manicure kit materialized from God knows where and, with professional expertise, Robert started cleaning the blue paint from under my fingernails. They joined forces in an effort to give me an intimidating appearance.

When my nails were dry and my hair cut super short Robert relaxed. The four of us huddled in companionable silence for a long time, our four noses nearly touching and the glow from the fireplace illuminating our faces.

The short hair made me feel exposed. Something touched my naked neck.

I shivered. "Do you feel him?"

"Yes," Zoe whispered.

"I do too," Robert said. "What's he trying to tell us?"

"*Keep away from my black widow*," Kyra said, lowering her voice.

I know she only meant to lighten up the mood, but I felt even smaller. I melted into her arms, sobbing, just as I had on New Year's Eve.

"Sorry, baby," Kyra said. "I'm here for you."

"What did I get myself into?" I asked.

"You don't have to go. We can be in Abu Dhabi tomorrow."

"Start packing," I said. Then I sat up straight and tried to act brave. "Tell me everything you know, Kyra. What is she like?"

"I wrote it all down for you," Kyra said. "I'd rather you read it when I'm not here."

12

"Dearest Carly,

Here's what happened the night Greg broke up with you. I never said anything about it, not to you, not to Robert or Zoe, because I felt guilty. That story was to be yours when you asked for it. I'm so sorry about the part I'd played in the breakup.

A few days before your almost-wedding I asked Greg to accompany me to an art show. You said you were too busy, that the wedding cake you'd both designed, with the impressionistic motif, had to be ordered at the local bakery and that Robert needed you for a dress fitting.

Knowing you, my dear sister, you'd made up excuses to get us both out of your hair so you could finish that huge portrait job before the wedding and maybe get paid for it.

The art show took place at the retired power plant on the beach. That rich dude with the big head did it up real fancy and turned it into a trendy nightclub and art gallery. The place was crowded with those who wanted to see and be seen. Lots of bling. Someone played a sonata on the piano, but no one listened because they were all too busy being important and waiting for the guest of honor.

The floor was made of a series of connecting metal platforms. I found it thrilling, dangerous. When I peered down into the underbelly of that ship-like interior, my heart raced. It gave me vertigo. I was moved by the massive old gas-fired machines, by their lifelessness. The place itself, its history, affected me more than any of the art pieces.

Greg was not impressed by the art either. I'll give him that: before his brain started rotting, he was as witty and bitchy as a schoolgirl. We exchanged the usual mean comments about everything in general and one big, ugly canvas in particular. Greg claimed that the artist was pompous-assed.

'You mean the piece is pretentious,' I corrected.

He insisted, 'No, the artist is.'

I remembered that remark later, Carly. The timing had irony, considering how soon afterwards Greg would become the grand master of pomposity.

I wanted him to explain. 'You don't know the artist.'

'Overproduction,' he said. 'Oil, charcoal, watercolor, splices of ropes. His grandma's lace brassiere is in it, for God's sake, saying, *Look how funny I am*. I want to give him Pepto, the way he pukes onto one canvas everything he's eaten since nineteen eighty-four. His other pieces are regurgitations of the same motif.'

'Can't you just not like it and be done with it?' I asked, feeling sorry for the artist, who might have been listening.

Greg said, 'My Carly expresses more in one pencil line than this man in all his pieces put together.'

For what it's worth, Carly, you were on his mind until the end. At least the end I know.

His next sentence was the last he would ever say to me, 'This hellhole blows. Let's see who's at the G-Spot.'

'There's this last section,' I said. 'It's probably worth missing, but let's have a peek.'

Had we left right away, nothing would have happened. You and Greg would have now been married and he would have been alive, so, you see, it was my fault.

As we elbowed our way through the crowd to the other side of the gallery, Anna Garibaldi, the Divine One, the great patron of the arts, appeared, and the world ended.

She wore this sleek dress, whiter than your wedding dress was before you ruined it. It would have made anyone else seem like a fugitive from a gothic insane asylum. The way she carried herself, even that *schmate* was divine. Among all those mortals in formal black, her presence had the refreshing effect of a cold Heineken on a sweaty day. A million candles in a dark cave.

At Garibaldi's side hulked the giant bodyguard, Hildi. On her other side strutted a stunning woman with skin the color of sweet chocolate, whose delicate beauty stopped my heart. I recognized her as Juliet Blair, Garibaldi's leading actress from her very erotic last film.

The eternal sunglasses hid Garibaldi's expression. Who would wear sunglasses to an art show? Was she a vampire, hiding her feline eyes? You know how such ponderables go through my head all the time. Besides, she was very pale.

Anna Garibaldi had her back to us. She was immersed in conversation. Then she turned around, as if someone had tapped her on the shoulder. No one had because no one would have dared with big Hildi hovering.

That simple motion of turning had such flowing elegance, Carly. Then I remembered she used to be a dancer. If that isn't a ballet move, I thought, it should be. I would have given it a fancy French name like *tourner*, to match *arabesque* or *pirouette*. That simple turn was phenomenal.

Two events followed simultaneously. The first: Greg stiffened. I could almost see his eyeballs popping out of their sockets and jolting back in, like in a cartoon. That was insignificant since every single pair of eyeballs in that vast space did the same, including mine.

The second event was so strange, it imprinted itself onto my memory. I've replayed each frame in my head, in split-second pauses, so many times, examining it at different speeds. I still believe I could have done something to prevent disaster. I didn't, of course. But I imagine I could have. You be the judge of that.

As she turned, she spotted Greg. She cried out, '*Rosso*!' and tore the sunglasses off her face with trembling hands. She also dropped her glass of wine. We were all drinking from plastic cups. Her glass was real; it shattered on the metal platform, and red wine splattered all over her white dress.

So much pain was in her eyes. She took a little step back. Before she could fall into the machines below, Hildi stretched a fat arm to steady her. Ms. Blair embraced her lovingly. Garibaldi, breathing raggedly, leaned on her for support.

I don't know what she saw in our Greg, but no doubt she saw something. Carly, it was as if she'd spotted a long lost loved one she had believed dead.

No, I don't know what she saw, and now I'll never find out what it was.

I pulled at him. 'Let's go.'

It was too late. He was lost.

Recovered, Garibaldi stood straight and regal again. The social smile was painted on her lips. It skipped her eyes. They remained haunted, filled with terror. Then the sunglasses were back on her nose and all seemed well again. 'I'm fine, I'm fine,' she said to Juliet and Hildi and all the other people wanting to fuss over her and her wine-splashed dress. She made a joke, and they all laughed and relaxed. What an amazing actress. She may have fooled them, but not me. Her hand came up, as if to reach out through the crowd and grab hold of Greg.

Greg was dipped in honey up to his chin, forever lost to you and to himself. In my head I was asking, *What about my sister?* I was seething with anger, wishing he'd choke on that honey so I wouldn't have to kill him. As it turned out, I was spared the effort.

The energy, the attraction between them, was a force of nature. They could have brought the defunct powerhouse back to life. I swear, even the dead machines buzzed under the metal platform. I knew enough to keep out of it.

I stayed, uncertain what to do. It was like witnessing a grotesque fatal accident, when there's nothing left to save and the body of someone you love has been pulverized into nothing, but you can't take your eyes off the empty space it had once occupied.

I have dealt with a few mental emergencies. When it came to my own I was clueless. What was I to tell you? It would have been easier to say that he fell off one of the platforms and died.

While genuinely worrying about Greg and what would become of you, my eyes searched the crowd for Juliet Blair. I'd meant to charm her with one of my pick-up lines and see where it led. Ms. Blair was gone.

I didn't talk to Greg the rest of that evening, nor, for that matter, for the rest of his life. He was glued to Anna Garibaldi's side, a zombie. Anna never graced any of the art pieces with one glance. I agreed that none deserved a second glance, but she should have looked once. The great patron of the arts, my ass. Such hypocrisy. She worked the room, a queen performing her duties, talking, kissing people on both cheeks. She was touchy-feely with everyone, only using one hand because the other clutched Greg. Her arm was looped into his like handcuffs. She couldn't wait to take him home and . . . *you know*. I always know.

I stayed on the scene, hoping for rescue that would never come. Then Sabine—an adorable budding artist with flowing red hair, legs from here to there and a row of real diamonds pierced along her exposed spine—got the impression that I stood frozen because I was so moved by her painting of a yellow bird. Soon Sabine would make me forget the lovely, elusive Ms. Blair by feeding me baked Brie and grapes with her long fingers. Good listener that I am, I let her tell me about the big tips she used to make as a lap dancer. I have no defenses against such stories. By the time I searched for Greg again, both he and Anna were gone. I drove Sabine home.

The next morning my cellphone played your tune. I had a hard time disentangling myself from Sabine's bracelet-clad arms and long, red curls. I found the phone in the bed.

'Where'd you lose my future hubby?' you asked me.

'Didn't he call?' I asked, groggy.

I couldn't believe he was playing dead, making you worry sick about his useless ass. I didn't have the heart to tell you on the phone. I said I was on my way.

Robert had just finished the last stitches of your wedding gown, and you were trying it on. You came downstairs in your bare feet to show Zoe and me. The dress was simple and gorgeous. No frills. You consider yourself plain looking, but in my loving eyes you were beautiful. You didn't have a touch of make-up on, yet I'd never before seen such a glowing bride.

Then your groom joined us. Actually, he was on TV, in footage from that cursed art show. The two of them were Super-Glued to each other, Garibaldi working the room and Greg following her like a golden retriever.

Who is La Divina's handsome mystery man? was the question on the evening news. It was obscene, seeing it with you there, in your wedding dress.

'Did she offer him a job? Is he going to work for her?' you asked, hope in your smile.

I shook my head no. You wanted me to give you good news. I looked down at my hands, my empty hands. I had nothing to give you.

'He went home with her?' your voice cracked.

I cleared my throat as I would in a difficult session. 'Carly,' I started. I stopped.

You gestured down at your dress. 'I'm wearing this shit and he went home with her.' Your voice squeaked and choked. 'Went home with her . . .'

I wanted you to lose it on me, accuse me, because I felt responsible, but something worse had happened. The glow was wiped from your face, as if the wind had been knocked out of you. You were so utterly vulnerable in your white dress, in your bare feet. I wanted to turn you into a little ball and protect you, enfold you in my arms, as I had when Mom died. But you didn't allow me that. One moment you were still a girl, my baby sister. Then I saw you growing up before my worried eyes.

I opened my mouth to explain. You interrupted in an uncharacteristic ice-cold voice.

'How long were you going to wait to tell me?'

'Carly, you tend to kill the messenger,' I said. 'I wasn't thrilled about it, but I'm here.'

'You knew last night,' you said. 'You went fucking someone instead of . . . Oh my God . . .'

'You're better off without him,' I said, which was the worst thing anyone could have said. 'Let's talk about it.'

'I don't need a blow-by-blow, Kyra. Not now, so cork it.'

I blinked, then I heard your bad muffler as you backed the Mustang out of the driveway and zoomed out to the alley. I called your phone, but it rang in the living room. Zoe, Robert and I, separately, went searching for you all over West Hollywood.

I was back in the house an hour later, my heart heavy. Mozart's *Requiem* was playing from the second floor. You were up in your study, still wearing your white wedding gown, humming the Lacrimosa sequence, Greg's favorite Mozart. He once mentioned that he wanted it played at his funeral. It seemed you were giving him his dream funeral. Your eyes were dry, your feet were bare and dirty, your hair was wild and one paint brush was held between your teeth, dripping red paint on your left shoulder. You were feverishly working an old canvas with a pastoral landscape, painting flecks of blood onto the formerly blue sky.

'Where the hell . . . ?' I was short of breath from hurrying up the steep stairs.

'I ran out of crimson red,' you said, your voice steady, the brush tight between your teeth.

'You're getting it stained,' I warned, pointing at the white gown, Robert's creation. I worried that you'd become Miss Havisham. You had, in a way.

Your reaction was vintage Carly, spare but dramatic. You took the very brush you were using, loaded with blood red, and wiped it on the bodice, leaving a dark slash against your heart.

'Now I like it.'

You smiled at me, changed by the grief you didn't want me to see. The drips of crimson on your chin made me cold. You know the rest.

Love you always,

Kyra."

13

At exactly five o'clock, a sleek, black Jaguar parallel parked next to my red Mustang. The driver uncorked herself out of it with difficulty. I recognized the huge bodyguard.

"Good evening," she said in a soft baritone. I did a double take to make sure the human mountain was really a woman.

"Nice to finally meet Bruna's twin," Kyra said with more charm than usual.

"It's Hildi," came out of the unsmiling pudgy face. "Which one of you is Ms. Rosen?"

We both said, "I am."

"The artist," Hildi clarified.

I raised the hand holding the packaged canvas.

"The original?"

I nodded. While I wondered how it would fit into the back seat with both of us without blocking view of the rear window, Hildi took it from me. She opened the trunk and laid it carefully inside. I bid it goodbye. She held the back door open and gestured me in. Kyra made a move to join me.

"The artist only." The lowest of Hildi's multiple chins trembled when she spoke.

"I'm also sort of an artist," Kyra said, "if you count mind-blowing—"

"Carly Rosen," Hildi said.

"Why, I wouldn't miss a ride in this fine machine."

Kyra stroked the top of the Jaguar, and her ring clicked on the shiny surface. Hildi's beady eyes got smaller and beadier. Kyra immediately took her hand off and blew on the moist hand print I imagined she'd left on the paint.

We sank into the softest leather seats. The car was immaculate, inside and out. And it was all wrong. Not only the grotesque way Hildi's baby face was stuck on top of a gigantic body, making her seem like the action figure of a sumo wrestler. Not only the way she had confiscated the painting. Kyra was wrong too. Taking her as a matching bodyguard would be an admission of weakness. I should do it alone.

“Get out,” I whispered.

“Yes, out,” said my warden, still propping the door open. “Signora should not be kept waiting.”

The way she said *signora* gave me a bellyache.

“Does signora hold her breath while she waits?” asked my sister.

Whose head rolls if she waits was the question on my mind. As the side of Hildi’s face twitched, I kept my musings to myself. This was not going to be a fun ride.

“We can run for it,” Kyra whispered.

”She took the painting hostage,” I said.

“Work for free this once to save your life.”

“I screwed up alone,” I said. “Let me handle it alone.”

I expected Kyra to resist. She hesitated. Then she smiled proudly, sadly, like a mother sending her grown-up baby to active combat.

“Shit, I almost forgot.” Kyra took the silver ring off her little finger—it was so shiny!—and showed me the inscription on the inside: *Carly and Greg forever*. “It took a lot of scrubbing.”

“Kyra!” I cried out. “She’ll see now.”

“Robert did a great job,” she said, slipping the ring onto my finger. “You have the hands of a real princess.”

Hildi cleared her throat.

Kyra asked, “Did you read my letter?”

“A few times,” I said.

“Are you mad at me?” she asked.

“Why would I be?”

“Because I’m the one who took him to that show in the first place, and when he wanted to leave I delayed him, and then she . . . and I did nothing about it, and then I went fucking someone instead of telling you right away, but you see now, he didn’t have a choice.”

“We all have choices. He loved me, but she glowed brighter and dazzled him and he made his choice.” I took Kyra’s face in my hands and looked into her hazel eyes. “Stop worrying yourself sick. Thanks for describing her, and him, in such detail and for letting me know what he said about me and my art. I can now confront her."

She hugged me, relieved, then hopped out and slammed the door shut on life as I knew it.

Outside, Kyra turned to Hildi. "You probably get it all the time, but you are definitely the better-looking twin." Next, my crazy sister totally crossed the line. She reached up and touched Hildi's fat cheek with the back of her hand. "Fabulous skin," she said.

What was she doing?

Hildi drew away wordlessly, squeezed herself back into the driver's seat and started the silent engine.

Kyra's fearful gaze held on to mine as we sailed away. I smiled at her and winked.

I texted, *WTF? Fabulous skin?*

I could see Kyra through the rear window, peering down at her phone and laughing.

Trust me, she texted back. *I want her to treat you well.*

Hildi turned right onto Wilshire Boulevard.

I guess it's a law office, I texted.

Share location on Facebook when you get there.

K, I texted back.

I expected Hildi to pull aside by one of the tall buildings, but the Jaguar kept up its silent glide toward the setting sun and the freeway.

No traffic on the 405 for once, I texted. *Must be a Jewish holiday we don't know about.*

Which direction?

South. I wish you'd come along.

Jeep keys in back pocket, Kyra texted. *One word and we'll come for you.*

K.

Last night we decided on Kyra's stiffest, whitest shirt, collar up and tucked inside my charcoal slacks. Zoe warned against the sexy heels. "You'll trip in front of her and fart." The JanSports were my only other option. When I wore them,

Robert made a scary kabuki face and raised the manicure scissors. Sexy stilettos it was.

As Pacific Coast Highway passed through the beach cities—Manhattan, Hermosa and Redondo—I was reminded of leisurely days in the sun and normal life.

Hildi turned right on Palos Verdes Drive, keeping south. The ocean thundered through the closed car window even before it appeared, vast and glorious, in the sunset. Trees with amputated limbs sent contorted extremities up to the sky, black branches against blazing reds, yellows and purples. One naked branch gave me the finger. I reached for the sketch pad I always carried in the inside pocket of my well-worn leather jacket. I quickly sketched a few impressions. In my head I was mixing a matching palette of dazzling brilliance.

The ring was loose on my little finger. I switched it to my ring finger and admired Robert's work. I got so used to oil paint in all the creases, my freshly manicured hands with the rose blush fingernails looked like someone else's.

Greg loved me as a child, when we exchanged rings. He loved me when she stole him away from me. He loved me when he found his death. Greg never stopped loving me. I was about to face Hades and reclaim, if not his life, the truth of his love.

I texted, *Thanks for polishing my ring.*

Good luck retrieving its twin.

BTW should have worn flippers instead of fuck-me shoes.

LOL. I doubt she'll drown you. Where are you now?

A place called Malaga Cove. Gorgeous, I texted. *She said nothing since WeHo.*

I would have made her talk.

You make them talk for a living, I texted. *I make them sit still and silent.*

LOL, princess. Hugs from all of us.

Dying to pee. Battery low. Bye now.

I took my pocket mirror out of my purse and touched up my lips with Zoe's lipstick. This shade of rose changed my eyes from hazel to emerald, or perhaps it was the effect of the dying sun. My short, dark hair was sharp, with one spike on top Robert couldn't control even with stiff gel.

"Spike it more," Zoe had suggested. "You may need it for self-defense."

All the colors of the rainbow gathered in my small mirror for one magnificent moment—dark hair, emerald eyes, feverish cheeks, rose lips and nails, and the silver ring. My life was ruled by rich, incredible colors.

Night fell quickly, leaving me in darkness. I was so comfortable in the soft leather seat, it would have been a nice ride had Hildi spoken to me or played music. Any music. The sensory deprivation was so unbearable, I closed my eyes and maybe dozed off for a minute.

Hildi's baritone startled me. "We're here."

I opened my eyes and gaped open-mouthed at a bizarre and magnificent view. Was it man-made or part of the mountain? The underworld was nothing I'd expected.

14

"Wow!" I cried out. "Is this her home?"

"Sure is," Hildi said with pride.

Long, slender crystals projected upward from the earth, like buildings in a fantasy city. The crystals were lit from within, shedding soft light on a rose garden and on the white cubic main structure.

"Signora Garibaldi's design," Hildi said. Then she blasted the magical illusion with the longest speech she'd made so far. "Quartz from Brazil and neon from around the corner."

She let me out onto the slate-paved driveway. The rose bushes on both sides of the pathway were of the wicked, thorny kind that could rip one's eyes out. I hobbled on my high heels, my mouth open in a big *O* at the simple brilliance of the house and its illumination. Hildi huffed and puffed behind me as she tried to keep up with me while carrying the canvas. A whiff of sweat (mine? Hildi's?) was mixed into the intoxicating fragrance of roses.

"Roses in January?" I tested to see if she'd talk again.

"Signora uses coffee as fertilizer," she said.

"That explains it," I said, as if I knew anything about gardening.

A small woman in her seventies greeted me at the door. Her gray hair was plaited and wrapped around her head a few times. A huge cross dangled from a gold chain and rested against her black dress. She looked like a Sicilian widow from those old Italian films.

"Come in, Ms. Rosen, I'm Flora," she said in a pronounced Italian accent. A hint of garlic wafted from her wet handshake.

My gaze searched for Zoe's gang of Amazons who were going to eat me alive and spit out the bones, or the deadly brutes with their spears, or all those Hildi clones I imagined protected Her Majesty. What actually happened was just as weird.

"The original?" Flora turned to Hildi.

Both of them lost interest in me. They frantically ripped the brown paper off the canvas and propped it up against the wall.

"Shouldn't *Signora* see it first?" I asked.

"Soon," Flora said.

Hildi flipped on a switch and halogen light washed the portrait, making me realize anew that the painted eyes needed more life and detail.

Flora crossed herself, as Zoe had, adding, "*Ave Maria, piena di grazia.* I think we found the one, Hildi."

The one portrait?

"*Blue Madonna*," I offered.

Flora nodded at me in approval. Hildi examined the piece the way an artist would, from all angles, checking its edges and texture by running sausage fingers on the furrows I'd left with the palette knife. *Blue Madonna* was indeed my best work. I should have been flattered by their excessive gushing, but the whole scene felt like a pelvic exam by two amateur gynecologists who scoped and prodded, pretending I wasn't there.

Something occurred to me. "Does *Signora* believe this is Greg's work?" I asked.

"Be real." Hildi's baby face twisted with ridicule. "These are the famous *Guidos*." She gestured widely toward the walls. I glanced at the pale paintings, then quickly looked away. What was left of Greg wasn't good. I didn't want to associate his memory with these piteous works.

"Signora is waiting for you on the deck," Flora said, extending an arm behind her.

The realization of having to face her alone dawned on me. I needed another moment to empty my bladder and pull myself together. I asked where the bathroom was. Her face still pressed close to *Blue Madonna*, Flora pointed down a dark hallway.

After getting myself together—and after I checked every nook and cranny of the bathroom, wondering if this was the toilet in which I might be drowned later—I made a last study of my reflection. Rather than formidable or intimidating, I seemed small and frightened. My hair was mousy, and that spike they all considered cute had become downright pathetic.

"Fail, Robert," I whispered.

My feet ached. I wished I'd worn the hiking boots.

"Shoes off, please," Flora called after me as I stepped into the hallway. With great relief I kicked the stilettos into a corner, as I would have at home. Flora immediately picked them off the spotless floor and cleared them away. Obsessive compulsive. Whose obsession was it, Flora's or La Divina's? In our house, mine and Zoe's, the floors served as shelf space. As I walked away from both women, my painting and the light above it, the hallway got darker. The ocean thundered. I stepped into a magical room, washed in eerie, soft light from the quartz crystals surrounding the house. I couldn't discern colors in the indirect light.

Simplicity and military order ruled here, along with hundreds of books. Thousands. I was used to clutter, and the total lack of it disoriented me. Books were piled up on the coffee table and in built-in bookcases covering the walls, but not on the floors. The floors are sacred here, I thought. I had a mental picture of rolling heads if a scrap of paper was found on the gleaming wood floors. Greg had been the biggest slob of all. How did he fit into such austerity?

A trio of double doors opened onto a stunning panorama of the small bay. An ocean of dark indigo was framed by bejeweled city lights. Anna Garibaldi had a perfect view of the famed Queen's Necklace.

Speaking of . . .

At the far end of a vast wooden deck stood the source of my fear, the owner of Greg's last months with all their sizzling secrets. Hades herself. She gazed out to the ocean, her back to me, not leaning against the railing, but upright, proud.

I was so alone without my buffers. Zoe wasn't here to restrain my out-of-control reactions with a loving hug of her skinny arms; Kyra, in her cowboy boots and tough attitude, wasn't here to stand between us and protect me. And I needed Robert to give my drab hair a last hopeful tweak.

Soon she'd turn around and see me, small and insignificant in this immense room, a guest in her tightly controlled private territory, where the rules would be hers.

I was as good as dead.

She turned.

Part Two

15

My enemy stood firm and regal against the inky blackness of the ocean, her pale hair hanging heavy to her waist. The lights of the bay twinkled and floated behind her like a scarf strewn with diamonds. She was all that I had imagined and feared, and her height! I didn't expect her to be so imposing!

I was trying to remember if I had a working tongue and what to do with my aimless limbs. I could barely breathe, because in front of my stupefied face my art came alive. My *Blue Madonna*, my Hades, my painted predator! Did she actually radiate light or was it a trick of the surrounding crystals and my feverish mind? Was she even human?

I wouldn't have been surprised had she bared a set of long fangs and said, *Good gloaming* in a low, seductive growl. I would have kissed my life goodbye, but that would have explained what had happened to Greg. A set of bared fangs would have made more sense than what actually occurred.

She took a step back, arm stretched out for support, and met the pillar behind her. The sound she made was either a fearful hiss or something that sounded like *Rosso*.

What was happening to her? I wasn't exactly Ms. America material, but I didn't frighten people either. Had I brought a ghost with me?

I remembered Kyra's letter of confession. In it she describes such a reaction and that exact sound. Rosso. What did it mean?

She immediately recovered, and her face relaxed with a welcoming smile. She twisted her hair up and knotted it back at her neck in a sloppy version of her usual style. As she moved forward to greet me, the illusion of size and otherworldliness evaporated. The soft sway of her long, clingy dress against her slender strength slowed time into a chain of freeze frames. She was no taller than I in her bare feet.

Her handshake was firm and business-like.

"Good evening, Ms. Rosen."

My ordinary last name sounded too intimate in her famous contralto.

Was I supposed to call her Mrs. Wheeler?

Not in this lifetime.

"Good evening, Ms. Garibaldi."

"I remember you from the funeral," she said. "We talked."

"Sort of," I said. How I hoped she wouldn't remember what an aggressive, insulting ass I'd been. I changed the subject. "The rose garden smells marvelous. Can we see it from here?"

"The roses surround the house in three directions," she said with pride. "On this side there's nothing but ocean. Let me show you."

She led me to the edge of the wooden deck. Down below, the rocks boiled in a soup of dark turbulence. An image from my colorless nightmare overwhelmed me. I leaned back against the support pillar. Frothy water pulsated in front of my eyes, making my limbs lead-heavy and weakening the muscles from my waist down. I was sandwiched between my two greatest fears: heights and this woman. A thin rail separated me from the former; the latter stood so close behind me, a whiff of her musk reached my nostrils, like a thin line of blood-red highlight in a blue portrait. It would only take a small push and my New Year's Eve musings of revenge would come true, only on me.

As if sensing my fear, she took me by the arm and moved me away from the edge. Her touch burned a hole through the sleeve of my leather jacket. Suddenly I had an urge to hold the entire length of her body to mine. Would that make me understand Greg? That out-of-nowhere urge made me queasier. What did he fall for first, her unforgiving beauty or the liquid seduction of her voice? I knew him as well as I knew myself. What was it like for him to willingly go under her spell?

I found my voice. "I guess children never come here."

"Not many adults either," she said.

"Don't you entertain?" I asked. "This house is made for parties."

"A writer needs her solitude."

My gaze slid down the defined muscles of her strong arm, down to her hand. Not the manicured hand of a bestselling novelist, but that of a woman who worked in the garden or handled wild beasts. A long scar of what seemed like a deep scratch adorned her forearm. Did she keep lions or feral cats?

On her little finger gleamed the ring. My ring. How dare she wear it in front of me? I'd had enough small talk.

"Let's get to business," I said. "First, the silver ring." I pointed at it with my own ringed pinky, meaning to claim it on the spot and be done with that most unpleasant part of my mission.

"Did you actually read it?" she asked, pretending to misunderstand, turning this into a discussion about her book.

"Sure did." I humored her, retracting my hand. I'd have to try another way to force her to pay attention. "Your poetry collection makes Fanny Hill's memoirs read like nursery rhymes. Especially that last one."

Her laugh came from deep inside her, rich and throaty. "Let's go inside and talk business."

We settled in front of the crackling fireplace in oversized, plush armchairs. The whitewashed coffee table between them was covered with stacks of art books.

"Flora, Hildi," she said in a normal voice, not particularly loud. "Bring it please."

They must have been eavesdropping, as both women marched in immediately, Hildi carrying my painting. They rested the canvas against the wall. Their mistress kneeled down in front of it and ran her fingers lightly on its surface from side to side and from top to bottom, as Hildi and Flora had done earlier. The sign of the cross? Was this a weird religious ritual I was expected to join? I didn't even bother with my own religion.

"Well?" she asked.

"Yes," the other women answered in unison.

What was the question?

"Let's celebrate," said the mistress, relief clear in her voice.

The painting was lit only by indirect light from the quartz crystals. Wasn't she going to turn on the lights and take a better look at what she was buying or praying to or celebrating?

Flora left and returned a few minutes later carrying champagne on ice. She filled up four rosebud glasses.

I was completely at a loss. "What are we celebrating?"

The mistress smiled. "A consensus."

The three clinked their glasses. I stayed away, expecting an explanation. None came. The champagne tasted wonderful, but its delicate flavor and texture didn't hit the spot. I would have killed for Zoe's Baseball Bat with that special twist, or for Zoe and Kyra's presence in this strange scene. What did it all mean?

"Leave us," Garibaldi said.

I thought she meant me, but both Flora and Hildi stepped out, leaving me with my enemy and her portrait. The light from the quartz crystals swallowed all the room's colors, disorienting me. The reigning goddess of this colorless underworld kneeled again and rested her hands on my painting. She remained silent, deep in thought. Praying? I was frightened. This woman was obviously a lunatic, a case for Kyra.

Something was terribly wrong.

Despite the blazing fireplace, a chill passed through me that had nothing to do with the cold champagne. In our loaded silence, I sensed the ghost between us. Greg.

"Do you know"—her cracked whisper finally broke the silence—"how many Carly Rosens live in the LA area alone?"

"Should I care?" I asked.

"I'm glad you sent me a sample of your work."

"A sample? I don't get it."

"My Guido surely told you."

Maybe at some point she'd explain why she'd changed his name.

"I haven't seen Greg or talked to him since . . . for a long time," I said.

"Haven't you?" she asked in disbelief, picking up her champagne glass and sipping daintily. "When they came to notify me about the accident, I expected to hear they'd found two bodies in the car. Yours and his."

"He'd been on his way to see me," I said. "That I know from a text message that he'd meant to send, but never did."

"A message?" She sat down. "I know nothing about a message, Ms. Rosen."

Her surprise was genuine. And I was confused. We seemed to be speaking different languages.

"Tell me what the message said," she commanded.

She hadn't seen the message because Kyra made sure she couldn't. That fateful night a West Hollywood police officer had knocked on my door.

"There's been an accident," she'd said, handing me a cellphone. Greg's phone, which I'd recognized at once by its goofy protective cover in the shape of a purple owl.

My name and address were on Greg's phone, naming me the first to be notified in case of an emergency.

I'd tried to read the unsent text standing up. I could only see every other word.

Coming over . . . something to show you . . . forgive everything . . . the only one.

I'd slid against the wall and down to the floor, reading and rereading that message. I had no idea what it meant. While I was falling apart and good for nothing, Kyra had pried the phone from my hands and read the message once. Officer Kimberly—one of Kyra's former intimate friends—looked away, pretending not to see as my sister pressed one command, sending the text to my cellphone, then another command, erasing the original from Greg's phone.

"His words, whatever their meaning, belong only to you," Kyra had explained. She didn't want his widow or the press to get a hold of his final message.

I'd wanted to keep the phone, but even my sister's intimate connections didn't help. Greg's belongings—his Rolex, his expensive Nikes, the totaled Jaguar—were all his widow's property.

"Do you remember the message?" the widow now asked.

My heart was wedged in my throat. That cryptic text had sustained me in my grief. I didn't understand it, but *remember* it I did. I swallowed hard, then I recited Greg's words, my *raison d'être* since his death.

Through tight jaws I said, "Coming to pick you up. Have something to show you that will make you forgive everything. You are the only one."

"Ah!" My enemy's perfect face relaxed into a smile of relief. "That explains it."

"What explains what?" I asked.

"I don't know what he meant by *forgive everything*," she said, "I do know what he wanted to show you."

I straightened up. "It was here?"

"Still is, Ms. Rosen," said my nemesis. "Waiting for you."

16

I came here, to this house, to this woman, to reclaim, if not Greg's life, at least his silver ring and the proof that he'd never stopped loving me. He'd been on his way back to make it up to me and confess that he'd made a terrible mistake in marrying her. He'd meant to show me the new home he had bought for us, where we would start a new life. *This place*?

That hope had kept me intact, stowed away and hidden, as I'd made my journey to truth.

Now, barely two months after his death, truth was battering my baseless dreams and fantasies.

"Why was Greg on his way to see me?" I asked, needing to know, yet fearful of the answer.

"I'd asked him to do some work for me," she said. "He believed you were more appropriate for it. Naturally, he went to fetch you."

Naturally. Greg's beautiful widow, who owned the last months of his life, was coldly informing me that what he'd wanted to show me, my last hope, was also hers. That he had gone to *fetch* me, and his opinion of me had been so low, he'd believed I'd allow myself to be fetched.

"Some work," I mocked, daintily nursing my rosebud glass, steadying my hands. "Did you ask him to take out the trash? He was never big on that."

"I can show you the work now," she said simply, ignoring my sarcasm.

I said, "You're missing the point."

"I'm missing quite a few points," she said.

My hugely fat bank account, the hefty inheritance he had left me on the last day of his life, was proof that he knew he was dying and that I'd always been his real love. Despite my promise to my friends that I'd never mention the money, I had to boast a little.

"You may not know," I said with a defiant smile, "he left me money. A lot of money."

"Yes, Ms. Rosen." She sighed. "My money."

"Yours?" This must be what it felt like having the dentist yank out your healthy teeth, one by one, without anesthetics. I held myself together, but I knew it wouldn't be for long.

"An advance," she explained. "I pay for work ahead of time." She pushed behind her ear a strand of pale hair that had come loose. "A silly habit that gets me the best performance."

I knocked back the rest of my champagne and pounded the fancy rosebud glass on the coffee table hard enough to smash it. Unfortunately, it remained intact. She flinched at the thud it made. Probably a family heirloom.

Some of that money must have been a gift from Greg! "A hundred grand is a big advance," I said, clutching at straws.

She coughed, then chuckled. "That's quite a lot, but typical. Dear Guido did like to throw my money around. He said that you were the only one he knew who could do the job right. You see? Thus, *the only one* in his text."

I refused to cry in her presence, but tears fought their way out. He had texted while driving, *You are the only one*, crashing before completing the sentence. *You are the only one who can help us*. I was the only one indeed. The only one left at the altar. The only one pushed off the deck. The only one jilted.

I wanted to blink and be back home, where it would be okay to cry and scream and get drunk to death on Zoe's Baseball Bats.

"The project is quite extensive," she continued with that mind-boggling calm, as if I cared a hoot about her project or her life. "Guido claimed that you'd refuse, but in my experience, no one refuses work if the price is right. I suggested that he pay you a convincing amount, and you were convinced! I gave him a free hand, but *a hundred grand*? You must be worth it. And now we have a consensus, so you are hired."

What a complete idiot I'd been. I sensed the gap closing between my eyebrows. My scream came out as a whisper. "You thought I came here for a job interview?"

"Why else would you request a business appointment?" she asked.

How stupid, stupid, stupid and desperate of me to give such credit to one text message, a text message that had come from a man who had dumped me without a word!

Greg had the love of this most talented, beautiful, desirable woman. How could I compare? What could I have offered him that he didn't have in abundance?

I had to get out. *Call a cab; call Kyra; call Zoe. What is the address here? Why hadn't I driven my own car?*

I realized that I was crying, that my careful make-up was probably smudging, that black mascara was dripping down my cheeks and gathering at my chin. I scrambled up and scanned the pristine room for a pack of tissues. The vast room of this rich woman was cleaned daily, organized into military order, and still I found nothing to wipe my runny nose on. I used the sleeve of my white shirt in front of her because I didn't give a shit anymore and my dignity was history. I was humiliated beyond humiliation.

I searched for a landline. Nothing. Where had I dropped my cellphone?

I glared down at her perfect oval face, so still and pale in the indirect quartz glow. I wanted to kill her, right there in the middle of her perfect fucking life with her perfect fucking memories about Greg. Those memories should have been mine. Greg should have been my husband, alive and far away from this perfect hellhole that didn't have a landline.

Her tranquility was unbearable. This uncanny beauty could have had any man, but she took the love of my life. What part had she played in his death?

What was it like, to hear the gasps of awe when you walked into a crowded room? Did adoration have a flavor, a color? Did it smell of the ocean or of musk and roses? Had I walked in your shoes, would I have walked any taller? Would I have smiled any wider? Would I have laughed now instead of crying?

The echo of my own choked voice in my ears told me the mortifying truth, that I'd said those things out loud, letting her into my innermost feelings. Yet I couldn't stop.

"Do you feel entitled to everything you want just because you are you?"

Everything else I'd ever wanted to say to her, to anyone, came flooding out of my mouth in a voice I'd meant to be loud, but ended up a jumbled whisper. "How can you resist constantly staring at your own reflection? You should have bright lights and mirrors in every corner to catch accidental glimpses of your face, your pose, your figure throughout the day."

She sat upright, her gaze on me, listening patiently as I kept talking, choking, drowning in the dark mire of the murky Styx. "You took him . . . You ruined my life and now you're telling me that . . . Shit. How many more times am I going to lose him because of you?"

Even in my state of terror and confusion, I was aware of how crazy I sounded. Nothing coming out of my mouth made sense, even to me. Yet I kept talking. Talking was breathing.

"Look at it once," I said, pointing at *Blue Madonna*. I wanted her to turn on the lights and soak in the venom of its colors, grasp the full extent of my anger and loathing.

To her credit, she did not make a move to call the police, her bodyguard, or even little Flora. She kept her gaze on me.

"Ms. Rosen, calm down," she finally said, great concern in her voice.

Another horrible realization dawned on me—she didn't know. He hadn't cared enough to tell her about our engagement. It was time to apologize and leave before I made a bigger fool of myself.

I smiled through tears and tried catching my breath. "Forgive my outburst, Ms. Garibaldi. I don't know what possessed me. My coming here was a terrible mistake. *Terrible*."

"I don't understand," she said. "Did you love my Guido? Did you two have an affair?"

Just as I was calming down, my head exploded. "A *what?*"

"You poor child!" she said in that famous voice. "Would you like some ice water?"

"Don't you *poor child* me! How dare you?"

I wanted to start smashing expensive objects at random—the rosebud glasses, family heirlooms or not, a few pairs of signature sunglasses she had lying around the room.

"Tell me what's going on, Ms. Rosen."

"All right," I said. "Here goes. The night the two of you met and fucked your brains out for the first time, I was trying on my wedding dress. We were . . . I was supposed to be Mrs. Wheeler."

"*Mon dieu*, my God," she said in two, maybe more, languages. "This can't be true. He never said . . . You must have misunderstood him."

"For twenty years? We grew up together. We loved each other, till you . . . you . . ."

She didn't believe me. I crossed the boundaries, the sacred space between us, bringing my left hand dangerously close to her face, revealing the shiny silver ring. In my heart I thanked Robert for having made my hands presentable.

She reached for my hand. She felt the ring on my pinky. "Like mine," she said, keeping my cold hand in hers, rubbing it, as if to warm it up.

"Like yours." I pulled my hand away from her in disgust. "Spare me your sympathies." I took the ring off. "Read the engraving on the inside of both rings," I said harshly. "*Carly and Greg forever*. His name was Greg."

She didn't take the ring. She remained sitting, her eyes slits of great concern. What was wrong with this woman? How could she keep so calm? Yelling didn't make her react the way other people reacted. Did the confidence of beauty make one immune to anger?

"Sit down and listen," she commanded in that celebrated contralto she used to boss everyone around her. *Not me*.

"I don't have to listen to you," I said.

Flora appeared in the doorway and asked something in Italian. My enemy stood and answered in what sounded like the same fast dialect. Despite the composure of her voice, I knew she was about to kick me out.

I'd make it easy. First, I'd return the money.

I grabbed my purse from the corner and, with a shaky hand, wrote a check for one hundred thousand. Most of it was still in my account, minus the money I'd paid Zoe. I wrapped my silver ring in the check and threw both at the widow's feet. The sound it made on the hardwood was too small to match my anger.

"Keep both rings," I blurted out. "And the money."

She didn't bother picking anything up. She stood stoic, infuriating, in the cold light of those quartz crystals, letting me have my tantrum. Her Amazons, I imagined, were on their way. They'd soon lift me by the scruff of the neck and throw me off the deck into the stormy ocean.

I'd destroy her first.

What I needed gleamed on the coffee table, sharp and serrated. She was an imposing fantasy queen who had the power and authority to sever heads. Mine was gone; the next would be hers.

"Kyra, help," I whispered, imagining my sister's face.

Kyra wasn't there to stop me when I seized the kitchen knife in both hands and, despite Flora's shriek, did exactly what I'd wanted to do all along.

17

A sudden gust blew through the window, flapping the pages of a fashion magazine, whooshing through Kyra's ears like a wailing lament. Someone was hurting Carly. Her text about not wearing flippers wasn't a joke anymore. She was desperate, drowning.

When the Jaguar drove off, taking her away, Kyra felt emptiness and great fear for her sister. She wasn't happy about Hildi, the car, the whole idea of an undisclosed location. For a while the sisters texted back and forth. Kyra watched a murder mystery with Robert and Zoe. The old episode started with a young woman in her wedding gown who is pushed into a van, never to be heard from again. Kyra shuddered.

"You are internalizing again," Robert said.

Dying to pee, battery low had been the final text.

"She's doing what Greg did, simply disappearing," Kyra said, knowing full well that she'd probably only let her phone die and wasn't willing to ask to charge it.

Zoe ordered food from their favorite Mexican grill to cheer her up. When the food was delivered Kyra could neither sit still nor eat. She was going crazy.

"Let your sister wipe her own ass for once in her life," Zoe said, biting into a burrito the size of her arm.

Kyra left them with an extra burrito to share. She was off to the G-Spot to talk to Bruna.

"Find Bruna a replacement for tonight," she said to B. J.

"I need her at the door." B. J., who had recently become the manager, was drunk on her own power.

"For one night," Kyra said. "Please."

B. J. smiled at her viciously. Kyra lowered her voice and scanned the bar, about to confide. "Listen, Beetlejuice, don't tell anyone, but Mona dumped me."

Kyra was lying. B. J. claimed she'd stolen Mona away from her, as if Mona didn't have a free will. Mona and Kyra had a one-night stand, but Kyra figured another lie wouldn't hurt anyone and might help Carly. "Bruna Bear is more my type."

"You and Bruna." B. J. started laughing so hard, she probably forgot how much she hated Kyra.

"You can laugh all you want. I can't explain this crush."

"I understand," B. J. said between snorts. "I went for butch once. Cookie Schwartz."

"Cookie may-the-Schwartz-be-with-you?" They both laughed, remembering. Kyra stopped laughing. "So . . . does Bruna have the night off?"

"Be my guest," B. J. said, back in hysterics. "You made my week."

"It's all new, so not a word," Kyra said, basically giving her permission to spread it on Facebook and Twitter and to anyone who walked into the G-Spot.

"Not a word," B. J. repeated, already texting on her cellphone.

In no time Kyra was buying Bruna her first drink at The Abbey. As Bruna dropped the burning tequila shot into a mug of Corona, Kyra sipped a Diet Coke.

"How do I get in touch with Hildi?" Kyra asked outright. "I need a phone number, an address, anything you can give me."

Bruna got all teary eyed. "My sister broke my heart," she said. "Do you mind if we leave it alone?"

"Sure thing," Kyra said.

She wasn't going to leave it alone. She called their server for more beer and felt like a shit. Sweet, innocent Bruna trusted her, and here she was pumping her for painful information she wasn't ready to face. Bruna was one of her few real friends, and Kyra was about to betray her and break her heart, just as Hildi had.

Kyra was seriously sex-starved and so desperate to prove to herself that she wasn't really deceiving Bruna, she talked herself into believing that Bruna wasn't really unattractive, only big. What's beauty, anyway? In the limited light Bruna was almost pretty, with her yellow and black check shirt. If Kyra half-closed her eyes, the Elvis sideburns and upper lip whiskers were barely visible. Perfect vision only gets in the way, Kyra thought. We all look better when the lights are out.

18

The kitchen knife lay where I'd dropped it, next to the ring, the crumpled check and the ruined painting. Flora let out a cry of anguish, fell to her knees and ran a shaky hand over *Blue Madonna*, now slashed across the throat. She ran the same hand on the gleaming hardwood, where the knife had left a visible dent.

Vintage Carly, Kyra would have called it. Real-life drama for this film and stage director, this novelist, this nemesis of mine, who watched me calmly from a safe distance.

"Keep it all," I said.

Her voice was instructive when she spoke fast Italian, asking Flora, I imagined, to get Big Hildi and drag me out like a criminal.

"Don't bother calling the Cosa Nostra," I said in the most commanding voice I could muster through my scratched throat and snotty nose. The realization of Greg's final betrayal soaked into my heart like watercolor into heavyweight paper. This place depressed me with its gloomy lights and its history of Greg's real love for this woman.

"Flora," I said, "please get me a damned cab."

Flora scurried out.

"Stay," said the enemy.

"What?"

"Have dinner with me," she said evenly. "It won't make up for the man you've now lost three times"—at least she could count—"but Flora cooks with such love, it's a real treat."

"I'm not hungry."

"I'd like to celebrate his memory with you," she said.

Flora returned, cradling a frost-covered bottle and throwing suspicious glances my way. I eyed the intricate bottle, recognizing it for a pricy tequila unavailable for sale in the United States. Kyra would die if she saw it. Flora filled two shot glasses to the brim while muttering what sounded like incantations. She handed her mistress a full shot glass and left mine on the table. She might cook with love, I thought, but none was wasted on me.

Anna Garibaldi took a small sip, then lifted her glass. "Here's to you working for me."

I picked up my frosted glass and eyed it with relish. Such liquid gold didn't come one's way every day. I drank it straight down like a big girl. The sacrilege felt good. As the hundred-dollar shot burned its way down my throat, my mind cleared up. My focus returned.

"I'll stay for dinner," I said, "but I won't work for you."

"You know nothing about the project."

"One more word about it and I'm out, Ms. Garibaldi," I said.

"For fuck's sake already. Call me Anna!"

"Now you sound like my sister, Kyra." I picked up the spiked bottle. "She'd just die . . . I'd like to know who smuggled this across the border."

Her rich, throaty laughter broke the solemn mood. "Of all the secrets Guido kept from me, you are the most fascinating."

"And please, Ms. Gar . . . Anna," I said, "not another word about that dead piece of shit you called *Guido*."

She sighed. "You are a tough dinner guest."

I needed to freshen up. As I washed my face clean of make-up, I realized I'd brought none with me. Zoe's lipstick was in my back pocket. I quickly applied it, grateful for the semi-darkness concealing my blandness.

Flora rolled in a dinner table and set it between us by the blazing fireplace. Mouth-watering, tangy smells filled the room. My stomach growled with hunger. I'd eaten nothing since her phone call the night before.

The experience of dining with the woman Greg had called his wife and the world called La Divina was both surreal and natural. While devouring the second course—a pasta dish with a long Italian name and white sauce way too rich for my stomach, but delicious—I could not take my eyes off her face. Her beauty, her elegance, her economy of movement all mesmerized me. After only a few bites, she pushed her plate away. As if having predicted this, Flora immediately appeared at her side with plain yogurt and black coffee.

"Is that all you're having?" I asked.

"Don't worry about me. Enjoy," she said.

I was anxious that my table manners had put Anna off her food.

I rested my fork. "Sorry. I don't usually make such a pig of myself, but this is fabulous."

"Flora will love you for it," Anna said. "She'll feed you till you burst."

Our conversation touched on poetry and contemporary literature, both her own and others. She elaborated when I asked a few questions about her second novel, *White Horizon*. She was pleased when I admitted to reading each book twice. Then she spoke of her new protégés and their art.

As she spoke, her calm manner put me at ease. Her voice relaxed me, deceived me, stirred me away from the past and lulled me into thinking I had nothing else to fear.

I was willingly lulled. And I couldn't blame what happened next on alcohol, since the second round of tequila shots I'd poured remained untouched.

19

I don't know when the pot of fresh coffee and the bowl of fruit appeared between us. Anna held up a navel orange and eyed it. With a paring knife, she made a hairline cut around the rind, careful not to injure the fragile flesh. She removed the crown, cut thin slits into the peel, then slowly stripped it down. The naked orange was whole in her hand, then she slipped a finger into its top and separated it into perfect segments.

She reached across the table and offered me the wedges. I could barely breathe in all those perfumes—the ocean, her musk, the rose garden and now citrus. As the sweet and sour flesh burst in my mouth, her steamy poetry book came to life in my mind, waking up all my senses.

She took my hands in hers. Her hands were calloused and strong, and now sticky from the orange.

"Close your eyes," she commanded.

"Is this one of your religious rituals?" I asked, bewildered. "Because—"

"Do it."

I did. A vision flickered in my mind. The colorless alien world of my nightmares.

"No." She blurted out. "Colors, please."

What? I tried to pull away, but her grip was tight.

She spoke Italian. Reciting poetry? I listened to the way she sang the words. I didn't know their meaning, but they were not meaningless. I could listen for hours, and maybe I did. Her voice trickled through my skin, even and safe. As she spoke, a brilliant rainbow gushed out of the darkness behind my closed eyelids and broke open into colorful specks of apple green, burnt sienna, aquamarine, purples, blues, and rich carmine red. Each stanza of poetry she spoke exploded with more colors and raw emotion. Flowers grew in the dark, opened up and bloomed in dazzling colors that made me laugh out loud. Then the flowers wilted. A ghostly blue figure emerged from somewhere, expanded and burst into nothing, drowning me in sadness.

Strange peace engulfed me, calm and sadness seeped into me as I soaked up her spellbinding voice. I became a naked orange, stripped of its skin, penetrated, ruptured into wedges. About to be devoured.

She let go of my hands and whispered, "You see so many colors."

I did, but how did she know? And why was her voice so rough? Was she crying?

I opened my eyes. One sparkling teardrop rolled down her cheek, and again I saw that brief expression of pain. I wanted to reach out and wipe that tear away.

Her face was calm when she said, "You see colors in richer shades than anyone else."

"I suspect that is true," I said, "but how could you possibly know that?"

"A shot in the dark," she said. "I'm an expert at that."

"What does that mean?" I asked.

"I could always see deep, Carly. Now I see deeper."

Everything she said, every cryptic answer to my open questions, became part of a seductive game leading to more questions.

Light and shadows danced on her face. She looked incredible.

"Keep still," I said. "Don't move an inch."

Not taking my eyes off her face for fear of losing this perfect angle, I found my leather jacket in the corner of the white couch and pulled the sketch pad from its inner pocket. I went straight for my comfort zone, a dark pencil in my steady hand.

I worked from the outside in, outline to detail, first seizing her proud pose, the glow from the fireplace on her right cheek, the defiant strand of heavy hair dangling loose on the left side of her face, her hand offering me wedges of that peeled, penetrated, violated orange.

When and how Flora had rolled away the table was a blur. With the table gone, Anna and I remained seated opposite each other in the same comfortable, oversized armchairs, warmed by the blazing fire.

I turned the page and started a new study.

My *Blue Madonna* did not do her justice. Now that I knew exactly how to strengthen the jawline while maintaining the daintiness of classic feminine beauty, I planned a new and more accurate portrait.

Anna kept silent and motionless, staring straight ahead until I flipped another page. She then leaned back, showing me a partial profile. She knew how to strike a pose. Hadn't she sat for Greg? Hadn't she once modeled for Vogue or Givenchy?

I quickly shaded the side of her straight nose. A woman who had been my enemy for months, now simply sat, willingly posing for me as if I hadn't come here to accuse her of murder and of stealing my happiness. And I had done exactly that, yet she sat for me. How did this happen? I couldn't explain that transition.

The page filled with quick impressions of her nose, her hair, the faint smile relaxing her lips. I left her eyes blank. Her eyes were the most complex portion of each composition.

A new page.

I held my pencil at arm's length to approximate proportions. I breathed in all the intoxicating perfumes in the air. As I rapidly sketched, an image flickered in the back of my mind—a cold, colorless world.

"Don't let it take over," Anna whispered, as if seeing the same cold image.

I gasped and paused. "Holy shit, how did y—"

"You are immersed in your medium," she explained slowly. "I, in mine."

"Peeling me like that orange?"

"Your peeler is sharper."

She changed her pose again, gracefully letting the soft dress slide off one sculpted shoulder. One long leg extended beyond the side of the chair. Her feet were strong and toned, and her ankle had one of those old scratches.

"Do you climb trees like a five-year-old?"

"There aren't too many trees suitable for climbing around here," she answered. "Were you afraid, before our meeting?"

"Why speak in the past tense?" I resumed my work, carefully rendering her bottom eyelids. "Were you?"

"I still am," she said.

"Because of my bad temper?"

"That's the last thing," she said.

Her eyes were perfectly shaped, but complicated. The top eyelids . . . The irises . . . I couldn't guess their true pigment in the dim light. Drawn in pencil, they were the color of the ocean on a rainy day.

I guessed at her dark secret.

"You've suffered a great loss," I said, frantically working, grasping for a clearer vision.

"So did you," she said.

"I only lost a man, a dream." My breath caught in my throat as the truth was becoming clear despite her not saying it. "Your loss is immense. Your books, their intensity, remind me of Beethoven's symphonies."

"Thank you." She straightened up, even prouder, then deep pain changed her face. It touched my heart.

I'd hit a nerve. So I continued. "Why do you write alternate endings?"

"Reality is cruel and confined," she said. "Fiction should be truth, but also an escape. If a writer is considered God, she should be a benevolent one."

"The way you see and understand the world is a paradox."

"I see more than I want," she said, "but not enough."

I paused in my drawing to focus on her. The sorrow on her face was brief but intense.

Still . . . still I heard—no, I *felt*—the truth in her words.

Flickering images of earlier moments streamed through me as I returned to sketching her face. Behaviors I had attributed to her grandeur, to her reserve and calmness, now seemed to arise from an obvious truth, a different truth. Doubting myself, I started to grasp why she'd held my hand and felt the silver ring. Why she expected to be handed everything—the glass of champagne, the shot glass of tequila. Pieces of the puzzle were falling into place, forming a clear picture on the drawing pad and in my head: the particular way Flora had arranged items on the rolled dining table; the way Anna ran her hands over my painting; the austerity of the house, the clean floor, that insane order everywhere; no dog or cat, nothing out of place.

More and more of the obvious flooded into me, until it became too much to handle.

The tip of the pencil broke. The sketchbook dropped to the floor. She didn't pick it up, didn't ask to see my work.

I knew that all my worries—of being beaten to a pulp, drowned or sued—were laughable. My careful preparations—the shoes, the hair, the power suit, the lipstick—were all a waste of time. So much for the theatrics of writing the check, throwing the ring at her feet, slashing *Blue Madonna* in front of her eyes.

Her eyes saw nothing.

"What is happening to you?" she asked.

All my nerve endings were exposed. A woman considered a Goddess by the world, a woman I used to hate, was simply posing for me and, without a warning, as I was using my eyes to draw her beautiful face, I found out she was blind.

Blind.

I took in and then released a deep breath.

This was so unfair and so fucked up. A yellow orchid lobbed jaundiced waves of nausea at me from across the room. The orchid was in a far corner, and even that fact was telling—there was nothing to block her way.

Colorful spots swam before my eyes.

I floated away from her, down the same hallway that now seemed to stretch and stretch for endless miles. I was carried by waves. I opened the door. The shiny, gray faucet gleamed as if from miles away and receded even as I stared.

Wash your face, I told myself. Regroup. Refocus. Don't you dare black out.

20

"Talk to me, Carly," commanded a calm voice. Musk was in the air. Wet fingertips moistened my forehead. "Say something."

I wiggled my fingers. My vision cleared up. The green and blue tiled ceiling and walls, the ceramic floor, everything was as cold as ice except for Anna's pale, worried face and her warm hands busy all over me—feeling the pulse in my neck, burrowing under my shirt, unfastening my bra. The lacy, virginal, useless, stupid bra Zoe had wanted me to wear, just in case someone saw it.

"What happened?" I asked.

"You passed out cold. How's your head?"

"*Where* is a better question." I sat up, mortified by my weakness.

Anna's eyes were closed against the strong light. She helped me up to my feet, steadying me, since I was dizzy. I searched my reflection, trying to remember what I'd learned in that long ago nursing class about the signs of concussion. The pupils meant something. My eyes were haunted, but both my pupils were responsive to light and equal in size.

Her strong arms embraced me. "What colors do you see?" she asked with apprehension.

I thought the question strange; nevertheless, my gaze ran along the walls of multi-colored Moroccan tiles. "All the colors, really," I said.

She sighed with relief, then she reached up and dimmed the bright lights. Only then did she fully open her eyes.

I splashed cold water on my face. Anna remained behind me. Her skin was white and silky without make-up. Her lips were ruby red without lipstick. I noticed something puzzling and unusual about her reflection. Whenever I searched for flaws in my paintings, I would inspect the canvas in the mirror and all the faults became obvious. But Anna's reflection was flawless, similar to her un-mirrored image. Her face was utterly symmetrical.

"Too much alcohol? Not enough?" she asked.

I turned around and took her face in my hands. I planted a gentle kiss on each of her eyelids. "Your eyesight, how bad is it?"

She stiffened. "You know," she whispered, tightening her arms around me.

"How bad?" I insisted. "Are you completely blind?"

"Not yet, but it's a matter of time. I know up from down. I can find my way here, at home. I can tell that you are standing, just as earlier I could tell that you were lying on the floor, but I wouldn't know your face in a crowd."

"Open your eyes," I said. "I want to see their color."

She obeyed. Her distant gaze rested far beyond my face.

"Light gray, as I thought. What's wrong with your eyes?"

"Nothing. It's all up here." She pointed to her head. "No cure. A long ago head trauma damaged my visual cortex and I lost my ability to perceive colors."

"I don't understand—"

"Let me put you to bed."

"Just put me in a cab, or have Hildi drive me home," I said.

"You aren't going anywhere tonight."

There was no point in arguing. Anna pushed me forward down the dark hallway and through a maze of doors, into a room fragrant with the scents of saltwater and sand. The thunder of breaking waves resounded through the open window. A stormy ocean was lit by the moon.

"Incredible," I said in awe.

The bed was a rectangular shadow. She made me lie on top of its covers. Good, because I was only going to rest a minute, then go home. She sat next to me.

"Do you have a diagnosis?" I asked.

"Cerebral achromatopsia," she said. "This means *nothing is wrong with your eyes, but your brain won't let you see colors.* The only color I could see, until recently, was orange. Then orange faded and the rest is just about to—"

I thought of how she'd held up the orange to the dim light, milking her dying eyesight for every speck, every hope of seeing color.

"—I used to see black and white, but those are fading along into dull gray. Imagine your car's windshield in a pouring rainstorm without wipers. I can't see art or the printed word or what's on a computer screen." Her voice broke, but she quickly made light of it by adding, "My blind typing is impeccable."

"Does sunlight help?" I asked. Immediately I thought of her line of designer sunglasses. Those wonderful sunglasses—each unique, amusing, outrageous and stylish—had a deeper purpose.

"*Protect your eyes à la Garibaldi*," we both recited the famous slogan of Garibaldi Eyewear.

"Sunlight gives me a gargantuan headache and makes it even harder to see." She shrugged her shoulders, dismissive. "When did you realize?"

"The clues are everywhere, despite your brilliant cover-up. When I was sketching, well, when I do I get these flashes and I put things together. You told me that you could see more than you want but not enough. And those freaky senses. You can read my words before I say them. How?"

"Only mental pictures, only with certain people."

"Should I be afraid?"

"I am," she said. "I could always reach deep with my senses and the accident sharpened my ability." She sounded neither happy about it, nor proud.

"My best friend, Zoe, is a nurse at Cedars Sinai. She may be able to help."

She chuckled. "Is Zoe willing to donate the occipital lobe of her brain?"

"I'm sure she knows someone who can help you."

Right. How silly of me. La Divina probably had the best specialists on speed dial.

"My condition is so rare, nothing can be done," she said. "I've given up on a cure. Instead I'm working on my collateral senses, which you called *freaky*."

From my reclining position, I saw Anna in a new perspective, painted by the moonlight in strong lines against the night's sky. I wanted a huge canvas. My arm moved in the air, capturing a memory of this image in wide brush strokes, black lines and shades of blue.

"You are so famous and visible. How and why hide your blindness?"

"*Shush!*" She tensed up, as if the mere mention of the word *blindness* would summon the press. "I don't volunteer this information."

Only Zoe's happy drink could make me understand the logics of that non-explanation.

"Do you play baseball?" she asked

"What?" I leaned on my elbows.

"Some words keep popping into your head in dark courier font," she said. "*Baseball Bat*, with capital Bs, and some numbers."

"Baseball Bat 911." A tickle of laughter started in my throat. "It calms Zoe down, it makes Robert pontificate like a DA on TV, and it clears my mind. Kyra gets royal hangovers from it."

"It's a drink?" Anna sounded amazed.

"A mighty one. I should try it on you to make you volunteer important information."

Again, even in this limited light, I saw that brief sequence of expressions on her face I'd seen many times before. First wonder, then deep pain. Then a throaty, hearty laughter started low in her chest and came gushing out, unrestrained. Soon I was infected by that laughter and we were lost in hysterics, holding onto each other on the big bouncy bed. I let months of tension drain out of me.

In the dim light she seemed like a friend I'd known all my life. That must have been the moment everything about her came together, the moment everything became easy and I fell desperately in love with her.

"You have to know," I said, "that I'm wearing my power suit to intimidate you."

"What a waste of time . . ." A new wave of laughter started in her throat.

"Right? I wore a pair of high heels too, but Flora made me take them off."

"Yes, she is very fond of the hardwood floors. You should have worn the hiking boots," she said, apparently reading the picture in my head with her inner vision. Yes, truly freaky senses.

"I tried to," I said in a whine, "but Robert threatened me with the manicure scissors."

"Is Robert a violent person?"

"Only when it comes to fashion. Otherwise he is the sweetest. We all worked so hard on this look, I'm gonna make you see it even if it kills me." I took both her hands in mine and ran them over my spiked hair. "Robert cut it really short, to make me look sharp and butch, but I don't." I guided her further, to the collar of my white shirt. "Kyra's shirt. Feel how stiff it is." On to the gray slacks. "Feel this itchy material."

I had a few more complaints, but she wasn't laughing anymore.

"Carly, if you don't mind," she said, sounding almost shy, "if you'll allow me, I want to really look at you."

What did *really looking* mean when *seeing* was impossible?

"Okay," I said, curious, my heart beating out of my chest.

"Please stand up for me," she said, her voice commanding again.

I slid off the bed and let her lead me to the window.

"Don't be afraid, Carly."

21

"Stand still and close your eyes," she commanded.

I held my breath and did as I was told. My heart thundered with the ocean. My muscles seized up, rock hard. With my eyes tightly shut, I felt on my forehead what I could only describe as the touch of a butterfly. Another butterfly joined, lightly grazing my hairline. I wanted to see them.

"Keep your eyes closed, please," she said.

More gentle wings fluttered circles around my eyes, traced the outline of my brows, slid down both sides of my face, gently trailing the paths of tears on my cheeks, moving slowly on my lips, down to my chin.

"Your skin is so soft," she whispered. "I had no idea how beautiful you are."

I let her believe it. She was not judging beauty by common standards.

I imagined a dozen tawny-orange wings with their black veins and their white spots flying around my head, touching my hair, my nose, the back of my neck all at once.

"Monarchs," she said.

"Yes."

"No peeking. No cheating."

I had to cheat. I opened my eyes a crack, curious to see her. In the moonlight she seemed ethereal, with her hair down, her eyes wide open, completely focused in a world deprived of most vision, but rich in touch, sound and fragrances. Her stunning beauty was so painful to see, I shut my eyes again.

She slowly peeled the stiff shirt off me, letting it fall to the floor along with my already unfastened bra. My skin tingled as she maintained her downward motion, pausing at my neck. Her fingertips increased their pressure on the pulse of my throbbing heart.

"Are you afraid?"

I nodded, unable to speak. All these new sensations were so loving, yet so wrong.

"Just breathe, Carly. Fill your lungs with air."

She stopped the *seeing* and wrapped her arms around me, holding me close, so close that the steady movement of her chest against mine guided my own breathing, calming me, until I could notice other things. Wrong things. For instance, that this was the closest anyone had ever held me in my entire life and that I shouldn't feel so comfortable but I couldn't help myself because any embrace before this shouldn't have been considered an embrace at all. For instance, I noticed that only the thin material of her soft dress separated us and that if I slid the dress off her shoulders, we'd be completely naked against each other, and that was wrong. I noticed that she smelled incredibly good and that she wasn't wearing a bra and that without my noticing, my hands were gliding up her sides to confirm this realization.

She released her heavenly hold on me, leaving me wanting, craving more, and that release was the wrongest of all wrongs.

"I want to see more of you," she whispered in that melted honey voice.

Her touch traveled on my bare shoulders, down my arms, lingered on an achy spot where I had bumped my elbow against a wall in my klutziness a few days earlier. How did she feel it? She kept moving her hands downward, lower, along my arms, pausing on every ache and pain and bump I've long forgotten. She found a childhood injury on my right lowest rib, the one I'd broken years ago when I fell out of a tree. It would still ache occasionally, reminding me. Now her hand lingered over the memory. She gently kissed the very spot on my formerly broken rib, learning with her touch what no one else could see.

My life became an open book, and she was turning its pages. Through her fingers I discovered my body anew, saw it clearer than any mirror reflection would allow, from all angles, all at once.

"No secrets from you," I said.

"No secrets."

My insides were turning to water. The rest of my clothes, piece by scratchy piece, dropped to the floor. She was bringing me back to life with the feathery touch of her hands, sending strong currents deep into dying parts. Those formerly dead parts were moistening the insides of my upper thighs. I didn't want her to stop. I was choking on tears, starving, craving any touch at all since, ever since . . .

What if I was getting it all wrong?

I knew all along where this was leading, yet I was surprised by my body's betrayal. I was afraid she'd go on and find out, but more afraid that she'd stop. Would she kick me out in disgust? Tell me this had gone too far? She wanted to *see* me, she'd say, not . . .

She'd soon realize; what should I do? Should I stop her, tell her it was a mistake? She ran her warm hands down my waist, my stomach, again lingering, this time on a small scar from a long ago minor surgery, a bump on my hip from a straying piece of furniture. She gently kissed away the memories of pain.

She kissed the path of her sensitive fingertips, down my hips, down lower. Suddenly both her hands were on the delicate skin of my inner thighs. One hand slowly slid up toward the place of widening moisture. It was too late. She paused, realizing, her hot breath on me, her perfect oval face upturned and pale in the moonlight.

"Carly," she said, a catch in her voice.

She stood up.

That was it. It was over. I was devastated. I wanted to explain, to apologize, but she stunned me into silence by pressing her greedy mouth onto mine.

I was again in her arms, and now all was allowed. A locked door opened wide, letting me into a secret room in a forbidden palace, where I was free to roam, free to explore, to kiss and touch precious art objects with my bare hands.

I knew this was a crazy combination, Anna and me, her touch and kisses and whispers in Italian and French. "Mi amore," she said. "Mon chérie." And there was another language of love that came so naturally to her.

I couldn't take being upright much longer. My knees buckled. She eased me backward onto the bed, then she slowly parted my thighs and her lips, those demanding, hungry lips, were on the wet center of my universe. I cried out in pleasure as she took all that I had become into her mouth, moving on me in circles of agonizing slowness.

At that moment of neither here nor there, Greg's memory flickered into my mind. Had this happened to him? Then I didn't want Greg in my head and he became a soap bubble and burst into nothing. What happened so far in my life or what would happen next didn't matter. Past and future dried and shriveled like figs and raisins in the summer sun, but the sweetness remained, and I became a plump orange, peeled and devoured wedge by juicy wedge.

My hands were in her hair. That magnificent, famous hair now streamed heavily, freely, between my legs, adding to the exquisite sensation of her mouth.

"Yes, please," I begged, my voice coarse. "Don't stop."

She did stop and came up, her eager mouth meeting mine, her tongue parting my lips, letting me taste myself. She very gently pried me open with her fingertips, then paused and too slowly invaded me, so slowly I could scream. I tried not to scream but I did, because she pulled out of me completely and her hand hovered over the hollowness I'd become, leaving me crazy with desire.

"What do you want?" She kissed my lips, her hand lightly stroking me.

"You," I begged.

"Say it," she demanded.

"Take me all the way."

I raised my hips to meet her and she did, all the way, ripping me open, splitting me apart, until I cried out in pain and pleasure and madness. And more was inside me, her entire hand, Greg's ring and all. How? I couldn't understand because in agonizing slowness something grew inside me and I could barely stand it. Had she clenched her hand into a fist? I became a big ball of craving. That fullness, that pleasure, was too much to take.

"Keep still for my surprise gift," she said.

How many more surprises could I take? What else could ever surprise me?

With her lips small-kissing my entire face and her clenched fist motionless inside me, she proceeded to recite in a whisper the four erotic lines of her shortest poem in the original Italian. Even when I'd read it for the millionth time, I couldn't imagine it spoken for me, just for me, in her celebrated voice. By the end of the second line my cries were wild and alien in my ears. By the fourth line, I was done and ready to go again.

"Beautiful Carly," she said in that smoky whisper, as though adding a fifth line to her short poem.

"It took the blind to call me beautiful," I said, short of breath.

She laughed that rich, throaty, sexy contralto and remained inside me, taking me again, this time silently, in slow motion, until my release that went on and on.

She held me, protective, until my heartbeat steadied. She then aroused me again simply by slipping out of me and sliding her hand up toward my belly.

"Again, my love?"

"Let me catch my breath."

Only a few hours ago I scorned and feared her, the all-powerful enemy who had destroyed my life. Now I would do anything to protect her. To see for her. I would give my eyes for her. Greg had only had to give me up, which didn't seem like much. Not anymore. Any residual anger I reserved for the man we both loved and lost now dissolved. I understood his lack of choice. Anna had owned him, now she owned me.

Yet how could I go from hate to this feeling of love and devotion so quickly?

I didn't know or care, because her soft dress still separated us. I finally slid it down her shoulders, and she was naked against me and completely mine.

"I also have a gift for you," I said.

I opened my eyes as wide as the window, my mind wider, soaking in, sensing, seeing for her the splendor of the night's colors, those colors she ached for. If indeed she could see through my eyes and mind, I was giving her the whiteness of the full moon, the indigo blueness of the Pacific with its white caps, the black infinity of the sky. As she climaxed around me, whispering in Italian, I gave her the glorious lights of the bay, the Queen's Necklace.

"Thank you," she said, her breathing ragged. "Oh, Carly, you understand."

I tried to imagine what was missing from her life.

"Nothing's missing." She said. "Now you are mine."

A mental picture flickered in my mind, of Kyra, Zoe and Robert waiting, worried.

"Call them," Anna said, seeing what I saw. "Let them know you're alive."

"But I died and went to heaven."

"And there you discovered . . . ?"

"Why . . . why they call you La Divina."

And we were at each other again.

Afterward we were silent, catching our breath, listening to the waves breaking against the rocks.

I drifted off to sleep in her arms and remained asleep until a scream woke me up.

22

"Zoe, what'd you put in that shit?" I muttered.

Another scream pierced the darkness.

A mean hammer pounded the left side of my head. I opened my eyes a slit, then wide, soaking in the breathtaking view of a stormy ocean lit by the crack of dawn. No curtains or blinds concealed the Pacific's beauty.

Then I remembered where I was. A smile stretched my face from ear to ear at the memory of last night. Not Zoe's mixed cocktail, but something rather strange and wonderful and so tremendously wrong in countless ways. I had dreamed I was flying above an inky cloak of water, but this time it wasn't a nightmare. This time I knew what it meant. My naked body—enclosed in musky flannel and satin sheets—felt longer, leaner, alive with new sensations.

Had I dreamed the scream?

A strong smell of sand and salt and the sounds of the breathing surf drifted in through the open window. As my eyes adjusted, objects took shape in the dark—two plush armchairs, a round coffee table and bookshelves. My gaze caressed the objects I wanted to see for her. This was La Divina's bedroom, and I was in love with her. Our wild night was evident in the chaotic room, in my strewn clothes, in the crumpled bed sheets, the blankets thrown to one side and trailing off the huge bed. Raw memories filled me with warmth and desire.

And fear.

I sat up. Where was she?

"Anna!" The scream came from the outside.

I stumbled out of bed and rushed to the open window. From it I had a good view of the wooden deck. At the edge of that deck, two silhouettes clung to each other—huge Hildi and little Flora. They gazed down at the rocks and the stormy water. From my stance at the window, I did the same. My heart quickened at the sheer drop of the rocky slope above the breathing waves.

"What's going on?" I asked, my voice coarse from sleep.

They stared at me from the deck. "She's done it again," said a baritone. Hildi's.

"Done what again?"

They didn't answer, too preoccupied.

From the short time I'd known Anna—less than twelve hours—I surmised it wasn't likely that she'd jumped off the deck to end her life. And certainly not more than once. Suicide wasn't in her character. Did she trip and fall?

Twelve hours ago I'd fantasized about pushing her off, now, immense grief rattled me at that notion.

The sky was painted pre-dawn indigo. A new Queen's Necklace of glass windows and buildings reflecting the rising sun formed across the bay and around it, from Malibu to Pacific Palisades, Santa Monica, and the south beach cities.

I imagined a much televised search and rescue operation: helicopters overhead, news headlines, emergency vehicles, police, and reporters asking to interview the last person who had seen La Divina alive. Me.

I scanned the room for something to wear. Anything. Anna's dark dress on the floor seemed like a lifeless body. I pulled it over my head. An intoxicating fragrance of musk enveloped me. I craved her, ached for her, wanted her alive and close to me.

Where was Anna?

23

Anna hadn't done this for so long. It's been ages since she'd found the courage to get so near the edge. Carly opened an old door for her simply by reminding her of those *freaky* senses. Carly gave her new hope.

She was happy to find the rocks still as familiar as a lover's body. She took deep breaths, letting the open air ease her claustrophobia. She remembered the narrow trail dropping straight down the cliff side. An access ladder ran along the storm drain, but she'd never needed it and she wasn't going to start using it now just because of her disability. She preferred touch-seeing the rocks with bare toes and sensitive fingers. Here, in the open air, she didn't dread that word. *Disability*.

She knew, still remembered, exactly where one rock ended and the next began. She checked each surface for steadiness and dryness before trusting her weight to it. She could approximate her location by the growth of vegetation, the thorns, the sound of the surf. She studied every rock, every edge, with her fingertips, her toes, nose, and her ears. The skin of her face sensed the wind.

The loud surf below was a comforting presence, reassuring her that she could still tell up from down, left from right, night from day. No eyes could feed her such a constant and rich stream of information. What Carly called *freaky senses* were as good, or better, than a pair of functional eyes.

Ouch. A thorn scratched her ankle. That one would bleed. Flora would be on her case again, tell her she was risking her life. Flora and Hildi didn't understand her need to scale the rocks like a wild animal. Flora called her *procione*. Raccoon. Would Carly get it?

Her ever-dimming vision had taken a turn for the worse lately. How long could she keep pretending that all was well?

Her bare feet sensed each rock below. It was safer to stay on the bigger rocks as the smaller were gravel-like and loose and hurt her bare feet. She reached thicker vegetation, then sand. She first felt it with her toes, then her entire foot. She was finally down.

It was still dark, too early for sunrise. She left her sunglasses on the deck above so as to sense the wind against her forehead. This was the best time for a swim. She splashed cold water on her burning face and chest, in desperate need to feel the deep blue she couldn't see or even imagine. These *swims* opened up the dark gray box of blindness closing over her face, suffocating her, but a real swim in the open Pacific was a thing of the past. Still, she was at home here. This cove was hers.

Photographers loved her face. Composers wrote music for her. Artists wanted to paint her portraits. The only man she married got rich on painting her nudes. But her beauty was never magical to her. She walked tall because that was the only way she could walk. Even now, in approaching darkness, she could handle high heels as easily as bare feet, all from years of dancing and the runway. Yoga elevated her movements to a science, helping her maintain balance, strength and flexibility.

She was angry at those who wasted their perfect vision on sleep. She envied those who could see color and took it for granted. She was jealous of Flora, Hildi, the waiters at a restaurant, and even the homeless sleeping on sidewalks. If one could see colors, what else would one need?

They said her beauty had grown with age, that she was perfection, elegance impersonated, *le beau ideal*, the beauty to which all other beauty was compared. Anna Garibaldi, the most beautiful woman in the world. When she heard all those inflated adjectives, she pushed the sunglasses up her nose, smiled with her lips and cried everywhere else.

What good was beauty only others could see or a perfect figure that made the clothes hang just right? She would have given her so-called beauty up for one year of clear vision. A month. A week. If she were fast and didn't sleep at all, a week would be enough to finish all of them. They were waiting for her, calling for her, her babies. When her work was done, she may even welcome complete darkness. She'd rest.

Anna could smell the tide coming in. The scent of watermelon and cucumber made her stop and listen for the rattlesnake that slept underneath the rock. The first time she'd heard it rattle, she'd filed away the accompanying smell. Now she knew how to avoid snakes. Live rattlesnakes smelled different from dead ones. Dead seabirds smelled different from rotting fish.

The sense of smell was a freaky sense indeed. It opened death and life and love.

Her loved ones.

They were buried far below sea level. She'd often visit them in their resting place, breathe in the air permeated with cold preservatives. The smile twisting her face tasted bitter.

Here, in the open air, she could expand her lungs to their fullest. Not so up there, in the house.

If no one knew about her loved ones, what did it matter? If no one could see them, did they really exist? Was it a crime to love the dead? Weren't they *hers* to keep as long as she lived?

The man she'd loved had been destroyed by her truth. He had seen too much and what he'd seen had killed him.

Carly was her new life. She wouldn't let the same happen to her. She'd keep her away, protect her from that deepest truth. She'd seen Carly's face through her fingertips and that face was now internalized; that forehead, smooth and wide, straight nose, chiseled chin. Anna imagined her cheeks, pale and hollow from recent heartbreak. She sensed her craving, the loneliness. She'd make sure those cheeks pinked up, filled with happy smiles. She'd succeed where she'd failed with Guido.

She could smell the approaching rain, the gathering clouds, the dreaded sunrise. She'd better start the climb, reach the top and the safety of her dark glasses, before sunrise.

The sun, her enemy, gave off a burning smell as it scorched its way up above the green hills. Soon the full morning light would hurt her eyes. Another splash of cold water on her face, and she'd had enough swimming.

The rock sloped and curved, familiar. One bare foot anchored, the other followed. This end of the rock was safe; the other end, much too jagged. She ran her entire hand on the smooth surface, tested its stability, then started up toward the deck and their worried voices.

"Anna!"

Flora's voice came from above, the sound splitting up in the brutal wind, losing velocity like grains of dry pigment. Flora never stopped fussing. She'd fuss till she made herself sick.

24

"I'm not deaf, I heard you." Anna's calm voice disintegrated with the wind and the surf.

Relief shuddered my chest. I didn't know I'd been holding my breath. I peeked out the window in time to see her agile body, wind in her wild hair, appearing and settling on the deck.

"*Procione*," Flora muttered.

"Yes, raccoon," said a baritone, not Hildi's, but a man's.

I saw him reaching down to help Anna onto the deck. Where did he come from? She sprang to her feet with feline grace, avoiding his help, either rejecting it or failing to see his offered hand.

All three—Flora, Hildi and the man—spoke at once, making it hard for me to understand.

The man bent over and tried to kiss her. She gently pushed him away.

"You should go, Joe," she said, using the same commanding tone she'd used on me in the throes of passion.

Hildi said, "These are not your championship days."

What championship?

"I remember the rocks with my eyes closed." She chuckled at her own quip.

"It's still dark," Hildi reprimanded. "And now you are almost—"

"Yes, yes," Anna said, impatient. "I like the dark."

"And barefoot. Your leg is bleeding!" Flora's voice trembled as she switched to fast Italian and continued scolding her mistress, alternating between calling her *Anna* and *signora*.

I watched and listened, unseen from my position at the window, amazed at the whole scene, at how the two treated her, not as their employer, but as a naughty child. And she allowed it while telling them to stop fussing since she could take care of herself.

All three of them flurried around Anna like ballerinas, speaking at the same time. She brushed them off. I tried to figure out who said what and what the strange dynamics signified.

Anna said, "Flora, can the boss get coffee and some breakfast?" She added, "And make it for two."

"I already had my breakfast," Joe said.

"Good, because you're going."

"I have some time for . . ." He finished his sentence out of my hearing.

"I did some climbing instead," she said.

He laughed out loud. "One of your new victims?"

"You heard Signora," Hildi said. "Out."

"Tomorrow then?" Joe asked, hope in his voice.

"I'll call you later," Anna said.

So I was a *new victim*, an afterthought, a one-night stand. A steamy all-nighter, the best-sex for me, but not for the Divine One who undoubtedly had scores of victims.

I retreated from the window and into the room to the sound of her cheerful voice telling Flora, "It's going to rain. I don't want you catching pneumonia again." That much Italian I could understand. I guessed Flora was in the habit of catching pneumonia and Anna was in the habit of finding victims, like myself, playing with them and telling Joe all about the experience.

I'd be in a cab headed home before a drop of rain dripped. I wasn't ready to be her victim yet again. One-night stands, according to Kyra—and by definition—needed to last one night. Anna was out of my league and heading places without me. I was worth less to her than a peeled orange, squeezed of its juice.

I ran my shaky hands through my short hair, in my distress counting all my fatal errors. How wrong this had been, the meeting, the portrait, the dinner, her *seeing* of me and into me all the way up to her divine elbow. Why wasn't I stronger? Why had I allowed myself to be seduced?

She was surely in a hurry to put me in a cab and have her life back. She'd say that last night was fun, but a big mistake—

too much alcohol and *her dear Guido*'s memory between us, he was always the one for her, and "let's never meet again." She was about to let me have breakfast, as she had all her other victims, then kick me out and call Joe. *I'll call you later*, she had just said.

Of course she'd have scores of lovers. A recently widowed, famous beauty who'd managed to keep her disability a secret was a hot commodity. I couldn't face her. It'd be easy to slip away. She'd never have to *see* me again.

But a shower first. I couldn't wear her scent into my real life.

The lively thud of her bare feet approached down the hall. I grabbed my clothes from the floor, crumpled and shame stained. I quickly locked the bathroom door behind me and leaned against it. *Damn*. A large bump grew on the back of my head where I had met the floor last night. Dueling hammers now attacked both my temples.

Apple green dominated the old-fashioned bathroom. It needed updating, but it was sparkling clean. Through a glass wall so clear one could easily walk into it, the ocean appeared as a dark blue birthday cake decorated with white foamy caps.

Anna's dress, loose at my shoulders, slipped down and dropped to the floor. I threw my own clothes on top of it. A full-length mirror reflected my naked body. The glaring white of my skin only added to my throbbing headache. She said I was beautiful. What did she know about beauty anyway? My body was too thin, my face too pale, my cheek bones too prominent. I lifted one hand to my chest; a dark bruise on my neck would tell Kyra and Zoe everything. I searched the vanity drawers for make-up and found a bottle of aspirin. I washed two pills down with tap water and gagged on the acid trail they left in my throat. I found everything I needed, including a toothbrush still packaged in cellophane. Anna was well prepared for one-night-standers.

I shut my eyes under the near-boiling water. What was it like, knowing there was something as wonderful as color but being unable to perceive it? Would it be worse than complete blindness? What if all I could see was this, the black inside my eyelids?

When I opened my eyes, a picture of my fear surrounded me. Through the steam partially covering the glass wall I saw that the ocean turned barren gray and the sky above it disappeared into lifelessness. The world was dead and terrifying.

I gasped in terror.

Instantly a light rap sounded on the door.

"Are you okay, Carly?"

"Fine. Nearly slipped."

I rubbed my eyes. It was raining. Nothing was wrong with my eyes, only the rain Anna had predicted with her nose and her freaky senses. The walls, the floors, the cabinets all retained their normal green.

That brief glimpse into Anna's world made me cold.

A touch of pink lipstick improved the color of my pale face. I brushed my short, dark hair back, away from my forehead, and styled it with a glob of muck I squeezed out of a mysterious yellow tube. Like me, I hoped it wouldn't come unglued at some point.

Hair and lipstick didn't matter to Anna. As far as she was concerned, it was quite enough for me to smell good. But I didn't care about what she wanted. I was leaving even if I had to walk all the way home in the rain. The primping was for the world I was about to face. A dull world away from a dream. For Kyra, Zoe and Robert, who were undoubtedly ready with a list of unanswerable questions. I was duped again, I'd say, but I got some bruises, inside and out, to remind me for a while of the sexiest night of my life. *Divine* sex. Yes, I'd brag. Because what else did I have for them? What explanations?

I took my time behind the locked door, waiting for my headache to dissipate and for my taut nerves to calm. Then I took a deep breath and stepped out to meet the rest of my life.

25

A pair of flaming sunglasses adorned Anna's face—red and orange flames were literally part of their design. Her shiny hair was already tamed and held back in a tight chignon, as if the wind had never been in it. She was just as elegant now, in her colorless T-shirt and shorts, as she'd been last night in her clingy dress. Too beautiful for me and totally wrong. Her hands, those rock-climbing hands with the sensitive, seeing fingertips, now held a cup of coffee. Those loving lips that kissed me into heaven now sipped morning coffee like any other lips.

I never reached the door. Anna, moving with feline speed, got there first and blocked my exit with her body.

"Why are you wearing your scratchy clothes?" she asked. "Why are you wearing anything at all?"

She smelled of fresh coffee, saltwater and sand. She was pure muscle and all over me, seeing, feeling me with her hands and mouth, knowing all about me, even the fact that I was about to slip away unnoticed.

"Stay with me." Gently she kissed me.

"As your new *victim*?" I asked when I could breathe again.

"You overheard my trainer," she said, free of tension. "Joe talks like that. He is harmless."

"A personal trainer with extra benefits?" I asked.

At that she laughed. "We were lovers for a short time. He is now a good friend who works for me."

"A very handsome good friend," I said, "who wants more than friendship."

"Handsome is wasted on me," she said.

"What *championship* is he training you for?"

"The ultimate prime time," she said, a lilt in her voice.

"Is the *prime time* happening soon?"

"Never, if we can help it," she said.

"What does it mean?" I asked.

"Top of the mountain." Her voice smiled, but her embrace turned into a grip of terror. "Depths of the ocean. Bottom of the well."

"Complete blindness," I said.

Her silence agreed with me.

"Why did you do it?" I asked.

"I went for an early morning swim. That's all."

"In the dark," I said.

"Light is also wasted on me. I know those rocks like the inside of this house."

Her hands framed my face, dulling the headache, melting away my fears of rejection.

"As well as I know you, Carly, inside and out."

An aroused ocean reflected the clouds, sending volcano-like foamy waves into a sky scattered with lightning.

"Flora and Hildi were worried." I buried my nose in her neck. "So was I."

"You all see too well," she said.

"You make good vision sound like a disability," I said.

"I have to. Otherwise I'd climb the walls."

"Which you do anyway," I said.

"Yes," she said.

The idea of scaling rocks, either up or down, made my legs weak. "You'll teach me one day," I said, without meaning it.

"Stay away from that edge." Her voice was clipped with fear.

A split-second vision crossed my mind, the same vision of being suspended in open air, groundless in an alien world. Anna sensed it.

"Promise you'll stay away from it," she said.

"You bet I will," I said. "I have a phobia."

"Good," she said. "Keep the phobia."

She brushed back a wet curl from my forehead. Her hand belonged hostage in mine. So warm. Fingernails oval, perfectly shaped. Musk and warmth against my cheek, my lips. I kissed every seeing fingertip, every scrape and scar caused by thorns or pointy rocks. I discovered the flavor of musk as currents of desire turned my insides to water. Anna's breath caught when my tongue invaded the tiny triangles between her fingers.

The world outside darkened. A real rainstorm started, hitting the windowpane mercilessly. Anna opened the window wide. In seconds the hardwood was flooded.

"What are you doing?"

"You are so hot," she whispered. "I'm going to cool you down."

She slowly ran her hand over my face, down my neck, then took hold of the first button and ripped my white shirt all the way down the front. I gasped in sheer surprise as she did the same to my bra.

"You won't need clothes for the next year," she said.

She ripped every stitch off me, whispering in all her sexy languages. She eased me down to the floor. The wet chill on my feverish back made me cry out. Cold air and water blew in our faces. She threw back her sunglasses and closed her eyes, breathing in the freshness, allowing the rain to wash us.

She said, "Tell me how you'd paint a fresh canvas of a nude."

Her hair fell out of its knot. It soaked water and became darker, heavier. Rainwater dripped on my face and chest as she moved on me, her eyes closed against the morning.

"*Oui, chérie,*" she whispered. "*Oui, oui, oui, oui, incroyable.*"

"Incredible," I echoed.

"Colors, my love," she begged, wild in her desire, closing her eyes even tighter against a lightning flare. "See colors for me."

Another flash zigzagged across the gray sky, painting the world, the room and both of us, in grays and whites. I described red cherries and green apples, making up real colors for Anna, who'd had enough of gloomy grays.

"Ah, Carly," she cried out and her hands in my hair guided me lovingly.

My description of a plump blood orange, dripping with sweet juice, made her cry out, "Oui, chérie."

She collapsed on top of me, her pulse rapid against mine.

She laughed, rich and throaty, thanking me in her sultry poetry voice in Italian, French, and a language I could only identify as Slavic. I was already used to her slipping naturally into any language and back to English.

"Let's go up to my bedroom," she said.

"This isn't—?"

"No, my love," she said. "This is only one of my bedrooms. The prologue."

"Prologue? I'll die!"

One red chenille blanket was tightly draped around both of us on our way up the stairs to the second-floor bedroom. A fleeting image crossed my mind: Greg and I were to be wrapped this way in a traditional Jewish wedding that never was.

"Life takes its crazy twists and turns," Anna said.

"What?" I started. She'd caught me by surprise again. "Did you see what I was thinking? How the hell can you do that?"

"I don't know how," she said. "I don't want to know why. We have a bond."

"But the bond only works in one direction," I said.

She lifted me off my feet effortlessly and carried me over the threshold into her bedroom. In the chilly air she lowered me onto the feather bed and gathered around me the corners of a white jacquard sheet. The bed was fragrant with her musk.

"Cherries and cream," I said, getting used to naming the colors for her.

"I liked the contrast when I could still tell the difference," she explained.

I was soon engulfed by the scent of fresh burning wood as she added logs to the blazing fireplace.

"I can help," I said.

"Don't worry, I'm not going to burn the house down."

I dozed for a minute. When I opened my eyes, Anna stood still at the open window, engulfed in flames. I sat up, frightened, but it was only the morning light, breaking in prisms behind her generous beauty.

She remained as still as a statue, allowing me to drink in the view.

"Can you do something for me, Carly?"

"Anything."

"I don't understand why they're making such a fuss of my beauty. It's been years since I've seen my own reflection clearly. Can you . . . Will you . . . ?"

"I thought you'd never ask." I jumped out of bed.

She saddened me simply by not wishing to do so. I ran my fingertips slowly, lovingly, on her hairline, along the thin line of worry on her forehead, down the pale hair flowing heavily to her waist.

"How do I put such beauty into words? How do I describe your famous face to you, who can't see it? If I stuck by the conventions of beauty magazines, if I painted your portrait using the most flattering pinks and whites for your skin, pale yellow for your hair, warm gray for your eyes, if I worked a thousand years, I could never be true to your real beauty."

"You've just written a love poem," she said.

"Your beauty is poetry," I said.

"What about yours?"

"My face is pleasant enough," I said. "Nothing special."

She said, "I'd give up my poetic beauty and all my treasures to see your pleasant enough face."

I was pleased by her words, but a shiver, very faint, passed over me.

Such bargains should never be made.

26

Kyra's right arm tingled and ached. A pool of light spilled into her eyes through the edge of a broken blind. Huge clothes were strewn all over the floor: a pair of blue jeans, a man's checkered shirt, socks and worn black sneakers. What was she doing in bed with a man? Then a flash of memory brought everything back. What she had done was worse than fucking a man.

Bruna slept. Kyra glanced at her smiling baby face. This wasn't the first time she'd wanted to chew off her own arm in the morning, but she'd never before felt dirty. She'd crossed the line for her sister's sake, with dear Bruna, who had a crush on her.

She checked her cellphone with her live hand. Nine o'clock and still no message from Carly. She had to catch the one o'clock to San Francisco for yet another boring conference, and yet more lectures she had to give on sex and violence. For once her heart wasn't in it.

Her dead arm felt like a wet dish towel as she slipped it out, inch by painful inch, from underneath Bruna's massive torso. She shook it vigorously, wincing at the pain. Honeymoon palsy would no doubt keep her arm tingly for most of the day, reminding her of what a whore she'd been.

Bruna's sound sleep allowed her to steal smoothly out of the bedroom. She dressed in the kitchen.

The night before she'd learned some important information. Hildi was an art scholar and she'd been employed by Anna Garibaldi not only as a bodyguard, but in an advisory role. She was at Anna's side in every public appearance.

"La Divina can't make a right or a left without my sister," a jealous and hurt Bruna had said into her second or third beer and tequila combo.

Kyra kept shaking her achy arm, searching for coffee, smiling at the memory of a drunk and tearful Bruna, saying,

"You'd think she's the President of the United States the way Hildi is glued to her side twenty-four seven."

Hildi had always been the golden child, the smarter one, the more deserving. She'd sucked up to their parents and made them love her more. Hildi had ignored her sister for months now, too busy to return her calls. Bruna's pain was obvious. Last night Kyra listened to her with professional empathy, interjecting words of wisdom, really trying to help.

Bruna's kitchen was small, functional and very clean. The white cabinets peeled in strips here and there, exposing the old green paint underneath. A noisy refrigerator was covered with car magnets, notes to self, shopping lists. A child's drawing was framed above the sink. The sun, a red-roofed house, and stick figures of two adults and two girls. Bruna's childish signature adorned the top left edge of the drawing. Kyra found herself doubting and hoping that it wasn't a recent piece.

Since Bruna wasn't a slob like her, Kyra didn't have to make an extensive search for the coffee. She checked out the cabinets anyway, just to be nosy. She found a can of Yuban among a chipped set of coffee cups. She filled the old Mr. Coffee with tap water, promising herself that when she was done rescuing her sister, she'd buy Bruna a top-of-the-line coffee maker and a set of white mugs.

Bruna huffed and puffed like a heavy smoker as she sat down at the chipped Formica table. Kyra poured her a cup of coffee with lots of cream and sugar, the way she liked it. What should she say? How should she break it off?

Bruna took one sip and smiled up at her with sleepy eyes. "I love you a lot, but you aren't really my type. Too . . ." She hesitated, searching for the right word. Or maybe just one that wouldn't hurt Kyra's feelings.

"Too vanilla," Kyra suggested. "You like it rough."

Bruna nodded. "Can we stay friends?" She sipped her milky coffee.

"Absolutely, Bruna Bear. We aren't exactly a match in the sack," Kyra said, then her phone rang its generic tune.

Carly, she thought in fear. She was calling for help from a land line, because her phone was confiscated. Or worse. This was a call for ransom.

Kyra's good hand shook when she answered.

27

Anna's breathing slowed down. It was almost noon and we both needed rest. "Another woman is on your mind," she said. "Athletic, tall, big hands and feet, cowboy boots, healthy laughter."

"My sister will be delighted with your description."

"Tell me about her."

"Kyra has been my mother, father, and confidant since we lost our parents. She's a natural linguist, speaks six languages fluently, and she doesn't mince words in any of them. Let's see . . . What else? She reads Einstein for pleasure and Freud in the original German. She is inquisitive, and she wants to understand everything. She exhausts me."

"I'm already exhausted," Anna said. "Call her. She must be worried."

She handed me her cellphone, as I'd left mine in the Jaguar the night before. I played with it, enjoying a few fancy apps for the visually impaired. My favorite was the VM Alert that detected motion and used a mellow tone to let one know when one was no longer alone.

"Does that mean I can never sneak up on you?" I asked.

"I don't really need it," she said. "My senses warn me way before this does."

It took a few rings for Kyra to pick up. I imagined her trying to identify the caller.

"I'm okay, Kyra."

"Princess." She sounded relieved. "Where are you?"

"In Palos Verdes. At . . . at Anna's." I uttered the name with hesitation, knowing how Kyra hated her. I was supposed to hate her too, but I'd failed at that. Some loves wanted to shout from the rooftops. My love for Anna was fragile, improbable, wilder than any dream. It wanted to remain silent.

Kyra said, "I'll cancel San Francisco and come pick you up."

"No you won't," I blurted out.

Anna was working her way up my thighs.

"You don't sound right," Kyra said. "Is someone pointing a gun at your head?"

Not a gun. Not at my head.

"Of course not." My loud laugh contained a cry of pleasure.

"You're probably burning to talk about it."

Burning, and how!

"Nothing really to talk about," I said, biting my lip so as not to moan. "We had dinner and drinks. I fell asleep and woke up this morning with the worst hangover—" Shit. I had to keep my lying as short as possible, because in truth, my legs were far apart—one in New York, one in LA—and the Midwest between them had become a tropical paradise.

"You got drunk with her?" Kyra asked. "Was that clever?"

"She never knew about Greg and me," I said.

"Bastard never told her? Then he was just as bad."

"It wasn't her fault, really." Keeping my voice calm, I said, "An . . . Anna really loved him. We had tequila." Yeah, I changed the subject that crudely. "You should've seen that bottle with all the spikes and—"

"Ley 925?" Kyra shouted in my ear.

Telling her about the bottle was like dazzling a baby with pretty colors and sparkles.

"You got drunk on the most expensive fucking tequila in the world? You're supposed to sip it slowly and remember its taste so you can tell me about it. How did she get a hold of that?"

"Someone smuggled it in from Tijuana," I said, adding a little yawn of disinterest. Good. She was off the subject of what Anna had done to me.

"I tried calling you," Kyra said, mollified. "This isn't your cellphone."

"I lost it somewhere," I said.

Lost it along with my purse, my shoes and my life as I knew it. Anna's hands were busy on me, and I wanted to get off the phone and participate.

"When I told her about me and Greg, she got all solemn and teary eyed. She was like, *Let's eat and drink to celebrate the life of the man we both loved.*"

"Solemn?" Anna said, her face upturned toward me, her lips swollen and smiling. "Let's eat, all right . . ."

"Your voice is all wrong. Tell me what the bitch wanted," Kyra demanded.

"You," Anna whispered, biting the inside of my thigh.

"Me," I said. "She has a job for me. She wants me to start right away."

"What could you possibly do?" Kyra asked. "It ain't cleaning or laundry."

I covered the phone with my hand. "Think fast, what job can I do for you?"

Anna said between my legs. "Pleasuring me."

"You're no help." I bit my lip to keep from crying out loud.

Anna took her ravenous mouth off me and said, "You have the lovely job of telling me when something is hanging from my nose and when my dress is stuck in my pantyhose."

I uncovered the phone. "She liked *Blue Madonna*. She wants me to paint her portrait and . . . a nude."

"Is she really going to take her clothes off for you?" Kyra asked.

She'll have to wear something first.

"An artist is like a doctor," I said. "It's all meat and potatoes."

"It ain't cooking either," Kyra said. "Unless she intends to live on chili and Baseball Bats."

"You keep insulting me," I said, "I'll hang up on you."

"Carly, what aren't you telling me?" Kyra asked in her shrinkiest voice. "I'm canceling my trip."

"Don't cancel," I said. "I have to work real fast to get the pieces ready for a show next month. Portraits of celebrities."

How had I come up with that story? I hoped Kyra bought it, because I was ready to hang up. Anna's whispers in Italian and French declared her need to see me.

"Who's talking smut?" Kyra asked.

"The TV is on," I lied.

Anna started reciting poetry. I knew what would come next.

"I have to go now."

"Are you fucking someone?" Kyra asked. "Tell the truth."

"Goodbye." I disconnected, letting out a cry of pleasure.

Kyra wanted the truth. The truth was off-the-chart bizarre.

The truth: Anna indeed wanted me for a job. The fact that Greg and I were to be married was news to her. In my rage, I destroyed *Blue Madonna* in front of her eyes, which turned out to be a big waste of time since she couldn't see my dramatics.

The truth: Anna kept her approaching blindness a secret from an adoring world. Her senses, those she called collateral and I called freaky, were so developed, she could reach into my soul with her mind and look at me, into me, using her fingertips and her mouth and everything *but* her eyes, and it was the most thrilling, touching, caring, loving, sensitive, wild experience of my entire life.

What would Kyra have said had I told her that truth?

You're straight, she would have stated the obvious.

I'm not done, Kyra, I would have said. *I saw the colors of the night for her*.

At that, Kyra would have blown my magic bubble with a sensible remark such as, *Blind mind fuck*.

Kyra believed that Anna was dangerous. An addictive drug that had caused Greg's death. If Anna was a drug, I was hooked long before making love to her, before walking into her house, even before painting *Blue Madonna*. I became addicted at Greg's funeral, when her heartfelt eulogy made me cry for the first time. I became addicted when I read her fiction with all those alternate endings.

What if we could write ourselves alternate endings? Would I? If I hadn't lost Greg three times, I wouldn't have Anna. Would that ending be better than the one I had now? No, no matter how long I'd dreamed of that other ending, it couldn't possibly be better than this.

I reached for Anna's hand and pulled her onto me.

No, a different ending wasn't guaranteed to be a happy one, even if we could orchestrate its details.

So the truth I'd share with Kyra? I was happy at last.

28

"Procione," Flora kept crossing herself, staring out the kitchen window into the dark night. "What if she falls?"

"Our raccoon can take care of herself," I said to calm us both.

Poor Flora was a mess and so was I. Indeed, what if Anna slipped and fell? What if she lost her phone? None of us could help her because none of us was in good enough shape to climb the rocks day or night.

I added oregano and basil to the Baseball Bat and took a swig from the pitcher. "Perfect. Have a drink and stop worrying."

I liked Flora right away, despite her constant prayers and self-crossings and her fussiness about the hardwood floor and her *tshatshkes*. She was especially fond of a colorful farmhouse ceramic chicken that used to belong to her mother and now decorated the kitchen counter. She carefully dusted it every morning. It took her more than a week to warm up to me as a long-term guest and another week to let me mix Baseball Bats in her kitchen, as long as I cleaned up after myself. We became fast friends only when she agreed to a taste.

"It is good," she said. She poured an unmeasured amount of 80-proof cheap grappa into my mix. "Now it is better."

I was helping in my limited capacity, loading up the dishwasher, wiping off the counters. Then we heard the tapping of bare feet on the deck, and Anna came into the kitchen, muddy and glowing with happiness.

"I'm getting the hang of it again," she said.

Flora relaxed and studied her. "Wipe your dirty paws."

Anna did as she was told, but she pulled rank. "I want dinner. And make it something I like."

"You'll eat what I cook for you." Flora's attempt to boss her back in that heavy accent made me laugh out loud.

I realized early on this was all a game, covering up the great love and trust they shared. Flora allowed the bossing, and Anna allowed Flora to scold her as she would a stubborn child.

Anna preferred eating at the kitchen counter, where all was familiar, where she could identify the foods. She liked black and white food: black coffee, white yogurt, white rice.

When Anna reached for a slice of bread, Flora handed her a green apple. "Eat more fruits and vegetables and you'll get less episodes."

"What episodes?" I asked.

"Oh, hush, old woman," Anna said, begrudgingly biting into the apple. "You'd be surprised," she said to me, "how unappetizing a pale Granny Smith can be, a black tomato, a black cucumber. I'd rather eat what's meant to be black or white."

"What episodes?" I insisted.

Instead of answering, Anna took another crunchy bite.

I found out about it the hard way.

The next night, as we sipped cabernet on the deck, enjoying the mellow evening breeze, Anna asked me what she would often ask, to paint in words what I was seeing. She held her breath as I described the sunset, the calm water with the silver ripples all the way to Catalina Island in the distance, the sky burning in red and purple. My words, she claimed, would turn to mental pictures in her head and she could almost perceive the colors she had forgotten.

A quick move somehow made her sunglasses fall off her face, down into the clear water below.

For a moment the setting sun blazed on her smooth complexion, into her gray eyes, allowing me to admire her in a way I hadn't before, in strong light.

Her eyes were torn open, then she cried out in pain and covered her face, quickly retreating into the protective semi-darkness of the living room.

"This hell," she said, unusually frustrated. "I can't take it anymore."

"What did you see?"

"A nuclear holocaust," she uttered, a catch in her breath. "What you called a sunset was a wrecking ball that came at me from that white emptiness you called sky. This is hell. *Hell.* I'd rather have complete darkness."

I thought again of something she'd said only two weeks ago, on our first evening together, while I was sketching her portrait.

I see more than I want, but not enough.

So that was what she meant. She'd welcome blindness.

"Now it's going to start again," she said, her teeth clenched. "That sunlight shines into my eyes and then it starts. It's already starting . . . "

"What's going to start?" I asked.

She didn't hear me.

"I'm not ready for another one," she said, clasping her head as she slipped down to the floor. "Not now that you're here."

"What's happening, Anna?" I asked, my heart pounding in fear for her.

"My head . . . Flora knows what to do . . ."

A suppressed cry escaped her throat. It was the loneliest sound, one not meant to be heard. She curled into the fetal position, right there on the hardwood floor.

"Get Flora," she said through clenched teeth, trying to control the tremble in her voice but unable to do so. "Then stay away."

There was no need to call Flora, who rushed out of the kitchen, having heard Anna's cry.

29

I watched with dread as Flora kneeled next to Anna, took her head in her lap and spoke gently in Italian. She reached into the thickness of her loose hair and, ignoring a choked cry, slid a steady hand down to her stiffened neck. What was going on?

I sat at Anna's feet, watching. Just watching.

"Show me," I said.

"Carly, go," Anna whispered, curbing the pain in her voice.

Flora glanced up at me in approval, took my wrists in her cold, bony fingers, and guided both my thumbs toward the sides of Anna's nape. "Push upward and hard," she said.

Anna's skin was hot to my touch. She cried out again, but Flora gestured to me not to take any notice and to keep applying firm, unrelenting pressure. It took about five minutes. At last Anna breathed in relief and sat up, still flushed, but smiling at us both.

"Thank you." She hugged Flora.

"I did nothing," Flora said.

"Carly?" Anna asked with disbelief. "You showed her?"

Flora shrugged. "I won't always be here."

As she stood, her joints creaked. Not for the first time I noticed how old and frail she was.

Sounding amazed, Anna said, "Everyone before you got scared. Not you."

"Everyone?" I asked.

"My others."

"Even him?"

"Even him," she said.

Anna had never mentioned Greg to me, as she'd promised.

"Tell me what happens," I said.

"That short exposure to sunlight causes unbearable, sharp pain in my head and eyes. If Flora isn't here to push the right spots, the pain could last days."

"We'll stay inside in a darkened room," I said. "I'll make love to you for hours. I'll read for you, sing, whatever, but no more sunlight."

"What about your own need for light?"

"Ever heard of co-dependence?" I asked. "Teach me how to be a night creature like you."

Her smile was faint, but there.

She fell asleep where she was, on the living room couch, completely exhausted from her episode. I sat still, watching her. Her arms framed her face on a pillow of her own hair.

My Anna.

Fame, beauty, and incredible talents were hers. Her films—all black and white—won critical acclaim and artistic awards. She wrote one compelling bestseller after another. She hosted art shows, helping new artists launch their careers. Whatever she touched turned to gold, and yet, no one knew. Her few insiders—other than Flora and Hildi, who lived on the premises—were sworn to secrecy.

Hildi served as more than a bodyguard and a driver. She and Anna had a brilliant system, all meant for cover-up on public appearances. Hildi would always walk a step ahead, clearing obstacles out of Anna's way. She'd secretly guide her with a set of brief spoken signs and signals, nudging her in the right direction, whispering the names of people Anna hadn't recognized in a voice barely audible to others.

In a gallery opening for new faces in art, I'd watched Anna—in a white feather boa, diamond-clad sunglasses and five-inch stilettos, and that over-the-top elegance adored by the impersonators—warmly greet her fans, pose smiling for photos and even autograph a copy or two of her last novel when someone pushed it toward her.

It was during our first week together, and I'd felt so proud. This beautiful woman was mine. She posed and performed for the cameras but later in our bedroom, she'd teach me that love was blind.

The evenings belonged to us. During the day the big house hummed and buzzed with Anna's people—agents, publicists—who all eventually ended up in the kitchen, where Flora fed them till they burst. A lively young assistant among them also acted as hair and fashion consultant. He spent a few hours a day in the first floor office, answering the phone and the mail.

A fat lawyer came once and took Anna away from me for an hour. Then came a banker who needed her signature on a few papers and didn't mind my presence. From the way he guided Anna's hand, I realized he knew her secret.

Joe Rowland, Anna's trainer, helped improve her balance, strength, and confidence in her other senses. Among the trusted insiders was an ophthalmologist, a neurologist and a general practitioner, Anna's personal physician and friend, Dr. Louis Bernstein, a big man with a big belly and an appetite to match. He would come to visit, not so much to keep an eye on Anna's robust health but to drink grappa with Flora and swap recipes in the kitchen.

Those employees and friends formed a wall around Anna and her dark secret, protecting her from prying eyes. La Divina had a public image to maintain and people who helped maintain it. La Divina could not be pitied.

The rest of the world, those who knew Anna only from public appearances, television interviews and glamorous magazine covers thought her the luckiest woman on earth.

They knew nothing.

I thought I knew, but Anna, so generous in her fiction, so outpouring in her writing style, kept her real sufferings even from me until she had no choice.

If everything she touched turned to gold, so did everything she feared. Even her great fear of the sunlight became a fashion statement. Garibaldi Eyewear.

I watched her stirring in her sleep. Her lips curved in the little smile. She wasn't La Divina now, but a very tired child, safe and innocent in her dream.

She opened her eyes with the same smile, seemed worried for a moment, then she touched my cheek with the back of her hand. A new, long thorn scratch adorned her arm.

I held her hand. More than anything I wished I could protect her from harm, from pain, from her future and its looming darkness.

30

"Read to me," Anna said, still lying flat on the living room couch, her hand in mine.

"What would you like?"

"There's a small book of poetry somewhere here. Very old. It has an inscription."

Anna kept stacks of books on coffee tables, in shelves along the walls, anywhere safe, away from becoming obstacles. I browsed the coffee table, the bookshelves around the room, thinking of everything her deteriorating vision had forced her to give up. She gave up films, dance, stage—but her greatest loss was reading, or so I believed. Books remained dear to her, even now. On a bottom shelf I found the small Italian poetry book. When I leafed through it, the book creaked like an old door. The brittle pages were withered and yellowed around the edges, musty smelling. A handwritten dedication on the otherwise blank front page said, *To Anna. JR.*

"Is this the one?" I handed it to her.

She sniffed the pages, then pressed the book to her chest. "It is."

I could read Italian, slowly. As I read, she remembered and her voice joined mine and she was smiling.

I asked, "Do you miss JR?"

"As much as I miss colors." She pulled me on top of her on the soft couch. "As much as I miss reading. As much as, eventually, I'll miss writing."

"Why would you give up writing?"

"Because writing is so visual, and the read-back feature has its limitations. Too rigid."

"Can't you hire an assistant?"

"I can't let a stranger misinterpret my meaning."

"Hildi? Flora?" I asked.

"Flora's English isn't as perfect as her Italian. Hildi is my art expert. I won't pile up more work on either one."

"What about friends? A lover?" I asked with incredulity. "Did anyone ever refuse?"

"I tried once," she said. "It was a disaster."

Another piece fell into place. Greg knew of my reading speed. Had this been the job he could not handle?

"I'll edit for you," I said.

Anna stiffened. "You said you'd never work for me. I was afraid to ask."

The great Divine was afraid to ask! I loved her more for it.

"That was a hundred years ago," I said.

"And now?"

"I read a lot and very fast," I said. "I've become sort of an expert on your style, your phrasing, your alternate endings. I'll edit your first draft and read it back to you as many times as you need to get it right."

"Are you really willing to do it?"

"You'll pay for it."

At that she tried to escape my straddle lock.

"I paid you plenty already," she said, pretending indignation.

"Not enough," I said. "You'll have to have sex with the editor." I planted gentle kisses along her perfect hairline, down to her eyes. I stopped.

"Why are you crying?"

"Carly, my love, welcome home."

The soft light from the quartz crystals glowed on her hair, sprinkling it with gold and silver. Her arms were around me and I was home.

We started working every day.

Private Hell was the working title for Anna's newest book. A woman dies and finds herself in a beautiful palace overlooking the sea. The palace is fit for royalty, filled with luxuries. Alas, her eyes are gone. Her other senses only serve to remind her of the beauty she is missing. She suffers immense cravings for light and colors.

She can hear and smell the ocean and she longs for its beauty. She feels free only while standing at the edge of a cliff, smelling and sensing the wind on her skin. She takes to descending the rocks down to the stormy water in her bare feet. She isn't afraid of falling, as she is dead already, but she has to return before sunrise, to avoid painful burns.

A secret passageway inside the palace, down below, leads to heaven. When she finds it, she'll get her eyes back. Frantically and blindly she feels her searching way down for the passage to happiness. Disappointment hits every time.

Anna and I worked together in her darkened office since she couldn't tolerate even minimal daylight. I was sprawled on the plush black leather couch, filled with a great sense of mission, a fresh printout of her last draft in my lap. I was correcting each feverishly written chapter.

The anger and frustration Anna never expressed in real life came out in her metaphors. Her struggle—to break through to a once known but now unavailable dimension—devastated me. The arc of the story was fairly sound at an early draft, requiring very few corrections, mainly adding a word or removing phrase repetitions. I left the raw style as it was.

I read a corrected chapter back to her.

"*The claustrophobia of forced darkness*," she repeated my choice of phrasing. "I'm impressed. Why this particular combination?"

"Because this is so obviously autobiographical."

"It is," she said.

"If an actual passageway to your heaven existed," I asked, "where would it be?"

"In the center of my greatest misery," she said, as if I should have known.

"In the basement?" I asked.

She coughed in surprise, the laughter dying in her throat. "Stay away from there. The rest of the house is yours, but stay away from that place."

"Why?"

"It's unsafe."

I stayed away.

31

Anna choked back the tears as she traced her way back up the spiraling staircase, up to the sounds of the world. Its warmth. How many times could hope die? Every single time. She felt every nook and cranny of the cylindrical wall with her knowing hands. The way down was easier. The way up threatened to entrap her. The walls would somehow constrict into a cone shape, a bottleneck, closing in on her.

She was frozen to the core and filled with disappointment. Hope was warm, the lack of it was cold, so very cold. The air was chilly, and even the stone stairs felt more worn out than usual.

Every visit broke her heart anew. Each time she expected her babies to come running to her, saying, *Peek-a-boo. We were playing hide and seek, but all is well.*

Yet they remained just as dead.

Down there, even with the dust and those other stifling smells, she was transported to a time when life had a purpose. The time before she'd lost all of them, all at once.

Up and up the stairs. Now she heard the ocean and the birds, singing their morning songs. Now she smelled the coffee Flora was brewing in the kitchen. She'd have one cup of coffee and go back to bed where Carly waited for her, warm and loving. She stopped for a moment to pull herself together, so as not to frighten Carly. She had to protect her new love.

The staleness dragged behind her, a clinging scarf of death.

Flora and Hildi wouldn't go there. *Ghosts.*

What a joke! Ghosts would be a sign of certain life, and there was no life in that place.

Dear Flora was getting too old to do all the cleaning and cooking by herself. Anna should hire someone free of superstition to clean the entire basement, sweep it clear of dust.

Who could she trust? Who would not run to the press and sing like a canary?

"I'm here." Carly announced her presence. She was seated on the top stair, waiting. It was their third week together, the end of February, but Carly was fragrant with the full blooms of April.

"Did you find the passageway?" Carly asked.

Poor Guido had been right. Indeed, Carly could understand. Anna would have to prepare her for the big revelation. Guido had been shocked and the consequences proved fatal. But once Carly was ready, they'd work together. Carly would be her eyes.

And Carly would help infuse life into her lifeless babies.

32

A moving shadow was thrown on the wall above the stairs leading to the forbidden basement. It moved downwards. I stopped at the small vestibule and peered into the dark well of the spiraling staircase. A vortex of frigid air whooshed up at me from below, permeated with the smell of turpentine. I'd kept my promise to Anna and never gone any further. I'd sit there and wait for her until she came up, her face cold and sad and streaked with tears of memories she wouldn't share with me.

That shadow wasn't Anna's, that much I knew because she wasn't home. That morning Hildi had taken her to an appointment in LA and I'd stayed behind to work on the full first draft.

So far, three weeks of heavenly honeymoon passed in total bliss. Anna and I could not get enough of each other. Those who worked for her came in and out and did their jobs, but Anna did not schedule public appearances. We would work on her book, or we'd stay in bed, talking, making love, just listening to the waves breaking on the rocks below.

While enjoying the happiest time of my life, I made sure to text my sister and my friends daily and keep my lies as close as possible to the truth. If I was to keep Anna's secret safe, it was easier for me not to see them at all. They didn't question me. As far as the three of them were concerned, I had a new, demanding job. Kyra's schedule, between teaching school and private therapy sessions, was booked solid, Zoe worked in the ER almost every night, and Robert traveled on business.

I peered down the stairwell, listening to the creaks and cracks of a cold morning when Flora limped by on her way to the kitchen, complaining about her bad arthritis.

"Did they already leave?" she asked.

"They did," I said. "There's someone down there."

"*Spiritos*." Flora crossed herself and muttered one of her Italian incantations.

"Why the crossing?" I asked.

"It can't hurt," she said. "Stay away from there."

I'd heard enough about staying away. I was going down to see why for myself. If I was to become Anna's eyes, I meant to see everything for her and give her a full report.

A glamor shot of Irena Garibaldi, the then-reigning Queen of Hollywood, leaning against a shiny Lamborghini caught my attention. The vestibule was a shrine to Anna's famous parents, Hollywood's dream couple, Irena and Marco Garibaldi. A black and white of their wedding day; Anna, a short-haired tomboy of eight or nine, posed with her parents. The most stunning photo was of mother and daughter, smiling, their hair pulled back in similar styles.

The sound of light footfalls up the stairs startled me.

Dragon's breath came up from the darkness below. My heart quickened. I managed to drop to the floor behind a leather armchair, in my klutziness taking down a stack of art books and making a loud clatter.

A willowy being emerged from the staircase. A ghostly woman. Her graceful walk barely stirred the air as she passed me. I instantly crossed myself. As Flora said, it couldn't hurt, even if you were Jewish and didn't believe in ghosts.

The ghost was carrying what seemed to be a heavy square object—a box, a large book, or a piece of furniture. I couldn't tell what it was. The dim light illuminated one side of her face. She was beautiful.

My heartbeat was wild. I got up and followed her silently all the way to the front entrance. I poked my head out. She had disappeared! I could see neither the woman nor what she had taken, nor a vehicle in the driveway. If she wasn't a ghost, she certainly disappeared like one.

Was she real? What was she carrying out of the house? Stealing! And why was I the one hiding?

In the kitchen I started asking Flora about her while making our morning coffee. As I did, the mysterious intruder came in and hugged Flora as if only now arriving. Her dark-chocolate complexion was so smooth in the morning light, I was sure she'd never had a pimple in her life.

"You aren't a ghost," I said.

"You're a bright one," she answered, sizing me up with disapproval.

"But weren't you just—"

Flora introduced us. "Juliet Blair. Carly Rosen."

Then I realized why she seemed familiar. "You must be the actress from *Divine Darkness*."

"Right on again," Juliet said, sneering. "And you must be the new piece of ass."

"Right on, back to you," I said.

What was her fucking problem? My anger flared and my fist wanted to meet the center of that perfect obnoxious face. "First you take shit out of here, and now you—"

"I'm here because my friend Flora promised to teach me her mama's pizza recipe."

"But—"

Flora intervened again. "Are you staying for the pizza, Carly?"

I knew neither of them wanted me to stay.

"You bet I am." I smiled and stared straight at Juliet. "I'd love to make pizza out of your —"

"Shut up, both of you," Flora said.

"You probably can't tell pizza from chicken parmesan," Juliet said.

"I know nothing about cooking," I said, now seriously pissed off. "But I can eat and *eat*." Something possessed me to make a rude gesture of wiping off my face.

"You are both so childish," Flora said. She then took me aside and said in a confiding tone, "Juliet and Anna used to be friends but they, well, they had an argument."

"I can see who's to blame for it," I said, glancing at Juliet.

"Can I trust you to keep this visit our secret?"

"Sure thing," I said.

"You can stay here and listen, but you have to relax."

I wanted to argue that *she started it*, but decided to shut up for Anna's sake. Either Flora really believed in ghosts or she was playing stupid and they were both in on something. I was going to listen and study the dynamics between them, and I had no intention of keeping it a secret from Anna.

I poured out my coffee and, in spite of the early morning, mixed myself a pitcher of Baseball Bats—slushy bats, to create as much passive-aggressive noise as possible. Then I dropped a tiny red umbrella into my frosted glass, brought in a deck chair and sat down, slowly sipping my drink, thinking of Zoe and her special twists, and her loud burps, clearing my mind and relaxing my temper.

Juliet moved about freely in the kitchen and followed Flora's instructions, occasionally giving me the stink eye, and my right fist occasionally itched to meet her perfect nose and add blood to their pizza. I didn't give a shit about cooking, but I owed it to Anna to see that nothing else disappeared from her house.

Flora, who barely let me mix my drinks in her sacred temple, allowed Juliet to cook and even that pissed me off. Many came here to pour out their hearts and learn her recipes, but only Juliet was allowed to cook.

Suddenly Juliet dropped the spatula and looked up, listening. A moment later I heard the crackling on the gravel road, announcing Anna and Hildi's arrival. Juliet threw me another glance of hate, then took off by the kitchen's side door without saying goodbye.

Anna sniffed the air. "Ah, pizza," she said. And then, "How is Juliet, Flora?"

Flora stiffened. "You heard her?"

Anna said, "Ylang Ylang and lavender are fresh in the air."

Nothing escaped her.

I grinned, childishly delighted that Juliet had been caught out.

33

A certain paragraph I was editing had more stray errors than usual. Just as I noticed it, I heard a crash of breaking glass from the bedroom. I skipped upstairs, three steps at a time, to find a frightened and bloody Anna, shards of glass all around her. The mirror was broken. It seemed she had put her fist through it.

"It happened," she whispered.

"What happened?"

"Prime time," she said. "I can't see."

She fell apart in my arms, frightened, saying she had opened her eyes to complete darkness. I examined her face, her body. The thin trickle of blood came from her left hand; I found no shards in her skin. I stopped the bleeding and bandaged her hand with supplies I found scattered in drawers. I treated her hand when all I wanted to do was fall apart with her and wail.

Complete darkness.

"Do you want to go to the emergency room? For your eyes? Your hand is fine."

"They can't help. Let's give Bernie a call," she said.

"Right away." I searched my cellphone contacts for Dr. Bernstein's number, but she stopped me.

"No, he can do nothing," she said. "Leave the bad news for tomorrow."

We held each other on the bed for a while, Anna, regaining her composure long before I did, calming me.

"It isn't really a surprise," she said first. And then later, "I knew all along this would happen." Eventually she asked, "Where's your *Blue Madonna*?"

"Here, in the bedroom," I said. "Do you want to pray?"

"I want to see her through you."

She kneeled in front of it, then ran her seeing hands on the palette-knife ridges. Her forefinger penetrated the slash across its throat.

"Did you do this?"

"Yes," I said, "but you have to put it in context—"

"What colors did you use?"

I wanted to protect her from it. "Mostly blue. Angelic blue."

"What else?"

"Crimson for contrast."

"Where did you use crimson?" she asked.

"A hint of a halo on the side of the head."

"And the background?" she asked.

"Shades of sweet licorice."

She didn't fall for any of it.

"Another name for black," she said, pressing her fingertips to the canvas, as if to hold on to a disturbing image in her mind's eye. "I do remember what colors do, Carly. Bloody aura, inky black. You believed I was sinister."

"I blamed you for Greg's death," I said. "I know the truth now."

"You know nothing." She spat out the words, distraught.

She started pacing the room, agitated. She searched her vanity drawer, knocking a bottle of perfume off in the process, disoriented in her complete blindness, until she found a pack of cigarettes. Not even a fancy brand, simply Camel Lights.

"Smoking is bad for your eyes."

"Nothing is wrong with my eyes," she reminded me. She lit up and inhaled. Quietly she said, "It was all my fault. You were right. No one else had known his frenzy, his fear, his pain."

"Why was he frenzied?"

"He saw . . . he couldn't handle . . . It ended his life."

"What did he see, Anna?"

She was pacing the room nervously, barefoot, finally starting to talk about Greg's last day, maybe the last minutes of his life. The time had come to ask the questions still gnawing at me, yet I wasn't sure anymore I wanted to know the truth. The love Anna and I shared was true; did anything else matter?

She inhaled again, as if the cigarette was life-giving oxygen.

"Exactly a month ago you made me promise never to discuss him."

"Break that promise. Tell me."

"Okay, Carly. Happy anniversary. No more secrets."

Her lips were glued to the burning cigarette, her gaze was far away, remembering long-ago events. Two months had passed since Greg's death and his funeral. A million years for me.

Anna looked lost. "I'll tell you everything first, then you'll be ready to see it."

"What will I see?"

Her cigarette became a long, burning pyre as she sucked deeply. I took it out of her hand and stubbed it out in a hideous ashtray that seemed to have been made by a child for a school project. She didn't argue.

"Sit and tell me," I said.

She sat down. "You came here to reclaim something that belonged to you. I invited you here for the same reason."

"I don't understand," I said, my heart racing.

"You had something I needed desperately."

She said *had* not *have.*

"Anna, everything I have is yours."

"It's too late, Carly. Hades has won."

She could have slapped me, my shock was so great at her mention of Hades. My life had become a row of collapsing dominos.

A knock on the bedroom door was the last falling block, hitting with a thud that made me jump.

Hildi said, "Guests."

"Offer them a drink," Anna said in her usual commanding tone. "I can't see anyone now. Literally."

"Not your guests, Signora. Carly's."

My guests? Without a word I took three stairs at a time on the way down, away from madness. Away from pain and darkness and truth. Those could wait.

Part Three

34

Kyra planned to meet B. J. and the rest of them for dinner before the party at the G-Spot. She couldn't wait to sink her teeth into a juicy New York steak and as she was also sex starved, she was envisioning a date with Zingy Lola. Lola was too kinky for B. J., but Kyra was horny enough to try once. While rinsing her super short hair and admiring her own six-pack in the bathroom mirror, her phone played the *Alfred Hitchcock Presents* theme.

"Bruna Bear," she cried out, answering the phone with wet hands.

"I have the Palos Verdes address," said the baritone. "You owe me big for the hell I had to take from my bitch sister."

It had taken Bruna two days to get the address. Carly had kept in touch through texting and she asked Kyra to keep away since she was working hard. Kyra was respectful of her wishes but come on, a whole month? Fuck respect.

Once they had the address, it was Zoe's idea to land on them unannounced. "How else will we find out if she has a gun pointed at her head?"

Kyra drove Carly's Mustang, and Zoe drove the Wrangler with Robert. The official excuse for their unexpected visit was to leave Carly her car and some clothes.

They arrived in full daylight. Hildi was waxing the spotless black Jaguar in the driveway. She looked up, alarmed. Then she recognized Kyra and raised a fat arm, either in greeting or as a signal for the mob to attack.

The house.

The white and blue structure looked like a giant crystallized form. Kyra thought it must have been designed by a mad architect with a minor in chemistry. She'd seen a mini version of it only once, in biochemistry class before an elaborate experiment went *kaboom*.

The house was surrounded by a cluster of blingy quartz minerals, much like those things the feel-good new agers wore around their necks. The aquamarine Pacific spread all the way to Catalina Island in the distance. Big rolling waves thundered on the rocks below.

The fragrance of an old-fashioned rose garden tinged the saltwater air. Frilly rose bushes climbed on trellises, spreading out and up in vines, like misbehaved children. Marble statues of nude females baked in the lazy sun. Kyra counted at least six of those.

"If this is Carly's prison," she said, "handcuff me now."

The three of them, stunned at the beauty of the place, followed big Hildi to the main entrance. It was open and inviting, and the wonderful aromas of cilantro and garlic wafted from the kitchen. Someone, a saint, was cooking Italian. Kyra was famished. She hoped that whatever happened tonight, life or death, included dinner.

Garibaldi's foyer could swallow her entire WeHo apartment. Hildi led them all to the bright living room. "Wait here," she said and headed toward the stairs.

"Fuck me," Kyra said.

"Fuck me twice!" Zoe embellished.

The polite Robert turned on his heel and whistled softly in amazement.

The room was spectacular, with views of the bay and the afternoon sun on the water. The only flaw—*flaws*—were those *Guidos* everywhere. Why did she even display his art, Kyra wondered, now he was dead? She must have really loved him.

An olive-skinned woman who resembled a shriveled-up Anouk Aimée—cook? housekeeper?—wiped her hands on her white apron. "Can I get you anything?" she asked in a heavy Italian accent straight out of Fellini.

"Whatever you're cooking smells to die for," Kyra said, signing with her fingers.

La Dolce Vita cracked a flattered smile.

"What's wrong with you?" Zoe asked. Then to the woman, "I'm sorry, ma'am. My friend's mama never told her not to beg for food."

"I'm starving!" Kyra said in protest.

Moments later, Carly skipped down the stairs barefoot, excited, dressed simply in a white T-shirt with a red design and faded jeans with rips in strategic places. Soon all four of them were entangled in a group hug. Carly showered them with kisses.

Kyra solo-embraced Carly, easily lifting her off the floor. She was skin and bones.

"Let me see you," she said, holding Carly at arm's length.

Kyra tried not to gasp. Carly seemed sick, very pale and super thin. Yes, her green eyes sparkled, but her hair needed styling again. Instead of the natural highlights she always got from the sun, its color was dulled. Was she kept indoors, indeed a prisoner?

And the red design on Carly's T-shirt wasn't at all a design.

"What's all that blood?" Kyra asked.

"We had some broken glass upstairs."

It looked more like the result of a fucking bloodbath. What the hell was going on in this house? What was happening to Carly?

35

I was locked in their hugs, happy to be grounded by the relative lightness of my former life. Zoe's hair was cut shoulder-length. Her small frame was squeezed into a short black leather skirt she had taken from my closet. A large white shirt—filched from Robert's closet—was tucked into it. She had the lousy habit of trying on other people's clothes and keeping them.

"The skirt stays with me tonight," I said.

"I don't have anything else."

"Tough luck." I giggled like a schoolgirl, delighted to see them all. "Robert's shirt is long enough."

"Talk to me," Kyra said. I might have told her everything had she not added, "You look like death warmed over."

A badly timed comment.

Anna's curious words, *Hades has won*, were still a verbal bullet, bouncing back and forth between my eardrums, wreaking havoc inside my brain. I should have kicked Kyra out as soon as I realized she hadn't come in peace.

36

Carly turned a shade paler. Then it dawned on Kyra what the problem was.

"You're in love." She hugged Carly even tighter, not only to restrain her own knee-jerk reaction, but to protect her. *From what?* "Who's the lucky dude?"

Carly said against her neck, "No dude."

"Did you cross over?" Kyra joked. Then she thought Carly really might have. And then the heavy certainty dropped from the cortex of her brain straight down to her empty stomach, nauseating her. "Garibaldi?" She choked on the name.

"Yes," Carly said. "Yes! We love each other."

"You *love* her?" Kyra couldn't believe her ears. She also couldn't control the angry diatribe that came out of her mouth. "I tried for years to get you to loosen up, date more, see the world, and *this* is what you bring home? This monster bewitched you, seduced you like she did him. How could you fucking fall for her?"

"Take a breath, Kyra," Zoe said in the voice she would use to calm distraught ER patients.

Carly ran her loving gaze over the three of them. Then she held Kyra's face in her soft hands and said, "It isn't what you think," and those soft hands told Kyra the whole ugly truth. Silky smooth hands, with long fingernails. The pink nail polish had peeled off in strips and was mostly gone, but her hands were as clean as they'd been a month ago, on the day Robert had given her a thorough manicure.

"Why are your hands so clean?" Kyra whispered in dread. "You told me you worked for her. You told me you were painting."

"I do work for her, but—"

"When did you last touch paint?" Kyra raised her voice.

Carly didn't answer. She was glancing up beyond Kyra, fear in her eyes. What scared her? Then she looked back at Kyra, smiled and playfully kissed the tip of her nose, the way she used to do as a little girl. "Trust me for once, big sis. I'm happy."

Kyra trusted her, but not that monster, that life-sucking vampire. Carly was in danger, and Kyra was here to save her. She prepared her slaying swords.

The vampire was gliding down the stairs, smiling, dressed appropriately in blood red.

37

I expected Anna to be too devastated for company. When I glanced up, she was halfway down the stairs, diamond sunglasses on her face, glossy hair pulled back and tied into a sloppy knot, one of her long dresses in a shade of claret clinging to her voluptuous figure. Once again she took my breath away with her beauty.

Yet something was off. I narrowed my eyes and assessed her.

Her lips were totally white! Had she mistaken the concealer for lipstick? Even that mistake added a sensational glow to her clear skin.

Only a touch of hesitation, the slightest sway in her graceful glide down the stairs, could have betrayed her complete blindness. Despite her wide, welcoming smile, I knew the pain she was hiding, the fear, the vulnerability. Her beauty and courage squeezed my heart.

"Here you are," I said, to warn her, then I caught her by her narrow waist and guided her carefully down the last few stairs.

A shudder traveled through me. How should I introduce unknown people to the blind Anna without revealing her blindness?

Robert and Zoe were easy, cordial, uncomplicated. Then I introduced Kyra, who had to be an inquisitive pain in the ass. To my horror, Kyra extended her arm for a handshake, which Anna couldn't see and appeared to deliberately ignore. I knew there'd be hell to pay.

"I've heard a lot about you," Anna said.

"And yet you're not kicking me out." The insulted Kyra let her arm fall limp by her side.

Anna raised a blond eyebrow above the rim of her sunglasses. "Is yet the operative word?"

Touché. Anna held her own and I was smack in the center of an awkward situation. Kyra stared at me in open question, not even trying to hide her disdain. How I'd hoped, craved, the first meeting between my two loves to at least be polite. My hope died in infancy.

"You and Carly have similar, melodious voices," Anna said to Kyra. "But you are so much taller."

Anna's freaky senses had kicked in. Could she also sense the hot hatred pouring out of Kyra like lava from an active volcano? Even I could sense its heat, its poison.

Seeing Anna rising to the occasion, holding her own, acting normally, my admiration grew even stronger. Hadn't she just fallen apart in my arms? How I loved this woman.

Kyra didn't approve. I knew my sister; I saw her sneer of hate and misunderstanding. It was obvious to me that Kyra passed judgment on everything: the sunglasses, the absence of a handshake, Anna's natural air of grandeur which even her fear could not suppress.

Kyra was too caught up in her protective mode to perceive weaknesses in Anna. And I couldn't explain those weaknesses—I had to protect my lover the same way, with the same fervor that made Kyra want to protect me.

What should have been a cheerful, joyous moment, with Kyra and Anna meeting, was heavy with undercurrents. Kyra was gearing up for confrontation. She was going to be her obnoxious self, while knowing nothing. What was the use of all those Ph. D.s coming out her ears and her analyzing eye, when she was more blind than Anna?

A loud wave thundered. I braced myself for a storm that might sweep in and drown us all.

38

Oh my God! formed on Kyra's lips. She avoided religious expressions, but this was a moment of humility. Her hate of the woman aside, Garibaldi was hot.

Airbrushed photos missed the staggering effect of her real beauty. The way she moved was a glide, a dance. She nearly tripped once. She held on to Carly and steadied herself, like a dancer correcting a near miss.

She also reacted to Kyra. It wasn't Kyra's great beauty—nonexistent—but rather the danger she presented. She'd been told she was cute, if you can so allude to a six-foot butch dyke with bad attitude, but she was not beautiful by any standard. Garibaldi must have reacted to her imaginary swords.

She completely avoided touch, not even offering a handshake. The Garibaldi Kyra remembered from the night she'd kidnapped Greg and turned him into Guido had kissed everyone on both cheeks. So why was she so rude to them? Yes, they landed on her unannounced. Still, they were Carly's guests. Wasn't Carly allowed to see her friends? See her only family?

Despite that hot red dress and that hot body, Garibaldi was wrapped luxuriously in a cloud of arctic air. Even Carly's heat hadn't melted her and maybe couldn't.

What bothered Kyra more than anything was the sunglasses in her own home. What was she hiding?

Kyra still felt humiliated by Garibaldi's refusal to shake her hand when she heard her say, "I hope you'll all join us for dinner."

Kyra might have just imagined her saying this because she was famished. The smells wafting from the kitchen made her dizzy with hunger and might have made her imagine things.

Still . . . "We'd love to have dinner," Kyra said, accepting for all three of them.

She'd planned to make it back to WeHo and the G-Spot before the party got strong, but this was turning into a whole-evening affair. She was so happy to see Carly and spend the evening with her, she brushed aside thoughts of the party and her maybe-date with Zingy Lola. She was more hungry than horny.

Garibaldi swayed once on the way to the deck. Carly held on to her arm and Kyra had the feeling she was trying to hide Garibaldi's drunkenness. Why bother? Kyra had seen all of them drunk plenty of times.

The housekeeper—introduced as Flora—popped open a bottle of champagne and poured it into rosebud glasses. She had one for herself and Hildi, who had joined. Kyra was dying for an ice cold beer, straight from a frosted bottle.

While they were all chatting excitedly, admiring the view, the sun started setting in crimson and orange. Soft, chilly neons gradually came on, washing the deck with the softest of lights, illuminating both the interior and the rose garden. The brilliant design made Kyra feel off balance.

"Isn't it majestic?" Carly asked. "Anna designed the crystal effect."

Garibaldi explained the lights in that beautiful voice of all accents, gesturing widely toward the bejeweled bay and calling it the Queen's Necklace, a florid title most of us reserved for tourists.

Despite the open space, the sunset and the far horizon, Kyra felt an overwhelming suffocation. She had to get away. She didn't want to leave Carly now she'd found her again, but hunger, the airless darkness seeping under her skin, and her craving for a cold beer won out. She decided to search for the kitchen and see if *La Dolce Vita* could spare something to nosh on before dinner.

Kyra would talk to Flora in Italian, certain that she was eager to tell someone like herself about the horrors of working for the Divine One. Kyra's Italian was decent, but the kitchen wasn't her thing—what if Flora made her help with the dishes or something in order to cadge a snack?

She slipped away from the others and started for the kitchen. She inhaled a long whiff of Italian spices—yes, it smelled so damned delicious that she would beg for something to eat and not even feel guilty.

Kyra never made it to the kitchen. Her vision blurred and darkened, and she collapsed into a leather armchair by the fireplace.

39

Kyra opened her eyes to the vision that had stolen her breath. A black angel, clothed all in white, kneeled in front of her. Her burning brown eyes searched Kyra's face with concern. Her hair was cut very short, showing off finely etched features. Her full lips were slightly open, ready for a kiss. She smelled of summers on the beach and of lavender.

"Are you okay?"

Her rich voice sent loops of warmth up and down Kyra's body.

The angel opened her hand and in it was a chocolate square. Kyra popped it into her mouth and was immediately revived by its bitter sweetness.

"Are you Lady Godiva?" Kyra asked.

"If you're Peeping Tom." One tooth was slightly crooked in an otherwise perfect set of pearly whites. Adorable.

"It's Kyra," she said.

"Juliet."

Kyra recognized her, but she wanted to play. Juliet Blair played the lead in *Divine Darkness*, Garibaldi's fascinating and plotless erotic study of a blind woman whose supernatural senses acquainted her with her lovers' deepest desires. Ms. Blair's cinematic wardrobe had consisted of one pair of diamond earrings, one pair of eight-inch diamond stilettos and —what else?—one pair of Garibaldi Eyewear diamond shades.

She took Kyra's hand in both of hers. "Why are you facing away from the sunset?" she asked in a sexy lisp.

Kyra had goose bumps. "I'd rather face you, Lady Godiva."

"What's wrong with you?"

"An overdose of my new sister-in-law, Ms. Divine Darkness." Kyra gestured with her head toward the deck.

"Are you really Carly's sister?" she asked, the barest hint of some tragedy passing over her face. "You are so much nicer."

"Carly's temper is a little . . . but once you get to know her —"

"Your sister threatened to make pizza out of my face. Or lasagna."

"Just bragging," Kyra said. "She can only cook chili."

Juliet smiled. "I actually deserved it."

Her hand in Kyra's was soft, except for the writing bump on the middle finger.

Kyra said, "You don't completely trust modern technology."

"I prefer to write longhand," she said.

"So do I." Kyra held up her right hand with the matching bump. Still studying Juliet's hand, she noticed the thin white scar on her wrist. She ran her finger gently over it.

"Why?" Kyra's voice choked.

"Never you mind," she said, pulling her hand away.

Then she stood up and up *and up*. She had a supermodel's body, long and limber and sexy. Kyra pushed the wire glasses up the bridge of her nose and ogled her shamelessly while remaining slumped in the fat armchair.

"Let me guess." Kyra stretched her legs forward. "Victoria's Secret catalog?"

"Nice try," Juliet said. That lisp was killing Kyra. "I guess you barely recognized me with my clothes on?"

She was definitely not Zingy Lola. Kyra would have to come up with better one-liners or try normal conversation for once. "You sure know how to peel an orange."

"Peeled enough of them to hate the fruit for life."

"Must have been exciting, working with La Divina."

"If you like total perfectionists."

"I am one," Kyra said, hypnotized. She had to get herself some of that brown sugar.

"Let me guess," Juliet said. "You play football or basketball."

"I did in college," Kyra said. "Now I'm a clinical psychotherapist who got through school with minors in art and linguistics." She sounded so pompous in her own ears, the blood rushed to her stupid face. At least she stopped herself before mouthing off about Simone de Beauvoir.

"My little passions, Lady Godiva," she qualified, certain she had just lost a potential date.

Juliet beamed. "I bet you also have your fingers in women's studies."

"Deeply," Kyra said, thrusting two fingers up in what could be considered a rude gesture.

Juliet's sweet smile proved she was not offended. "If I show you something big, a secret, you aren't allowed to tell," she said, her lips slightly open, her voice sultry.

"Not telling is what I do for a living," Kyra said.

"Problem is," Juliet's voice softened to a whisper, "it is down, much lower, in the forbidden place."

"*Verboten* means all the more attractive." She'd follow this woman anywhere.

Kyra got a head rush from standing up too quickly and from inhaling the summer of Juliet's fragrance. She glanced back at all of them on the deck. Robert was talking to Garibaldi, his hungry gaze playing on her face, her dress, her hair. Kyra knew he was dying to work for her. Carly was engrossed in conversation with Zoe. She'd catch up with her later.

Her boots clicked on the shiny hardwood. Juliet was leading her deeper into the vast house, through a hallway and to a small vestibule. Its walls were covered with old photographs of Anna's parents, the Garibaldis. Irena, a living legend, was one of Kyra's favorite dead actors. Anna was lucky to have inherited both her mother's beauty and her voice.

Hearty laughter gushed from the deck, uninhibited, Irena's laughter, familiar from movies of the fifties and sixties. Juliet and Kyra glanced back at the same time. All of them were laughing and gesturing at the beautiful red sunset. The longest-lasting laughter was Anna's.

Kyra said, "I could have sworn Irena was behind—"

"I've always found that laughter haunting," Juliet agreed.

She clasped Kyra's wrist and pulled her down into a dark stairwell.

"You are very strong for a little girl."

"You have no idea." Juliet laughed.

As Kyra laughed along, an echo answered from the cave-like hollowness below.

40

Robert, delightfully enamored, discussed fashion with Anna, who leaned against a support pillar. I kept one eye on her, making sure she didn't trip. The other eye was on Zoe, who was telling me I'd sold a few paintings in my absence.

"Keep the profits," I said.

"Thanks," Zoe said. She held my face. "Are you happy?"

"Very."

"And the sex?"

"Divine," I said. I glanced around. "Where's my sister?"

"I just heard Kyra flirting with my friend Juliet," said Anna, who could talk and at the same time listen to every word spoken around her.

41

"Let's go down," Juliet prompted, sensing Kyra's hesitation.

Kyra obliged, too embarrassed to admit weakness to the beautiful woman at the end of her hook who obviously knew her way around the house. The staircase spiraled down along with Kyra's stomach. What was down there? Coldness surged up from the darkness. It wasn't formaldehyde. She'd never forget that creepy smell from her visit to the morgue in med school. What she smelled now was just as cold, but happier. Turpentine.

Another smell, musty and wet, like the fountains in old Rome, attacked her nostrils as they descended into complete silence and darkness, at least three floors down. Kyra was warmed only by the hope of soon tasting Juliet's kissy lips. She wasn't disappointed. They reached a flat landing, then Kyra's back was pressed against a cold wall.

"Quick," Juliet said, honey in her voice.

An angular object with a sharp edge dug into Kyra's calf. She didn't care. Juliet's tongue was already in her mouth—no buildup, no foreplay—and her hand, that hand with the long fingers, was ripping through the fly of Kyra's jeans. They were wild, devouring each other whole while standing upright in the midst of dust, turpentine, and whatever else lurked in that chilled darkness.

Afterward, as they held on to each other, catching their breaths, Kyra's eyes gradually got used to a darkness lit only by a thin sliver of light from the stairwell.

Juliet said in a cool voice, "Now to the highlight of the evening."

Kyra sneezed once. "That was pretty much it for me," she said, her voice raspy from all the dust they'd stirred up.

Juliet clicked on the light and turned Kyra around to meet the canvas whose edge had dug a hole into her leg.

Kyra was stunned.

To admit that she was stunned by anything other than what had just happened between them was big. They'd met less than thirty minutes ago, yet they'd just had frenzied, mind-boggling, dirty sex against an unsuspecting wall. To find out that it wasn't a mere wall, but this painting, was racy even for Kyra.

Kyra held Juliet's hand close to her pounding heart. This woman was her goddess. That she could fuck with such fervor and then turn around, literally, and consider an acrylic painting the highlight of the evening, that fact alone made Kyra feel that she'd known Juliet for years.

"The highlight of my life," Kyra said.

Juliet squeezed her hand. "I knew you'd like it."

"Love it. Is this why you dragged me all the way down here?"

"Hell, no." Juliet buttoned up her shirt. "I was horny."

"Rebound?"

"Revenge."

"Why here?" Kyra asked.

"Long story," she said. "I owed myself a good one, right here at this spot."

"I'm glad to be part of your sweet revenge." Kyra's admiring gaze caressed Juliet, then the painting.

Four life-sized intertwined female nudes suggested a slow turn, a sequence from a dance. The piece blurred the boundaries between painting and sculpture since the images were raised above the canvas. The edges were damaged by smoke and fire. It had been painted with love, rich in color and depth, and the model was the one and only. La Divina. The painter was fascinated, obsessed, with her movement and stance. The first nude showed the back of her head and body, the second, half profile, then profile, with the last figure full frontal. Her horror-filled face was only a sketch, but the emotion was evident. What had frightened her so?

"*Tourner*," Kyra said, thinking out loud the title of a dance move she would have given it.

And then she thought of another turn, the night La Divina had lured Greg away from Carly.

"Exactly," Juliet said. "*The Turning*, by Rosso."

"What?" Kyra's teeth chattered from the tension.

"That's what it's called." Juliet shrugged one shoulder. "Look at the signature."

Kyra ran her fingers across the acrylic surface. The thick ridges, the palette-knife action, made it a wall sculpture. Carly said she was working for Anna. Was this her work?

"This piece has Carly all over it, even those white patches here, yet it can't be hers because her hands are too clean."

"Oh, this has been here since long before the Carly era," Juliet said. "Sorry for calling it that, but Anna is a serial monogamist. A chain smoker of love."

Kyra's head played with that gorgeous metaphor. If Anna was a chain smoker, she, Kyra was a multi-smoker, discarding burning fags left and right after one hit. Once she smoked four together. Only once. Too much smoke suffocated her.

"Who did you say the painter was?"

"Someone named Rosso," Juliet said. "I heard Anna talk about him once." She gestured toward the turpentine-saturated hollowness. "There are more surprises here."

"Show me."

"Not now," she said. "I have to leave."

"You're not staying for dinner?" Kyra asked, disappointed.

"I'm persona non grata here." Her eyes burned at Kyra in the semi-darkness. "Besides, it would be hard not to eat you at the table."

Kyra didn't want to let her go. "*Then move not, while my prayer's effect I take.*" She kissed her. "*Thus from my lips, by yours, my sin is purged.*"

Juliet squealed with delight. "Show off." She easily slipped into character and said, "*Then have my lips the sin that they have took.*"

The next line came to Kyra naturally. "*Sin from thy lips? O trespass sweetly urged! Give me my sin again.*"

Again they kissed, slowly, deeply.

Kyra said, "*You kiss by the book.*"

"You're stealing my lines!" Juliet laughed out loud. "Go on. What comes next?"

"That's all I remember from that school play," Kyra said. "I think Juliet's nurse enters and shit hits the fan."

"Why don't you ditch them all and come home with me?" Juliet whispered. "I have disco lighting in my bedroom, and I can recite Shakespeare's sonnets and fuck all day and night."

"What a romantic," Kyra said. "Tempting, but I haven't seen my sister for a whole month. I need to spend some time with her."

Juliet tore herself away from Kyra, her forehead creasing in sadness. *"Parting is such sweet sorrow that I shall say goodnight till it be morrow."*

"Good grief, I ain't staying here all night!" Kyra had an idea. "Meet me at the G-Spot tonight at ten."

"Sure." Juliet pointed down. "Your jeans are still around your boots, Romeo."

Kyra pulled her jeans up, then she snapped a shot of *The Turning* with her cellphone. "Our first surface."

"Now who's waxing romantic?" Juliet asked. "But fair warning: you'll need a photo album the size of Manhattan." She shrugged that one and only shoulder. "I'm a nymphomaniac."

Kyra circled her slim waist with one arm, burning with lust. "You are me in black."

42

Background music played during dinner, an eclectic blend of Bach, Chopin and techno. Flora was clearing the table, about to serve the second course, when Zoe admired the lasagna and asked for the recipe.

"I cook in Italian," Flora said, gathering the dirty dishes with Zoe's help. "Never a recipe, only a lot of love." She winked at Zoe—an unnatural expression for her pointy, grumpy face—and said, "I'll write it down for you."

When strands of Anna's hair came undone, Robert asked permission to fix it, then did something amazing. He braided a long strand from her nape, looped it up and twisted it. Then he did another. He braided those together and weaved them to hold her hair back. It took only moments. It was brilliant and stylish, and Anna enjoyed being fussed with.

"Are you the Robert who threatens women with manicure scissors?" she asked.

"For fashion atrocities," he said.

"You're hired."

Robert was beside himself. He took out his cellphone and started showing Anna photos of his work, both clothing and hair. I quickly came to her rescue and took the phone away from him, pretending to scroll through the photos while changing the subject of our conversation.

Anna picked up an orange and held it up to the light. A little tremor of her bandaged left hand gave away what I knew already. She couldn't see even a sliver of her beloved fruit. Then she did her usual sexy peel, and all of them at the table stared, fascinated, having no idea what all of it really meant.

Anna's longing for the orange, her dead hope of seeing its color—of seeing anything—transformed her moves into a sensual act. What a waste that she couldn't see the effect of her actions. Kyra, Zoe and Robert were all transfixed by her hands. As was I.

That was the high point of the evening, before Kyra threw a monkey wrench into a perfect, spontaneous gathering.

43

Carly barely had a bite, Kyra noticed. She was busy attending to Queen Garibaldi, her lover, her mistress, her *warden*, a woman too important to do anything for herself.

Robert and Garibaldi got on like a house on fire. He played with her hair, and she actually seemed to enjoy it. She said, "You're hired." Maybe it was in jest, but Robert could not contain himself in the presence of the reigning queen of hair and fashion.

Carly wasn't happy about it. About something. When he started showing Anna photos of his work—yes, bragging, but why not?—Carly intervened. She confiscated his phone, as if to look at the photos that she had seen many times. Deliberately she changed the subject.

Why put the kibosh on his glory?

Sometime between the first and the second course, Garibaldi picked up a paring knife and started peeling an orange. No big deal—peeling fruit is peeling fruit, right? Wrong. As Kyra followed her hands, sensual, obscene forces invaded her body and made her want to take off her clothes. Suddenly everything felt too tight—the boots on her feet, the jeans against her crotch. Kyra observed Anna like a novice, re-learning the art of seduction, fantasizing about Juliet Blair in the basement, and later, in her bed.

Kyra took another sip of red wine and tried to relax, but how could she? She remembered Garibaldi's film. In it Juliet peels an orange and tells a simple story about her childhood with that adorable lisp. It's a most erotic scene.

Juliet. The only thing keeping Kyra from reaching across the table to strangle Garibaldi was the thought of ten o'clock, the G-Spot and more Juliet pleasures to come and *come*.

Garibaldi's voice maintained the tone of cordial conversation as she slowly ran a long finger around the naked fruit. A quiet and pale Carly watched her; so did Robert and Zoe. They were all bewitched by that *pièce de résistance*, by the orange and Anna's hands. Had she fed them Ecstasy? A hallucinogen? And why was her hand bandaged anyway?

Kyra must have been under the influence of *some* drug, because she blurted out, "Why keep *The Turning* in the dark?"

"Carly." Garibaldi gasped, dropping the paring knife.

"Kyra!" Carly reprimanded. Or had she informed?

The sisters had similar voices, but they were both there. So the Divine One had name confusion.

During dinner, Garibaldi had called everybody *love*. Kyra overused *honey* in bed to avoid errors, so she couldn't really blame her for it. She could have trouble remembering names. Or maybe it was part of being rude to Carly's guests. When Garibaldi dropped the paring knife, Carly was immediately at her service, under the table, like a good golden retriever. Couldn't Divine Darkness pick up her own shit?

Kyra strummed that major nerve again. "Such a brilliant piece, even damaged, shouldn't remain in the basement."

Something landed hard above the spur of her boot, Carly's fist, making Kyra cry out in surprise and pain.

44

I hoped Kyra's foot was in agony. She was hurting Anna! How dare she go snooping where I wouldn't? I sat, letting the hardwood cool my burning anger. How hard it was, keeping Anna's secret from Kyra, who sensed lies and secrets, who ferreted them out for a living.

From under the table I glanced up at Anna, seeing her graceful neck, the longing in her face as she sniffed the orange, the glow from the blazing fireplace caressing her gold and platinum hair. She reached down, searching for me, aware with her special senses that I had a problem. She ran the back of her citrus-fragrant hand on my cheek. I handed her the knife.

"I need fresh air," Kyra announced. Then she grabbed my elbow and hoisted me to my feet. "Come with me."

Instead of the breezy deck, Kyra headed deeper into the house, toward the forbidden place.

I resisted. "The deck has enough fresh air for you to choke on."

"I need to ask you a few questions about something in the basement."

"No one goes there!" I jerked my arm away from her death grip. "Anna asked that I stay out of that part of the house."

"Do you always do what Divine Darkness says?"

"She is entitled to a private corner in her own home."

"What about your corner?" Kyra asked. "What are you protecting and from whom, princess?"

Kyra's questions were so infuriating. "Anna from you."

"She can protect herself," Kyra said. "I'm here to make sure you don't become Greg."

That was crazy. I said, "You blame her for his death, but I know the truth."

Did I? Anna had been about to open up—confess?—about Greg's last day. What had she meant by *you had something I needed desperately*? What about *Hades has won*? What else had she been about to throw at me when the knock on the door interrupted?

I was doubting Anna, right there at the top of the stairs leading into the innermost core of her pain. If that wasn't disloyalty . . .

"I blame her not only for his death," Kyra said, "but for stealing his soul and his name when he was alive."

"He had his choices."

"So do you," Kyra said. "Your hands are clean. If you don't paint anymore, what do you do?"

"I actually work for her, editing her new book." I was still protecting, justifying, explaining myself to my sister who didn't have freaky senses but could see through my bullshit and knew I was hiding something crucial.

"Let me understand," Kyra said. "She has acquired another pair of eyes, a free editor, who also picks up her shit from the floor. What do you get out of it except a heavenly abode and an ocean view, Palos Verdes to Malibu?"

"You may not know a thing about true love," I said, clenching my jaw, "but you surely know what one gets out of great sex."

"I was in love once," Kyra said. "Remember Saori San?"

"Who went back to her husband and left you for dead," I said, just to be mean.

"Yes, yes," Kyra said, unmoved by my cruelty. "The point is, I've been in love, but I don't give up the other things I love, like my work."

I was seething with anger. Kyra didn't know a thing about the truth. How dare she walk into my happy life and make me question it?

"That's because, Kyra darling, your work is talking, talking, talking and *prying*. You can't live without sticking your nose in someone else's business and messing up their lives because you have nothing of your own. How does it feel to be analyzed back, *huh?*"

"You sound very angry," Kyra said. "And they can hear you."

Her cool professional manner hurled me flying into that state of madness in which there's no air to breathe but you can scream. None of my insults would shake Kyra, not with her treating me like one of her clients. How infuriating! Instead of calming down, I went ballistic.

"I don't care who hears as long as you do," I said with venom. "You'll be forty next year with nothing going for you but work and one-night stands and stupid cowboy boots and that tough butch-girl act with Bruna and B. J. and the G-Spot every night! You'll soon be old and wrinkly—look at the corners of your eyes, at your fat ass—almost forty and all alone because of your Oscar Wilde and your one-wife-is-one-too-many crap!"

Kyra held me firmly by my shoulders. "Sweet princess of mine." She gazed into my eyes. "You stopped painting, eating and going out in the sunlight. I'm going to talk to your new lover and let her know how thin and pale you've become. Because clearly she doesn't have the fucking eyes to see for herself!"

"You're pathetic!" I cried out.

"Obnoxious and outrageous," she said. "Never pathetic."

How nice it would have been to simply say, *No, she doesn't have fucking eyes*, but that story wasn't mine to tell. As much as I could hate Kyra, I truly adored her. She was genuinely worried even when there was nothing to worry about.

I took her in my arms. "I'm so sorry, Kyra. Your life is great. You are beautiful, no wrinkly eyes, no fat ass. I apologize for everything I said. You know my temper."

"What else?" she asked, narrowing her eyes.

"You are the best psychotherapist west of the San Andreas Fault and, from what I've heard, the best fuck in WeHo."

"What about insulting my cowboy boots?" she asked.

"Those are what I love most about you," I said. "I love the spurs and the clicking and that stupid little buckle and—"

"All right, all right. Not so thick. Now, you know how I hate dark enclosures—and that claustrophobic hellhole below beats the Roman catacombs—but will you kindly go down with me?" Kyra's eyes bored into mine, not pleading, but demanding. "If you haven't been down there, seen what's there, you should."

Down below was the cold unknown. The belly of that huge beast contained the answers Anna kept from me. She said she was going to show me something, but what if she'd changed her mind?

I caved. "What's down there?"

"Something you'll never forget."

"I'm not staying more than a minute."

Kyra remained a step behind, lighting our way with her cellphone. The stone stairs were cold and worn beneath my bare feet. As we descended lower and lower into the hollowness, I was lured by familiar fumes. The old longing tugged at me, the yearning to hold a paintbrush or a palette knife and go berserk on a white canvas. We kept going down and down, into a spiral of sensory deprivation—was this long swath of darkness the true Styx?—gradually separating from the world above. Silence replaced the constant crash of waves against solid rocks. The only sounds were those made by Kyra's boots behind me. The light from her cellphone sliced my peripheral vision. Was this how Anna felt, trapped behind her blindness?

"I know Flora never vacuums here," I said, suffocating on dust.

Kyra squeezed my shoulder in response. "We're here."

My bare feet touched solid concrete. Kyra flipped a switch, and halogen light washed the darkness. I squealed. We weren't alone! The place was populated and sizzling with life!

"Relax," Kyra said. "It's only a painting."

The huge canvas covered the wall. On it, life-sized female nudes interlaced in a dance, rich with colors and movement. I expected all of them to leap away from the canvas, merge into one warm body and rush the few feet straight into my arms. All four were one and mine. I knew this body, its complexities, its strengths, its weaknesses. The piece was lovingly rendered with a palette knife. The full frontal image was a younger Anna in rich colors. Her face showed the fear of witnessing horror.

And her eyes were blurred. The artist knew!

The painting was singed by fire. Why? I stared down at my hands.

"Did I ever work in my sleep?"

"This can't be yours," Kyra said, "because your hands are prissy clean."

"This isn't Greg's work either," I said.

"Got that right," Kyra agreed.

Joe Rowland, the trainer with the extra benefits, crossed my mind. Did he also have extra talents?

Kyra pointed at the corner.

The Turning. Rosso.

She let me take it all in before saying, "He was a sculptor. The lines . . ."

A sculptor? I thought of all the nude statues in the rose garden, all in Anna's image. She would run a loving hand on the marble surfaces, smell the statues, as if trying to re-create something wonderful. A certain day? A long-dead lover? I thought of her stoic, calm face in the moonlight and that single silver tear trickling down her cheek. Did she miss him or only the days filled with color and light? She'd blamed the tears on allergies. "When the Palo Verde blooms, my itchy, watery eyeballs remind me of those yellow flowers."

It was clear, she loved him and this, his magnum opus. Even now, unable to see it, she kept coming down here to the core of her happiness and her grief. No wonder she wouldn't let me be part of it.

This was beautiful, Anna in a way no other had captured her. This painting did her justice. It featured her essence in a way no photographer could, not only her uncanny beauty and regal posture, but the gracefulness of her movement—how brilliant!—with those four separate yet intermingling images. I wished I'd been the one who had created a piece so worthy of adoration.

This artist, who had loved Anna with *my* intensity, was the real deal. Like me, he couldn't get enough of her. I could channel him in this cold space, could feel his presence in the air.

"You're shaking," Kyra said.

"This chill—I swear I can sense his ghost."

"No talk of ghosts or I'll shit," Kyra said, showing me a side of her I never knew.

"Scared?" Now I had the upper hand. She'd had enough, but I was only starting.

"I feel something too," she said, her voice trembling. "Let's get the fuck outta here."

"Wait till I tell them at the G-Spot what a chicken shit you are," I said.

I looked back at the painting. It needed a huge wall and light to do it justice.

"Why is this beautiful piece hidden where no one can see it?" I asked myself more than Kyra. "It's damaged, but so what?"

"My question," Kyra offered, "is what else is buried here? What do you really know about her?"

"Everything. Or so I believed." I touched the rough surface. The smell of turpentine made my feverish brain radiate currents all the way to my fingertips. I knew how to repair the damage. The eyes, the background. It didn't need much. I could do it.

Then I got it.

"*The job!*"

45

Kyra agreed with Carly. Poking her nose into other's business was her life. Here she was, shitting her boots at the mention of a ghost, and still, curiosity won.

"Tell me about the job," she said in the careful tone she'd use when a client had just dug out a devastating childhood memory.

Carly pressed her fingers to her eyes, as if doubting their existence. "How did I not see it?" Then she held Kyra by the forearms with hands soft and telling in their cleanliness.

"Remember the money in my account?" she asked.

"Yes. Greg's money."

"It was Anna's money, an advance for a job she wanted me for." Carly coughed, probably choking on dust, fumes and a crucial understanding. "Greg recommended me to her. He said I was the only one who could do it. Remember that phrase—*the only one*—that we all fried our brains on? That was it."

"How did she find your account?"

"He moved the funds the day he died, but under her instructions." Carly chewed on a cuticle, immersed in thought. "Anna saw the print of my *Blue Madonna*. She saw . . . Well, she somehow saw . . ."

Carly repeated *saw* as if it was the wrong choice of verb. "She realized the dead-on similarities of styles and meant for me to restore and finish this work."

They both focused on the lifelike human forms leaping out of the damaged painting.

"So she believed you'd mailed her a sample of your work as an audition." Kyra thought out loud, putting it all together. "A hundred grand to restore one painting?"

"You don't think I'm worth it?"

Carly's eyes got even larger in her thin face as she feigned hurt.

"Every penny," Kyra said. She thought of what Juliet said earlier, about more works. "But what if she meant to hire you to restore that guy's body of work?"

"Rosso," Carly said, voice and posture dreamy. She then turned to Kyra. "What made you come here, down to the basement, in the first place?"

"An angel named Juliet."

What happened here, against this masterpiece only a little while ago, kept playing on a loop in Kyra's head. She was so looking forward to her date tonight.

"Juliet Blair, the actress?" Carly asked. "I can't stand her big, bad mouth."

"Her mouth was mighty fine," Kyra muttered to herself. "Why don't you like her?"

"I hate the way she moves about Flora's kitchen, cooking with her, like she owns the place."

That made Kyra envision a bright future in which Juliet would fill her kitchen with the heavenly aromas of Flora's cooking.

"Why did you stop eating?" Kyra asked.

"I'm in love."

"I have another theory. Would you like to hear it?"

"No"—Carly was pissed again—"but I'm sure you'll tell me anyway."

"That woman . . ." Kyra tried unsuccessfully to restrain the hate in her voice.

"Careful what you say."

She had to hear it. Kyra didn't care if Carly went crazy on her again. "Painting is your lifeblood, yet Divine Darkness sucks out your life and blood and who knows what else, the way she sucked Greg dry. Alas, even he of the tiny talent painted and you don't. I see your lack of creativity, the submissive behavior and yes, downright—"

"Stop. I don't need another dose of your clinical *crap*." Carly screamed out the last word.

Crap, crap, echoed back to them from all the corners.

"—downright slavery," Kyra said. "You've become her handmaiden. I don't like the way you talk and act and how starved you are. Starved because you stopped painting. I know how one can become blinded by love. I once dated this chick, a real babe—"

"Don't you dare." Carly's voice was harsh and alien in Kyra's ears. "Don't talk to me about chicks and babes. Anna isn't one of your semi-literate idiots, so keep her out of your experience."

"True," Kyra admitted. Carly was right when she was. Still, Kyra didn't trust Garibaldi. "What does she actually want from you?"

"She loves me! Is it so hard to believe that someone would?"

"What does she want, Carly?"

"My eyeballs," Carly blurted out, adding in a softer tone, "Joke, joke."

Kyra raised her left eyebrow. "Life is funny, but there are no jokes in therapy."

"That totally was," Carly said.

"And yet you stopped painting."

"Yes, Carly"—a cultured voice from above startled both of them—"why don't you paint anymore?"

A shiver passed through Kyra, the sense of someone walking on her grave. Invisible hands closed around her throat. Slowly, she turned.

Garibaldi seemed to hover, one foot above the ground. How long had she stood there, on that step, listening? Dust swirled around her regal form in the red dress, like smoke around a long-gone fire.

46

"What, you can't let her out of your sight?"

Sight . . . sight . . . Kyra's voice echoed through the basement, microspittle sprouting from her lips.

"Kyra, shut it!" I cried out, choking on dust and on my sister.

Shut it, shut it, answered the echo.

"You need Carly to pick up something for you?" Kyra kept at it.

Anna listened in her usual stoic manner, allowing Kyra to express her anger. I had to hold back. Anna could take care of herself just fine.

"You killed my friend Greg," Kyra continued, dust balls lit by halogen swirling around her angry face like dialogue bubbles in a comic book. "I'll make damned sure you don't kill my sister."

"Please do," Anna said, calm.

Kyra's arms went up in the air, as if to gesture *What's the point?* She turned to me. "You know my number if you want to talk."

She stormed out, letting us know how angry she was by the clatter of her spurred boots. *Wild West Kyra.* I was relieved to hear her click away; my ears were ringing.

"I'm so sorry, Anna," I said as soon as we were alone. "We weren't supposed to be here."

"Not Kyra," Anna said. "Only you."

My stomach dropped to my feet. "What?"

"Tell me, my love," Anna said in her head-spinning calmness, "why don't you paint?"

"Why?" The bug in my ear buzzed loudly. Kyra claimed that I'd become a slave to Anna, that I'd given up the best part of myself, my own dream. Kyra's hard words in this suffocating enclosure and her unconditional love for me had infused me with poison, turning me against Anna. That was the only explanation for what I said next. What was the point in painting when the most important person in my life couldn't appreciate it?

"Why bother?" I asked, and now the truth was out and it was too late to unsay it.

"You don't paint because of me and my useless eyes?"

I kept silent.

Anna straightened up, majestic in her clingy, blood-red dress. "You paint because an image burns a hole in your belly," she said slowly. "I write because a story eats me alive from the inside and I'd go insane if I don't. It isn't my choice. I'd write if you, or the whole world, were illiterate."

"Of course." My throat was getting sore. "Writing is your true love."

"My true love." She laughed bitterly. "My true love is dead."

Greg. Or Rosso. She still loved one of them or both.

Her voice cracked when she said, "Carly, I dreamed of the day I'd take you down here by the hand and show you, but I hesitated, and your sister was quicker than me." She sighed. "This is just as well."

She smoothed her seeing fingers on the surface ridges of *The Turning*, unable to resist a *glance*. She slid her way farther to the left, beyond the painting, up the wall, and clicked the main switch. Full light flooded a space which, I realized, spread beneath the entire house. A rippled ocean of white sheets covered long, tidy rows of furniture or boxes.

Juliet's ghostly visit crossed my mind for a second.

"Get ready for dust," Anna said. "Flora and Hildi are terrified of the spirits. They won't come down here."

"I don't blame them," I said.

She stepped into that huge hollowness, imperial and fearless in her bare feet, a beautiful, wild creature in its natural habitat. This basement was as familiar to her as the insides of her mind. She reached out from her personal darkness, aware of everything in its place, and pulled on the edge of one ghostly sheet. The sheet slid off, sending clouds of dust into the already dusty air.

"Welcome to the Land of the Dead," she announced.

Dead, dead, dead . . . answered the echo.

47

As the first white sheet slid off, a long row of canvases appeared, resting like fallen dominoes against each other, all the way to the wall.

"Can I look?" I asked, unsure of what she wanted me to do.

"Knock yourself out."

She pulled more dusty sheets off more rows of canvases, saying excitedly, "Take a look here, and here."

I became transfixed by the first painting. It was a jungle scene, wildly colorful and teeming with life: lush foliage, birds, butterflies, orchids. Its clever perception of depth made me dizzy and disoriented. Its colors were wrong, confusing, joyless. Yet it was brilliant.

"This isn't Greg's work," I said. "And this one's also burned."

"Yes to both." Anna coughed, wiping dust from her face and hair. "Is any of it salvageable?"

"Let me see more." I was estimating the damage, my hands itching to start.

I picked up the first canvas and rested it against a vacant patch of wall, then I sat crossed-legged on the cold concrete. The next painting was more damaged than the first, its corners seared in an all-around brown aura. Granny Smith apples were strewn within long blades of green grass on a hot summer day. My taste buds shrieked at the crispness of those apples. A caterpillar of yet another green crawled along one of the blades, bowing it down with its weight. If I half-closed my eyes, the caterpillar actually moved and made its way toward one of the apples. I could almost feel its fuzzy, furry texture. Blades of grass swayed in the summer breeze and their fragrance reached my nostrils.

This was a celebration, an orgy, an act of pure love for all that was green. That artist, Rosso, was enamored with various greens.

I tore my gaze away from it with difficulty. I so wanted to explore it longer, but there were more.

I set the green painting against the jungle scene and studied the next. A fantastic sunset turned into a love affair with reds and purples. I gave it a few minutes, ran my hands on the aura of smoke damage, in my mind planning how to repair it. I leaned it against the green painting and continued.

The same fire had wounded the next one with black and brown burns. The painting was a tender act of love for reds and whites. A female nude on rich, red brocade. Anna? It was hard to tell, as the face remained blurred. Another rendition of the red nude had small variations. The artist—very familiar with the reds and whites of Anna's bedroom—was trying to achieve the contrast between the softness of her skin and those stark reds and whites.

He, Rosso, loved her.

I moved through those precious art gems with the pleasure and greed of a pirate sifting through buried treasure.

How long was I at it? Hours? Days?

Time passed. Hunger and thirst gnawed at me, but I couldn't stop examining and then setting aside one canvas after another, each beautiful and disturbing in its own way, each a world of wonders laden with emotional depth, heavy with craving and suffocation. Each painting had some degree of fire or smoke damage.

In my excitement, I planned how to repair each as I set it aside, estimating the time it would take to fix one of them, then multiplying it by dozens, hundreds. It could be done, but I'd need years to repair them. I tore my gaze away from the red painting and scanned the yet untouched rows of canvases.

It would take years.

Rosso's time had come. Such greatness, dead or alive, deserved to be known. His name needed to be displayed on banners and ads in the streets of New York, Vienna, Paris. Everywhere.

The strong smell of turpentine permeated the air, propelling me back to reality. I had to share my excitement with Anna.

She stood behind me, corking back the bottle

"Are you sniffing solvents?" I asked.

"I so love this smell," she said, reluctantly lowering the bottle to the floor.

She caressed random canvases, the way she would lovingly run her hand on the statues in the garden. I saw it then, the yearning for what wasn't, and my heart stuttered. She had said, *My true love is dead.* That great loss was written on her face, thrumming through her body. And three things were abundantly clear.

The mysterious Rosso was an artist out of my league, he was dead, and he was Anna's true love.

She had seen his art and she remembered it. She could never see mine. Even if my talent could measure up to this, she would never see my work. She would never . . . Oh God, I wanted to cry. Her blindness had broken her heart, and now that same damned blindness was breaking mine.

I turned to examine the red nude again. My envy of Rosso was less for the fact that she still loved him and more for his artistic accomplishments. I could mix pigments into black or white to achieve the illusion of depth, I knew the rules and all the tricks, but this connection between colors and emotions was sublime. Nothing I'd done had come close to this haunting brilliance. I was running out of adjectives.

The reds generated heat; sweat ran down my face. My throat was sore from the dust, my vision blurred from straining my eyes, yet I couldn't stop moving more and more paintings aside, examining each with covetous eyes, wishing to have been the one who'd painted them.

Succulent oranges were casually strewn on yellow sand, a love affair with warm colors tempered by the horizon of aquamarine water. The damage here was an easy fix; it was reduced to a few spots near the edges. One of the oranges was peeled and separated into wedges; yellow and orange invigorated my taste buds. A mouth sore from having bitten my tongue the day before screamed with pain, as it had at dinner when Anna fed me her favorite fruit, wedge by zesty wedge.

I sat down cross-legged on the concrete floor, my gaze glued to those oranges, unaware of time passing, letting a new knowledge saturate me.

Not Rosso's work.

Anna came here alone. She would climb back up smelling of turpentine, dust and grief.

Not Rosso's work. Anna's . . .

"Carly, you're crying."

She startled me. I'd lost track of her, just as I'd lost myself in the paintings.

I looked up at her from the floor. Through my tears she became a column of burning red. What did she remember of all these art treasures? Her blindness robbed her of everything she'd loved—dance, film, stage—but this was what she grieved for most. The loss of all her loves all at once. She'd written of that loss. Her novels were the literary expression of that loss.

"They are all salvageable," I said. "I'll do it."

"Thank you," she whispered, still standing proud, but curling a notch into herself in relief.

I stood up and held her in my arms. Her wide gray eyes gazed far beyond me. I kissed each eyelid gently.

"What you lost, your true love, is painting."

A brief sound of pain escaped her throat.

"This one can only be yours," I said, pointing. Then I remembered that she couldn't see. I added, "The oranges are yours. Their colors—"

"My last color," she said.

"*All* these are yours. All except *The Turning*."

The sculpted nude loomed in a frozen dance on the wall behind her. Who had painted her into such a masterpiece? Who had seen her face so frightened and survived the agony?

But he didn't survive, did he?

"Who is Rosso?" I asked.

She slowly said, "Rosso, my love, is you."

48

Open grief was easier to take. Open grief with its wailing, crumbling hysterics that bounced off the walls in hundreds of keening echoes. Anything but this quiet madness.

Rosso, my love, is you.

What was that supposed to mean? What a strange sentence for Anna, who was so exact with her phrasing. Had grief made her use words as bullets to kill with?

This one sentence—*Rosso, my love, is you*—spoken quietly and with dignity was hard for me to take. I was afraid to find out what was behind it. What had been behind the earlier, *Hades has won*? Maybe our month's anniversary meant Anna saying weird things and me just listening.

I needed silence to spin it all in my head.

I untangled myself from her embrace.

"Where are you going?" Her voice was laced with fear as she held me tighter.

"Up," I said through clenched teeth. "Just up."

"You should have never come down here," she said, mostly to herself. "Every loss—every*one*, every*thing*—has to do with this cursed place. I can't lose you too."

"Lose me?" My voice cracked. "I'm choking on dust. I need fresh air."

"That's what he said." Her lips were cool on my burning forehead. "You're feverish, frantic. That's how he was. He couldn't take it."

"I can take it," I said through the thin windpipe I had for a throat. "I can help you, but I have to think about it alone. I have to breathe."

She released her hold. "Go, Carly. I want to stay here a little longer."

I started up the spiral staircase, measuring each worn stair carefully, expecting a minefield of more surprises. Living with

Anna, loving her the way I did, was a journey of constant discovery. She would drop a shoe and then another, and another. She was a centipede, with hundreds of feet and shoes on all of them, and she kept dropping shoes. Just when I thought no more shoes were left, another one dropped. This last one was a boot. Not Kyra's cowboy boot, but a combat boot of heavy leather, with toe and heel irons, and long hobnails.

That's what he said. That's how he was. He couldn't take it.

I could imagine Greg's reaction to the art, the greatness of it, and Anna's pain of losing it. But Anna's insanity? I'm not sure how he would have reacted to that. I was angry. Not at Anna, but at the cruelty of her fate. I wanted to scream for her.

Anna's talent was enormous, haunting. She was going insane because she couldn't paint—literally climbing those walls of rocks and risking her life—and here I was, not painting in spite of my intact visual equipment. How wasteful I'd been!

Suddenly the narrow stairwell became alive with sensation. My bare feet on the cold stone stairs, the palms of my hands on the uneven walls, became sets of eyes, and I had a look into Anna's world of freakish senses. With my ascent the space narrowed and darkened, but new senses brightened up, reminding me of the time I went snorkeling. The familiar world above water was gone and the silent underwater world appeared, richer in its colorful, astonishing strata.

This dark, silent stairwell was neither dark nor silent. I could hear, imagine, feel, sense down to the insects swarming in the spaces between the stones. In my extreme state of alertness, what I sensed and felt and heard was overly detailed, enhanced, as Anna had promised would happen one day if I allowed it.

Scents aren't only pleasant or not, Carly. There is more.

The stones had an old smell I'd never before noticed.

The texture of your skin, your warmth, your reaction to my touch tell me how to love you, she'd said. *Teach me*, I'd begged, blindfolded, to keep even the faintest moonbeam out. *Teach me your freaky senses.* And she had, with great patience. She would make me touch and smell and listen. And now all this knowledge was realized, flooding into me, making me see what she was trying to teach me.

The uneven old walls had a rough texture, yet in spots they were worn—like the steps—from hands tracing up the stairwell for years.

I could not hear Anna behind me. Had she, back with her paintings, forgotten my existence? Was she touching, caressing them as she would a lover's body? As she had mine?

My ears popped. I heard the waves breaking against the rocks.

The sighted treat sounds as background noise, Carly, but sounds are so much more than that. Listen to the ocean. Can you hear the approaching storm? Open your ears and listen to nature's voice. Hear that mockingbird? He longs for a mate. Can you hear the cars on Palos Verdes Drive? I can tell Hildi's driving before she makes the turn on the gravel road.

I listened. A truck braked in a screech and started again at the stop sign down the road.

"*Carly, Carly, Carly . . .*" I heard my name like another echo. Was Anna calling me back? It wasn't her normal commanding tone, but rather a lament distorted by the walls, thrown back more than once.

"*Carly, Carly, Carly . . .*"

I knew I shouldn't turn around because of some old myth. I skipped up the stairs all the way to the top and found near silence. They were long gone, all my buffers—Kyra, Zoe and Robert.

A crazy urge grabbed me, demanding that I spread my wings and fly above the vast black and white of my nightmares. I had to do it, at least once, to understand Anna's brilliant madness.

I found Flora on the deck in a big chair—the way she would normally sit at the end of a working day. Her sore feet with the pronounced bunions rested on another chair. She was smoking, eyes half-closed.

"Carly?" She crossed herself with the hand holding the cigarette. "You smell of that place."

I wasn't sure what she meant. The basement smelled to me of dried oil paint and turpentine, both of which I loved. Did she mean the dust or the smell of grief and desperation?

I took the cigarette from her hand and inhaled. A coughing fit racked me.

"Easy," Flora said. "Sit down. Tell me what's wrong. Where is she?"

"There must be something they can do for her," I said, my voice as taut as the strings of a violin. "This cosmic joke is too cruel."

"You saw the paintings." Flora lit another cigarette for herself.

"How can she take her blindness so calmly? I'd be screaming my lungs out . . . on tranquilizers!"

Flora let the smoke out in a series of perfect rings. "She's done enough screaming." The cigarette dangled from her dry lower lip. "Now she needs you. You understand her greatness. You are the best person for her."

"What about the other way around?" I asked. "Is she the best for me?"

"You'll need all your strength."

"You are too loyal to answer truthfully."

"Where is she?"

"She stayed. I had to leave."

"The ghosts?"

"The ghosts," I said. "So many."

I sat on the edge of the deck under the thin railing, the way I'd seen Anna do dozens of times. Clouds gathered to cover the full moon. The Queen's Necklace twinkled hazy lights at me. *You can do it.*

I gazed down at the great turbulent beast of the ocean below and I wasn't afraid.

Anna could barely recognize a face, could barely tell up from down, but the dangerous rocks under her bare feet were hers. The rocks were the only freedom she still had, the only justification for the powerful title La Divina. Even the air was hers. Here she could breathe.

I took the cigarette out of my mouth and inflated my lungs with the cleanest air. I smelled the approaching rain, heard the ocean below—storming, soothing, cajoling. My fear of heights was numbed. My fear of death was gone. I was exhilarated. Alive.

I sensed solid rock with the toes of one bare foot. If a blind woman could do this as easily as brushing her teeth, so could I.

Flora's voice warned behind me. "You've never done it before."

"This makes two firsts," I said, the first cigarette of my life dangling between my lips.

"Anna will be so angry," she said.

I craned my head back to look at Flora, who seemed comical and dramatically older when seen upside down, illuminated by the lights from the quartz crystals. Her contorted expression was the last thing I saw before closing my eyes.

The cigarette between my lips made me feel tough and ready for anything. I reached down with one bare foot to feel the rock below.

I traced the memory of Anna's words, her description of how she easily found her way down the cliff side. The top section was very steep. "Don't ever try it," she'd warned. "You see too well."

Eyes shut, I felt the wind on my face. I listened to the surf, studied every nook and cranny with my fingertips and toes before trusting my weight to them. I avoided the rock on the left—too jagged. I stayed away from a slippery surface. The thorns, as Anna had said, grew only at the top half of the steep trail.

How easy it was, descending the rocks toward the stormy water. What a beautiful experience. Even the air smelled different to me here, caught between sea and sky.

Anna had lost her sight and, with it, what she loved most, but here was this one joy no one could take away from her, this freedom of moving in open space, of being suspended like a sea bird above the coastline. Here no one could reach her, and she loved it.

As the surf got louder, my toes touched soft moss. I knew I was getting closer to the water. The access ladder was somewhere along the storm drain, but I couldn't reach it and didn't need it.

I use my legs more. My arms may get too tired.

I imagined becoming one with Anna's mind, her memories, her senses. My head swam with pride at my accomplishment.

A small rock rolled down from above, skidded and passed me. A cold gust of wind blew my hair forward. In a moment of weakness I opened my eyes and glanced behind me at the vast, indigo night. That was all it took for panic to set in.

What had I gotten myself into, and why? I tried to hold on to the boulder near me, but its jagged edge stabbed my hand.

I lost my footing.

"Shit!" I cried out.

A free fall through the black night was not in the least romantic.

49

Kyra waited for Juliet at the G-Spot. She'd missed nothing here, as the weekend parties were only beginning. The bars and the restaurants on Santa Monica Boulevard were abuzz with people. As she sipped a Diet Coke, Kyra considered her dramatic exit from Garibaldi's house. What purpose had it served other than drama? Their trespassing had been her idea. She shouldn't have left Carly alone to explain it to her demon lover. She was worried about Carly and curious. She would have liked to have been a moth, or rather a bat, hanging above them in that dark basement.

Something leathery touches her cheek. She recoiled, her mind filled with images of upside down bats. It was only a leather glove belonging to Zingy Lola.

"Let's dance Kyra," she said.

"I have a date."

"I bet she isn't as much fun as me." Lola inched toward the counter with a pout and draped herself around B. J. like a growing vine.

Then all the noise stopped. Even the jukebox was silent for the first time.

Juliet Blair had stepped through the doors.

She had changed into jeans and a black leather jacket. Someone wanted an autograph. Kyra could tell Juliet was enjoying it, so she sat, witnessing the grand entrance along with the rest of them, sipping her Diet Coke and delighting in the splash her exotic date was making in the neighborhood dive. *Divine Darkness* had been very popular in the last gay and lesbian film festival, acquiring a cult following.

Juliet peeled off her jacket.

The love of women is more complex than adoration of the breasts. However, here was Juliet in a white tank top. What a view.

"Look what is walking into my bar," B. J. bragged, leaning forward on the counter. "She's as much of a knockout with her clothes on."

"Watch your mouth, Beetlejuice." Kyra got up to welcome her date.

B. J. said, "I saw her first."

Kyra felt a personal triumph when Juliet pressed her close, giving her a sexy kiss in front of B. J.'s sinking eyes.

She guided Juliet to a private booth in the back, away from the jukebox and the gawkers. B. J. herself brought the beers and said, "On the house."

Juliet saved Kyra the old beating around the bush. "What went on at dinner?"

"I took Carly to show her the painting, and Anna caught us in the verboten place. I believe she heard everything we said about her."

"No way!" Juliet exclaimed.

Kyra smiled. "Those who eavesdrop deserve what they hear."

Juliet leaned forward. "What exactly did you say?"

"You go first." Kyra took a swig of Heineken. "Tell me the long story you promised."

"How much time do you have?"

"My whole life," Kyra said.

Juliet laughed, showing off her perfect teeth and that one adorable, crooked one. Yet there it was again, that hint of tragedy in her eyes.

"I'm sorry to interrupt," said a kid with spiky dark hair and a pale face. The vampire style. She'd probably showed Bruna a fake ID at the door. In Kyra's book she was barely out of diapers. She took a white baseball cap out of her pocket and handed it to Juliet for an autograph. Kyra wished they'd all disappear and leave them the hell alone. Juliet was flattered.

"Great movie," the kid said. "Wasn't it kinda weird to be naked all the time?"

"Honestly," Juliet said, still enjoying the attention, "with the cameras up my nose and the glaring lights, I was more worried about going blind for real."

The kid noticed Kyra. "Would you mind?" she asked, handing her the cap.

"Sure," Kyra said, wondering who she was supposed to be. "How did you recognize me?" She asked before signing.

"From the playoffs," the kid said.

Kyra signed her own name, still having no idea. The kid donned the cap and joined her gaggle of giggly girlfriends.

"You want to go somewhere else?" Kyra asked.

Juliet shook her head. "The publicity can only help." She smiled. "You more than me."

Kyra took Juliet's hands. Short fingernails. That pleased her. "I don't want to pry, but I'm going to."

Juliet eyed the swinging exit door, as if about to bail out. Quickly Kyra asked, "Did you and Anna have an affair?"

Juliet gestured at the beer. "I'll need something more medicinal."

Her sweet lisp drove Kyra nuts with its cuteness.

"I have prescribing privileges," she said, motioning to B. J. She didn't have to motion long since B. J. was buzzing around them like bees around honey. "You got Ley here?" Kyra asked.

"Sure do." B. J. grinned. "You don't expect that to be on the house."

Kyra turned to Juliet. "I can make Benjamin Franklin stand on his head."

She took a crisp one-hundred-dollar bill out of her wallet and rested it on its side. It stayed up. The bill had to be new for the trick to work.

Juliet laughed. "You don't have both chopsticks in the chow mein."

"I don't know a psychotherapist who does," Kyra said. And to B. J., "The bottle, Beetlejuice."

B. J. accepted the money, shaking her head at Juliet. "You gonna fall for it?"

"Too late," Juliet said with a shrug.

Minutes later the spiked bottle and two shot glasses gleamed between them on the scratched wooden surface.

Juliet sipped. "You're worried about your sister."

"Should I be?"

"Eventually we all drop from the heights," she said.

"Tell me what you mean by all, by drop, by heights," said the 24/7 therapist in Kyra.

"We who love her fall from figurative or literal heights."

"By choice or by accident?"

"Ah, that's my story."

Juliet ran her fingers through her short hair, took another polite little sip, rested the shot glass down, then picked it up again, emptying it all in one go.

Once she started talking, Kyra could not shut her up.

50

The fragrance of damp sand and agitated saltwater tickled my nostrils. Had I been knocked out for seconds? Days?

I was sprawled like a sunning crab on top of a rock. I turned onto my stomach and stretched. I was unhurt. A wave moved up, slowly covered parts of the rock and then cleaved into smaller foamy swirls in little tide pools. As the water receded at the same hypnotic pace, I heard hectic *click, clicking*. The wet rock was alive and bustling with little caverns.

I held on to the rock, delirious and fascinated by the breathing ocean. The water engulfed me, saturating my T-shirt. I was one with nature and unafraid. A night creature, like Anna. I bathed my face in cold saltwater. I was hot, then cold. A breaking wave splattered and crushed into white nets of froth. I remained still for a minute, or an hour, collecting strength, listening to the waves coming in, going out, and the tiny marine creatures *click, clicking* inside their caverns and tide pools.

My face rested on the rough, prickly surface of the rock. Sharp points dug into my skin. I heard the little creatures that lived, clicked and died inside this rock. I closed my eyes against the fluid rocking. Cold air cleared my lungs with smells of salt and sand and musk.

"Carly!" Anna's voice was frightened. "Where are you?"

"I'm here," I said.

"Are you hurt?" Her hands moved on me, head to toe, tenderly checking for injuries.

"I don't think so," I said.

"Get away from this rock," she said, her voice urgent. "The tide will be in soon."

She led me into the small cove, to a dry area protected by a natural wall. She'd brought with her the red chenille blanket from the patio, and I was happy for that as my teeth were chattering.

"Take off the wet clothes. It gets too cold here."

I did. She wrapped the chenille around my shoulders and kissed me.

"We've both lost enough," she said. "I can't lose you too."

"Why would you lose me?"

"You want the long or the short answer?"

"I've had enough short answers from you," I said.

Her dress was tied between her long legs, to facilitate her climb down, I guessed. She now untied it and dropped to the dry sand, tucking her legs beneath her. I did the same. I looked out into the night, at the twinkling diamonds of the Queen's Necklace along the bay, then back at the queen herself. My blind and beautiful queen.

"Why didn't you show me your paintings until now? Why has Hades won?" I held her face as though she could see me. "What did you mean by what you said in the basement? Why? Why am I Rosso? "

"No, no. You are my only, my Carly," she said, her lips on my face, down my neck, her hands sliding down, trying to warm me up and only turning me on. I so wanted her, here in the cold sand, in the dark night, both of us sprinkled by the frothing waves, but I wanted, needed, answers first.

"Why, Anna?"

"It's a long story and the night is cold. Would you like to go up to the house?"

"Here and now," I said.

If we had to negotiate the way up, Anna might close up again and I'd lose this opportunity to hear the honest truth. Anna felt safe here, in her home grounds. Here, she'd tell me everything.

She reached into her bra and produced the flattened pack of Camel Lights and an elaborate lighter bearing the face of Donald Duck. I lit two cigarettes at the same time and passed her one. I saw it done once in a Bette Davis movie.

She took a long draw and coughed. "*Yuck.* I can't really smoke these things," she muttered, burying her cigarette in the sand with agitation.

"Why do you, then?" I asked.

"This, the cigarette, is part of the story. I want to tell you the whole truth, my love, but I don't know where to start."

"Start by telling me who you are, La Divina."

Part Four

51

"I admired art before I could read," Anna said. "I started drawing and painting as soon as I could physically hold a pencil or a paintbrush. My world was visual, colorful. Very early I noticed how colors affected my emotions. I became fascinated with the quality of the light, the richness of reds and purples. You know the landscape here in Palos Verdes—the greens, the blues and all their in-betweens. Those colors were unforgettable, glorious. They still are, but I have to speak in the past tense. The sky and the ocean changed during the day from aquamarine to shades of dark blue. The mountains turned from white to yellow to orange to red. Until sunset."

She paused to catch her breath, as if she'd run for miles. "Now all I can remember is the names of the colors and the sense colors used to give me. But color itself, nothing. You take it for granted, Carly."

"I do," I said. "I'm also grateful for it."

She said, "It's getting colder. Do you see anything to build a fire with?"

I gathered a few damp twigs in a spot protected by the rocks and used the Donald Duck lighter. The twigs crackled and spattered. A small fire started.

"Forgive me if it comes out all jumbled and confused," she said. "This is difficult for me."

I leaned my back against a smooth rock and tightened the chenille around me.

"First, let's nix the myths. Number one: I'm a California girl, not born, but raised here, in this very house from the age of six." She gestured upward toward the house and the neon pillars illuminating the night.

"But your worldliness," I said, surprised. "And all the languages you speak."

"In my twenties, after . . . well, after Johnny Ross . . ." Her voice cracked, as if she hadn't spoken for years. She paused.

"Rosso?" I asked.

She nodded. "I went back to live and work in Europe. Myth breaker number two: My adored, famous parents, Hollywood's golden couple of the time, were too busy with their film careers to remember my existence. Irena Garibaldi was a talented actress. A mother, not so much. Papa was just absent. They weren't abusive, and they loved me in their way, but they loved each other more. I was an inconvenience they tolerated. When they worked, they did nothing else. I understand, because I'm the same."

"Yet you didn't choose to have children!" I said, ever defensive for her, even against herself.

"They didn't either; I just happened." Anna laughed sadly, rubbing her hands above our little fire. "I'm not complaining, only getting the facts straight so that you won't expect me to waste time talking about those who were the least significant in my childhood. They gave me life, money and freedom, which is really a lot."

"Your mother also gave you her looks and voice," I said.

"So I'm told. I missed nothing, thanks to my dear Flora, my surrogate mother, who loved me and cared for me from the day I was born and still does. When I was six and Mama made it big in Hollywood, Flora left Italy with us and raised me right here, in Palos Verdes. I owe her my happy childhood. She was the one who encouraged and supported me, the one I'd run to with a scraped knee or my good grades. I'm trying to be as much comfort to her, now that she's getting old, but I'm a handful. Flora saved my life more than once. When I lost everything . . . When Johnny . . ."

Here was that name again, a name that made her otherwise steady voice waver. She was silent for a while, her hands hovering over the embers.

"Tell me about him," I said.

"Johnny Ross," she said dreamily. "The boy next door." She started humming Judy Garland's famous song, and her melodious voice was velvet against the rolling waves and the crackling fire.

"Johnny's parents, like mine, were rich and neglectful. We raised ourselves and each other, and we had Flora. While our classmates played football and basketball, Johnny and I painted together, Johnny ever the perfectionist." She smiled to herself. "In bursts of anger at his own imperfection, he would destroy his best works."

Anna's paintings were singed, some burned to dark brown and beyond recognition.

"Did he . . . ?"

"No," she cried out. "His anger was directed only at his own work. Eventually he would branch out into sculpting, claiming that marble was more durable."

"The nudes in the garden?" I asked.

"Yes. There were more, but his family took most of his works. Our first love was art, our second was rock climbing. Our third . . ." Cold wind blew in from the ocean. She turned her face into it and her long hair blew back in waves. "We dreamed of surfing distant oceans and climbing Everest and Kilimanjaro, but in the meantime, we got to know all the rocks around here and we surfed Palos Verdes. Flora called us *procioni*, and fussed and worried, much as she still does. That's my childhood in a nutshell. That was how I grew up—wild, happy and free.

"Johnny and I had our own language. We would transfer whole images to each other in a look or a touch. We believed it to be normal, an ordinary way of communication between close friends."

"You can still do that," I said.

"To an extent, yes. One day I was gazing at him from the window—my bedroom window on the second floor—as he was hammering away at a crude block of marble in the rose garden. His long hair was wild and streaked with gold from the wind and the sun. At that moment, I recognized that Johnny wasn't a child anymore. His powerful beauty was new. He took my breath away. New muscles had appeared overnight. His olive-tanned legs were strong. He called out to warn the gardeners of a falling piece of rock, and the tenderness in his voice, a man's voice, overwhelmed me with feeling. A new feeling.

"Johnny felt my eyes on him. He stopped hammering and squinted in the sunlight. We were at eye level, I on the second floor, and he on top of his stone. He dropped his hammer, this time without a warning, and he lit a cigarette, all the while looking straight at me. He'd light a cigarette when something new, an idea, occurred to him. I thought I knew what he was thinking. He used his T-shirt to wipe rock powder and sweat off his face, revealing his chest muscles. And I hoped I knew what he was thinking.

"Then the morning sun moved directly behind him, and the sun ignited the sky and set his body afire in front of my eyes. *I'm going to lose you*, I thought in great fear. I rushed down the stairs and toward the garden to save him. By the time I got to him, he'd come down from the rock, the sun had shifted and the light changed from red-orange to yellow. The illusion of fire was gone, but the power of it still moved within me. 'Anna, you're trembling,' he said, enclosing me in his strong arms."

I shivered in the cold, imagining the moment. Imagining the man I'd never met. Imagining the strength of a nascent attraction.

Anna's hands were instantly on my face. "You're hot. Feverish. Should we go up?"

"Let's stay." I was delaying the inevitable. The idea of scaling the rocks made my stomach sink. The excitement I'd felt on the way down was gone, and I was left with my old dread of heights.

Anna framed my face between her hands. "Here in the dark I can almost see you."

As her blind gaze bore into my very seeing eyes, I imagined she was seeing someone other than me. A gust of wind cut across my face like a cold knife across an oil painting.

52

"It started on the day I went to audition for *Divine Darkness*." Juliet said. "A woman entered. Her golden hair was styled in an extravagant, one-sided coif. She was so strikingly beautiful, she could carry that crazy hair well. Her clothing was austere by comparison. Her white collar was stiff and up to her ears; her dark gray designer's suit was perfection. *La Garibaldi*, I thought. *La Divina*."

Someone turned on the jukebox and k.d. lang crooned another country-western. A few couples took to the dance floor. Kyra moved across the booth and sat next to Juliet, not wanting to miss a word.

"She turned and stopped midmotion when she noticed me. She took off her sunglasses and let her gray eyes slide shamelessly down my body. She then announced to no one in particular, 'We have our Leila.' I looked around, and my heart was squeezed dry of blood when I found she meant me."

Juliet exhaled, the air fluttering out of her like a cry.

"Production began immediately, as Anna had only to cast Leila. When she realized I could act, Anna confessed that she'd been prepared to isolate me for as long as necessary, just the two of us, to give me private acting lessons. She added, barely moving her lips, 'I'm disappointed you don't need any.' I was ready to let her direct me on and off camera. I gave myself to her completely."

Juliet was silent. When she spoke again, her tone lost its natural fullness and became that of a shy little girl. Her lisp intensified. "Kyra, I don't know if you remember that autoerotic scene . . ."

"Remember? That scene fed my fantasies through many a one-night stand. Here at the G-Spot they play it on a loop in every party."

"Really?"

She smiled at that. Kyra poured two more shots. Behind the counter, B. J. stared at her in reproach, gesturing with her hand, *How many more?* Kyra lifted the spiky bottle, suggesting that she take it back.

Juliet continued. "Anna would command complete silence. The lights were dimmed. She'd hold my hand and lead me to the bed. She made me feel like we were all alone. I'd sit on the edge of the bed, naked, as I was the entire film. Right in front of everybody, Anna would kneel down and slowly smooth her hand on me, like this, Kyra."

Juliet demonstrated the touch along Kyra's thigh. As she looked into her eyes, Kyra wanted to repeat what they'd done against a damaged masterpiece, below sea level, only a few hours ago.

"'Be subtle,' Anna would say. 'You are blind, so you can never be sure you are completely alone. Do it for me.' And I did, Kyra. In my mind I was making love to her."

When Kyra looked up it was half past midnight in the parallel universe of the G-Spot. The dancers on the floor howled and hopped to an Aretha Franklin classic.

"I peeled hundreds of oranges until I got the trick right."

"I tried it once," Kyra said. "Big mistake. Juice squeezed out and nearly blinded me."

"Maybe that's how Leila lost her vision," Juliet said.

They both chuckled, then they drank in silence. B. J. took the bottle of tequila away, replacing it with two Cokes. Kyra's mind was flooded with stark images from Garibaldi's film, Juliet's perfect body, nude but for a pair of stilettos, its smooth darkness contrasted with the snowy-white bed linen. Each frame somehow featured a bright orange in full color. In a white bowl on a black kitchen counter; in Juliet's hands as Leila, a blind nymphomaniac obsessed with oranges, since it was the last color she had seen.

The black and white movies of the forties seemed colorful. Not so Anna's film with its eagle-eye details and its jarring bareness.

"Anna demanded perfection and got nothing but. She paid me very well, but the price I paid . . . "

Juliet emptied the second shot into her throat. "In less than six weeks the filming was done, and then it happened between us."

Kyra knew exactly what she meant by *it happened. It* was supposed to be exciting and wonderful. *It* was love realized. Why would the smoothness between Juliet's eyebrows crease into two vertical lines? For a split second Juliet seemed old and sad. Then she smiled and she was an adorable kid with a lisp and one slightly crooked tooth. Kyra's mind was all mixed up with Juliet's lavender and the sweet chocolate of her skin and something Oscar Wilde had said and the fact that she was a sworn bachelor. Kyra Rosen did not fall in love.

53

"I still put my nose to his statues," Anna said, "but they are sleek and wind chiseled and that smell, his scent, washed off long ago. When I smoke I almost relive his first touch, the feel of that day. I come closest to it when I'm down here. That day he smelled of a swim in the ocean, of rock dust and the sun and a whiff of cigarette smoke."

"Camel?" I asked.

"Camel Lights." She pulled me to her. "Let me warm you up."

She made me lie down in the sand, my head in her lap. She tucked the chenille tightly around me.

"Johnny and I started down to the water, down the rocks—these very rocks—to the sand. The world was ours. The green mountains and the sky belonged to us on that day we became lovers in our private heaven. Right here, in this cove."

"Here?" I cried out, torn from the story into reality. "*Here?*"

"Sorry," she said, holding tight to me. "I did spring it on you."

"And I'm sprawled so casually in this place," I said, up on my feet, coughing, rubbing at my scratchy throat. Either the dust of the basement or the chilled air was giving me a problem.

"We were fourteen," she said, dreamy.

"Greg and I were fifteen. We had no idea what we were doing," I said.

"You grew up with your Greg," Anna said. "I had my Johnny. Kyra was your surrogate mother. I had Flora. We both had painting very early on. You and I are very similar."

"But *here*," I repeated, glancing around me, absorbing the beauty for myself, and for Anna who only had memories.

It hadn't been so picturesque for Greg and me, only my narrow bed in my childhood room. I looked around again—at the water, the sand and the rocks, and up to the lights radiating from the house above. This place was sacred ground. Anna had seen it when she could still see. When she came here, again and again, she was trying to recapture the love she'd felt that day. Was it the love for *seeing* or for Johnny? When she touched me here, anywhere, who was she touching?

"Can you still see through me, even now?"

"Now it is all memories," she said without melancholy. "I get a mental picture through you here and there." Then she was on her hands and knees, frantically searching, moving her seeing fingertips on the smooth surface of the rock. "There's an engraving here. Johnny chiseled an image of both of us for posterity. Help me find it."

She moved her fingers on the hard surface with butterfly gentleness, trying to read it, as she'd often read my face. My body.

"In this rock . . . Or maybe here . . . I don't remember. It's small, but you can't miss it."

We searched for a while, me with my cellphone light and Anna feeling the rock with loving, gentle hands. "You'll be able to see it in the light," she said.

She sat back down, her hands measuring in the air, as though still searching for the engraving in her memory. She was far from calm. "Is it too much for you? Do you want me to stop?"

"Don't stop." I wanted to stay there, my ears filled with her magnificent voice. "You're quite a storyteller."

Her smile was a sad one. "He's quite a story." Then she remembered. "Call Flora. She shouldn't worry about us."

I did. Flora was indeed waiting on the deck, happy to hear my voice. Next a big ball fell from above and opened when it hit next to us. It held a thick blanket, a bottle of water, and a chocolate bar, plus flannel pajamas for both of us. I put mine on right away.

We huddled inside the blanket, keeping each other warm.

Anna continued.

"'Even death shouldn't part us,' I told him. Johnny pondered my words a moment and then said, 'I'll come back to you as another person. But you'll instantly recognize me.'

"Now remember, we were fourteen with the magical thinking and knowing that we'll live forever and, well, I made him the same promise. That was our ceremony, our pledge to each other under the clear sky, by our rocks and our aquamarine ocean and my parents' house, our home. We considered ourselves married at fourteen."

Pain was in her measured speech, in each carefully spoken word. A light drizzle started. Tiny raindrops fell on my face and Anna's, like tears yet to be cried. I braced myself for the coming heartbreak.

"Johnny and I used to go to the movies a lot. That same night, really our wedding night, we went to see my parents in a new romantic comedy. I told you they worked constantly, that they were as attentive to me as they could be long distance. They were voices on the phone, fictional characters on the big screen in one box office smash after another. The tabloids loved them. They maintained their image as Hollywood's golden couple—loved, adored, and envied by millions of fans. But I had only as much of their time as any of those fans."

I thought of all the glamor shots adorning the small vestibule, the film stills and snapshots of Marco and Irena Garibaldi. Those images were as meaningless to Anna as those real people had been in her life. Her real life was below that small vestibule. Way below sea level.

"You take after them in a way," I said, digging my bare feet in the sand. "I heard a rumor that you have a bad temper. What a joke."

"I twice lost my temper in public."

"When?" I asked.

"About three months ago. It was bad."

Three months ago. I did a quick calculation. "Greg? Did you lose your temper on him?"

"Yes. I wish I could take it back." She paused. "Back to Johnny. Seven years passed. Our love grew and matured. Those were the happiest years of my life. For four of those, Johnny and I were high school students, and for the last three, we belonged only to each other and to our art. We went to the local college, nothing fancy, and studied art together. We lived like a married couple, in this very house. We did everything together —we wrote poetry together, we painted, we listened to the same music, any music. We loved all of it, classical, dance, rock 'n' roll—"

"Music?" I couldn't help interrupting her.

"Oh, yes. Music and parties all the time. Our friends from art school would come here and we'd sit for each other in the garden, or in the basement, and have painting parties. Flora was everyone's Italian mama . . . and how she loved to cook for our friends and fuss over them when they'd come to the kitchen and tell her their problems. The parties lasted for days—"

"Go back a minute," I said. "The music. You don't listen to music now. Why?"

"My ears are my eyes," she explained. "I can't afford to block the constant information I get from my ears with music. The same goes for fragrances. Musk is gentle on my nose. I can't, I won't, confuse my sense of smell with anything else."

Behind the logical explanation, a world of tragedy opened up. With her vision gone, she'd also had to give up music. Such losses were too much for one person.

"Don't feel sorry for me," she said. "The ocean is my music now and the birds and nature and . . ." She took my hand, constantly touching me when she spoke, reassuring herself of my presence. "And your voice is my music, Carly."

She sighed. "Yes, I had to adjust. But back then, Johnny would chisel away on a series of marble nudes in the rose garden. Sometimes I would paint in the natural light, next to him, calmed by the sound of his hammering. The wind would blow the marble dust, and I'd let it texture my painting. I can now feel that roughness and almost see those paintings with my fingers. And him."

"What you have down there is only seven years' worth of paintings? But the number of pieces! I could have sworn—"

"I worked like mad, nonstop, because I was having so much fun experimenting, studying the effect of colors on the emotions. On mood. The calm of blues and greens, the hot-tempered reds and black. I loved what orange and yellows did to passion and appetite. You've seen some of those pieces, Carly. They were meant to be my life's work, my greatest achievement." She played with the sand, letting it run between her fingers. "Now it's all lost."

"You can't lose what's inside you," I said. "Your use of light and shadow has gone beyond Caravaggio."

"Has it?"

"You've taken *chiaroscuro* in a new direction."

"So much for the revolution." Her caustic laugh cracked into a brief sob. "Carly, you understand me. Painting is the most intimate form of creation."

"For us it is," I said.

"For anyone. That metaphor for a starting point, a blank canvas, relates to painting, but all artists understand it. You start literally with a blank canvas and when you're done, it's all yours. You were alone with your mind, beginning to end. No choreographers, no team of writers, no accompanist, only you and the result of your perfect vision."

She waved a hand, lightly touching her eyes, then let that hand drop, as if to say, *What's the use?*

"I'd forget to eat or rest. I'd play the music loud and paint until I dropped from exhaustion or until Johnny's arms enclosed me, his embrace redolent of ocean and sun. We would love each other on the beach, in the basement, in the garden. Forgive me if I get carried away here, but it was a dream. A living dream. Seven years of heaven, then *wham*."

She gestured an explosion above her head. The moon emerged from behind the clouds, and I saw solid drops of silver rolling down her cheeks. I wiped the tears away with my thumbs—something I'd learned from Kyra. I shivered. My entire body ached, reacting to the fall from the heights and the cold and to Anna's story.

"*Wham*," she repeated.

A wave broke, its millions of tiny droplets hitting our faces like splinters of wood.

54

"Everything I knew and loved exploded into bloody pieces all at once, in one vicious, cruel moment," Anna said. "I loved my world exactly as it had been, Carly, with rock climbing, painting, parties, writing poetry, swimming and Johnny and Flora. My parents should have stayed where they belonged, characters on the big screen. Why did they have to come back for one evening, for one fucking evening, only to take it all away?"

At that, Anna sounded soul-deep angry for the first time, the sort of anger I'd only seen, so far, expressed in her fiction.

"Hollywood's favorite couple sure had a gift for drama with a special twist. On that one evening I realized what life should and could have been, only to lose it, along with everything else I treasured." She fastened the chenille and the blanket around us and trembled along with me. "This is my first telling of the whole story, Carly. And here, in this cove, of all places."

"Why haven't you told anyone?" I asked with incredulity. "What about Flora, Hildi, or Greg?"

"Flora knows. Flora lived it with me. Hildi does her job without asking. I don't know what I would have done without them. Guido loved me with the sort of infatuation that asks nothing. I never tell because this telling is torture."

"Why me?"

"Because you were wise enough to guess my secret within two seconds of seeing me; curious enough to venture to my Land of the Dead; brave enough to overcome your own fears and find this sacred spot. It's only fair that I connect the dots for you."

"That's all?" I asked.

"I trust you completely." She kissed me softly. "I love you, Carly."

That was all we needed. The day, the evening, the night, the paintings all gave way, turning us into a wild tangle of arms and legs, hands and mouths. Our whispers and cries merged with the howling wind and the breaking of the surf and a lone night bird.

Eventually our breathing calmed, our passions satiated, but only for a little time because once was never enough. Once was only the start.

"You greedy girl," Anna whispered. "Aren't you sore from that fall and the cold?"

"I'm sore from you," I whispered back, kissing her swollen lips. "But I wouldn't have it any other way."

"Let's get some energy for more," she said.

We ate the chocolate bar in two bites, then we were naked against each other inside the blanket, warm and protected and in tune with the wind and the waves and the spattering fire. A moonbeam played across our secluded spot, washing the cove with an eerie glow, illuminating the rocks above us and the glistening sparkles of a breaking wave. I spoke steadily in Anna's ear, as I always had when our passions were spent, telling her of the night and its deep colors, showing her in words what she could not see.

Anna listened, her breathing calm against my chest.

"This is my happiest place in the world," she said.

"That makes two of us."

"Paint me here," she said. "Now. In words."

She ignored my protests and freed herself from my embrace, standing up graceful and naked and strong above me. Her smoothness, her curves were engulfed with the moonlight.

From my position, I extended one arm to measure her proportions, as I did when starting a new canvas with a new sitter.

"Anna Lighting the Moon," I said. "Subject, a mythical goddess; medium, oil on canvas; colors, iridescent blue with the shimmering gold sprinkles of a breaking wave. One lengthy, white line runs unbroken down the perfect curve of her neck and shoulder, down her back and gluteus maximus, down her well formed calf and tendo Achillis . . ."

As I spoke, both her arms slowly stretched above her head. Very gracefully she bent her entire body backward until her fingertips found the sand behind her. I watched amazed as she held the perfect wheel. I'd seen her practicing this spectacular pose with her yoga trainer—it had some long Sanskrit name ending with *asana*. Here, naked in the moonlight, it took on a different meaning. Slowly, effortlessly she came up from that backward wheel, breathing normally. She paused a moment, arms up, then she brought her palms together into the prayer position.

I was transfixed by what I'd just seen, but Anna didn't let me indulge. She turned again into a normal being and gave a little squeal.

"I'm dying to pee, aren't you?"

I was. And we giggled, peeing naked in the sand, then washing ourselves and each other in saltwater—which burned like hell, giving us more giggles.

"Warm me up," she said.

We fell asleep wrapped up in each other inside the blanket. When I woke up it was still night and her face was pressed into my chest, her calm breathing against my neck.

"Where was I?" she asked, meaning in her story.

"Here, with me," I said, meaning in my heart. "Do you want to go up?"

"No, Carly. If I don't tell you here and now, I never will."

I kissed her forehead and felt the tremble in her body. She was frightened.

55

"Mama was asked to speak at a Children's Hospital charity event. I was twenty-one and they wanted me to join them. Since I spent my days climbing rocks—swimming, surfing, painting—I didn't own fancy clothes. Mama let me try on her evening gowns and they all smelled of her delicate French perfume. Mama and I wore the same size. How happy I was when she made a big fuss over me. Her dress, a shade of orange, set off my great tan. Mama's stylist pulled my hair away from my face—"

"I saw that photo in the vestibule," I said. "You two look like twins."

"Yes, that photo . . ." Anna said. "The woman teased me about the oil paint staining my hands. She took a long time cleaning under my fingernails, as if they were never to be dirtied again. An omen. Ah, the chills this still gives me."

A chill also passed through me as I thought of how Robert had cleaned my fingernails and that I hadn't painted since. I promised myself to start tomorrow with Anna's nude against the moonlight.

"That evening, for the first time in my life, I had loving, attentive parents. We actually liked each other and we had fun. Then all, *all of it*, was torn away from me."

"How do you mean? What happened?" I asked.

"All three of us got into Papa's car and headed for the Beverly Hills Hotel. The evening was magical for many reasons. For starters, the lights and the colors. It was a children's event, made for those who loved children. I was a child, dazzled by colors. Those man-made colors were different and new to me, as I was used to nature and its colors. I could taste the brightness, feel it with all my senses. I planned a new canvas to capture all that blinking luminosity.

"I was used to solitude, with only Johnny or Flora for company. Yes, parties broke that solitude, but only occasionally. When you paint or write you have to be alone with your mind, so all that attention was overwhelming. Yet I smiled a lot in real joy and not for the cameras they kept shoving in our faces. In my mind I was telling Johnny everything.

"I realized how adored my parents were, how respected. I don't remember Mama's actual speech, only her melodious voice and the way the crowd reacted. Papa kept glancing at me, as if discovering me, maybe comparing us. I saw the pride in his eyes, the adoration. 'This is your mama, Anna,' he said, as if introducing me to someone new. She received a standing ovation. She was glowing and so stunningly beautiful.

"That evening their glamor stuck to me, the tomboy. A Spanish director offered to get me a screen test. He wanted Mama and me to play sisters in his next project. People noticed me and commented on what they called my *exquisite beauty*.

"And I was a little girl, excited to be told I was pretty, happy to be included in the magic, happy to belong to my parents, who were lavishing more attention on me than they had in my entire life."

"What a waste," I said, my hands running down her back, "to create a divine being like you and never realize it."

"Just as wasteful as creating many masterpieces, realizing it, but being barred from ever seeing them," she said, pressing me to her, protective.

She insisted that we dress, but finding our clothes was a task as all were scattered by the wind and by our passion. Anna's red dress was tangled up and covered in wet sand. My jeans and T-shirt were soaked, and the flannel pajamas Flora dropped for us was at the edge of the water, one splay-legged, the other crumpled up into a ball, but dry.

We wore our pajamas and huddled inside the big blanket, using it as a sleeping bag. "A question about that night has bothered me for a long time. Had they really discovered me that evening, really found me lovable, or were they actors acting as loving parents?"

"Oh, Anna. Did you ever find out?" I asked.

"No, but that unusual parental behavior continued on the way home, away from the cameras, so it felt real. I never knew for sure. They left countless films I can only hear. I hear their laughter, their voices reciting well-rehearsed lines as movie characters. In that brief time I knew them, before it all ended, I thought how easy it would be to learn to love them. One night, Carly. That's all I had."

What of my own parents, I thought. Would I have loved them had I known them? What did it feel like, having parents for a day? I'd been too young when I lost mine to remember even one day. I remained silent, my fingers playing along her lower spine, absorbing Anna's pain, making it mine.

A fleeting memory passed, of a loving face smiling down at me, a hand reaching down to hold mine. Was it a vision of Kyra? Of my mother?

Anna sensed my mental pictures. She kissed the tears I didn't realize were running down my face.

"I want to wipe out all those losses and give you only happiness."

"You already have," I said.

We were both silent, listening to the wind, to the waves hitting the rocks, to the call of an owl.

This was odd.

"Where's the owl?" I asked. "Isn't it up there in a tree, too far away for us to hear above the noise of the breakers?"

"Welcome to my weird existence," she said. "Happy anniversary."

"One month and I'm a freak like you."

"Together we'll rule the world."

Her embrace shielded me from the wind.

"On the way home I told them that Johnny and I were married. They were shocked for a moment. Not legally, I clarified, but we would be soon. Mama was going to help me plan the wedding, choose my dress. We laughed a lot and acted like a normal family. Mama asked if I was interested in acting at all. 'You really dazzled them,' she said. They'd help me get my foot in the door if that's what I wanted. I said maybe eventually, but that I was presently working on a new technique in painting and had to finish my life's work. They were actually interested in my work. Papa chuckled, saying I was too young for talking about a life's work and that my life would include a lot of works I'd love. I had no idea he was so knowledgeable about art history. He knew Caravaggio's work and the Dutch painters quite well.

"Carly, they didn't try to sway me away from my choice of painting over acting, for my decision to get married so young. They were happy for me. I promised to take them down to the basement and show them my work as soon as we got home.

"Papa hit something in the road. He swerved and lost control of the car. The coast road up to Palos Verdes, as you know, is dark and serpentine. It all happened so fast, I remember little of it. The last thing I saw was a bright light from a passing car and my own orange dress."

"Is that why you . . . ?"

I didn't know how to phrase my question without weaving the word *see* into it.

"Yes," she said. "That's why I focus so much on the color orange. It was the last full color I remember seeing, the only color I could see for years after the accident. Now the color I most long for." She shook her head. "I recall neither the crash, nor the rescue. I woke up in the hospital with a headache, having suffered only a few scratches and a mild concussion. Johnny and Flora were by my side. I was the only survivor in a crash that had instantly killed both my parents. I stayed in the hospital a few days, sleeping on and off, confused, heartsick, in disbelief."

"Did they tell you right away?" I asked. "How did they break the news to you?"

"It was so horrible and surreal, the actual hearing about it is a total blur," she said, sitting up, wrapping one edge of the blanket around me and the other, around herself. "I only remember anything now because of what Flora has told me since then.

"Back to the moment of waking up . . . A few things seemed strange as soon as I opened my eyes. Johnny and Flora seemed flat, two dimensional. Everybody did—nurses, doctors—like they were painted on a canvas. The depth was sucked out of objects. When I got up and moved around the room, I felt odd. Imagine the contents of a room sweeping behind you like veils in slow motion.

"I stayed in bed. I asked for the newspaper and Johnny got it for me, despite Flora's protests. The story of my parents' deaths was splashed on the front page. I knew what I was looking at only because of their photos and mine. I could read nothing. The text appeared to be in Hebrew and Greek. All the hospital signs were similar, so I thought nothing of the strange alphabets and wrote it off to concussion.

"I was too overwhelmed by everything else to pay attention to those visual irregularities. I wanted to go home to my normal life. In a day or two I could read again. People regained their depth, and objects stopped flowing behind me in nauseating waves. I was back at home.

"Something big was still missing, but I didn't know what it was. I was so preoccupied with the obvious disaster, my greater tragedy didn't hit yet."

What could be a greater tragedy than losing both parents at once?

Now, having seen Anna's paintings, I knew.

56

As Juliet spoke, Kyra admired the delicate curve of her neck, the smoothness of her milk-chocolate skin.

"We were done filming. Anna had a party at her house, a spontaneous celebration of mutual admiration. We were toasting this and that and each other. I felt high, proud, accomplished, and I was dressed for a change, dressed to the nines. We were all standing on the deck at sunset, wine glasses in hand, when Anna came behind me, pressed the length of her body to mine, and asked in a whisper if I'd stay when everyone else left.

"You can imagine my excitement, my anticipation. Then Anna and I were alone. For the first time alone, with no others between us or surrounding us or needing us. The sun had set and the air got cold. She took off her sunglasses, slowly, put them on top of her head. Her eyes were light gray and misty. 'My Leila,' she whispered. Then she kissed me with great love."

"Self-love," Kyra said.

"What?" Juliet was shaken from her state of reverie, surprised to find Kyra next to her.

"Falling in love with one's own creation is the absolute statement of narcissism," Kyra said. "She looked at you and saw herself."

"I didn't care if she saw Attila the Hun and called me Cleopatra, because it was all so incredible. We barely made it to her bedroom. We spent the next week devouring each other, insatiable. Never in my life was I so worshipped. We made love everywhere. On every surface—vertical, horizontal, you name it. She has those hands . . . She could sense my every desire with the tips of her fingers."

"Yeah, I bet her hands are fucking magic," Kyra said through clenched teeth.

"It's more than the obvious. I swear she has healing powers. She knew when and where I ached, and she could take away any pain with a touch of her fingertips. It's hard to explain."

"Spare me." Kyra pushed her empty shot glass away in disgust, gulped Diet Coke and let out a loud burp that would have put Zoe to shame. She hated that the vampire had touched the beautiful woman she adored and already considered her woman.

Lost in her recollection, Juliet was oblivious to Kyra's suffering.

"Champagne for breakfast, sensual massages for lunch, and all day long her hands on me and those gray eyes seeing straight into my core."

"But in the end it wasn't worth the trouble, right?" Kyra asked hopefully.

"I know that your sister and I aren't exactly friends, but no one deserves this. Get her away from there before—"

"Before what?"

"Before she becomes another sucker, like me."

"Don't blame yourself. How could anyone resist?"

Juliet stared down at her scarred wrists. "Soon afterwards, the change started. My love kept growing, but hers was dying. Whereas before she looked into my core, now she looked through me, eyes distant, like she didn't see me. Or didn't understand what she was doing with me."

"What about *La Dolce Vita*?" Kyra mimed stirring a pot and then tasting the spoon.

Juliet seemed puzzled for a split second, then chuckled and bit her lower lip. "Dear Flora remains my close friend. She has a heart of gold and she is very loyal to Anna—practically her mother. I love sitting in the kitchen, watching her cook."

"Doesn't Anna mind?"

"Anna doesn't know."

"She must know," Kyra said. "Wouldn't Flora tell her mistress?"

"Flora keeps my visits a secret. I hide my car. When I hear the crackling of the Jaguar on the gravel, I split through the kitchen. I have a great system."

"Why invent such a system when you should use your inventive energy to find a new lover?"

"One doesn't exclude the other," Juliet said coyly. "Last night Flora called and asked me to help her cook an unexpected dinner for five, but Flora cooks dinners for fifty at the drop of a hat. She wanted me to meet someone new."

Kyra pointed at herself, raising her eyebrows. "She pimped us together?"

Juliet nodded.

"I knew I loved her for more than her cooking," Kyra said. "Why, Juliet? Why do you keep going back?"

"I want to understand exactly what happened."

Her eyes were so sad, Kyra's heart went out to her.

"I want to tell you, but it may sound pathetic. Totally pathetic."

"Try me."

"Once, when Flora went out to the garden for tomatoes, I climbed the stairs to Anna's bedroom, opened her closet and stuffed one of her dresses into my purse."

Kyra gasped. "You *stole* from her closet?"

"It was a fluke. It isn't like you hooked up with a klepto."

"Okay," Kyra said, not so sure.

"Well, it was a clingy, flimsy dress she'd wear with nothing else. How easily I could slide it off of her . . . It weighed nothing at all and it smelled of this musk she wears. I slept with it on my pillow for a long time, until the musk wore off. But now I can't be around musk at all."

Kyra didn't want Juliet to take her farther down that road and, mercifully, she didn't.

"I need to get a life," Juliet said.

Kyra pulled her onto her lap. "If I can be of any help, sweetie, you just got yourself a life." Her big hands covered Juliet's entire back, protecting her. "You're not going back to that house, if I have to restrain you in my arms." She was doing exactly that.

"I'm not going back," Juliet repeated, melting into Kyra, as if having needed permission to relax. "Did you notice," she asked, "how the sense of smell leaves us with the most potent memories?"

Kyra more than noticed. Her doctoral thesis included a section on the erotic power of perfumes. She slid the white tank top down and gently kissed Juliet's fragrant shoulder.

"Lavender," Kyra said. "Forever etched in my memory." She was eager to put an end to *that* love story and start her own. "How exactly did it end?"

"It was brutal," Juliet said. "One night it was over."

"Did she fall in love with someone else?"

"Yes. Do you mind if we stop now?"

"Tell me this." She held Juliet's thin wrists and kissed the linear, white scars. "Is that when you . . . ?"

She nodded.

A chill ran down Kyra's spine. She'd had all the tools to help Juliet, but she hadn't known her then. Had she succeeded . . . What if . . . ?

That notion was unbearable.

"Thank heavens you failed," Kyra said, choking on emotion.

"Oh, Kyra . . ." Juliet let a giggle slip into a sob. "What do you think about such pathetic behavior?"

"You want my educated opinion?" Kyra cleared her throat. "Well, there are two schools of thought." She pushed her sliding glasses up and put on her lecture face. "One philosophy believes in simply a bed, but reaching one may take too long. The quick fix will be the back seat of my Wrangler."

Juliet smirked. "Will you photograph the back seat of your Wrangler for that file?"

"Sure. For the *hot surfaces* file that will soon be the size of Manhattan."

A new group of noisy girls had swarmed into the G-Spot, filling the place with squeals of laughter.

"Two a.m.," B. J. announced. "Last call for drinks."

Juliet, still in Kyra's lap, rested her head on her shoulder. "Let's go fuck," she said. "But forget the Wrangler. My bed or yours?"

Kyra said, "My bed is only two blocks away."

"You win." Her full lips were soft and warm on Kyra's and so alive. When Kyra opened her eyes, B. J. was glaring at her from behind the bar, wiping off glasses, closing for the night.

You suck, Doc, she mouthed.

Kyra didn't even smile in response. This was not one of those one-nighters she'd boast about in the morning. Even if all they had was one night, Juliet was different.

57

Anna woke up startled. "Don't let me fall asleep again," she said. "The sun may come up, and I'm screwed without my shades." Then she laughed bitterly. "But what does that matter now?"

"Can you see anything at all?" I asked, waving my hand in front of her.

She didn't flinch.

"Nothing," she said.

"Are you sure you don't need to see a doctor?"

"So to speak." She chuckled. "Hildi called Bernie and he'll come today, for what it's worth."

She sat up, sniffing the air, listening. "What time is it? The tide sounds and smells like three a.m. or so."

I checked my cellphone. "You make clocks obsolete," I said. "Exactly three oh one."

"We have an hour, no more." She pressed herself closer to me and I was warm.

"The funeral of Hollywood's dream couple was a real shindig, a true media circus. I was showered with the love of famous strangers, my parents' friends and colleagues, other actors I knew only from movies or from occasional dinner parties my parents had given at home. I wanted only Flora and Johnny. They would help me find myself again. I wanted to go back to a semblance of a normal life, to my work.

"I knew there was something wrong with my vision, even allowing for my grief and physical recovery. Colors seemed distorted, at times bursting like rainbows out of objects. At times colors were lacking altogether. I blamed it all on my crying.

"Flora, Johnny and I were finally alone and in front of the TV. It was almost like the old times. All the channels kept playing footage from that children's hospital charity event, replaying Mama's speech, the standing ovation, saying that Marco and Irena died together, just as they'd lived together. They kept showing clips from their famous *Romeo and Juliet*. Clips from the event, of the three of us together. They called me the stunning girl who would now have to live without the most important people in her life. They made such a big deal of how my orange gown seemed like autumn leaves against the blue sky of Mama's gown. *Such closeness between mother and daughter, such harmony. What a loss.*

"About two weeks after the funeral I found it in me to go back down the spiral staircase to the basement. There I was dealt the greatest blow yet. I could see the canvas I'd been working on, and I knew what should have been on it, but I couldn't see it, the image. I could see straight lines and edges, but the painting itself was just a gray surface with a black or white line here and there. I could see orange where I'd used it, but the image, my creation, was flat and meaningless.

"My unrestrained scream froze the blood in my own veins. Instantly Johnny was down the stairs and by my side. I was more hysterical than I'd been at my parents' double funeral. He was wearing a vermillion-red scarf, so red I had to close my eyes against it.

"I said, 'Rosso' in my distress and confusion, naturally slipping into Italian. He asked why I was calling him Rosso. I said, 'Because you are red.' As he held me, the red split into more colors, becoming an aura that surrounded both of us. The aura shifted, moving the air with our movements. We were engulfed by a bright rainbow. 'Can you see it,' I asked. But he didn't. It was me. My vision."

"You've painted it," I said, remembering the canvas with the image of a man wearing a red scarf.

"I did, didn't I?" Anna's sharp intake of breath told me she was reliving past horrors.

"You captured the wild colors and the moment of fear."

"You're right. When I glanced back at my paintings, they were distorted, not exactly true to color, but I could see them well enough to realize what had been missing before. I stared at the paintings and then at Johnny. With my back to the paintings, I pushed him away, made him leave, go up the stairs to where I couldn't see him. And I turned back to my canvases. The colors were again gone, leaving only black, gray and dull brown. I called for Johnny to return. Color returned with him."

She shivered and so did I. I ran a shaky hand across her back, needing to comfort her. Looking for comfort for myself.

"When Johnny wasn't present, the colors were gone. Everything was flat." She shook herself and turned to me. "The name *Rosso* stuck. I called him Rosso till the day he died. He was my colors."

She said *my colors* as one would say *my life*.

"The lack of colors confused and sickened me. It's one thing to watch an old black and white film—your mind fills in the gaps and you make the extrapolation into color. But a three-dimensional world without colors is disorienting, morbid. The walls, the sky, the *ocean* were either black or white. Flowers were the worst. A black rose seems dead. My world became an alien planet, foreboding, frightening. And what happened to the sun, black in a white sky, turned every morning to an apocalypse. My disaster dawned on me."

She ran her hands on the back of my neck, where tension from the fall was spreading. Those seeing, feeling, loving hands kept searching my body for injuries.

"You'll be sore tomorrow," she said.

"Already am."

"Let's go up," she said. "Here I am, talking away instead of putting you to bed."

"I'd rather stay here and listen to you," I said, dreading the climb. "Please go on."

"Only a little longer, then up," she said. "As the daughter of the late, beloved stars, nothing was denied me. Flora and Rosso took care of everything, scheduled appointments with the best specialists in ophthalmology and optometry. Nothing was wrong with my eyes. A neurologist, after tests, revealed the bad news.

"I was told I was lucky to have survived the accident, lucky to see anything at all, because the concussion had injured my occipital lobe, the part of the brain responsible for visual perceptions. My eyes were fine, but I couldn't see, remember, or as much as imagine colors. I could see the canvas, but not the image painted on it. Flat images—paintings, films, photographs, even a mirror's reflection—became meaningless to me.

"'But when Rosso is with me,' I said, 'I can see colors. When Rosso walks in, he turns the world red, then to psychedelic colors.' At that, the neurologist referred me to a psychotherapist, assuming that I was going insane from grief. He was right about that.

"The psychotherapist was next, but she only wanted to talk about my parents, as they all did. She was more interested in their fame and their tragic deaths. A session with her felt and sounded like one of those TV interviews. I quickly gave up therapy. I tried ridiculous pathways instead. I went to a hypnotist and a medium, hoping to communicate with my parents—a Ouija board, can you believe it?—I gave up on that also. They barely had anything to do with me when they were alive; why would they bother now?"

I ran the back of my hand on Anna's soft cheek, feeling the sadness seeping from her words.

"I tried drugs, even illegal street drugs. Nothing. Only Rosso's presence helped me see color. Distorted, inconsistent color, but it was better than nothing. He was the first of only three people who would give me hope. He was my green, yellow, blue, and mostly red."

"How exactly did he make you see with his presence? Did you ever figure it out?"

"It was a mystery we didn't want to unravel. We were afraid to break the magic. I kept painting, but it wasn't the same. I would mix red and black to achieve that mystic quality of burgundy, but I didn't see it. I *couldn't* see it.

"I'd been robbed of a chunk of my life. Color blindness wouldn't have been such a big deal for anyone else—people adjust, they learn to live in black and white and even enjoy the benefits. For a while my colorless vision became very sharp, with marked edges, dramatic corners, supersharp details. At night I could see like a hawk, spot a fly on top of a building.

From the deck I could see a fish under water. But that talent was wasted on me, as I had no interest in catching flies or fish.

"Rosso started painting *The Turning* on that very wall down in the basement. We still had each other, yet I was more dependent on him. Even my dreams were in black and white. I became entombed in a gray concrete prison, with stark black bars in my window. Dull brown was gradually replacing lively orange."

I played with her hair, feeling with my fingers the braids Robert had weaved in it only hours ago, but which seemed like years.

"What about shades of white?"

"White came in through the blackness as bright light only to give me headaches and to throw a glare on the page. Reading made me nauseated, and I could only paint in Rosso's presence. I tried to live with the loss. Some days I was depressed, some days hopeful and child-like as I discovered new perceptions and abilities. You call those *freaky senses.* I call them collaterals, the affirmations of life in the presence of death. Pleasure and pain were intensified. Johnny and I became even more sexual, the way I am with you."

"No complaints from me," I said, kissing her lips.

She responded, pressing me to her—eager, warm, soft. I pulled her on top of me and this time we didn't even bother taking off our clothes.

"No complaints at all," I repeated afterward, calming my racing heart. Then I said, "*The Turning* is really a wall sculpture. He worked thousands of ridges into it with the palette knife."

"He wanted me to see it with my fingertips."

"In case you lost your vision completely?"

"In case I lost him."

It started raining. A powerful downpour washed over us, drenching us in the wet sand, inside the blanket. I couldn't help but cry with her. The love, the beauty, the sorrows she had known so long ago, now belonged to me.

58

The climb back up the cliff was a dreamy haze, with the flannel pajamas sticking to my achy body, the slippery rocks looming grand and threatening above my head, the access ladder and the storm pipe running on both sides, and Anna's instructions sounding calm in my ears.

"Don't look up, don't look down, just listen to me," she said. "You're doing great, love. We're almost home."

I imagined a steamy bath, fluffy towels and a warm bed waiting for me at the top. When I opened my eyes, we were both sprawled on the deck like wet trout on the bottom of a fishing boat.

"Did you carry me up?" I asked, exhausted beyond exhaustion. I knew she was strong and capable, but she wasn't superhuman.

"Don't be silly," she said. "We did it together."

When I next opened my eyes, bubbles covered me up to my neck. A blurry creature spoke to me with concern, her golden-platinum hair dripping wet.

"You're not bad looking," I said, my voice groggy. "But why do you have two heads?"

"Because you're burning with fever."

"Did you hoist me up the stairs too?"

"That's ridiculous," she reprimanded, washing my face with warm bath water. "In-house hoisting is Hildi's job."

"You drag me up and down rocks at night," I said, "and now you drown me."

"You think you can get out of the water by yourself?" she asked.

I laughed. "Off to our next adventure!"

"Straight to bed." She wrapped a big towel around me. "And no more hanky-panky for you tonight."

"But it's already tomorrow," I protested.

Satin sheets met my nakedness. In the dark, her healing hands began at my still-wet scalp, gently moving down my body, rubbing every muscle with her musk oil, as she had many times before, yet carefully, as though I'd become fragile. She didn't rush. When she was done, she slipped in next to me, her naked body radiating delightful warmth into mine. I ran my hands down the curve of her lower back, feeling small spasms of arousal within me. She gasped a little, held my wrists down and kissed my forehead.

"Rest now, my love. We have forever."

Her arms enclosed me. Rain pounded on the windowpane, waves thundered against the rocks and I was safe. Anna spoke to me in all her loving languages until I slept.

There are no jokes, said Kyra. Her green eyes leaped out of her face and into a jar. Eyeballs stared at me from more jars on shelves along the basement walls. Kyra's. Greg's. Zoe's. Robert's. Anna's. Mine. Eyeballs everywhere! One pair of eyeballs, dark and burning, I didn't know. Johnny's . . .

I woke up in spasms of a dry cough, the air wheezing through the thin straw of my sore throat, my heart pounding. The red digital display of the clock had just clicked five. Dawn lit the sky and the ocean. Anna woke up next to me.

"I had a dream about eyeballs in jars."

"Can you dream me up a working pair?" she asked.

No jokes.

She reached for a water mug on her bedside table and passed it to me, spilling most of it on the bed. "Can't trust me with open containers," she said, laughing.

She turned back to the table and fumbled in a drawer until she found a red paperback copy of John Cheever's short stories. She smelled the pages longingly, as she did every book she picked up. She started flipping through the pages.

"I lost them," she said, terrified.

"What are you looking for?"

She sighed with relief. "These are all I have left."

The photos she handed me were old, dog-eared, washed out. In the first one I could make out a man sleeping on a colorful beach towel. Dark face; wide forehead; long hair, streaked with the sun; full eyelashes; slight dark circles around his eyes; tight bone structure at his cheeks; ears and nose too large for his face.

"Tell me what you see," she urged, eager. "How would you paint his portrait?"

She exclaimed with each detail I described. "Yes, this is my Rosso. Yes, big ears and nose, and long hair. I'd moved it away from his face, before taking this photo, careful not to wake him."

I'd never seen her so excited, animated, so childlike.

I said, "He's wearing a white T-shirt with a soccer ball and a name. Marco something."

"Tardelli. Rosso loved Italian football." She laughed, giddy.

"His right hand is bandaged, resting on his stomach."

"Ah," she said, remembering. "He injured his hand with the chisel. What about the other photo?"

"It's only black and white." I regretted what I said as soon as the words left my mouth.

"What a shame." Anna chuckled. It was hard to offend her.

A boy and a girl posed by the water, holding hands. The boy's head rested on the girl's shoulder. Light streamed between their outlines from behind, reducing them to ghostly silhouettes. Rosso's head seemed to move. The sun sprinkled gold in the girl's short hair where it would later go silver. A giggle. A squeal of children playing.

I shook off the feverish image. Anna's hand came between my eyes and the faded photo. She ran two fingers on it, caressing its surface, then gently touched her fingers to her lips. Jealousy stabbed me. Rosso was dead, she hadn't seen him or his photo for years, but something—alive beyond reason—made me afraid for Anna. For myself.

59

In the kitchen I set the coffee pot to brew and took some aspirins. My throat was sore. My muscles were seized up from my neck down as a result of the fall down that slippery slope. Last night I'd lost my mind for a moment, long enough to feel exhilaration at facing a phobia. Yet instead of conquering that phobia, as I should have, I'd left my courage down at the cove, rolled up in a big blanket soaked with our love and tears and the rain.

As the coffee brewed, sending its delicious aroma into the cool morning—Anna ordered it especially from Puerto Rico—I watched the bay through the glass wall of the kitchen. In the distance, the Santa Monica Mountains touched the cobalt blue water.

Anna stood behind me, embracing me. She owned this heaven, worked and paid for all of us to enjoy it, while she remained in the dark.

"You opened a window in my darkness," she said simply, still surprising me when she responded to my mental images.

"I wish I could break the walls open for you," I said, taking her in my arms.

"But you have," she said.

As the sun didn't frighten her anymore, she didn't wear her sunglasses. This was the first time I saw her gray, slightly unfocused eyes in full light, and they were beautiful.

She ran her seeing fingers over my entire face, fleetingly, as if a glance was all she needed.

"Even now . . ." Her voice broke. "Now that it's too late for me to dream of painting again, I still sense the bay and its vast cobalt-ness and aquamarine through you. You make my senses sing, Carly. You are my LSD trip."

"LSD?" I gaped at her, surprised. "You did . . . ?"

"And everything else." She smiled. "When you looked through my paintings, did you happen to come upon a jungle scene?"

"I sure did," I said. "Lush, magnificent, brilliant. It has clever perception of depth, but the colors are confusing, psychedelic."

"That's it."

Her phone rang. She made an appointment with her neurologist for the next morning. He wanted to run some tests, find out whether something could be done about her vision. Another phone call came regarding a scheduled weekend-long celebration of her literary works.

I knew she dreaded public appearances when she could still see a little. What would she do now?

As she rested the phone down, her hand bumped into a coffee mug featuring a partially peeled orange, the logo from her award-winning film. She searched for the cream and missed it simply because it wasn't exactly in its usual spot. I poured it for her and stirred her coffee. Here was a woman strong and capable enough to carry a grown person up a wall of slippery rocks, yet she messed up a job a ninety-year-old could easily do.

"Look at me, bumping into things in my own home." She dropped her face into her hands. "I don't know about appearing in public, now that I can't tell night from day."

"This may be a good opportunity to come clean," I said. "Tell your fans the truth."

"Out of the question," she said sharply, sounding like the Divine One again. "I have a week to practice my blind walk in high heels with you on my right and Hildi on my left."

She paced the five steps to the window, faced the gorgeous morning, the purple mountains on the other side of the blue bay. She saw nothing. Her hand went to her face as a habit, to push up the sunglasses that weren't there.

"Look, Carly, no shades!" she said with a new realization. "I feel naked without them."

"Are you sure you don't need to wear them?"

"No headache yet," she said, pacing the floor barefoot. Five steps to the window, five steps back to where I sat having my coffee, wondering in amazement how it was possible that she strode so confidently, seemed so proud and sure of herself, when deep down her fear was immense at each step.

I said, "I'd like to paint your portrait, here and now, if you'll sit still."

She was distracted. "I used to love painting in full daylight," she said dreamily, "After the accident, when light hurt my eyes, Rosso and I moved my studio to the dark basement. He had given up sculpting, temporarily, until I'd adjusted. We worked well together. He didn't exactly mix my palette, but his presence, his voice and smell and touch, turned into colors. Does that make sense?"

"No, but I've heard about LSD trips," I said.

"One morning we were tripping a little from the previous night, still jumpy, but happy. I'd been immersed in painting my jungle scene; Rosso worked on *The Turning*. Then we were hungry. I decided to fetch us some lunch. As I ran up the stairs, he called me. I turned back to look at him. He said, 'Hold it there.' Then he worked rapidly for a few minutes before he blew me a kiss. Carly, for a moment, he was engulfed in that crimson aura I'd gotten so used to seeing around him, only, that particular time, as I was looking down at him, it was frightening . . . like . . ."

"Like a premonition?"

"Yes. On my way back from the kitchen, I smelled the fumes. Then a white tongue leaped from the black mouth of the staircase. Have you ever seen a completely white flame? Of course not. You can see colors. I cried out and started down the stairs, but Flora grabbed me from behind and dragged me away —she was very strong twenty years ago. Someone, maybe the gardeners, called the fire department. It was too late. When the fire was extinguished, Rosso's . . . when it was extinguished . . . Carly, the smell stays with you. It never leaves. . ."

Anna came close and touched my face, as if to feel my reaction. Something nagged at me.

"Do you think your face was the last thing he sketched?"

"I don't know," she said. "I just saw him sketch rapidly."

"Your face in the painting is frightened."

"Is it?"

"Haven't you seen the fear . . ." I stopped myself. "I can't believe how dense I am."

"I've never seen it finished," she said. "He'd planned to paint my expression in minimalism, he'd said. 'A few quick, clean lines would do you justice.'"

Her naturally pale face was now drained of blood, so ashen, I feared she'd collapse.

"You say I look frightened in *The Turning*?"

"Terrified."

"I caused his death," she said slowly. "His death had been a direct result of my turning."

"How's that?"

She spoke slowly, recreating a lost memory. "When Rosso got stuck on a problem, he'd worry about it for days. When he worked his marble in the garden, I'd seen him raise his index finger in the air, as if saying, *I got it!* Then he'd automatically reach for a cigarette, celebrating his success."

"But surely he didn't light up in an enclosed space filled with solvents!" I said.

"That LSD the night before may have screwed up his judgment. I turned to glance at him. He quickly sketched something, then blew me a kiss, and I went up the stairs. Had I not turned, he would not have lit that cigarette, he would have lived. I kept up the stairs, but I can imagine him saying, *I got it*, then absentmindedly lighting that one last cigarette."

She covered her face and I tried not to imagine a room igniting with instant flame.

"It seemed the whole fire department was there, in the smoke-filled basement. Flora tried to stop me, but I pushed my way through the rescuers. Rosso's charred body was . . . his entire face was gone. I can still smell the burning flesh . . ."

"I fell to my knees in front of him. They all gazed at me with pity and compassion, but, unfairly, so alive. More than anything I felt this huge disappointment. Rosso and I believed our great love for each other had protected us. We thought we were immortal. I supported his head in my lap . . . tried to communicate with him in our usual way, through mental images, but the joining thread was gone."

I watched in dread as Anna dropped suddenly to her knees on the kitchen floor and stared down at her hands, wide-eyed.

She whispered, "Dead? It can't be."

A chill of dread and amazement went through me at the sight of her. In her mind she was back at that basement, many years ago, cradling Rosso's burned body. She wore an expression of disbelief and defeat, her face the marble white of Michelangelo's *Pietà*.

"*Perché?*" she whispered, her cheeks wet with tears. "Why? It's a mistake. He's mine."

I crouched next to her on the kitchen's immaculate floor, watching her disintegrate, fall completely apart. I was mesmerized and, more than anything, guilty. Because as Anna was re-living that terrible moment, I could not help but admire her beauty.

I touched her gently. She started, realizing I was there.

"Oh, God. Carly." She dropped her head on my shoulder, exhausted. "I don't know what came over me. Forgive me."

"Hush, love," I said.

She was very silent in my arms, both of us unmoving on the floor.

"How lucky Mama and Papa were, not to be parted by death. Don't leave me, Carly."

"I'm here," I said.

Then she sat up tall.

The morning sun beamed on her paleness. Long locks of hair had come loose to frame her face. Despite the turmoil in my heart, I thought what a shame it was that mirrors were useless to her. She sat motionless for so long, I didn't have to ask her not to move. With a black marker Flora used for the grocery lists, I quickly sketched—on a paper towel—a preliminary study for a work I'd title Beautiful Grief.

"I lost Rosso. I lost painting. Reading nauseated me, but I could still see well enough to use a typewriter. I was twenty-two when I wrote my first novel."

"*Scorched Earth*," I said. That novel had started my nightmares of a world burned of its colors.

I stopped drawing. We held each other on the floor, rocking slightly back and forth.

"Carly," she said. "Carly, Carly, Carly." The sound of my name reverberated like a sigh of pain.

"Not Rosso?" I asked.

"Only you, my Carly," she said. "Thank you for helping me see and remember."

As we rocked together into peacefulness, her hands slid under my T shirt. "Enough sadness." She kissed my forehead, my eyes, the tip of my nose. "Enough art and artists . . . fuck the Dutch masters, the Italians, your cobalt-blue ocean. There's only us, in love, right here."

"Right here," I repeated, hypnotized by the rocking motion, lulled into peace by the music of her voice. "Us . . . Here?"

"And now."

She kissed me slowly, deeply.

I could hear Flora upstairs, getting ready for another day, the hardwood creaking under her old feet in her big slippers. Soon she and Hildi would be in the kitchen.

"You're crazy," I said, breathless, my insides turning to water.

Then she pulled me up and off the floor and, with one sweeping motion of her arm, she cleared off the kitchen counter, barely missing Flora's gaudy ceramic chicken, neither seeing nor caring that a glass crashed into the sink. Despite my protests, she pulled down my shorts and lifted me onto the cold, marble surface with the fine Carrara grain.

"Someone may come in," I whispered, but I didn't really care.

Her voice was coarse with desire when she said, "This is *my* house, damn it, and if I want to eat you in my kitchen, they should all stay away."

She took me there, on the immaculately clean marble counter, where Flora had, only the previous night, prepared her famous Sicilian vegetable lasagna.

And even as Flora's ceramic chicken was digging into my back and the cold marble pushed hard against my ass and Anna's hungry mouth and wild whispers were on me and in me and above and beyond me, making the world and everyone in it irrelevant, fear still gnawed at me and I remembered.

Deep down below was the Land of the Dead. It had remained dark and dormant for many years, but now I'd seen it glowing with light, more brilliant than the sun. Anna's imprisoned art revealed and set free. Only last night I'd been touched to the core, changed forever. I simply could not get those paintings out of my mind.

Even now—maybe because she was making love to me—the memory of those vivid colors stirred all my other senses and made me hear and feel and taste magnificence.

And I knew that it was up to me to take that brilliance out of its captivity. I was the only one who understood what colors did to her and what she was expressing in each painting. I was the only one who could restore those works. Greg knew it first, then Anna, and now I knew it too. The deep honor was mine alone, the responsibility to restore Anna's paintings and take them out to the world.

There, below, in that place of brilliance and shadows, lurked my private Hades. He had something that belonged to me and he was holding fast to it, unwilling to give it up.

60

The light on my face woke me up. The rain had stopped, and the afternoon rays slowly traveled along the red and white bedroom; along a bookcase filled with volumes Anna could not read; along her dresser, on which her smashed mirror reflected polygons of broken light. So much had happened since she'd put her fist through it. Only yesterday I knew nothing about her and now . . .

I wanted to stay like this forever, spooned, naked and warm in her arms, knowing no more. Knowledge meant disaster.

"I did a good job on that mirror," she murmured, her face buried in the back of my neck.

"You can see again," I said, excited.

"Not in your terms. I see glimpses through you, not much, but you have no idea . . . no idea what this little bit does to me and how crazy you make me . . ."

Her knee parted my legs from behind. I tried turning around to face her, but she held me still.

"I want you like this, my Carly," she whispered, her voice urgent. "You see for me, now come for me. Like this, if you can take it."

Then I was face down on the pillow, and both her knees parted my thighs wide, and her hands, those strong hands, calloused from rock climbing, and very warm, caressed and stimulated me gently for a new adventure.

"Did I tell you what it feels like, seeing through you?" she whispered in my ear. "Your impressions inside me turn into colorful butterflies and travel through my mind stretching rainbows, squeezing oil paint out of tubes . . ."

As she spoke she became aroused along with me. She slowly invaded me in a whole new raw and sweet way, then in another way, and it felt like she was turning me inside out.

"Ah . . ." I cried out. "I'm not a bowling ball . . ."

She paused. "Should I stop?"

"Don't you dare . . . don't stop . . ." I moaned.

I became a prisoner in her arms as she took me whole, all of me, until pain and want twisted together into a wild and powerful vortex of intense surprise and savage pleasure.

Then I free-floated, weightless, in another dimension luminous with stars and vivid colors.

And I knew she saw the same stars, because she cried out with me and collapsed on top of me and she was crying with me.

We remained still a long while, catching our breaths, calming our hearts.

I finally recovered enough to say, "That move made me faint, I think."

"My anniversary gift to you." Her voice smiled although my cheek was wet with her tears. Then we faced one another, and I kissed her tears away.

"Your reds and greens thrill me," she said. "Your blues blow my mind. But what I've only now seen, what made me insane, were those purple spots with the red edges."

"Those vermillion pulsating edges?" I held her face, astonished. "You saw that?"

"In my mind." A catch shook her voice. "It was overwhelming."

"You can see through me, you really can," I said. "I admit I had some doubts until this moment. Wow. Vermillion edges, alive and pulsing and dripping greens and pinks and—"

"And orange," she said. "Here you are, starting me all over again and we both need rest."

"Did you drop acid?"

"This was wilder than acid. Just the two of us and this bond, our love."

We stayed like that, dozing and waking, the sweet soreness from her loving still inside me. Then the sun was lower in the sky, shining brighter into my eyes, when I thought again of what she had said.

"What did you mean by *Hades has won*?"

Anna didn't answer. I fell asleep again until her voice woke me up.

"The whole world has been my Hades, Carly. I invited you here to be my eyes, and that's what you've become. The night you walked into my life, loathing me, even the hot crimson of your hate filled me with light and warmth. You made the stubborn, filmy veil fall off my face."

Just as Rosso had.

She said, "That first shock of color is very sudden, intense, like the first high of cocaine. Eventually that intensity wanes and I crave that same effect. That same sensual pleasure of bright red or blue."

Strong waves crashed against the rocks below. The wind whistled through the cracked open window.

I asked, "What happened to you when he died?"

"Imagine twenty years of stark black and white, of everything people rave about appearing as a visual threat. The ocean, the sky, the sunset—even the sunrise—all seemed like a nuclear holocaust, an alien planet. What you call white and blue gave off a painful glare with luminous, blinking spots. Red and purple turned black, and the horizon was a black blanket wrapping the world.

"I'd keep going down to the basement to see if anything had changed. As soon as I'd start down the stairs and smell the oil paint, the turpentine, even the dust in the air, I'd be transported to the work I loved and to the memory of Rosso's arms. I'd get disappointed again and again. I knew those canvases contained the heart and soul of my life, yet I couldn't perceive any of it. They remained meaningless with a dark line here, a dull spot of orange there.

"I danced, I made films, I did stage. I wrote fiction. As soon as I'd perfected a new form of art, my vision would drop a notch and I'd have to let it go. Who wanted to see a dancer who tripped all over her own feet, a film made by a director who couldn't see farther than her nose? Then even black and white started their slow fade into gray. Dirty, hateful gray."

"What do you do as a public figure with obligations?" I asked.

"What you do is keep your crappy vision to yourself, but what about the fear in your eyes? You turn dark glasses into a fashion statement and get rave reviews at Cannes about your style. You start a signature line and people copy you.

"Every morning you open your eyes in trepidation, expecting to see one less definitive detail. Then you don't even want to open your eyes, because you fear what will be missing that day. Will it be the corners of your desk? The edges of a table? You blink, but the dark film remains and thickens. You wish for complete darkness, because it's easier than losing your sight bit by bit. The depth, the meaning, the substance are stolen from everything you see. One day Flora's face was gone . . ."

She let her chest rise and fall against mine.

"One day Flora was only a voice. That face I loved that had smiled at me since I was born was gone. And I didn't want to tell her, couldn't break her heart, but Flora knows me too well, and I heard her cry that morning as she cooked my breakfast. 'Why are you crying?' I asked, and she said, 'Sicilians don't cry.'

"Twenty years of visual winter with its constant snowstorms and grays, and I am trapped in it, dying for the spring. What I saw made me cold. I wore fake furs over my swimsuit and next thing I know, fake fur over swimwear is in, getting rave fashion reviews. I couldn't win. I couldn't lose. And I couldn't stay here, at home. Flora and I moved back to Europe."

Anna paused and waved her hand. "It's no good. I sound so pathetic. It isn't like me to talk like this."

"Be pathetic all you want," I said. "It's me you're talking to, not the damned press."

"Make me your 411 Hockey Stick," she said.

"Baseball Bat 911? I'll make a pitcher."

We were down in the kitchen where Flora was busy cooking dinner. I eyed that part of the counter she was using for cutting the salad and thought, What one doesn't know doesn't hurt one, does it?

It took minutes to mix Zoe's most potent drink with all the bells and whistles. It took Anna less time to kill the first glass—

for which I'd used a heavy beer mug, to avoid accidental spills. I offered Flora some, but she declined as she was working on a huge shot of her 80-proof grappa.

We settled on the deck chairs. I described the darkening horizon, the Queen's Necklace, now brightly visible in the post-storm evening.

"Even the fish smell different in this clean air." Anna sipped her drink. "This is strong and perfect. Where was I?"

"You and Flora moved to Europe," I said.

"Yes." She started pacing, restless. "In Italy and France I did some modeling, writing, acting, some dancing—everything to keep myself from going crazy. The name Garibaldi opened doors. I found work easily, but not peace. Peace was a whole different thing.

"We lasted two years in Europe and then I wanted to go back home. To my babies buried below ground. So long without painting, and the need to pick up a brush and go to work on a canvas was eating me alive."

"You could have changed direction," I said, topping off our mugs with the slushy cocktail. "Charcoal, pencil, pen and ink, sculpting. It's all art."

"I'd never found joy in colorless art. It felt like a precursor, a teaser for the real thing. I held on to Rosso's promise that he'd come back to me. I'd spent those twenty years waiting, living for the moment of recognition, busying myself with secondary activities. I wrote and directed plays and films—"

"Amazing plays and films," I said. "An Academy Award nomination, two Indies, a Palme d'Or, and a Pulitzer aren't secondary achievements for most of us."

"Those were definitely nice," she said. "But I craved the impossible. My blues and greens and yellows. I wanted back what was mine: to be alone with my mind, a full palette and a canvas in front of me, painting. In my black and white desolation I had a certain vision of glorifying, eroticizing color. I wrote *Divine Darkness*. Enter Juliet Blair in a white leather tube dress. That was a white-on-black contrast I could see. We made the film. We fell in love."

"Juliet Blair!" I cried out.

"Juliet is an incredible, brilliant actress," Anna said. "I hear her sneaking out through the kitchen door when she visits Flora, and I can always smell her unique mix of soap, shampoo and Ylang Ylang."

"We had an altercation because I saw her taking something from the house. Well, we didn't exactly hit it off."

"She doesn't know about my vision and my extra senses. She thinks I don't know about her visits, and I don't want to embarrass her. Yes, and she is a bit of a kleptomaniac—"

"You knew she stole from you?"

"Not only from me, but what's the harm? Well . . . Juliet is so good to my Flora and, I did hurt her. So she steals." Anna chuckled sadly. "I never missed what she's taken."

"That's not the point!" I could not understand Anna's nonchalance. I asked, "Could she see colors for you?"

"No, but we became inseparable," Anna said. "I so loved her, I nearly came to terms with my colorless life. I planned to show her my art, tell her—and the world—everything. The very night I planned to come out to her, Rosso waltzed back into my life."

"Greg," I said, immediately feeling a pang of inexplicable pain.

She nodded.

61

"Call in sick," Kyra begged, her nose nestled in the sweetness between Juliet's breasts.

"I'll lose my job." Juliet sat on her in protest. "It isn't like those movie contracts are falling into my lap nowadays."

Kyra's hands ran slowly down the smooth trail starting in Juliet's navel and ending in heaven.

"Then tell the truth."

"Mmmm . . ."

"How often do we fall in love like this?" Kyra asked. "We should take time off for real happiness. Later comes first argument, first Christmas, first fart, and before you know it, we'll become an old, boring, married couple ordering pizza and watching *I Love Lucy* reruns and sprouting prickly chin hairs and pot bellies."

Juliet hopped out of bed. Kyra heard her fumbling in the office, searching frantically, opening and closing drawers. *What's she up to?* Kyra dozed off, exhaustion numbing her limbs.

Then Juliet was back, straddling her.

"What were you stealing from me?" Kyra asked, keeping her eyes shut.

Juliet moved on her sexily, wordlessly.

"Really, little girl. You should give an old lady some rest between rounds."

She still said nothing. Kyra opened her eyes and couldn't believe what she saw. Santa Claus sat on her, mustache, beard, belly and all.

She howled. "Where did you find this old thing?"

"A real klepto knows where to search," Juliet said. "I'm giving you a glance into the future."

Kyra pulled her close, searching for a mouth to kiss in all the dense facial hair. "Let's get married today."

"Let's fuck more first," said her bad, bad girl.

Kyra ripped the costume off her and they were at it again.

They rested when, out of nowhere, Juliet blurted out, "He was a nothing, nothing, *nothing*."

"Who?"

"How could she have dumped me for him?"

Kyra said, "Love is blind."

"Maybe she is," Juliet said with disgust. "Do you see the artists she supports? I could never understand her. She is such a perfectionist when it comes to her own work, but those people —"

"Totally useless," Kyra agreed.

"Now I'm over her, I want to tell you about this." Juliet stared down at her scarred wrists.

Kyra gently kissed the thin, white scars. "Tell me."

62

"My Rosso kept his promise," Anna said. "He came back."

We were quiet. I held my breath until it hurt, tightening a blanket around my shoulders, gazing out at the vast and darkening bay, at the Queen's Necklace.

"I like being around artists, hearing them talk about their work, smelling the paint. Those art shows I sponsor get me as close to painting as possible for me. One of those events took place in an industrial space converted into a nightclub and gallery. The huge place was filled with new artists and their colorful works. I assumed those were colorful, for me all was as usual—stark black, boring gray, and glaring white lights.

"Juliet was on my left, knowing only that I loved her and wanted her near me. Hildi was on my right, watching me as always, making sure I didn't trip, aware that my vision was deteriorating. We were greeting people. I was engrossed in conversation with a woman whom I'd recognized only by voice and whose blurry face was stretched in a featureless smile. Then red flashed in the corner of my eye."

She was silent, taking a small sip of her cocktail, then another.

"Red? Just like that?" I asked.

A huge wave thundered below, sending up strong smells of fish and saltwater.

"*Intense* red. So intense, I felt hot and faint from the shocking appearance of color, any color. Only a few feet away stood a stranger who wore a cloak of bright colors. The space between us came to life, filled with rich blue, cerulean, carmine red, aquamarine, burnt sienna, vermillion."

As she named each pigment, I heard the longing in her voice, the bleakness of her colorless existence.

"All those colors danced and sang before my starving eyes. My glass of wine dropped from my shaky hand, and even the sound of its crashing to the metal floor turned into a splattered chromaticity of metallic blues and greens dissolving into each other. It was so fabulous, so utterly amazing, I welcomed even the burning pain in my eyes. I couldn't tell if the stranger was a man or a woman, old or young. I cried out for Rosso!

"By then, Hildi, or maybe Juliet, picked up my sunglasses—which I had dropped—and put them back on my face, but the rainbow of colors remained, the full spectrum. People were fussing around me, wanting to get me this or that. I guess my white dress was spattered with Cabernet. I calmed them down, made them laugh with a silly comment, hoping to be left alone to follow that rainbow."

The wooden planks of the deck creaked under her bare feet as she restlessly paced. She reached me and stopped, then gently ran her fingers through my hair.

"Some think in words; we strange ones think in colors. Light generated from that one person and jumped onto the walls, splashing colors onto the art, infusing the glory of spring into my frozen veins. The pain in my eyes subsided. I could see that the stranger was a man, still, I couldn't tell age or features. His blurred face turned to me, and he reacted right away."

"How? How did he react?"

Even as she played with my hair, my heart squeezed at the memory of the old pain.

"He knew," she said. "It was all so sudden and great and colorful. We shook hands, and his touch . . . I had no doubt. Even he felt it."

And suddenly I smelled the earth, and Greg was there, sandwiched between us, as if having pulled himself out of his casket and six feet up and out of his grave.

"Oh, Carly . . ." she said, letting go of me, frightened at what I was showing her. "Where did *he* come from?"

"From nothing," I said and his image disappeared back into nothing. "I've seen you make an entrance." My voice sounded harsh through my sore throat. "And Greg . . . La Divina picked him out of a crowd and paid him extra attention. He was dazzled by you, like the rest of them, and flattered out of his mind. He felt nothing else."

"Let's stop," she said. "I'm hurting you."

She was right. I asked for the truth, I wanted to know all of it, but I was hurt.

Night was falling, the second night of Anna's story, but I was wide awake and ready to hear the part I feared the most. The chapter of Greg.

63

Juliet leaned against the scalloped headboard, an elaborate piece Kyra had found in India, hand carved with rich patinas and imbued with traditional scenes from the Kama Sutra. Juliet's dark beauty was life imitating art.

"Here's my heartbreak in a nutshell," she said. "Anna wanted me to accompany her to all these events. She isn't a great fan of social functions, but we needed to promote the film. My presence, she said, my arm in hers, simply stabilized her as she was thinking of what she would do to me later."

Kyra stiffened. "Where was Hildi?"

"On her other side, always, like death and taxes. What's with the bodyguard anyway? She isn't a rock star or a head of state."

"Narcissism has a theory." Kyra gently ran a hand on Juliet's smooth thigh. "Go on."

"It was one of her charity art shows. Twenty new artists, a lot of noise and wasted paint, not a smidgen of talent. In that black-tie event, Anna was the only one wearing white. A simple clingy, flowing white dress."

A white dress.

Kyra had a flash of memory that scratched a groove the size of the Grand Canyon across her brain. She and Greg were giggling, bitching about some paintings they both hated, then Garibaldi made her entrance. Her pearl-white dress was later ruined by red wine. Kyra didn't want that memory. It wasn't that same evening at all, it couldn't be. She probably wore white a lot.

"The cameras were in our eyes, lights blinding us," Juliet said. "Rather, only me, because Anna was always protected by those bionic sunglasses. She claimed that bright lights gave her headaches. I tried those shades on once and they are almost opaque. It's a mystery how she gets around. Another thing about her is that complete lack of vanity. Looking at her, you'd think she spends half her life primping in front of the mirror."

"Doesn't she?" Kyra asked.

"Anna barely owns a decent mirror. She'd literally throw something on, wear some lipstick and that's it. Anyway, that night we'd made the usual splash with the cameras and Anna kissing both cheeks of each person and the people kissing her ass. You know, the works. Then she and this guy locked eyes. She dropped her shades, her glass of wine, and everything else, including me."

Kyra's professional reserve was the only thing between her and a raw scream. Yes, it *had* been that very evening! She still had to verify. "Where was that show?"

"That dead powerhouse on the beach."

"Did she cry out *Rosso*?"

"How did you know?"

There was no doubt in Kyra's mind. "I was there."

Juliet leaped out of bed, making the headboard hit the wall in a thud.

"What . . . Where . . . Why . . . Dammit, how?"

"The next night my sister tried on her wedding gown, but she had no one to marry because Garibaldi had stolen her motherfucking fiancé from under her."

Juliet screeched a sound Kyra didn't know she had in her. "Carly was supposed to marry Guido?"

"She was."

"And now she's with her. Ain't that fucking awesome and crazy and . . ." Juliet sat back down. "Whoa, I got a head rush."

"Let's eat. Keep telling me at breakfast."

"It's dinner time," Juliet said, her breath warming up Kyra's naked chest. "See the sunset?"

Kyra squeezed her and said, "*But, soft! what light through yonder window breaks? It is the east, and Juliet is the sun.*"

"*Arise, fair sun, and kill the envious moon,*" Juliet mumbled. "*Who is already sick and —*" She sat up, her brown eyes two large saucers. "Tell me now."

"My story later. First yours, and food." Kyra was frantically trying to remember if she'd left dirty dishes in the sink and when she'd last cleaned the kitchen floor.

"My sad story is done," Juliet said. "It was like curtain down on act two. I didn't stay for act three."

"I stayed till the last curtain call," Kyra said.

"Tell me before I burst," Juliet said.

"Okay."

And Kyra told about that evening, the gallery, the art, how Greg wanted to leave and how there was one more thing she'd wanted to see, and how Anna Garibaldi had walked in, and turned, and saw him, and Carly's life was ruined.

"That was the ultimate Orphean turn," Juliet said. "Like the painting."

"And now she's with her and it is my fault." Kyra laughed out loud, too loud, as she realized how one apparently small event, that one turn, was related to more than one broken heart and many changed fates, including her own.

"Okay, I'm hungry," she said.

"Got eggs and chocolate sauce?" Juliet asked.

"Sure do, Lady Godiva." The combination turned Kyra's stomach. "Something Italian you learned from *La Dolce Vita*?"

"Some of it from Flora, some from *the Divine One*." From her mocking tone, Kyra knew she was definitely over the heartbreak.

"Glad to see you're getting a life."

Juliet wore the white apron Kyra had bought at a WeHo street fair around B. J.'s time. Its front said, *Drink, fuck, eat, in that order*. She pushed a fleeting image out of her mind, that of B. J. cooking breakfast and how she looked like a dude in this apron.

"Do you cook?" Juliet asked, getting busy at the stove.

"Heavens, no," Kyra blurted out, appalled.

Juliet bent over to search for utensils and Kyra so enjoyed the stunning rear view, she didn't help.

"Who wears this lovely apron, then?" Juliet asked.

"Marita used to make this mean chili, but most of it would end up on the floor. Sometimes I can still see the brown spray-splash on the fridge."

"You let a woman throw food at you?"

"It wasn't a temper thing," Kyra said. "Marita was a big slob."

"Who else cooked for you?"

"Saori San did. We used to eat sushi off each other."

"Yuck. Sushi in bed," Juliet said. "How do you get rid of the fishy smell?"

"You don't," Kyra said, reminiscing, leaning back against the wall. "Saori was straight, and she was *my* heartbreak."

Saori had left her husband, children and conventional life to move in with Kyra. They'd had a fiery month in which a tormented Saori fluctuated between the two worlds. Kyra remembered the smell of gardenias, a blue-green bedspread and Saori's cool hair streaming between her fingers like fibers of black silk, so heavy and sleek it squeaked when she played with it. How she'd wanted to hold on to a flower so rare and exotic. Alas, the husband had won. Saori returned to him, leaving Kyra bereft. Carly had picked up the pieces and put Kyra back together.

"At least she didn't offer me a chocolate omelet."

Juliet wore a dirty grin. "Don't be frightened, cowboy. You have an empirical mind. Experiment."

Kyra knew there was a catch. Something had to be fucked because no one could be as perfect as Juliet. She was imagining a scrambled egg with chocolate syrup on top or worse, chocolate filaments marbled into a thick omelet. She gagged. What if Juliet decided to feed her, piece by disgusting piece? Would she be able to fake an appetite to spare her feelings? Could she make up some allergy she'd forgotten about? If worse came to worst, she could always learn to cook, to keep this otherwise perfect woman away from the stove.

"I can't believe you were there," Juliet said.

"I saw you hanging on Garibaldi's arm." Kyra gazed up at Juliet with a smile. "Your exquisite beauty and fragility touched me so deeply, I wanted to approach you with one of my stupid pick-up lines."

"I would have told you to fuck off," Juliet said. She opened the refrigerator. Her tight ass was a perfectly round black peach. Kyra kissed it.

"Forget dinner, Lady Godiva," Kyra said. "I want to dip all of you in chocolate and eat you."

The evening was cool, but they were boiling hot. Kyra took her in front of the open fridge. They held each other a minute longer.

"I'll never have enough of you," Kyra said.

Juliet opened the freezer. "You need to relax and let me work here." She fumbled in the freezer. What was she looking for? Kyra sat back, obedient. Then Juliet turned around and Kyra nearly passed out, seeing what she was holding. The precious spiked bottle of tequila. Ley 925.

"Did you steal it from the G-Spot?" Kyra asked. "Beetlejuice will have my throat!"

"Relax," she said. "Flora gave it to me last night on the way out."

"How could you manage to hide it from me?" Kyra asked.

She smiled and raised an eyebrow. "Practice, practice."

She poured Kyra a shot, then was back to breaking eggs over the stove. "Ask me anything, but don't get in my way anymore. I'm hungry."

"Okay." Kyra sipped. This woman was priceless in many ways. "How did Anna explain the break-up? Did she apologize?"

An egg dropped to the floor.

"I'm sorry," Juliet said. "My hands were shaky."

"No prob." Kyra was down on her knees, cleaning up.

Juliet glanced down at her. "Exactly my point. When an egg breaks, you can explain and apologize. La Divina does neither." She turned back to whatever she was doing at the stove. "I'd heard nothing from Anna for a week. My wrists were still sore, but healing; my heart was trickling blood. As I sat at home, feeling lower than when my mother died, a delivery arrived.

Twelve yellow roses with a white bow, bearing a handwritten note: *Thank you for the good time, AG.*"

"Fuck me," Kyra said, stunned, tossing eggy mess into the trash can.

Juliet stopped scrambling. "The note smelled of her musk, which totally added to the insult. What she'd forgotten was a wad of cash for my services. I felt cheap, discarded, like Marguerite Gautier in act two when what's his face—"

"Armand," Kyra said.

"Yes, Armand—when he throws the money at her." Still facing the stove, Juliet paused and took a deep breath. "My whole body, everywhere she had touched with her love, ached each time I looked at those roses. Still, I couldn't toss them. Moron that I am, I even dried one of them upside down from the light bulb."

Her voice broke. Certain she would cry, Kyra was ready to hold her, console her, but when Juliet turned around, any trace of sorrow was nonexistent.

"Now eat."

Her face wore the proud smile of a French chef. What an actress!

Kyra took a bite, gingerly, and was delighted. The omelet was perfect, seasoned right. They sipped expensive tequila and looked out the window on a bustling, busy West Hollywood night. Kyra savored the fabulousity of the best ever breakfast she'd had for dinner.

Her plate was licked clean when she said, "I couldn't even taste the chocolate."

"In the omelet? *Yuck*, what's wrong with you?"

Kyra wiped her mouth and sighed in relief. "There's no chocolate here, after all that?"

"Oh, but there is." Juliet produced a squeeze bottle and started rubbing it slowly between her hands to warm it up.

"It was all a show," Kyra said.

"Straight to Broadway," Juliet whispered, kneeling between Kyra's legs, spreading her knees apart. The wicked smile smeared on her face hid more painful secrets Kyra had yet to find.

64

The cocktails were gone and we were now working a bottle of merlot. Flora served our dinner in the kitchen. I promised to clear up and do the dishes, so she'd left us there and went upstairs to watch Italian soccer, but not before she whispered to me, "Don't let Anna help. She always tries to be nice and clean up after herself, but this morning I found broken dishes in the sink, and my mother's ceramic chicken I brought all the way from Italy is now chipped."

I swore to protect her kitchen from further damage, then I crossed myself for reinforcement, thinking I should.

"Aren't you Jewish?" Flora asked.

"It never hurts," I said. She relaxed and left.

Anna sipped her red wine with a smile. No whispering was low enough for her ears.

"You shouldn't have promised," she said when Flora was gone. "I had some sweet desert for us in mind."

"Can't we have it in bed for a change?" I asked.

She spread her fingers wide. "What would be the fun in that?"

We ate in silence for a while.

"That first night with Greg, at the gallery, could he show you the art works?"

"As in other people's canvases?" she asked. "Not exactly. That evening passed in a blur, for reasons other than my bad vision. Faces remained blurred expressions, and I could see sparks of color from the displayed pieces, but I couldn't wait to take him home and find out if he would show me my paintings the way Rosso had.

"Guido and I didn't talk much that night. I worked the room—striking conversations with people I could barely see, hearing nothing they said—holding on to his hand, so as not to lose him in the crowd. At home, in the basement, I was deeply disappointed. I remained too blind to see the paintings, and he passed out."

"Because he'd found out you couldn't see? Not his face, not the art, not even a reflection of your own insane beauty?"

I recalled my own epiphany. *I'd* passed out.

"He was simply drunk and enamored," she said. "The other realization came shortly before he died. That first night, Hildi—who hates the basement—had to shlep down and carry him up the stairs all the way to the bedroom."

"What a sexy night for you," I said with a snorty laugh. "Did you go back down there in the morning?"

"No. I was frightened of another disappointment. I kept hesitating till it was too late."

"How could he not know about your eyes right away?" I asked.

"Some don't pay attention until their egos are involved."

"Some? We're talking about your husband!" I said in disbelief. "When you walked arm in arm on the beach, didn't he say, 'Hey, look at the pretty girl'? Greg and I used to ogle beautiful people all the time. Didn't you dance? Admire art? Didn't you have favorite TV shows? How did you hide it?"

"I'm an expert," she said with the pride of achievement.

"The neighborhood used to come to Greg's M and P—movie and pizza—nights. Academy Award parties were his specialty, with the red carpet in the living room, the finger foods, the costumes. He loved old movies. His prolific sense of humor was based on movie quotes for every occasion. Bette Davis, Joan Fontaine, Hitchcock, all the classics."

"I know the movies by heart," Anna said. "I could recite the lines with him."

"But how did you . . .? How could he . . .?" I was shocked. He hadn't known!

"What are you asking me, Carly?"

"How could you not tell him?"

"He knew that I was shortsighted and that prescription glasses caused me headaches, as did the light. He didn't know how rapidly a veil of darkness was falling over me."

She paced the kitchen in barefoot elegance, pausing her story only to revisit her wine and take another sip.

"I enjoyed being with him, sensing colors through his eyes." She started slurring her words. "I sat for him, but I couldn't actually see his work. Hildi and Flora, my art advisors, saw how happy I was and spared me their opinion of his paintings. By the way, they both love your *Blue Madonna*."

Clouds rapidly covered the sun, the day fogged up and darkened, but my mind was clearing up. My mind was hyperalert.

"When you and I went out in public that time, Anna, I walked a tightrope to keep your secret. How did you and Greg manage public appearances, what with the blind leading the blind?"

"He never left my side, always holding on to my arm. Like with Juliet before him, this was our agreement. He was aware of my vision issues; he'd warn me about stairs and walls. We played the game for the cameras, for Hollywood, for the world. Our constant physical closeness was accepted because we were in love."

"We were four months into our marriage, at the top of his popularity as an artist, when my truth was forced on him. We had a TV interview with Lisa Colemann. Those interviews are a no-brainer for me. I always insist on strict Q and A, nothing I can't handle—no dancing, cooking or visual presentations. That appearance began as a run-of-the-mill interview. Greg and I held hands, in love. Lisa said she'd become a great fan of Greg's work.

"Then lights flashed, and the audience was clapping and cheering. Greg squeezed my hand in excitement. I had no idea what was happening, but I could sense that something had gone terribly wrong and that Lisa Colemann was straying from the allowed format. The way Greg was clutching my hand, I knew he was in on it. Was he tricking me? Had his fame gone to his head? I told him I wanted to leave, but he fastened his grasp and whispered, 'Not to worry.'

"But I was very worried . . . incensed. Then Lisa asked the dreaded question, 'Which one of these is your favorite, Anna?'

She was gesturing toward a huge wall, but I could see nothing on it. I was trapped, backed into a corner, the cameras on my face. I tried joking and changing the subject, but Lisa wasn't giving up.

"You know how sometimes my face takes on a disdainful expression? I have no control over it. After a long, silent moment, Lisa said, 'You don't seem to be too fond of your husband's famous nude of you.' Carly, I wanted to die."

At that, her face turned pasty green. "Your Baseball Bats don't mix well with red wine."

Suddenly she was up, hurrying through the kitchen's open door, out to the deck. She crouched down and was sick on the earth, the shrubs, the boiling turbulence of water below, onto the path she had scaled up and down countless times since her childhood.

Not the wrong mix of alcohols, I suspected, but that of alcohol and the remembered taste of humiliation.

65

"Anna looked like she was going to throw up right there on stage. Colemann's entire costly collection of *Guidos* was screened on that wall, and Anna held on to his hand for dear life. Colemann kept questioning her, told her how much she paid for each one of those horrible paintings, and Anna looked disgusted."

"I saw that interview," Kyra said. "That part must have been edited out."

Juliet's long body stretched next to Kyra's in the dark.

"I sat in the front row, watching every nuance on her face, on his, through my new opera glasses. How beautiful she was, even angry, and how she ordered him to get up with her and leave the stage. It was embarrassing. The audience was silent, then Lisa cut to a commercial—"

"Wait a minute," Kyra said, leaning on her elbow, staring down at her crazy girl. "You bought opera glasses to watch a television talk show from the front row?"

"I didn't exactly buy those."

"A gift?" Kyra asked, hopeful, but she had a feeling they hadn't been.

"Cost me five minutes of elevated pulse at Best Buy, WeHo."

Kyra laughed. "Pray tell, why did you steal those?"

"To spy on her, silly," Juliet said, as if that was obvious. "There's a blind spot in front of Anna's house, where you can park and see straight in without being seen. I'm surprised Hildi never noticed it. I'd find myself sitting in my car at night, listening for their voices, hoping to see them or hear them argue, looking up at their bedroom window—"

"OMG, you're a stalker."

"Yes, Anna's stalker, still loving her while hating on him and wishing him dead. One night Flora found me in my car crying . . . you know, with my nose dripping all over the place and all the heaving . . . completely pathetic. Dear Flora is an angel. She has the face that comes from a hard life—can you imagine working for a high-maintenance diva?

"Without scolding, she pulled me out of the car then she noticed my bandaged wrists . . . Freaked out on me, Kyra. Got all Italian mama on me and shit with her self-crossing and prayers and the Ave Maria. I never had anyone . . ."

Here Juliet choked up and her voice trailed off. Kyra simply waited. "Flora sat me down in the kitchen and made me eat because I was too skinny. She cared so much . . . No one gave a shit about me for so long, so I didn't know how to take it and, well, I was crying and eating and crying and it's like my appetite returned just because someone cared enough, so she kept piling up food on my plate and she even poured me a big shot of that awful eighty-proof shit she drinks . . . Like drinking fucking gasoline, but I drank it.

"Flora told me that I was better off without Anna. 'But I love her,' I said. And this is what she said, 'Let the dust settle,' or something else in her Sicilian dialect. 'Come learn my recipes. You have the talent and I don't want my cooking to die with me.' I thought Anna would object, but Flora said, 'I'm the boss in my kitchen.' And that cracked me up. Flora made me laugh out loud when she said it."

"I love her for that," Kyra said.

"So I took cooking lessons from her. Still do. I thought about how easily I could slip poison into his food, if I knew which food he liked and Anna didn't. Oh, don't give me that face, Kyra. I didn't kill him, but sure as shit I was tempted. I was only tempted.

"One day I wandered down to the basement and found *The Turning*. I asked Flora who the artist was. She crossed herself, said an extra-long Ave Maria and made me swear I'd never go down again. That request made the place more irresistible."

"Naturally." Kyra shrugged.

"I used to sneak into their bedroom. It was practically my bedroom for so long, I'd convinced myself it was fine. I . . . I would steal things."

"I thought you only stole that dress."

"And a few trinkets," Juliet said, lifting one shoulder sheepishly. "A bottle of perfume, a scarf, a pair of earrings. Souvenirs."

"Earrings aren't souvenirs!" Kyra cried out. "Jewelry can be valuable, family heirlooms!"

"She barely wears any. She won't miss it. And remember those paintings I told you about, by that guy, Rosso? I took one or two."

"One or two?" Kyra asked.

"Two paintings."

"You own two paintings by him? Smaller, I take it."

"Of course," Juliet reproached. "*The Turning* was too large to get up that stairwell and into my car. Maybe in your Wrangler . . ."

"Right," Kyra said, sitting up in bed, shaking her head in disbelief. "Because the only reason not to steal *The Turning* was its size."

"It isn't like she appreciates it, the way she hides it." Juliet smiled. "Wanna see them?"

Kyra scrutinized the bedroom, its red curtains, the Kama Sutra headboard, the suggestive leather gear decorating the walls that was never used and was only there for ambiance and dramatic effect. Her gaze softened, caressing the graceful being she hadn't planned on, the sylph, the fairy who had lost her wings and landed naked smack in the center of her sanctum of pleasures.

"What did I get myself into?" Kyra asked. "A stalker, a poisoner, a klepto—"

"Don't forget nymphomaniac," Juliet said.

"You are my package deal, Juliet Blair, my bread and butter. You'd pay off my student loans if they weren't already paid. Didn't your mama teach you not to take what isn't yours, even if the owner doesn't appreciate it?"

"Take a breath, Doc," said the mad sylph. "If it makes up for my sins, I can recite for you their last conversation. Remember the night he died?"

"How could I forget? Good thing I was with my sister when the cops came to her door."

"I overheard what turned out to be their last argument. It was wild."

"And an eavesdropper!"

"It was their fault. They came to me."

"You were in their bedroom!"

"Actually, in their basement," Juliet said. "I had no time to run upstairs. They surprised me."

"They . . . Oh my God!" Kyra got out of bed, wearing nothing but a serious, professional expression. She stared down at Juliet in disbelief.

"What's wrong?" Juliet asked.

"I'm a therapist," Kyra solemnly said. "I've heard confessions in my life, but fuck me if I ever . . . I'm not sure what to do with this."

"You can't be disbarred for listening, can you?" Juliet asked, worried.

"Of course I can, for not reporting you to the authorities immediately."

"Not the police!" Juliet leaped out of bed, covering her bare breasts with a T-shirt.

"I'll let you off the hook if you recite what you heard, word for word."

Juliet jumped on her and, as light as she was, managed to wrestle her to the floor. "Don't you dare fuck with me!"

"I love fucking with you." Kyra tightened her arms around Juliet's slim waist. "Now, story time, you big fat criminal."

"I'm hungry again." Juliet must have had the metabolism of a hummingbird, the way she could put away food.

Kyra gazed up at her sylph, her fairy, who—with her sweet lisp, her silky voice, and the dark chocolate of her skin—filled this private bordello with class and whimsy and fabulous madness.

Juliet was too fucked up, even in Kyra's world.

66

Anna sat cross-legged on the deck, her green sheen visible even in the dim light of the crystal neons. I wiped her face with a cool towel.

"Let's go inside," I said. "It's too cold here."

"No, I may be sick again. I need to think straight about what this all means for you and me." She shook her head. "'I'm sick,' he said. Can you believe that? 'Sick of consulting you about everything. I'm sick of being called Mr. Garibaldi. I'm your husband, not your slave! I make a good living, and I can make my own decisions.'"

Aghast, I asked, "In front of the audience?"

"On the way out, but not out of earshot. He was loud."

I remembered Greg's anger, that voice, that contorted face. Anna could not appreciate the petulant expression, but she sure had heard the high-pitched whine. Not my favorite trait of his.

"When we were safely in the back of the Jaguar and Hildi started the car, I said, 'You should have consulted me about this.' Then I confessed that I'd faked it all along, that my vision was nearly gone. That I'd never seen his art or even his face in the conventional way and that I'd been using him as eyes. I apologized for lying to him all those months. He was silent, then he admitted he'd never suspected that much."

Anna grasped my hands.

"Carly, the things you noticed right away, sensed easily within one hour of being with me, took him a grand fiasco that nearly killed us both."

"You should rest," I said.

"I need to tell you everything," she said, "exactly as it happened."

She leaned back against the support pillar, looking tired. I expected her to be sick again, yet before I managed to ask how she was feeling, her strong and agile body was up and out of sight and quickly descending the rocks down to the stormy water.

"This is not the best idea right now," I hollered after her.

"I need a swim," she called up at me, already many feet down. "Don't you dare come after me; I'm too drunk to carry you up again."

So she had carried me. I knew it.

The moon came out. When I gazed down the cliff I saw her, my wild and incredible night goddess, standing still at the edge of the water, staring blindly into the darkness. Her loose hair was blowing in the wind. Was she shedding tears at long gone days? Did she miss her Rosso, her Guido, her paintings? Did she try to remember colors?

She kneeled down, scooped up water from the ocean and washed her face. Her version of a swim.

Just as suddenly she turned around and was on her way back up the cliff with the natural ease of a nocturnal animal. A raccoon or a bird wouldn't have been quicker. Within minutes she was up on the deck, not even out of breath, her face relaxed, refreshed. Back to her normal self.

I wrapped her shoulders with one of the old blankets Flora always kept folded on the deck. I forced her to sit by the fireplace.

Her face, wet from saltwater, glistened in the blazing fire.

"That night, after that talk show and my confession, I took Guido down to the basement for the second time. I showed him my canvases, as I did you, Carly. It took him a long time to go through the paintings. He kept commenting, exclaiming breathlessly, sounding greedy, as if devouring a succulent fruit and letting the juice drip down his chin. Finally he plopped into a chair, overwhelmed."

"But wait," I said. "The Greg I knew would have explored. He would have found the paintings way before the fourth month of living here."

"I'll never know if he had," she said. "He reacted as if seeing them for the first time."

"And could you see the paintings through his eyes?"

"Nothing. Guido never showed me anything but bursts of red and yellow, but that was more than I'd had without him." She rubbed her hands together in front of the fire. "That's when the idea first came to me. I asked if he thought he could help me restore the paintings and introduce them to the world. 'I wouldn't dare,' he said. 'This is too much art for me, but Carly Rosen could.'"

I gasped as my full name popped into her story without warning.

"I asked who you were, and he said that you were someone who would understand, who would grasp the magnitude and the meaning of the paintings more than anyone, but that you weren't available. When I asked if you were dead, he said you might as well be, because you'd never forgive something."

"I wouldn't have forgiven him, but I would have done the job."

"Would you have?" she asked.

"Not for you or for him, but for the sake of great art. Even pro bono."

"And yet he paid you a hundred grand," she said, amazed.

"Was that the worst thing he'd done?"

"The best, because you came to me." She smiled and tied her wind-blown hair back into a knot. "Well, I thought he'd pull another fast one on me to prove he was his own man."

"And did he?"

"What he did next was worse," Anna said.

In the light of the blazing fireplace I saw brief anger washing over her expressive face. I thought of what hell it must have been for Greg to realize he'd married divinity.

67

"I'd never seen the Divine One go ballistic, and I don't care to see it ever again. Here, Kyra, hold this still . . ."

Juliet handed her a green mixing bowl Kyra didn't even know she had. "Flora adds grappa. Let's try the same recipe with tequila in the mix."

Juliet, in her attempt to domesticate Kyra, insisted that she learn the alcoholic version of chocolate chip cookies

"Cooking is an enigma for me," Kyra said in dismay. "The kitchen is only another room for sex."

"Don't expect me to always be stuck by the stove. Tomorrow morning it'll be your turn to cook and tell and I'll be sipping a cocktail and gazing at your ass."

"Does that mean you'll call in sick again? Yeah!"

"Apparently the daily calendar is another enigma for you." Juliet batted her eyelashes at Kyra, wearing half a smile. "Tomorrow is Saturday."

She threw all kinds of mysterious powders into the bowl, one of which Kyra identified as sugar, then she added vanilla-fragrant liquid to the mix.

"All that will make cookies?" Kyra asked. "Magic!"

Juliet mixed expertly, silent for a moment. "Your friend Greg died a broken man."

"Meaning?" Kyra held the container still, but her face was far from still while she licked white sugar powder from Juliet's chocolate shoulder. "Tell me everything, oh fabulous stalker."

Juliet measured more sugar and mixed it in.

"He had a show in Beverly Hills. You see, I'd google their itinerary, as a stalker worth her salt. I became their shadow. That evening they made their grand entrance, holding on to each other, and I could just imagine her telling him how she was thinking about what she'd do to him later. I hated them both.

"I wore a clingy, bright orange dress to remind her of all those oranges she'd made me peel. Maybe, I was hoping, she'd see what she'd given up for the talentless klutz she called *my dear Guido*."

Juliet mocked Anna's cultured voice so perfectly, Kyra laughed out loud. They weren't only soul mates, they were hating mates!

"I stood in front of her, signing an autograph for an old man who recognized me. I was practically blocking their way on purpose. Anna looked through me, either ignoring me or blinded by her love for him. The gallery was full. His paintings were like stick figures drawn by a child. I don't mean to disrespect your dead friend, Kyra, but—"

"I know," Kyra said. "His work stinks."

Juliet tossed more ingredients into the bowl, angry. "I didn't understand. Why was she supporting that shit when she was hiding such great art in her basement? Now that I knew about the treasures by that other guy, some of them owned by me, I was so confused."

"*Some* of them? You've taken two," Kyra reminded her.

"Yes," Juliet said. "Hold the bowl still when you're mixing, or it'll be all over the floor. I was wandering aimlessly among the people in the gallery, frequently glancing at Anna because she'd been the only thing worth looking at. The *Guidos* . . . Seen one, seen them all. How he could claim they were nudes of his gorgeous wife was beyond me. Each piece sold for a small fortune. And just as I was thinking of those art treasures hidden away, there they were, clustered on one of the walls."

"*Rossos* and *Guidos* side by side?" Kyra asked. "You gotta hand it to him."

"Yes, I was surprised at that. He was allowing the works of a superior artist in his show. Rosso's other paintings are better than even *The Turning*. Their colors, depth, perspective are more sophisticated. People crowded by the *Rossos*, gawking and I thought, at last, she was releasing the real thing.

"One was a magnificent red nude. I'd been in love with that piece, with the whole series. I decided on the spot, before anyone else realized the greatness of that painting, to cough up the five grand and own one red nude fair and square.

"As I was fishing for my credit card, a woman asked loudly if Mr. Garibaldi was finally growing some talent. People can be so rude. They laughed. Anna stretched up next to him, standing even taller than she typically does. She seemed to be disgusted. I was too. I expected her to tell those rude people off for insulting *her dear Guido*. Instead she sniffed the air. Like a dog, Kyra, I swear. Like a goddamned dog. She checked one canvas closely, way too closely, running her hand over it. It was like she didn't believe what she was seeing. Then she roared."

"Not too divine," Kyra said, astonished. This did not sit well with her imagination. "Is this the *ballistic* you were talking about?"

"Kyra, she sounded like a wounded, wild animal defending its cubs. Suddenly everything spiraled out of control. She grabbed Greg's shoulders, too near his throat. Again she was angry and unbelievably beautiful, like the Red Queen about to say *off with his head!*

"Hildi said something to her, and Anna took her hands from his throat and regained control. When she spoke again, her voice was as calm as a lake. 'How many of those are you showing?' she asked, like she couldn't count. Like she had to make him say it. Confess. Exactly five pieces were on that wall. He murmured something, a deer caught in the headlights. 'This isn't your work, how dare you?' she asked. Those were her exact words—this isn't your work. I felt bad for him. His face, he was devastated. Despite what happened to me, I felt sorry for him."

Kyra couldn't bear it. She hated Greg for fucking her sister's life, but there was a time she'd loved him as a little brother. "Do you think he tried to pass the other works as his own?"

"I don't know." Juliet dropped into a kitchen chair, and Kyra followed suit. "Someone wanted to buy one of those paintings. Anna announced in a totally normal voice that they weren't for sale, or even for viewing. The scene was horrible. Complete chaos. Hildi started taking paintings off the wall and carrying them to the car. I offered to help her, and she accepted.

"I drove straight to Flora, to tell her before she heard it on the news. I had to see her. Flora has all these old Italian insights that make me laugh and feel better. I parked my car in my secret blind spot. Flora was cooking. She listened to me and said something sharp in Italian. As I'd been a permanent guest by then, she told me to stir the pot for her a little longer, then turn it off. 'And take some home for your dinner,' she added. She went to take care of business, leaving me in the kitchen.

"I did as I was told and stirred the pot for ten minutes, then turned the flame off. I was going to go home, but then I heard the gravel crackling and it was too late. One last time, I told myself as I ran for cover. Had I run up to the bedroom, they would have seen me. I could only try the basement. I quickly went down when I heard their voices coming in. Those old stairs are so worn out in places, I nearly tripped in my high heels, so I stopped to take them off and continued barefoot. Fuck, Kyra, their voices got louder and they were heading my way, down the stairs!"

Juliet put the tray of her alcoholic cookies in the oven, then she sat down, breathing heavily, reliving the night.

"I skipped two or three stairs down to that basement, risking my life, promising myself not to ever do that shit again. I stumbled and ran behind the last row of covered paintings. I crouched down on my knees, hiding, hugging my shoes, freezing cold in my evening dress, praying not to sneeze from the dust. "

Kyra's teeth hurt, thinking of Juliet having to hide like a burglar.

"Get us a drink," Juliet said.

Kyra wondered if she would ever repeat all this to Carly. She pulled the Ley out of the freezer and took the first swig.

68

A coughing fit woke me up. I was sprawled on the living room couch, covered with Anna's musk-saturated pink cashmere scarf. In the light of dawn I saw her pacing the room, restless.

"I know there was no malice in his actions," I said, my voice coarse from sleep or laryngitis. "No attempt to claim your work as his own. Greg couldn't paint to save his life, but he knew brilliance when he saw it. What if he wanted to show it?"

"Without my permission," she said.

"I would have done the same," I said. "Those paintings are your children? Fine. I would have freed those beautiful, brilliant, abused children from the closet you've locked them in for twenty years!"

"That's harsh," she said, stopping her pacing.

"Why don't you show your art?"

"Damaged?" Her eyebrows lifted into her hair line.

"Yes, with every scorch mark. They are yours and they are as magnificent, as brilliant, as beautiful as you are. And no more damaged than you."

"I can't. Not without restoring them."

"What happened next, Anna?" I asked. "You insulted him in front of his crowd, you made Hildi take your paintings down and away. How did you go from that to having a dead husband on that same evening?"

"Are you well enough for a walk in the rain?" she asked.

We strolled arm in arm in the rose garden, among rain-dripping statues. We were both barefoot. Anna because she could sense her way better without shoes and I, to check out that claim.

"That night my love for him died," she said.

"Anna, my beautiful Anna," I said, my voice barely audible through my sore throat. "You don't stop loving someone in an instant unless you didn't love him in the first place."

"I loved him at first sight, Carly. No pun intended."

I walked with most of my weight on the outsides of my feet. A pebble pricked my big toe.

"And at his funeral"—a cough clipped my words—"when he was lying dead in his casket, tell me, did I walk into church wearing Rosso's rainbow scarf?"

"Yes," Anna said, wiping raindrops from her face. "I could barely stop myself from running to you, taking you in my arms and leaving everybody there—"

"Even then, before you loved me?"

"Even then, but I had a eulogy to give, a dear husband to bury. Then you spoke to me and the splashes of color brightened up my gray existence."

I remembered her heartfelt eulogy, my tears, my yelling at her, the angry stares I got from people. She didn't care how rude I'd been or what I'd said, because I showed her colors. And now I knew why she'd sent Hildi after me. Kyra had practically lifted me off my feet and carried me out, away from the terrifying scene, and into the driver's seat of her Wrangler. And I had driven away from the church ceremony, from Greg's corpse, from his widow.

We stood still, arm in arm, in her garden, among statues made in her image.

"What happened when Hildi removed your paintings from the wall?"

"We didn't stay at the gallery," she said. "The party was over for both of us. We left. In the car we neither spoke nor touched. As soon as we got home, I headed down the spiral staircase. I needed to touch *The Turning*, make sure it was still safely there. Guido followed me to the basement, where the whole evening—the stress, the hurt, the betrayal—came to a head. We made love." She shook her head. "We had sex."

A troubled, ragged coastline was painted gray aquarelle by the pouring rain. Both Anna and I were soaked through our clothes, part of that aquarelle, part of that crazy nature scene.

"You said you stopped loving him. How could you . . . ?"

"Sex is sex," she said, as easily as she would say *food is food*. "Then I told him to go and fetch you."

"You told him what?" I asked, my sore throat emitting a cracked whisper.

"You knew that," she said.

"Not the circumstances!" My entire body trembled with tension. Or fever. Or fever plagued with tension. "He had just made love to you. You hurt him, lied to him, humiliated him, and he did nothing but love you!"

"He loved *you* more, Carly."

"He dumped me on our wedding day to marry you!"

"That he did, but you were constantly on his mind."

That maddeningly calm contralto of hers whispered with the rain. "I could sense your presence on his mind."

I kicked another prickly pebble, wishing for a pair of flip-flops. This seeing with bare feet was Anna's thing, not mine.

"You knew nothing of my existence!"

"Deep down I knew you. We first connected through him, in his life. You had the power to show me the truest colors, to help me restore my paintings. Even he said that."

Something snapped in me.

"Your paintings," I said. "Always your paintings."

"Painting was my greatest happiness, and it caused all my losses."

"You blame the wrong thing," I said.

"Carly, you were his true love till the end. Isn't that what you wanted to prove when you came here? Aren't you happy about it?"

"Listen to yourself!" My scream was an agonized croak. "A man loves you, yet his love is only the arc of some sick, tormented, idiotic game you play on the rest of the world!"

"You are not well, love. Calm down."

It may have been the fever, the knowledge, the pouring rain, or a combination of all, but the truth came to me like lightning.

"Texting and driving didn't kill him, Anna. *You did.*"

69

"I heard her killing him."Juliet took a long swig straight from the spiked bottle and passed it to Kyra.

"What do you mean, *killing him*?"

"I had to listen to everything. Every damned thing. Remember I told you I owed myself a revenge fuck at that very spot?"

"I was happy to oblige," Kyra said. "This is big, Juliet. We all speculated for months, but you actually heard everything they said."

"And every noise and cry and murmur. And they were wild. My face was pressed against the rough surface of a painting. It took them so long, I got a little bored and very cold. I decided to warm myself up with some art appreciation. I shone my cellphone light on the painting. It was a gorgeous sunset and in my mind I made it mine."

"You are un-frigging-believable." Kyra rested down the bottle. "So is this shit."

"They went for each other again. I thought, such sex, they'll make up, go to their bedroom and let me leave in peace. It was the one time I prayed for their happiness. But it wasn't that easy. They were done fucking. For a while they whispered, and I heard nothing. I believed they'd fallen asleep on the floor. My teeth were chattering so loudly I was afraid they'd discover me, or worse, find me frozen to death in the morning. Then Anna told him to go fetch Carly Rosen if he had to bring her back from the dead."

"My sister? From the dead?" Kyra cried out. "What in hell did that mean?"

"I don't know. Anna told him to pay her whatever it would take. When he refused, saying that money wouldn't convince the Carly he knew, Anna said, in that calm tone she uses when directing her crew, 'I want you out of here tonight, Guido. It's over.'"

"What the fuck," Kyra said. "*What?*"

"Exactly," Juliet said. "He had a similar reaction. A big *what the hell.* From behind those long rows of art, I cried out with both him and with the echo. All my caution was gone. I couldn't help but crawl on all fours and peek out from my hiding place. He was sitting on the cold floor, as I had been, his face in his hands. That was the night he died."

"A broken man," Kyra said, again pitying him.

70

Anna stood still in the pouring rain. I regarded her—that angelic oval face, that statuesque figure, that constant elegance —wondering just how broken she was within those regal pretenses and calm demeanor.

"Those reporters swarmed your house, waiting for something, and you gave them what they wanted," I said, my voice a mere whisper. "You served them Greg on a platter. You could have used your great powers to call a tell-all press conference. Here was the chance of a lifetime to come clean, the power to take his pain away, to reverse his humiliation. Why didn't you?"

"I can't stand pity."

"No. You don't *have* pity."

"Carly! What are you saying?"

"Greg died for your fucking pride," I said. Rain soaked my hair and dripped into my eyes—reverse tears. "He died for your secrets. I was wrong to cover for you, Anna. I won't do it anymore."

Her pale hair came loose and darkened in the pouring rain, framing her face in long, wet strands. Her colorless T-shirt clung to her in wet folds. Still, she was stunning.

I said, "Your secrets kill everyone who loves you. All that hidden drama around the loss of your vision. You, pretending to be so calm, joking about it and fighting the truth all the same.

"Blindness is tragic for a talented artist, yet artists go blind and survive. Athletes lose arms and legs. Musicians lose their hearing. Why can't you be blind like other blind people and stop lying and breaking hearts just to cover up? Why can't you come out and be truthful? You keep on as if all is fine. It's your responsibility to tell. Instead, you selfishly worry about your image, living a big, fat, unnecessary lie. You hurt those who adore you. You hurt your fans. You owe them the truth."

"Why do I owe them?" she asked.

"Those fans made you who you are, that's why. If you don't explain why you wear sunglasses, why you don't shake hands, why you don't comment on art, people get hurt. Kyra was worried about me because she took your affectations for aloofness and rudeness."

Kyra. Couldn't she shut up? Did she have to open her analytic eyes and her mouth? I was happy. Wasn't that enough for Kyra?

Anna listened with dignity, with that small smile on her lips, never seeming insulted, only interested and more beautiful.

I had to try harder to sway her. To make her understand.

"People listen to you, are inspired by you. Tell them about your blindness and be done with it. Don't unfold the truth slowly, like you do your yoga mat. Shake it like a blanket—*I'm blind*—then see what happens. The way the world treats anything you do, people may start popping their eyes out and making blindness the new fashion.

I swallowed hard and continued through what felt like shards of glass in my throat.

"No one should pity La Divina, you say. So let them pity you, then let them realize they don't have to.

"Your real divine talent is your healing touch that cures pain. Make your wonderful talent known, then watch your house become a home, your quiet, isolated and lonely hiding place become a Mecca to the suffering. You will be their prophet, their healer, a one-of-a-kind stylish guru for anyone with a disability. Then you'll become divine for real."

The sicker I felt, the harsher my voice sounded. She listened, soaked by the rain, as I laid out her life.

Finally she said, "I can't do it. I just can't come out and say it."

I fought dizziness. My head throbbed in a dull ache. Anna sensed it and her hands moved to me, steadying me.

"Don't touch me!" I couldn't stop when in sudden disgust I backed away from her.

"Carly, my love, what has changed?"

"You should know, you who stopped loving your husband in an instant, be—"

"Have you stopped?" she asked, pain choking her voice. "Have you really stopped? Fever and the truth are a toxic combination!"

I was crying, and I couldn't calm down. I said, "When you were telling me your story, I didn't hear the pain of loss. Not for your parents, not really for Johnny, not for Greg. You grieve only for the loss of your precious life's work."

"Is it wrong to love one's work?"

"There's passion for one's work, even love, but people feel pain and they come first. In all the heartache Greg caused me, I loved him. I still do. When I fell in love with you, you came first. But I've been somewhere way down the list for you. You love us for our ability to show you colors."

"Yes," she said, "but not only."

"What did Greg Wheeler really mean to you? What do I mean? Greg died because you lied to him for months. You would have let me die too rather than t—"

"You knew, Carly."

"No thanks to you."

Heavy breathing interrupted us. Hildi's bulk materialized out of solid sheets of rain. "Is everything okay?"

"Wait inside, Hildi," Anna commanded. "All is well."

I scanned the scenery around me, the luxury from which Greg had been hurled, vomited like a bad dinner, this rain-absorbed beauty—the house, the ocean thundering below, the rose garden and Anna in it. Rainwater dripped from her face like tears from the marble statue looming behind her. He'd loved this beautiful liar who had first convinced him of his talent and then humiliated and crushed him like an aphid on one of her roses.

My eyes followed the big woman into the house, and I was angry at Anna. *Now* I was angry at her. Was it a sudden memory of my love for Greg or my unfinished business with him? The memory of my own humiliation? I didn't know.

"I'm no different than Hildi," I said. "I've been your paid employee, a member of your staff, with extra benefits. Our month of magical love was nothing to you. From the beginning you wanted me to work for you. You never loved me or Greg, not even Rosso. You loved only our eyeballs."

I pointed at my eyes, probably looking as insane as I felt. The gesture was lost on her.

Anna said, "Carly, things constantly change for me. My vision, my art forms. Some loves die, others are born. You should know only that my love for you is alive and burning."

I felt wired enough to jump out of my skin. "Your love for me will go *poof* the minute someone shows you a glossier shade of red."

She didn't deny it. She couldn't see at all anymore, but she didn't deny it.

My throat was sore from talking, but I had to somehow move her, make her react. "You are blind, all right. Blinded by pride."

And Greg was there again, multiplied by my fever and agitation.

In my delirium all those statues around me became him. Greg was not only between us, but clones of him sprouted everywhere within the rose bushes, by the cubic form of the house, Greg at the edge of the cliff, and more of him, and more of Anna and Rosso, everywhere. I could hear her loving whispers to all of us, her loving words multiplying in the whooshing wind.

And all her words were false, because she did not love any of us.

She felt her way up my face.

"You are burning, hallucinating," she said. "Let me put you to bed."

"He'll be there . . . they'll all be there in the bedroom . . ." My throat felt rough, raw.

"Who will be there, Carly?" Asked Anna or Rosso or Greg.

Her lips felt cool on my forehead. I shuddered.

"Away, I can't," I said, my achy throat forcing out a ridiculous sound.

The sculptures swayed. The surrounding garden—with Anna and all her *Rossos* and *Guidos*—flattened and squeezed around me like a straitjacket, compressed my chest, sucked the oxygen out of my lungs.

And in all this turmoil, my sister's voice egged me on.

What do you really know about her?

Now I know too much, Kyra, and I have to give up my happiness because this place of my happiness has become the Land of the Dead.

Not the basement; that was only a large space filled with art. I'd had it right when I arrived here a month ago. Hades was Anna. Hades was inside her. So far I'd only grazed its edge. The edge of her pain, her darkness, and her heartlessness.

I ran.

I reached my Mustang, barefoot, coughing and feverish, Anna's cashmere scarf blowing in the wind, a pink, warm cloud around my shoulders.

"Carly!" she cried out behind me.

I turned to deal my last blow. "You said that your true love was dead, Anna, but your true love is very much alive. Your true love is you."

As I spoke, her image was slowly fading. A trick of the rain and the tears in my eyes.

Part Five

71

"Let's take two cars," Juliet suggested. "If you start hating me, you can get away."

"Why would that happen?" Kyra asked. "I've had three blissful days."

"I've been talking for three days, yet you know nothing."

"You have a huge husband with a murderous temper? Three cute little boys with a pet boa constrictor? S and M gear hanging from the ceiling? Something worse?"

"No, no, no and yes."

"Hop into my Jeep," Kyra said. "I'll take my chances."

Juliet strapped herself into the passenger seat and laughed nervously.

A rainy drive on the 405 freeway brought them to the tree section of old Manhattan Beach, a strange, affluent place with street names such as Palm, Oak, Elm, Pine. The houses were modest, mostly bungalows from the fifties, but the neighborhood oozed old money.

"Turn right," she said.

"I know your secret, little girl." Kyra beeped the horn in excitement. "You are a mogul, a tycoon, the sole heiress of Coca-Cola!"

Juliet laughed. "Not even close! Turn left on Valley Drive . . . and now into this driveway."

Kyra parked before an eight-foot wooden fence corroded by the ocean air.

"Who are you?" Kyra lowered and darkened the tone of her voice.

"I'm the same tight fuck-up from yesterday, only tighter," Juliet said.

"But you live five blocks from the beach."

"Oh, calm down, Doc. I'm renting from a generous friend."

Then she started kissing Kyra, buying time.

"We can do it in the Jeep," Kyra said, "but you promised disco lighting in your bedroom."

Juliet swallowed hard and put her flip-flops back on. "Fine. Let's get it over with."

The creaky gate revealed a small yard with weeds taller than Kyra's head. The rain was pouring, soaking them.

"And here's my luxurious abode," Juliet said.

"A dandelion garden," Kyra said. "Was that your big worry?"

"Those don't bother me." Juliet glanced around, as if noticing the weeds for the first time. "I let them be."

The little house, once Kyra could see it, proved to be a very private hideaway, a rustic wooden cabin one could find in the mountains or near a lake. She wouldn't have been surprised to see *Hush . . . Hush, Sweet Charlotte* approaching with a shotgun, but what she saw when Juliet unlocked her creaky red door made Kyra gasp out loud.

The place was a hoarding shed. Not for junk or empty food cartons—the single room was immaculately clean and smelled freshly of lavender and Ylang Ylang. The only piece of furniture in its center was a king-size futon with white bed linens and whiter blankets. The rest of Juliet's belongings were packed solid on her walls. Paintings. Canvases of all sizes wall-to-wall and wall-to-ceiling, barely a gap between the paintings to show the color of the walls.

"Your work?" Kyra asked.

"In a manner of speaking," Juliet said with that adorable, one-sided little shrug.

"These are your 'one or two' Rossos?"

"One or two each time I visited," Juliet explained.

"Sticky-fingered from Anna's basement."

"And from her closet." She pointed at a flowing white dress suspended from a padded hanger among the art pieces. Anna's *schmate*. A white feather boa was wrapped around its imaginary neck. It was splattered with red wine stains. A historic artifact from an ill-fated evening on which Garibaldi had taken Greg prisoner.

"And from the gallery in Beverly Hills." Juliet gestured up. One painting was somehow attached to the ceiling, to be viewed from below while lying down.

"I thought those weren't for sale," Kyra said.

"I told you how she went mental on her *dear Guido* and demanded that Hildi remove those from the show at once. In the chaos no one noticed that I helped."

"You helped yourself to it," Kyra said, earnest. "You have a real problem, Juliet."

"I was willing to buy it!" she said in protest, her kissy lips pouting. "It has two sisters, two more red nudes that belong next to it, but it will take another trip, or two."

"Fuck me," Kyra said with amazement at the vibrant colors, at the beauty of these pieces, at the sheer magnificence of this mighty, crazy woman. "*Fuck, fuck me.*"

And for once, someone took Kyra up on her demand.

When they came up for air, their clothes twisted awkwardly, the rain drummed melodies on the roof. They gazed up at the red nude adorning the ceiling. The woman was reclining on rich red brocade, a teardrop ruby dangling between her white breasts. The painting was an orgiastic celebration of crimson, maroon, rose, burgundy, cadmium, candy apple, cardinal, carmine—more reds than Kyra could name. More shades of red than she had seen in all her years of loving art and being her sister's sister.

"Eroticizing the reds," Kyra said.

"I'll never get tired of staring up at her." Juliet stretched leisurely on the futon, dark brown against the blinding white sheet, long arms framing her face.

"You're nuts, dipped in bittersweet chocolate," Kyra said, starting to kiss her again.

"You gonna call the cops on me?" Juliet raised an eyebrow in a question.

"Hell, no. They'd take you away and I'd go hungry." Kyra bit Juliet's lower lip playfully. "At least you steal from the best." She looked around again, quickly this time. "Hey, you lied. There's not a bedroom here, nor disco lights."

"That's one of my pick-up lines." Juliet giggled. "It worked on you!"

Kyra gave the room an all-inclusive glance. "I wish I knew what she did to him."

"What she does to all of them," Juliet said, wrapping long limbs around Kyra from behind in a four-point embrace. "All her lovers flame with creativity, then they're off the map. She has poetry books, written for her. Where are those poets?"

Juliet kissed the back of Kyra's neck.

"You may have heard of this trip-hop artist called Delirio. He and Anna were together for a time. He disappeared. Did he die or just stop writing music? His last big hit, *Crash and Burn*, was about a night with her. What happened to him? She's a black widow, not only of lovers, but of careers. Why would she climb to the top—an Oscar nomination, for God's sake!—then let it all go to hell? What's wrong with her that she drops everyone and everything?"

"What is love?" Kyra asked.

"*Here's what love is,*" Juliet whispered. "*A smoke made out of lovers' sighs. When the smoke clears, love is a fire burning in your lover's eyes. If you frustrate love, you get an ocean made out of lovers' tears. What else is love?*" She stopped. "Come on, Kyra, darling. You must remember the rest of that scene."

"You just called me darling!" Kyra said. Then thinking hard to pull out the words, she said, "*What else is love? It's a wise form of madness. It's a sweet lozenge that you choke on.*"

"Good memory, old lady. We should play out the whole thing one day."

Juliet slipped out of bed, next Kyra heard her fumbling with dishes in the small kitchen.

"Chocolate omelet?" Kyra asked, hopeful.

"Coffee first. Take your time looking around."

Kyra examined each painting closely, all oils that had dried many years ago, in her estimation. She could not take her eyes off those wall-to-wall treasures. Hyper-realism, surrealism, amazing abstracts. Each painting held more than its initial impression. But what? The works were a study. Each painting was part of a bigger picture, a theme. Their colors could be perceived with her other senses. She could taste the lemons. What was Rosso trying to do here? Music was soon piped into the room, a trance-inducing track she didn't recognize.

"Are you playing that trip-hop guy, Delirio?"

"I'm not playing music," Juliet called out from the kitchen.

Disbelieving, Kyra tuned her ear to listen; indeed, no music was playing. Not outside of her own body.

"Those colors have a way of fucking with your head. They pluck at your nerves and your emotions and make you perceive music and fragrances." She handed Kyra an aromatic cup of coffee. "This smell of vanilla hazelnut is totally real."

Juliet called in sick again the next day. Kyra canceled more appointments. They ordered Chinese for lunch, pizza for dinner. They had each other for dessert. They drank a fabulous bottle of Valpolicella Superiore, which Juliet swore she didn't steal from Anna's wine rack. "A gift from Flora for helping with a complicated recipe." They made lazy love on the white futon bed, lying in each other's arms, staring up at the gorgeous red nude above their heads.

"You need soft lights, pointing up."

"Remote controlled," Juliet agreed.

"How did you manage this grand heist all by yourself?" Kyra asked in awe.

"I told you," Juliet said, her head in the crook of Kyra's arm. "I used to visit Flora and cook with her and do neurotic things. I'd sneak downstairs and go through all the damaged art. All that talent needed to be seen, so I helped myself to the best. But there are more! The art was lonely, hidden in the dark like that. It needed light, it needed me. We needed each other." She shifted and hugged Kyra tighter. "Isn't it weird that I thought of art in terms of a feeling entity?"

"This definitely makes up for your many shortfalls," Kyra said.

Suddenly Juliet was up on her feet.

"Let's go get it," she said, pulling up her jeans.

Kyra had to get used to this impulsive behavior. Juliet had no time for a smooth transition between decision and action.

"What are we getting?"

"*The Turning*. It needs us. Get up, Kyra. It'll fit in your Wrangler if we let it stick out a little."

"I've never done anything like this." Kyra swallowed hard. "Not before my morning shower."

"We'll clean up later. Get dressed," commanded her insane woman. "There's nothing to it. All we need is an Erickson and a Van Staal." She stared down at Kyra's horrified expression and laughed out loud. "Pliers and a ratchet strap. Come on, I have a toolset."

"Is the stairwell even wide enough to pull that canvas out?" Kyra asked.

"Of course not, but we'll find a way."

"How?" Kyra's heart quickened

"We could roll it off the canvas like a carpet," Juliet said. "I'd seen it done."

"When you worked for the mob?"

Kyra pulled up her jeans. *What had I gotten myself into* crossed her mind for the hundredth time. As she gaped at Juliet —the obsessive, maniacal gleam in her eyes, her graceful, slim body ready to spring into action—Kyra knew she'd follow her to the depths of hell to rescue the great masterpiece from oblivion.

Life had a way of foiling plans. They were already in the Wrangler, Juliet's professional toolset on the back seat, when Kyra's phone rang.

"Did Carly get in touch with you?" Zoe sounded tense. "Anna just called looking for her."

Kyra speed-dialed Carly. What answered after the first ring was definitely not Carly. The famous contralto ran shivers down Kyra's spine.

"Carly? Thank God you called back," said the devil, mistaking Kyra's voice for her sister's.

"Where is she?" Kyra hissed at her.

"Is this Kyra?" The devil didn't play games. "She drove away distraught and sick, like him."

"And you let her?" Kyra barked, thinking of Juliet's words: *He died a broken man*. "Where did you send her? Did you break her heart like you did his?"

"Calm down," said the devil. "Let's think together how to find her."

"You should have followed her!" Kyra was out of breath. "Can't you even fucking drive for yourself?"

Kyra hung up, seething with anger and fear. What Garibaldi had done to Rosso, Greg and Juliet festered her hatred.

Now she'd done it to Carly.

72

Palos Verdes Drive snaked north before me, too empty of traffic for lunch time. Anna once described her vision as a windshield on a rainy day—back and forth went my noisy wipers. She'd sat dressed in orange in her father's car and talked to him about her art. I passed the lighthouse and Golden Cove Shopping Center. The accident that had blinded her had happened around this bend.

I kept north, passing the beach cities, the airport, north on La Cienega. I was barefoot. I had no purse, no phone, no license, nor any ID on me.

When I arrived at Zoe's driveway, the rain was still falling hard. Four vaguely familiar figures huddled in chairs on the porch, apparently waiting for me.

Out of the hazy blur Kyra approached me with open arms.

At the sight of her, my anger surged like boiling water. She'd made me see Anna with analytic eyes. She'd made me doubt her. She made me lose her. I slapped Kyra's face with all my strength, which wasn't much. Kyra, used to crazy people attacking her, caught my hand and tried to embrace me.

"Let's have a quiet talk." She spoke in her clinical, infuriating voice.

I was choked up, my words faint. "I had my beloved back. Why'd you make me turn around?" I pushed her away. "Why'd you make me look?"

"Make you turn? Baby, you're burning with fever. Listen—"

"I'm done listening. Your psycho shit fucked me up but good. I was happy picking up from the floor for her, cutting up her food, editing. I would have given her my eyes . . ." I stopped myself before revealing more, still keeping a secret that should never have been a secret in the first place. "I was happy. Why didn't you leave it at that?"

They all turned to stone at my gibberish, all except Kyra.

"Come inside and have a Baseball Bat to clear your head."

"I've had it with clarity," I said. "Let me be confused for once."

My hand still hurt from slapping her face, and I was awash with regrets. We'd argued before, but this fight was a first between us. I went inside.

Up in my bedroom my unmade bed was strewn with clothes someone had tried on exactly a month ago. That someone was a messy girl who'd been going to Hades to reclaim her beloved. She'd died, and I had the dirty job of clearing up her mess.

I started putting clothes away, garment after garment, filing fact after fact in my head. Anna's scarf remained around my neck, her musk tickling my nostrils, keeping me breathing, breathing in and out. Keeping me from dying.

Which one of us had lost the other? Was it my fault for wanting to know the truth or Anna's for keeping secrets in the first place? Supposing she had not kept secrets? Greg then would have stayed alive, and I would have never gone to search for him.

My head hurt from *what-ifs*.

I was hanging skirts, blouses and pants back in my closet, the memory of her perfect, stoic face, her eyes, her touch, the calm sound of her voice, going through my mind. As I straightened up my bed, tucking in hospital corners—the way I'd learned in nursing school—because it relaxed me, I imagined taking off her sunglasses and kissing those gray eyes that could see nothing and everything. I took another deep breath of life-giving musk and thought of the moonlight she could not see washing our naked bodies. Her hands, her seeing fingertip on me, in me. Her whispers urging me in so many languages of love, all encouraging, all *yes, yes, yes*. No one measured up to the Divine One. No one could. I'd rather live like a nun than let anyone else touch me.

I collapsed on top of the blanket, sobbing.

I craved all that she was, a predator, a seductress, a liar who cared about nothing and no one. I loved her.

73

"My dear Carly,

Yes, I meddled. Yes, I pried and poked my nose where it didn't belong and acted like a garden variety whore and an accomplice in a grand heist and now I'm a stalker. I did it all, but you have to believe me, Carly—I only meant to save you.

My cheek still burns from your slap. I don't understand what provoked you, but if I had, consider this letter an apology.

Now, much too late—almost three months after Greg's funeral and only a day after you slapped my face—I keep writing, in fits and starts, the truth. All the truths.

I can't sleep or eat or think straight and my eyes are bleary from the tears but I have to explain myself and if I'm a bit verbose, what's new about that? Now I wish I had shut up for once in my life. Maybe then I would have kept you.

Carly, I can't help pouring my heart out to you longhand whether you'll read this or not.

Your old pastel drawing is staring back at me, and I marvel again at your love for colors. At the trust between us that you captured as a six-year-old. That trust has always been immeasurable. Until yesterday.

All of it—even our memories—is gone now, torn away.

If you read this and get my gist, know that my sense of loss is unbearable. The imprint of your slap on my cheek faded, yet not its sound. *Whack*. Even now, and through the lively noise of Santa Monica Boulevard, I can hear that slap. I'll never stop hearing it as long as I live. I may have to revise my theory about the power of fragrances. What lasts forever is sound.

There's no way back. So here I am, writing to you, but mostly to myself.

I want to tell you everything from the beginning. I've already written what you didn't know about you and Greg, about how Garibaldi took him away from you, about me, and now about Juliet and me. We are inseparable and she keeps trying to get me away from my desk to eat or sleep, but I'm in this manic state of writing.

I have to tell you about my obsession with Anna fucking Garibaldi.

Obsessions start because of love. Mine started with deep loathing. The month you were with her, busy falling in love, I've watched all her movies more than once and read all her books again. Now I want to know about her, and not what she tells the world but what she doesn't. Because there's something big there. I keep googling the hell out of her name, reading every article, every advertisement. What I want to find, what I think I know, isn't there.

There's something she isn't telling anyone, maybe not even you, and I'm going to find out what it is if it kills me.

Love you,

Kyra."

74

I woke up thirsty. My breath came in and out through a soft cloth. In the pitch darkness all my senses spiked like antennae. I listened for the ocean, the rain, the owls. Instead, the sounds of West Hollywood came in through the open window. I knew it was late evening, maybe night. The rain had stopped. I heard traffic in the alley and beyond it, on the boulevard, the harsh sounds of beeping cars and people laughing.

A man shouted, "Let's go dancing."

A giggly voice answered, "To the Abbey." Giggles turned into wild laughter.

It was good to hear a living city that had something to celebrate, people who could see each other across the street.

I reached under my bed and pulled out an old bottle of Evian I'd left there long ago, took one sip and was nauseated again. The smell of roasted garlic wafted in from the Thai restaurant down Santa Monica Boulevard. My favorite in good times, now the smell made me sick. I covered my face again with Anna's cashmere scarf, thinking how musk had been woven into it in heaven. Musk calmed my turning stomach. Musk was life.

I couldn't tell night from day. I got up to pee once or twice, caught a glimpse of myself in the mirror and thought how ridiculous my pale face and puffy eyes seemed above that pink cloud of the fancy scarf. I drank straight from the faucet and splashed cold water on myself to reduce the burning heat. Again I slept.

I dreamed of Anna—standing tall and tense. *Let me see you,* she said, her blind gaze on me. She unclenched her fist and from it fell eyeballs. She opened her other fist and more eyeballs rolled out—mine, Greg's, Kyra's, Zoe's. As I was losing her in the pouring rain, I marveled at the dignity of her posture.

I opened my eyes a crack. A shadow sat next to my bed in the dark, a reassuring presence. I turned away from it. A cool hand stroked my face. I slept more.

A knock on the front door. Could be little Timmy, wanting to shoot hoops with me. At night? Zoe and Robert must be out. The knocking got louder, too loud for a five-year-old. I floated, as in a lucid dream, toward my bedroom door, down the steep stairs to the living room, to the front door. Someone was behind it, knocking ceaselessly. Then I realized I was still in bed in the same position. I hadn't moved a limb. The getting up happened only in my drowsy, sleep-filled mind. With great effort I lifted my lead-heavy head and pried the horizontal blind open.

A shiny black Jaguar blocked the traffic in the alley.

What was she doing here? I closed my eyes.

75

Kyra waited in Bookworms. The West Hollywood bookstore was gearing up for a weekend-long celebration of Garibaldi's literary works. In-store displays of all her books and films, online promotions, and signed-books and DVDs giveaways were part of the festivities. Kyra wasn't.

Kyra was there to ask questions only the devil could answer. What did you do to break Carly's heart? What have you done to Rosso? Why did you bury his brilliant art? What is this thing about you, this one humongous thing you aren't telling any of us?

Those were only a few of the million questions floating in Kyra's crazed mind. Which one she'd get to ask before Hildi picked her up by the hair and threw her out, she didn't know.

Juliet—not a stranger to madness and obsessions—was too wise to trust her and she was on her way there. One question, Kyra promised Juliet. If she could get anywhere near the Divine One, she'd get her answer and be out in no time. They'd have the rest of the evening for themselves.

Carly's slap had hurt, but not physically. Kyra found herself stroking her assaulted cheek, absentminded, the last contact she'd had with Carly. The last ever, because Carly will never again have anything to do with her. Despite Zoe's suggestion that she let her be, Kyra went up to her room and sat by her bed for a while, hoping she'd wake up in the mood for a quiet talk. Carly burned with fever. She's been asleep for two whole days now and those were the longest two days of Kyra's life.

The well-advertised shindig attracted everyone, even those who wouldn't be caught dead buying a book, let alone reading one. For instance, Beetlejuice. Kyra spotted her in black leather, a pair of handcuffs hanging from the back pocket of her jeans and Zingy Lola dangling from her neck like bondage. B. J.

cracked her up with that S and M façade. She was so totally vanilla in the sack, a good orgasm made her weep like a baby.

Kyra blew kisses to five ex-lovers, ecstatic they *were* exes. Two clients and her pretended to ignore each other, per protocol.

A steady trickle of people turned into a downright flood, packing the bookstore like the G-Spot on New Year's Eve. They were all there for love of the devil. Kyra was there for love of her victims—Juliet, Greg and the mysterious Rosso, whose genius paintings she so adored. Kyra was there for Carly.

As she waited for the devil's grand entrance, pushed and shoved by the thickening crowd, Kyra found herself in the drama section. Shakespeare. She gave the room another once-over to see who else she knew, then she turned to the shelves and searched for *Romeo and Juliet.* She found the paperback and quickly leafed to Act 1, Scene 1. *Here's what love is: a smoke made out of lovers' sighs.*

"Kyra San," said a soft voice.

She swung around in dull recognition. Saori was gazing up at her, eight years older but still ravishing with her black hair and her clear skin. Still fragrant with gardenias.

That smell was harsh. The memories those fucking gardenias provoked . . .

Eight years ago Kyra had declared this woman the love of her life. What did she know? Saori still had great hair, only Kyra didn't want to run her fingers through its silkiness, inhale her gardenias, or eat sushi off her naked body.

"Saori San, what are you doing in WeHo?" Kyra asked in Japanese.

"My kids are grown up," she answered, also in Japanese, in that sweet voice that used to make Kyra swoon. "I never forgot you."

"I wish you the best," Kyra said, managing a polite smile. She had too much on her mind to deal with Saori or with how she had ripped her heart to millions of bleeding strips.

Bookworms was packed with beautiful people, but Kyra had eyes only for one. Her lovely sylph, Juliet, was pushing her way through the growing crowd, her worried gaze locked on Kyra's.

Nearly a week together and Kyra loved her more every day. Juliet had her full blessing and admiration for stealing and transferring such a bulk of art all by herself. That grand larceny had its own brilliance. And they had more work to do. A fabulous masterpiece was still buried alive, waiting for rescue. Their plan was perfect. They'd pay Flora a visit when she was alone, supposedly to celebrate her matchmaking talents. They'd get her drunk on her favorite grappa and when she fell asleep, they'd go to work.

The glamorous author finally entered in a cloud of fame—the hair, the sunglasses, the airs all in place. It seemed the bookstore, the world, was too small for her. A man who could have been a Playgirl centerfold was affixed to her side like a fashion accessory, apparently infatuated with her as Greg had been, as Juliet had been. And as Carly had been. Or perhaps as Carly still was.

Juliet rubbed her scarred wrists absentmindedly. "This is Joe Rowland, her personal trainer," she said with clenched jaws, clinging to Kyra. "I guess she's with him now."

In the big kerfuffle, Garibaldi dropped her black feather boa. Joe Rowland immediately picked it up and rewrapped it around her neck.

Kyra wanted her to die.

"Isn't it nice to be so fucking wonderful," Kyra said, "and to always have someone to pick up shit you drop?"

She had a feeling Garibaldi heard her, the way she cocked her graceful head.

"How easily you've gotten over her," she added with venom.

Kyra had lost two loved ones, while the devil sacrificed nothing. She didn't seem at all bothered by the loss of Carly, if indeed she had lost her. Kyra assumed she had, because, as far as she knew, Carly was still asleep at Zoe's, sick and alone.

"Let's go," Juliet begged. "This whole scene takes me back to where I don't want to be."

"You're with me now," Kyra said. "You have a life."

The devil smiled at the silent crowd and sat down on a bar stool. She crossed her long legs. Her famous voice was barely raised above a whisper when she said, "Nothing can replace the pleasure of reading in solitude. I'm going to skip the reading."

A chorus of protestation and begging voices followed. She acknowledged the love with a smile. "All right, I'll give it my best shot." She waited for the applause to die down. "Here's the first chapter of my still unpublished next novel, *Private Hell.*"

She looked down at her cellphone screen and started reading.

That must be the book Carly helped edit. Judging from the first chapter, it was Garibaldi's best work yet.

"She doesn't take off her sunglasses even now," Kyra said to Juliet. "And she hasn't touched the phone screen even once. I bet there's nothing on it. I bet she's reciting from memory."

"Who cares? Let's get the fuck out of here." Juliet was pulling frantically at Kyra's arm. "Why are we even here?"

"What's with her?" Kyra asked. "I want to understand what happened."

"This is what happened." Juliet kissed her passionately, but she was trembling. "Let's go back to your place and light the fireplace and park ourselves on the couch under the fuzzy blanket, like the old couple we'll be in twenty years."

Kyra stared into her lover's dark brown eyes. Such beautiful eyes. Then she turned back toward Garibaldi and her dark shades. At the same time, Kyra remembered Carly's eyeball joke at the basement, which wasn't really a joke. And even when Carly slapped her, even then, she'd said something else eye related.

I would have given her my eyes.

Who talks like that?

Juliet, phenomenally strong for her size because madness gave her strength, was now pushing Kyra toward the exit in the ever-growing crowd. People were still coming in. "Let's go, let's go, let's go," she said through clenched teeth.

It was like something possessed her, the need to be anywhere but here, whereas before all she wanted was to be with Garibaldi. Stolen opera glasses, for fuck's sake!

When the two finally reached the exit, Kyra glanced back at Garibaldi, who was still reading. Kyra paused to think how totally fake her *reading* was. But what was fake about it, she didn't know.

Juliet was losing it. "Let's go," she kept chanting, "let's go, let's go, *let's go*," as though that had become her life-giving mantra. She expertly picked Kyra's pocket for the keys to the Wrangler, then Kyra found herself strapped into the passenger seat and tires screeched on asphalt still wet from the recent rains.

While letting Juliet whisk her away, Kyra observed her with a professional eye. Most people flip-flopped occasionally in their feelings, but Juliet's emotions were intense, erratic. If they were to stay together, Kyra would have to either ask one of her colleagues to be Juliet's therapist or get used to the strong duality in her personality.

76

"Your fever is down."

Zoe's hand was warm on my face. I smelled chicken soup. I opened my eyes.

"You've been asleep for the last three days. Here, eat."

The soup hit the spot. "This is great, Zoe." My throat didn't hurt anymore, but my voice was gone.

Zoe started the bath for me. I could smell vanilla bubbles with a touch of lavender. My nose had become so sensitive in the last month, I knew that she'd dropped only a dab into the water.

She said, "They were here."

My heart became a hummingbird, flapping her wings. "Who?" I knew who.

"She didn't get out of the car, only the big bodyguard. I said you were out, which wasn't a lie."

The same heart grew into a huge condor and it was trying to fly out of my throat and choke me. I wanted to shake Zoe and ask her why and how and what, but I didn't actually have the energy for it.

"Well done, Zoe."

I stuck my nose back in Anna's fluffy pink scarf and sniffed it. I missed her desperately. Either the musk had faded or my nose had adjusted. I had to think about everything she told me. About her twisted reasons and her straight lies. About my burning love for her.

"They'll be back," Zoe said over the noise of running water. "What happened between you two anyway?"

"It was good."

Oh, so good. I slowly peeled off my jeans, hesitating because when I'd put them on I'd been sore from her loving and now I was healed and I craved her seeing fingers and her mouth and the taste of her . . .

"It was good, Zoe, then it wasn't. I'm glad you're here for me."

"You two need to meet somewhere neutral and talk and listen to each other."

"Yes." I would wait for Zoe to leave before I took off my T shirt and stepped into the bath. We were never shy in front of each other, but now things had changed. Now my whole body had been marked by love. Now the only eyes that should see me were the eyes that could not.

The tears started, so I said in what I thought was a light tone, "I want the biggest fucking double cheeseburger, dripping with BBQ sauce." Even that statement sounded way too intense in my ears, but when I said it, hunger became true and I craved exactly that.

"Perfect bubbles," Zoe said. "We ordered Mexican, if you want some of that."

Then she was out and I could hear her skipping down the stairs loudly in her bare feet. Anna's bare feet on the floor sounded so different, not only serving for getting from here to there, but for seeing and identifying and warning and sensing and . . .

I bathed in vanilla and lavender and felt like a human being again. I put on a white button-down shirt and an old pair of blue jeans so loose, they slid off my hips. My face in the mirror was thinner, with prominent cheekbones and big haunted eyes. I must have aged a thousand years.

Still, I was going to live. And I was really hungry.

Downstairs the fireplace blazed. Zoe and Robert cuddled on the couch, eating and watching *Wheel of Fortune* by the sound of it. They were addicted.

"I'm going to see who's at the G-Spot," I said. "Wanna come?"

"We're in for the evening," Robert said. "But it's good to see you back to life."

The evening was warm. I walked the few blocks on Santa Monica Boulevard, passing Gelson's, Joey's Cafe and the busy La Boheme. My stomach was growling in hunger, my mind forming an irresistible image of a cold beer bottle dripping with frost, and B. J.'s triple cheeseburger, juicy with spicy-hot barbecue sauce. I couldn't get there fast enough.

Bookworms was bustling with more life than usual. A book-signing, I guessed from the long line spilling out of it and coiling around the block. My head buzzed with something I'd forgotten, something I was supposed to know about the event, but I didn't bother poking my head in. I was thirsty for a beer.

A busy B. J. smiled behind the counter. "I heard you crossed," she said. "Congratulations."

"Right." I smiled back. "I crossed to light beer."

I carried my food to a corner booth so I wouldn't be interrupted. As I took no time making the cheeseburger disappear, my eyes and nose were running and barbecue sauce now stained my white shirt. I didn't care because it so hit the spot and I couldn't remember ever being so hungry in my life. Then I relaxed with my beer and picked my teeth, watching a springy, slim woman dancing all by herself among couples. She twirled and turned and swayed in front of the mirrored wall. Her fingers ran through her short, dark hair, sliding slowly down her body in a self-caress. She was her own best audience. Everything about her was tight. Her tank top stretched on small breasts. An entire knee poked through a large tear in her jeans. Her belly-button ring gleamed and fascinated me. The night was mine, and we both needed a dance partner.

I could seduce her like Kyra, I thought, only to see if I could.

I stood behind the lone dancer, making sure I was reflected in the mirror, the only place she cared to look. I rested my elbows on the counter behind me and opened the top two buttons of my white shirt. I tried to pour beer down my throat and missed by a mile. Ice-cold, fizzy liquid streamed between my breasts, down my stomach, evaporating immediately from my body heat. My white shirt was a mess.

I could go a step farther and lure her elegantly, like Anna would. Eyes closed, I imagined the woman's pelvis against mine. I shuddered. In front of me, gray eyes, pale face, pale hair streaming heavy down to her waist, black silk dress that would slide off so easily. Anna's hands rested on the small of my back and slipped down, reducing mountains of passion into one point, swaying both of us with the music. A bruise on my hip ached.

"Anna," I whispered, "you don't belong here."

"It's Sibyl," said a scratchy voice with a pronounced lisp.

I knew about Sibyl from Kyra. Sibyl would get stoned and tell the future. I looked down. The ripped hole in her jeans gaped at me, promising adventures I didn't want. I matched my rhythm with hers. Her fingers stroked my lower back, but I wasn't excited.

"Are you the famous Sibyl?" I asked. "The psychic?"

"The very one," she said. "You need a reading?"

"I do."

"I need to smoke a little first," she said, sounding like she'd already smoked a lot. "I live a block away. And you have a sexy voice."

"It's temporary."

"Then let's go."

When Sibyl pushed me against the wall in a dark hallway of a decaying apartment building, I still felt nothing. When she kissed me, I felt her tongue ring, but nothing else. Her door lock needed jiggling. She had a marijuana leaf tattoo above her right nipple, and she bragged about the one on her shaved pubis. "A tattoo of what else but Michelangelo's Delphic Sibyl. Cost me a fortune."

I didn't get as far as seeing her pubic tattoo. Anna was irreplaceable, as if I'd needed proof.

"I'm sorry," I said. "I can't."

"No worries. Want a smoke?" Naked from the waist up, Sibyl pulled a carefully rolled joint—probably the only neatly done thing in the messy apartment—out of the back pocket of her jeans.

"One hit and I'll be out of here," I said.

"How about Coke?"

"Diet, please," I said, assuming she meant a soda.

Sibyl left in a skip and came back with two cans of Diet Coke. Her small boobies above her visible ribs only reminded me of Anna's majestic breasts and strong, upright figure.

"Rebound?"

She dropped to a seated position on a shaggy, colorless carpet that needed a Hoover and flea bombs.

I nodded, sipping, sitting in a chair.

"Same here," Sibyl said. "Bitch left me for a dude."

"I'm so sorry," I said again, buttoning up my shirt, all the way up to my neck. "I shouldn't have."

Sibyl sucked on her joint, closing her eyes in pleasure. She passed it to me. "Here's your chance to talk about it with a perfect stranger. What's your name?"

I inhaled deeply and gave her back the joint. "Eurydice."

"That's a good one." Her laugh was too loud. "And your Orpheus lost you to Hades because he turned to look too soon?"

I said, "My Orpheus is blind."

"The turning broke the contract, not the seeing," Sibyl said.

"She didn't lose me," I protested, thinking of Anna's frightened face in the painting. "She didn't."

Sibyl had misty eyes. "I remember this blind chick. Desiré. Sex with her was fucking awesome because you gotta feel what you can't see. She fucked dirty, like a whore on meth, but she wasn't mute, so I had to listen to tons of bullshit."

I half-listened to Sibyl's description of her *awesome, amazing* blind sex. As she spoke in a tough-girl lisp, I glanced around at the murkiness of unopened windows, at a sink filled with unwashed dishes and at a table covered with dirty bongs and half-burned incense sticks meant to cover up unpleasant odors with an assault on the senses. My love for Anna, our passion, had nothing to do with Sibyl's adventures. Anna's darkness had never been as dark as this cave. Anna's blindness was colorful; Anna's foreign languages were never as alien as Sibyl's talk of awesome sex. Making love to Anna was poetry spoken in a heavenly contralto. Anna.

" . . . never stopped looking for the same high," Sibyl concluded. "Our first date lasted a week. How long was yours?"

"A month."

Sibyl whistled. "Fucking awesome."

I was short of breath. My hands went to my neck, desperate for a fluffy pink scarf that wasn't there. Her musk was life. I'd left the scarf at home, and I couldn't breathe without it.

Sibyl offered me the joint. "Here, you need another hit."

"Thanks. I'll be off now."

"Your blind Orpheus won't make it without you. She will die."

"She's stronger than all of us!" I said, my voice squeaky and frightened and unconvincing.

Sibyl took another lazy hit and lay back on the dirty carpet. "You have working eyes, Eurydice. Use them or lose her to fire."

I shuddered at the way she spread her fingers and let the joint fall to the carpet at the word *fire*. I backed away and toward the door.

"You don't know what you're talking about. Fire happened in her past."

"And yet I tell the future." Sibyl arched her upper back and looked at me upside down from the carpet. Her eyes got big, misted up, then closed.

For some reason I needed to argue. "In my Bible, if I remember any of it correctly, they stoned the false prophets."

"I'm stoned already." A gargling laughter started from the bottom of her belly, wiggling the marijuana leaf above her breast. "Fire!"

I jiggled the doorknob. It was stuck, and I needed the pink scarf to breathe. I couldn't inflate my lungs without Anna's musk, with this woman shouting *fire*. The door finally gave in.

"Leave it open for air," Sibyl said, slurring her speech, laughing more. "Fire!" she kept crying out loud in that loud scratchy voice. "Fire!" Laughing.

That laughter ran shivers down my spine all the way down the dark hallway, down the stairs to the bustle of a busy Santa Monica Boulevard.

"Fucking junkie," I said, my voice hysterical in my ears, my head ringing with her laughter.

I ran all the way home to call Anna. She still had my cellphone and I had to call her and I couldn't breathe at all, or live without her musky pink scarf.

The truth didn't dawn on me even when I spotted the first thing out of place. The black Jaguar, waxed to a shiny perfection, blocked my Mustang in the driveway.

Zoe and Robert still sat on the sofa, munching on crispy tortilla chips, watching TV. Zoe raised her eyes toward my bedroom, and I knew in an instant.

"Here?"

Zoe nodded and smiled.

I grabbed my car keys from the bowl, but Zoe caught me from behind. She was very fast and strong from lugging ER patients and heavy equipment.

"Go deal with your shit, Carly," she said, steering me up the stairs.

I hid my face in her shoulder. "How'd you let her into my messy bedroom?"

"Don't worry about the mess," Zoe said, adding with surprising simplicity, "She's as blind as a bat."

"Did she tell you?" I asked, my heart racing. "How did you know?"

"A nurse can tell, silly," she said. "She moves in her own house different from how she moves here, in an unfamiliar place. Here she needed help." Zoe screwed up her face. "*Phew.* You stink of dope."

I gazed up toward my room, short of breath, wishing I'd had another hit of that grass. I'd gone up this steep staircase thousands of times, but never like this, with Anna up there, waiting for me. She was blind, I wasn't. The stairs seemed more worn out, the walls suddenly needed a fresh coat of paint, and I was freaking out.

77

I found Anna leaning against the open window, blowing cigarette smoke out into West Hollywood's night air. Her pale beauty, the regal line of her neck and shoulder against the city lights, transformed the simple room into a palace.

Her presence in this room felt wrong.

Here I'd made love to Greg. Here I'd cried out her name for the first time in front of a freshly painted *Blue Madonna*. Here —

Then I was locked in her strong arms. We fell onto my bed, greedy, hungry for each other. Desperate. We didn't say a word until that hunger was satisfied, the desperation eased.

"I can't make it without you," Anna said, breathless. "I will die without you."

"Why are you using her words?" I asked with growing fear.

"Whose words?" she asked, still kissing me with swollen lips, still wanting more.

"Sibyl, the stoned prophet."

"Are you delirious?" she asked, feeling my forehead. "You still sound sick."

I moved the long hair off her face and gazed down at her in the chaos of my unmade bed, in the midst of our strewn clothes. A limp, red sock lay next to her ear. This was my truth, my mess, the dichotomy of our existence, and she could not see it.

"I was cruel to you," I said.

"But you were right, Carly." She turned us both and lay atop me and her hair fell forward, cascading, trapping both of us in a protective veil. "I've just been to the bookstore. I was humbled by the adoration of complete strangers who love me for what I've given them in books and films. I want to give them truth."

"What truth, Anna?"

"My new novel, my old paintings. A tell-all autobiography with the truth of my blindness."

And just like that, she uttered *my blindness* for the first time.

"If you are willing, Carly, you'll restore what you can of my burned paintings. What can't be restored we will show as is."

"Damaged?" I asked.

"As damaged as I am, with every scratch and scorch mark." She held my face between her hands. "Even if it takes years, I'd like to entrust my life's work to you. And—"

"It doesn't have to take years," I said.

I'd cheer up the basement with bright lights, hip-hop music and long work tables, and find artists to help me. The ghosts would disperse along with the dust balls, and Flora wouldn't be frightened to bring us all lunch and join us there and hang out.

"Long work tables," Anna said, seeing what I was imagining. "Music."

"We should start right away," I said. "Tonight."

"Or tomorrow, my eager, hot-blooded Carly." She softly kissed my forehead, my eyes, my mouth. "My love, I'd like for you to do your own work, to paint for yourself. And . . ."

I wanted to fall down on my knees and apologize for my cutting words, for my cruelty, for leaving her standing in the rain, for doubting her love. But falling down on my knees became superfluous, because that was exactly what she was doing.

"Carly Rosen," said Anna Garibaldi, kneeling down at the very spot where I'd painted *Blue Madonna*, where I'd rested my forehead on still-wet cerulean blue paint and uttered her name in anguish for the first time.

"Carly Rosen," she repeated, holding my hands, her famous contralto mine alone. "If you don't mind damaged goods, will you do me the great honor of becoming my wife?"

In her voice, even that question sounded like a command.

She remained at my feet, as still as a statue, allowing me a moment to contemplate my response. I had nothing to contemplate, or to doubt. My silence was only an awed reaction to her beauty. In the single street light her heavy hair became a yellowing wedding veil she had kept in a dark closet for years and now put on just for me.

"Yes," I said, choked with tears, breathing in the musk in her hair. "I'll marry you, Anna. We'll have our wedding and your show on the same day."

She laughed out loud in relief, then she removed a ring from her finger and slipped it onto mine. "This used to be my mother's," she said, wrapping her strong hand around mine. "Now it is yours."

The old-fashioned diamond glittered in the semidarkness like millions of stars. It was a perfect fit.

"Yes, my Anna," I said again. "Yes, yes, yes."

"I've never been so happy, Carly. *Carly*." She repeated my name as if deriving strength from its sound. She ran her seeing fingers yearningly from my forehead down to my chin. "If I could see your face only once, now, I'd file it in my memory and shut up about it forever."

"My face is one big smile," I said. "Ear to ear."

She said, "Let's tell them."

We quickly put on some clothes. She twisted her hair into a sloppy knot. "Do I look presentable?"

"My beautiful Anna." I brushed a strand of hair off her worried forehead and planted a kiss on her lips. "Most of us work very hard to reach your starting point."

We shouldn't have left my room. We should have stayed in my bed all night.

78

Zoe and Robert looked up at us and turned off the television. I held on to Anna's arm, making sure she didn't trip in the unfamiliar house, then I went for it.

"You were right, Zoe," I said. "Anna is blind."

"No shit," Zoe said.

And I had to wonder if she would have kept her bare feet on the coffee table had she not known of Anna's blindness.

"Are you okay, Anna?" Robert asked.

His gaze darted to the diamond on my hand, and his face broke into a smile.

"I'm perfectly fine, thank you," Anna said. "Now to the good news." She pulled out her cellphone and quietly said, "Hildi."

Within seconds Hildi was at the door and then inside.

"We want the three of you to be the first to know," Anna announced. "Carly and I decided to get married."

"I knew it," Robert cried out.

Big excitement, hugs and kisses. Hildi wiped a tear, and her huge face stretched into a smile. Zoe did a few dance twirls in the air and around the living room, which I was trying to describe to Anna with difficulty. Robert brought out a bottle of champagne. "Sorry for the shitty stuff, Anna," he said, uncorking it. "Had I known, I would have had Cristal Brut chilling."

"You can pay for this faux pas by doing my hair, make-up and wedding dress," she simply said. "Only, I'm very particular."

His eyes lit up. He was beside himself. "I'd kill to dress you. This figure, this hair, this face, I'd simply kill for it."

"No need for violence," Anna said, laughing.

Zoe rolled her eyes at me. "I have a gay boyfriend and didn't even know it." Then she froze quickly, like a cartoon character. "Violence!" she said. "We should call Kyra." She crossed her arms and stared at me. "I mean you need to call Kyra. You fucking slapped her."

"I'll go there now," I said, knowing that Kyra might need some maintenance before giving me her blessing.

"Don't be too long, love." Anna kissed me. "I miss you already." She took my cellphone from her purse and shoved it into my hand. "Don't forget it again."

That quickly, Anna and Hildi were off to tell Flora.

And Robert was on the phone with Sunset Caterers.

"It's one o'clock in the morning," Zoe said.

"They're booked for ages," he explained. "We want the best."

Zoe helped me pack up a trunk with clothes and art supplies.

She hugged me. "Are you sure, Carly?"

"I've never been so sure," I said. "I love her."

Then I was in my car. A few minutes later Juliet Blair opened Kyra's door to my knock and sighed with relief when she saw me.

So they were playing house. I needed to catch up with Kyra's life.

"Carly, thank God you're here."

I saw her white-knuckled grip on her cellphone.

"She's been writing you a letter—started it right after you showed up at Zoe's—explaining what happened and apologizing and . . . you are going to forgive her, right?"

"What for? I'm the one who slapped her, and she actually did me a favor."

"I wish she'd kept writing. This, I don't like."

"*This* what?"

"Oh, Carly . . . She's in Palos Verdes, waiting for Anna."

Fear choked my inflamed throat. "What! What the fuck?" I let out a squeak I'd meant to be a scream.

"She wants to ask her a question or a favor or something. She's gone a little crazy."

"Why can't she ask it like a normal person? Why the creepiness?"

"I don't know." Juliet's eyes with their long lashes filled with tears. "I've been on the phone all night, begging her to come home, but she's a mule. I tried calling Flora, but it's one thirty and she's asleep."

When I freaked out, I wasn't thinking of other overly motherly things Kyra had done on my behalf, like the time she'd embarrassed me in front of a full classroom, calling an abusive teacher *an incompetent who shouldn't go near little kids*. No, I wasn't thinking of Kyra's overprotectiveness.

This was more than that kind of thing. This was weird.

I wasn't worried about a verbal confrontation between the women I loved, because Anna could hold her own against Kyra, against anyone. But still . . . My heart was racing in a bad, bad way.

Words can't kill, nothing is going to happen I repeated to myself. My sister would confront my future wife, then Anna would diffuse the confrontation and I'd find the two of them on the deck, sipping tequila together and laughing. New sisters.

But instead of being reassured, my thoughts stirred my agitation. Dread squeezed my throat until I couldn't breathe.

"Why did you let her go there, Juliet?" I asked. "What does she want with Anna?"

"She needs a confrontation and . . . and revenge."

"Revenge? *Shit.*" My voice was strangled, desperate, stifled by dread. My hands clamped into fists as I tried very hard not to kill the messenger. There wasn't time to kill her or to ask if she wanted to come with me.

I ran to my car, gunned the engine and fussed at Kyra in my head. I called her number, but she didn't pick up. I kept fussing, arguing, cursing her out loud in the private space of my car, which wasn't very private because people stared at me from the street, from other vehicles, as I fell apart. I didn't care. What the hell was my crazy sister going to do?

Everything felt too late, too slow, too sluggish against my speed. Urgency flooded my system with adrenaline, grew demanding by the minute, made eighty miles per hour on the 405 freeway feel like a crawl. My ass barely grazed the seat as I stepped on the accelerator. Nothing would ever be fast enough,

I thought, or early enough, and life happened too late, always too, too late.

Your blind Orpheus won't make it without you. She will die.

My right foot pushed the gas in a spasm of desperation. Suddenly unable to see, I wiped a hand across my eyes. I didn't know when I'd started crying.

"No," I wailed. "No, no, no."

79

Kyra was going to do what she did best. Talk had never failed her, until it started failing constantly. As she waited, parked at that secret surveillance spot Juliet regretted pointing out to her, she thought of the poor example she'd be setting for her clients if word of her irrational behavior ever came out. What news she'd make if she got arrested for stalking a celebrity. Her only explanation was that she'd been driven nuts by this woman. La Divina was to blame for everything.

Juliet had recovered from her Garibaldi obsession, leaving Kyra with a bad case of it. Juliet's stalking had to do with her own experience, but Kyra was going global, for all of them: Greg, Carly, Juliet and Rosso. She narrowed all her questions for the devil down to a single one—What happened to Rosso?—and if she didn't get thrown out, one request—a permission to see all the paintings in the basement. That was all. Quite civilized.

The calming sounds of the waves were interrupted only by the *hoo-h-h-hoo* of a lone owl. She'd been mulling over the night's events—Carly, heartbroken again and burning with fever, alone in her bed, while the glamorous devil was hanging on some man's arm, surrounded by her fans, having already forgotten Carly.

Juliet called a few times, begging Kyra to come home, threatening to leave her, sweet-talking her with phone sex, promising food sex. "I made your favorite chili, chocolate sauce for dessert."

As Kyra was glued to her post, she used the time to continue that email letter to Carly on her cellphone. She needed answers. She needed to know what was going on here.

It was getting late. What if Garibaldi decided to stay in town for the night? Fifteen more minutes, then home, Kyra promised herself. She searched the inside of her jean jacket for chewing gum, and found the paperback of *Romeo and Juliet*. She'd never paid! Her new lover had given her more than a bad case of Garibaldi obsession.

The house and the gravel road leading to it were illuminated by the eerie light of those white crystals. It was all very sci-fi. Crashing waves soothed Kyra's urban ears, lulling her into sleep. Her cellphone woke her with the theme song from *Divine Darkness*, Juliet's ringtone.

The digital display said one thirty a.m., March 15. Not a good date for big decisions because the soothsayer said something and then someone was assassinated. Julius Caesar, Kyra thought.

The phone persisted. She picked up.

"*Beware the Ides of March*," she said in a dramatic tone, hoping to lighten Juliet up.

"Stop!" Juliet cried out. "Your sister was just here. She apologized."

Kyra heard the crackling of tires on the gravel road.

"Good, good," she said, distracted. "They're here."

She clicked *send* and emailed Carly everything she'd written while waiting. Then she stepped out in her socked feet, leaving her spurred cowboy boots in the car. The phone was glued to her ear.

"You can listen if you want," she told Juliet.

"All is well now. Come home." Juliet's voice had a touch of hysteria. She could definitely use some therapy.

Hildi got out of the Jaguar and opened Garibaldi's door. She stepped out alone. Where had she lost the muscle-dude who was so attached to her side in the bookstore?

Anna held on to Hildi's arm and let the big woman lead her toward the house. Kyra frowned. Hildi was actually *leading* her. Helped by Hildi, Anna was still imposing and elegant, the ruling queen of this fantasy dreamscape. Only . . .

"Fuck me," Kyra whispered. "I'm slow as shit, but I finally got it."

"What?" Juliet asked.

"I got my answer. This all makes sense now. When you thought she stopped seeing you, you were right, she had. When you stood in front of her wearing orange and she ignored you, *she didn't see you.*"

"How?" Juliet's voice was clipped by fear. "She's the eye behind the camera!"

"That's the craziest thing," Kyra whispered. "She may not have even seen you when she directed you in *Divine Darkness.* She's blind, Juliet. Do you read me?"

"My darling, you are in a bad, scary place. You are losing your mind. I've been there."

"Yes," Kyra said. The raw gravel hurt her socked feet. "I've lost it, like Greg and Carly and you. Maybe even Rosso. Hey, guess what? I'm a klepto. I stole a book."

"Kyra!" Juliet shouted.

Another call was coming in. Kyra didn't care because she had a mission. She shoved the phone into the back pocket of her jeans, leaving it on. Garibaldi held on to Hildi's elbow and smoked a fag all the way to the house. Kyra's doubts were dispersed. She was using Hildi as a Seeing Eye dog.

Kyra followed closely behind them, waiting till they reached the house. The advantage of surprise meant she'd get the truth. The disadvantage would mean a knee-jerk reaction.

She advanced, keeping one hand on her back pocket, as though that would keep Juliet silent. She saw through the big window that Hildi was slowly hauling herself up the stairs. Anna stayed alone. Perfect. Kyra slipped inside.

Anna headed toward the small vestibule with the family photos, the one containing the staircase leading down to all those art treasures Kyra so wanted to see.

Kyra glanced around her, taking in the beauty of the interior in a way she hadn't on her first visit. The eerie light of the tall crystals, the moonlight on the ocean, were truly magnificent. Yet that beauty, like an iridescent oil painting, looked fake. Garibaldi's beauty was real. She stood still, head tilted, listening, her cigarette burning in her hand. Kyra knew the blind developed special senses, but could she really hear her socked feet on this hardwood? Maybe she could hear Juliet's screaming coming from the phone.

Garibaldi took off her ever-present sunglasses—now Kyra knew why she wore them even at night. She held on to the metal balustrade—exactly where Kyra wanted to go. She inhaled the last of her fag, dropping a wad of ash she could not see on the gleaming hardwood floor.

Kyra said, “Good evening,” in her softest, least threatening voice.

“Carly?” Garibaldi turned to face her, a smile of satisfaction on her lips, a blissful smile that made Kyra think of the state following a mind-blowing orgasm. “That was quick, my love.”

A brilliant idea flashed in Kyra’s head. Anna was mistaking her voice for her sister’s; why not milk her confusion and discover all the secrets?

“I’d like to see the paintings,” Kyra said.

“You want to start on my paintings tonight?” Garibaldi asked.

“Yours?” Kyra started coughing from sheer surprise.

Her paintings? She was so madly in love with *her* paintings? Kyra cleared her throat, and then the trail of cigarette smoke and the cloying scent of turpentine had her coughing in earnest.

Garibaldi had been facing away from her, about to stomp out the cigarette in an ashtray positioned in a wall niche. She whirled on her heel. “Kyra?”

It was the first time Kyra had seen those light gray eyes. They opened wide in fear, utterly beautiful and completely blind. Anna took a step back. Her high heel caught on the worn stone stair as she lost her footing and tumbled down. Kyra instinctively reached out, racing to catch her and crying out for Hildi. The burning cigarette butt flew from Anna’s fingers in a perfect arc, passing through the cool air coming up from the basement, then continued its descent into the turpentine vapors.

The sequence of events took seconds. So did the explosive blaze flashing over them.

80

Your blind Orpheus won't make it without you. She won't make it . . .

My phone rang. I snatched it off the seat, but it wasn't Kyra.

Hildi's howl was a soul-shattering release of pain.

I went light-headed, turning the wheel and moving back into my lane when a car horn blared at me.

I couldn't hear Hildi. I couldn't hear . . .

Her big baritone was a mere whisper when she said, "It happened so fast, Carly. The fire spread, burning so fast, destroying so quickly . . ."

"Anna? Is she . . . ?" I was unable to speak. The image of a maniacal Sibyl flashed in my mind, shrieking in stoned ridicule, Fire! *Fire!*

"I don't know." Hildi huffed and puffed and sobbed all at once. "They're working on both of them."

The coast road snaked up through Palos Verdes Drive. A few weeks ago Hildi had driven me here and I'd been afraid of Anna. Now . . .

My lips desperately chanted, "Be alive, Anna. Be alive."

Only Anna was on my mind, not Kyra. Never Kyra.

All my senses, those Anna had taught me to enjoy, were crying with me. At a distance, my eyes saw the flames lighting up the night sky. As I pulled close, my ears heard the wails of emergency vehicles. But my nose was the worst.

My nose told me, as soon as I jumped from my car, that the scent so dear to Anna, the one that reminded her of her unseen loves, had turned on her.

Turpentine fumes told me that everything was lost.

Epilogue

I've stopped screaming. I have no more nightmares. My nights are quiet, restful. My dreams are made of white emptiness, foggy, soupy spaces of silence and weightlessness.

I find myself unable to stop speaking to you, telling you, *showing* you what's happening around me. I haven't given up my need to share my life with you.

If only we could write ourselves alternate endings. Now, in hindsight, enveloped in darkness bleaker than yours ever was, I wish I'd told Kyra everything right away. Maybe then we'd all be here and happy.

The nude woman gazes down at me from the red painting. Her mouth is moving. Is she telling me something, or is my vision swimming after staring fixedly for so long? Is my mind going bonkers again? There's nowhere in the world I'd rather be but here. Your paintings, their colors, flavors and music, explode inside me in rich sensations. Only here, as I lie motionless on this white futon, surrounded by your art, do I remember I'd once been touched by absolute love.

The memory of your hands sets my skin afire, your healing hands, warm, loving and rough from years of climbing rocks. I miss your seeing fingertips, fragrant with musk and tangy with the juice of oranges. Your hands fluttered on me like the tiny wings of monarchs, stirring all my senses at once. Your voice was rainwater running down a wall of rocks through a secret cove and out into the ocean.

I want you, Anna, not memories. One day you'll come back to me and I'll know you. I'll recognize you in a majestic pose or in the sound of rich, throaty laughter.

When I crank my neck back until the room turns upside down and I squeeze my eyelids into narrow slits, I see you standing there in a white dress, a feather boa framing your shoulders. When the sun sparkles gold and platinum through the white lace curtain, I can just about imagine the big, flamboyant hair.

Your face I can't imagine no matter what I do. Such perfect beauty can't be imagined nor remembered nor painted. Some died trying. Your beauty was the sum total of its features—warmth, movement, voice and laughter.

Your last laughter stays with me. Your gray eyes, wide and alert, were the only recognizable feature in the sooty mess you'd become. You reached up with a shaky hand and touched my cheek. Your famous contralto was only a whisper when you said, "My wish . . . has come true . . . my love. I see you with my eyes and you are beautiful . . . So beautiful."

I smiled down at you even as my heart was dying with you, because I wanted the last face you saw, and your first glimpse of me, to be happy.

"Put coins on my eyes," you said. "For the ferryman."

"Tell Hades I'm coming for you," I said.

"Just don't look back, Carly. Never look back."

Your rich, throaty laugh rasped with your dying breath.

Juliet lies next to me, also silent and beyond tears, hugging one cowboy boot and a paperback copy of *Romeo and Juliet*. We stare up at the red nude, both insane with our losses. The pink cloud of cashmere around my neck retains a faint hint of musk. Juliet keeps sprinkling it for me with a bottle she'd once appropriated from your closet. Thank heaven for kleptomaniacs.

"Did I ever tell you about the flavor of musk?" I ask.

"You did," Juliet says. "Kyra had a long, exhausting theory about fragrances."

"Fragrance killed them both," I said.

"How so?" Juliet asks.

"Anna used to sniff turpentine. She kept an open bottle in the basement because she so missed painting."

Yes, I remember the longing on your face when you inhaled those fumes, much like my longing now when I inhale your musk.

"Tell me again what happened," I say to Juliet.

She'd heard everything through Kyra's phone. First the gravel road when Kyra followed you to the house wearing only socks. Along with Kyra, Juliet learned about your blindness, then they discovered whose works they were actually obsessed with. Kyra's emails and letters, which by now I've read countless times, have a running vein: her love for your paintings.

Juliet brings my sister back to life with the retelling of her last moments for the gazillionth time. So did one of the EMTs who worked on Kyra, but couldn't save her life. She managed to tell him about the burning cigarette, your heel that got caught, the blaze, and something she had discovered about the paintings. Something he did not understand, but I do. And I share everything with you again, Anna.

Your paintings are worth dying for, but you two didn't have to be so literal about it.

"Good thing she left these behind," Juliet says, tightly hugging Kyra's boot. "Now it's your turn to tell me what *should* have happened. Your voice gives me some of Kyra back."

"If only you two had stolen *The Turning*," I say, "I'd have some of Anna back."

Juliet springs into a seated position. "We do have it!" she cries out, animated for the first time since our tragedy. "How could I forget *Hot Surfaces*?"

"What?" I'm also up, infected by her excitement.

Juliet scrolls through photos on her cellphone until she thrusts the phone toward me and says, "Here."

I gasp at the sight of *The Turning*, the most accurate rendition of you, my love. My chest threatens to burst with both sorrow and joy.

"How did you . . . Why do you . . ." I can't find the words.

"Kyra took this. We shared each other's photos. We have a whole file of places where we . . . Well, never mind about that. The point is we have this. We can blow it up to its original size."

She lays her hand atop mine.

"And maybe, maybe you can re-create it."

"Art conquers all?" I say, trying to sound cheerful, but Juliet has seen what *The Turning* did to me.

She runs the back of her hand over my cheek and says in that sweet, honey-rich voice, "Let's dream up the happiest of happy endings, Carly."

I swallow my tears and smile. "A new fairy tale?"

"Yes, please," Juliet says.

We tell each other plenty of those. The stories, and what's left of the expensive tequila in the spiked bottle, keep us both away from the loony bin, at least for now. Yet only for now, because we're starting to believe the stories, and they get more elaborate and improbable with each telling.

"Make it as maudlin as you can," Juliet says. "I'll get the bottle."

Each time I tell the fairy tale, it acquires more ridiculous details. In one of the versions, Kyra and I perform the Native American Radical Forgiveness Ceremony, in which we acknowledge our shadows and welcome our full selves into the light. That storyline made Juliet laugh out loud, because even in fantasy it was hard to keep Kyra quiet through a long, non-verbal ceremony.

In another version, Kyra heroically saves you, and you regain perfect vision while retaining your beauty, with only a tiny scar on your left arm to show for the fire and your fall down the stairs. A Thai monk, whose orange robe matches the glorious sunset, performs a double wedding ceremony in a hospital room high above Los Angeles.

Juliet and I face each other on the white futon. Her brown-eyed gaze meets mine.

"I know why Kyra loved you so," I say.

"Tell me again, Carly. Take it all the way this time."

"What, a double wedding wasn't a big enough fantasy? I need to work in three happy couples?"

"Yeah, Zoe and Robert too. Three happily-ever-after couples; Entertainment Tonight covering the festivities, rolling out a red carpet in the hospital hallway and stopping to interview each of us; and maybe you could throw in something about me and Kyra adopting a baby boy and giving Flora the grandson she always wanted."

"Poor Flora," I say. "At least she didn't suffer." I hope she didn't suffer.

"I have her recipes." Juliet's eyes fill up with new tears. "I'll put them together in a cookbook and she'll always be remembered."

I know what Juliet needs, I know what I need, and yet it can never be enough. Without you, Anna, I can never make it enough. That very day I fell in love with you, I asked why you wrote alternate endings. You said that reality is cruel and that fiction should be truth, but also an escape. You said that if a writer is considered God, she should be a benevolent one.

Where, Anna, is my benevolent God? Three loved ones lost in less than a year is a hell of a cruel reality. This isn't the first time I get a funeral instead of a wedding. We can dream up alternate endings all we want, but we are not meant to live happily ever after. We never were.

Still, as an expert on your fiction, I can imagine the most saccharin, schmaltzy idea of a happy ending for you and Kyra. It will please Juliet, if not me.

"Okay," I say. "How about . . .

"After a few days in the ICU, Anna finally woke up. I was a mess from staying up without showering or eating. I'd shower today, now that Anna was awake and recovering from the smoke inhalation.

"I hadn't yet forgiven Kyra for her role in the fire and for almost getting Anna killed. Hildi and Flora pleaded her case, describing Kyra's heroic efforts. Anna's agility and general good health were the reason she managed to stop her own fall and not end up a crispy critter at the bottom of the stairs. As for the smoke and fire, Anna had made it out of both only thanks to Kyra, who'd proved super strong, fast and resourceful. Kyra had risked her own life to get Anna up the burning stairwell, drag her out to the fresh air, and put out the fire in her long hair."

Juliet smiles in pride at that storyline, so I keep at it.

"My sister, a true hero, had braved the flames to carry my love out of hell. But she'd dragged me through hell too, and even her hangdog expression and burns weren't penance enough for me to let her off the hook. Not yet. Not quite yet."

"You have to forgive Kyra," Juliet whispers next to me. "You just have to."

I pretend not to hear her, and continue with the tale.

"Still, if anyone could get me to make a big production out of forgiving Kyra, it would be Juliet, as dear to me now as another sister. Juliet had saved a large portion of Anna's art. If not for Juliet, Anna would have lost not only her house, but her life's work.

"I sat next to Anna on her hospital bed, stroking her arm and her hair, unable to stray too far and shivering each time she spoke in that smoke-damaged rasp. I confessed to Anna that Juliet had tamed Kyra, had brought love and contentment to her, a prospect I'd given up on years earlier. But it was true; Kyra truly loved Juliet. And Juliet, she . . ."

I blink. How long have I been silent? Has Juliet fallen asleep? No, she is wide awake next to me on the white futon. Silent tears stream down her face.

"We had two weeks together. Only two weeks," she whispers, clinging to me. "Sometimes I wonder how I keep breathing."

"Me too."

I close my eyes. I listen to our breathing, those in-and-out sounds of ongoing life. Painfully empty life.

An eternity passes. Nothing changes.

"We're doing it all wrong, Juliet."

"Of course we are, but it helps."

"No, we can't let it end without a fight." An idea is taking shape inside me.

"What are we fighting?" she asks.

"It worked once, why not again?" I grin, certain I look like a madwoman. "Get up, we're going to do it," I say, already on my feet, determined and out of breath from sheer excitement.

Juliet laughs, uncertain. "For a moment, in this light, you looked like Kyra, the way she did when we'd decided to go back for *The Turning*."

"We're going to Hades, Juliet, to free both of them."

"Do I need my toolkit?"

"We need mine," I say.

"Where is Hades, Carly?" Juliet asks.

"In our hearts and all around us, on these walls and above us, on the ceiling."

I know I speak the truth. It rings clear and true in my soul and comes boldly from my lips. It's what you showed me. I finally understand it all. Hades is in me and in you. So are Orpheus and Eurydice. She will always call out to him, and he will always turn back, because their love for each other is greater than reason. And so Hades always wins. And we are all of them, forever intermingling, constantly playing all parts of that old love story for each other. Forever lost in the underworld.

I look around the room slowly, my loving gaze caressing the part of you Hades could not and will never have. I will keep my promise. I will show your work. In hundreds of years, when we are all dust, people born into the world will see your brilliance, Anna Garibaldi, and they will know why we called you *La Divina*.

#

THE END

An alternative ending for this book is available on amazon kindle

About the Author

Victoria Avilan studied art and nursing in her native Israel, served as a nurse in the IDF, and later studied novel writing in the UCLA Writers' Program's Master Sequence with the famous Aussie writing guru Claire (McNab) Carmichael. She lives with her wife and her dog in Redondo Beach, California.

An Alternative Ending is available on amazon kindle

Contact email : victoria@vicavilan.com
Author's website : www.vicavilan.com
Visit Victoria Avilan's author page on facebook

Also by Victoria Avilan
A Small Country about to Vanish

Source of Inspiration:
The Case of the Colorblind Painter By Oliver Sacks and Robert Wasserman.

Quotations:
William Shakespeare's *Romeo and Juliet,* Act 1. Scene 1
William Shakespeare's *Julius Caesar* Act 1, scene 2

61543202R00207

Made in the USA
Lexington, KY
13 March 2017